PARADISE PASSED

PARADISE PASSED

A NOVEL BY

JERRY OLTION

🌾 **Wheatland Press**

http://www.wheatlandpress.com

Published by
P. O. Box 1818
Wilsonville, OR 97070

Paradise Passed

Library of Congress Cataloging-in-Publication data is available upon request.

ISBN 0-9755903-2-4
Printed in the United States of America
Cover painting by Frank Wu.
Interior by Deborah Layne.

For Jenny Leon Goodrich

Jackie McKennan

and Kathy Oltion

with love

CONTENTS

INTRODUCTION

THIS IS MY FAVORITE NOVEL. I like my other books, too, but this is my baby. This is the one I've worked on for years, the one I've poured my heart and soul into. It has also been the most difficult to get published.

I got the idea for it about twenty years ago. The character came first, and then the starship he lives on, and then the worlds he eventually has to deal with. I didn't write the book immediately; I did three chapters and an outline and shipped it around to various publishers to see if anyone was interested. It spent about five years travelling from publisher to publisher. (That's right, five years. Publishers and glaciers have a lot in common—at least New York publishers.) Everybody said, "We'd have to see the finished book before we could make a decision," so I sat down to write the whole thing. That took another five years or so, inbetween other projects. Once it was done (in the early '90s), I sent the finished novel around to the same publishers who had seen the proposal.

I got back what I call "rave rejections." Editors told me they loved the book, and wished they could publish it, but they couldn't get it past their bosses, or "Our marketing people wouldn't have a clue what to do with it." Time after time, year after year, I watched this novel come close to acceptance, only to lose the race to something safer, something less controversial, something that better fit into a marketing niche.

One time, it came so close to publication that I thought I had finally defeated the jinx. The editor who had already bought two of my other books said he liked this one, and would publish it if the sales figures for the one that had just been released were good enough to justify buying a third book from me. So I waited on tenterhooks, praying (in an agnostic sort of way) for good sales and good reviews. And my prayers were answered! Reviewers loved *The Getaway Special*. Word of mouth spread world-wide. Sales were great.

So great, in fact, that the editor, either on his own or acting on orders from above, told me that he wanted a sequel to *Getaway* rather than an independent novel. I was now too successful to publish my favorite book!

In the two decades since I came up with the idea, the rest of the world didn't sit still. NASA orbited the Hubble Space Telescope, and I worried that astronomers would point it at Alpha Centauri and tell me there were no planets there. Or that there were planets there, but not where they had to be for my story to work. Fortunately (for me), there was a glitch in the mirror, and they couldn't focus the thing. They later fixed that, but it turned out they still couldn't resolve planets around Alpha Centauri. Not quite. *Paradise Passed* had dodged that bullet.

In the late '90s, astronomers turned to other methods for detecting planets around other stars. Reports came in by the dozen, but Alpha Centauri wasn't among them. There were either no planets there, or they were too small to detect (i.e. they were the size of Earth or smaller—just what I needed!)

Astronomers were chipping away at the novel's foundation, but they hadn't really disturbed the edifice yet. If anything, they had added a tantalizing promise of possibility to it. There were undoubtedly planets out there, even in double-star systems. Planets around Alpha Centauri *could* exist.

Not surprisingly, other writers noticed this. They began writing stories about interstellar colonization. Some of those stories involved the people on board the starships during the long journey, what they would do to occupy their time on the way and how they would feel about leaving the confines of their ship once they got there. John Hemry did the latter with a short story in *Analog* magazine called "Generation Gap," and Ursula Le Guin did the former with an anthologized short story called "Paradises Lost."

"*Paradises Lost*"! Can you believe it? I couldn't. How could she come so close to the same idea that I had—so close that she chose nearly the same title for it!—without ever seeing my novel? There was no doubt she had done just that, for the only people who had seen *Paradise Passed* were editors and a few of my close friends. And Ursula has no need to write other people's ideas even if she had somehow heard about it. She has plenty of excellent ideas of her own.

No, this pretty clearly was a case of "steam engine time," as in: when it's time for the steam engine to be invented, someone will invent it. Several someones, in fact. James Watt gets the credit for the steam engine, but several others were working on it at the same time.

That's clearly what happened here. I would like to claim that I was first, but it's not who *thought* of it first that matters; it's who published it first, and I wasn't that person. Ursula and John may not have been first, either. An extensive search of science fiction archives would probably turn up something quite similar by Poul Anderson or Andre Norton or one of their generation. We don't call that the Golden Age of science fiction for nothing. Those guys thought of practically *everything* first.

But *Paradise Passed* is finally seeing print, and despite a few other people already making forays into its territory, it's still everything it ever was, and maybe a bit more. I've gone back through it one last time, polishing rough spots and bringing it up to date with our current understanding of extrasolar planets, starship design, and human interaction. (In the twenty years since I began this, sociology has become enough of a science to have some meaningful impact on the story.) One thing I *didn't* do: I didn't change anything just because someone else had already done something similar. Paradise Passed is still true to the vision I had when I first wrote it, and it's my sincerest hope that it will be complete, organic, and true for you as well.

Jerry Oltion
June, 2004

CHAPTER ONE

TIMBERLINE

THE TREE WAS BOTH the physical and the spiritual center of Ryan's world. Growing as it did in *Daedalus*'s open central axis, reaching nearly half the hundred-meter length of the starship's rotating lifesystem, it was truly the one living entity about which everything else turned. The symbolism was simple and obvious—and intentional. The Tree was as much a part of the ship's design as the drive or the airlocks, but Ryan didn't mind. It was no less perfect for having been planned.

He sat cross-legged in the hollow of grass and pine needles beneath it, smelling the fresh, spicy mixture of plant-filtered air while he held his guitar against his right thigh and fingered slowly through the chords to *Home on LaGrange*. He didn't have to play them; the silence there beneath the Tree was so complete that just pressing the strings to the frets produced sound enough to evoke the song. The rest of the music—the parts for flute, bass, piano, and drums—played in his mind, as did an edited version of his own guitar. It sounded wonderful, better than it would have if he *had* played it aloud, and that, too, was a simple, obvious truth. Ryan wasn't that good.

He really didn't have an ear for it, he supposed. Or the inclination. He wanted to play, but not bad enough to practice at it for the hours each day that it would take to make any real progress. The mood to play didn't strike him that often, and when it did he usually found himself, like today, sitting under the Tree and simply fingering chords.

A rustling in the branches overhead made him pause in mid-song and look up just in time to see a gray and white blur disappear behind a tuft of pine needles about a third of the way up. Nova, one of the ship's cats, was making her way down. The branch flexed under her, springing back as she jumped for another one, but in that same instant both Ryan and Nova realized that something was wrong. Her target branch was not there.

Nova yowled her surprise and stretched out for the trunk, but her claws were still centimeters from the bark as she sailed past. She reached for another limb below, caught just enough of it to start herself spinning, then drifted out away from the Tree.

Ryan considered trying to catch her. In the axis the only acceleration came from the drive, straining to provide a twentieth of a gee straight aft, but even at a twentieth of a gee a falling cat could build up a respectable velocity from a third of the way up the Tree. It took time, though, enough time for Ryan to think it over and decide against it. Catching a falling cat was a good way to get slashed, no matter what the gravity.

She was doing a beautiful job of taking care of herself anyway. Her tail whirled in counter-rotation as she tried to keep her feet aimed downward, but she switched tactics when she realized that wasn't going to be enough. With another plaintive yowl she let herself roll partway around without correcting, then in the final moment before touchdown she writhed her entire hindquarters in a dying-gyroscope twist that spun her end for end and left her with feet once again pointing aft.

She landed with a thump and a spray of pine needles. Ryan winced at the impact, but Nova was evidently made of bouncy stuff. She stood up, shook herself, and stalked over to rub against his leg. Ryan set down his guitar and picked her up, and she began to purr.

He ruffled the fur between her ears, then got up and moved out from under the branches for a better look at the Tree, carrying her with him. The ship's spin-induced gravity began to rival the drive's feeble push only a few meters away from the axis, which meant that the farther Ryan got from the Tree trunk the more spin gravity tended to throw him toward the cylindrical wall. To keep that from happening, the ship's designers had curved the deck to compensate for the varying pull, which meant that as Ryan walked away from the Tree he also walked up the side of a bowl, save that the direction of *down* was always perpendicular to the floor wherever he stood. He stopped about halfway to the wall and looked up. Sure enough, there, on a Tree that now leaned over him at nearly a forty-five degree angle, was a bright yellow circle on the end of a half-meter-long stump where the limb had been cut off.

Ryan closed his eyes to visualize the Tree as it had been before and realized that the missing limb was the dead one, the one he'd killed by accident when he'd anchored his storage-crate tree house to it with carbon composite cable nearly fifteen years ago. Somehow that made him even angrier than if it had been any other limb on the Tree. That one was *his* limb; it carried memories for him, and someone had sawed it off.

What for? He hadn't a clue. Sean Little Bear had once mentioned that it would make wonderful carving wood, but Sean wouldn't have taken it without asking the rest of the crew first. Nor would anybody else who had a legitimate use for it. The Tree was an object of reverence, but it wasn't inviolate; if someone could convince the rest of the crew that the branch was more useful off the trunk than on it, then they would have been given permission to take it. But nobody had asked about it. Someone had simply cut it off when nobody else was around. Someone had vandalized the Tree.

Ryan was still scowling up into the branches when, a third of the way around the bowl-shaped deck, the observatory door opened and

3

David Bonham stepped out. The expression on David's face was as close to the opposite of Ryan's as an expression could be. He beamed. He carried a strip of printout in his hand, and when he noticed Ryan under the Tree he waved it like a flag.

"Ryan! Come see this!"

Ryan kicked off with his toes and bounced around the curve to David's side. "What have you got?" he asked.

"Spectra from A-3. The first ones I could get through the drive flame. Look!" He pointed to the bands of light and dark on the paper, their wavelengths marked along the bottom.

A-3 was Alpha Centauri A-3, the third planet out from the brighter of the two major stars closest to Sol. It was the starship's primary destination, and the planet upon which the hopes of the entire crew rested. Ryan looked at its spectra for a moment, then shook his head. "What are they, hydrogen lines?"

David laughed. "You'd better hope not, not in a planetary atmosphere. No, what you see here are nitrogen and oxygen lines. *Strong* nitrogen and oxygen lines, which indicate air that may—may, I point out—be breathable."

"You're kidding."

"No. And see here—" David pointed "—carbon dioxide. And *methane.*" He emphasized methane as if it had special importance.

Nova squirmed in Ryan's arms, and he scratched her behind the ears. "Methane? That's not good, is it?"

"Sure it is. It means something's alive there."

A momentary thrill shivered its way up Ryan's spine. "Alive?" he asked. "How do you figure?"

"On Earth, atmospheric methane comes from the digestive tracts of ruminants."

It took a moment for that to connect. "Ruminants? You mean like goats? Goat farts?" Goats were the only large animals besides humans on the ship. From goats they got milk and wool and the occasional steak, though most of their meat came from rabbits.

4

David's smile grew even wider. "Exactly. So finding methane on A-3 means there's probably something like ruminants there, too. Come on, I'm on my way to tell the captain."

He reached out to a maglev handle protruding from the wall beside him—a wall that, because of its cylindrical shape and distance from the axis, seemed to slant away at an angle a determined person could have climbed. The maglev handle looked like a single stair step with a waist-high grab bar rising from it; David slid the step from its resting place over to the vertical blue stripe painted on the wall, stepped on the foot rest, pressed the button in the end of the handle with his thumb, and the maglev began to carry him up through the ship's axis.

Ryan set Nova down on the ground, took a handle for himself, and followed. "What about gas giants?" he asked as they rose past the ring-shaped landings leading to the outer decks. "Don't some of them have methane in their atmospheres without having life?"

"Certainly," David said, "but their methane makes up a much higher proportion of the atmosphere, and it comes from a completely different source. It's mostly—"

The sudden wail of the emergency siren drowned him out. There were three long bursts, then the ship's Monitor and Control program, its synthetic voice amplified far beyond its normal speaking level, said, "Fire in level G, East. Fire in level G, East. Exact location indeterminate." The siren wailed three more times, then dropped to a softer note that repeated every few seconds.

David stopped his ascent, forcing Ryan to stop just below him. They looked at one another for a moment before Ryan voiced the obvious question: "Drill?"

"Probably," David said. He grinned, and Ryan knew just what that grin meant. It meant, *What difference does it make? We still have to respond.*

Ryan looked back down the way they had come. The upper branches of the Tree still blocked the labeling on the walls, but he didn't need labels to know that East quadrant was directly opposite them, or that they had already passed the point where G deck's parabolic curve intersected the axis. Neither did David. In unison they grabbed handholds set in the walls, detached their maglevs and transferred them over to the red descending stripe, and dropped back downship, this time with Ryan in the lead. He abandoned the maglev as he neared the landing, dropped the last few meters to the deck and kicked off around the axial wall toward the east side door as soon as he touched down. David was right behind him. The maglevs waited where they had been abandoned; in thirty seconds, if no one reactivated them, they would move back to their niches by themselves.

The doorway was recessed in the wall at a slant so it would be vertical to a person standing before it. Ryan nearly smashed his nose into it before he remembered that in a drill, automatic machinery acted to isolate the ship into sections. The pressure doors between decks and between the decks and the axis closed automatically, confining the source of danger to as small a volume as possible.

He palmed the sensor and stuck his head through while the door was still opening, but his reflexive back-step at the stench that assailed him nearly sent him out into the axis again.

"It's for real!"

"What?" David moved up behind him. They both looked through the open doorway into the corridor, where faint wisps of smoke drifted gently toward them.

"We'll need suits," Ryan said.

David nodded. "You're right."

Ryan opened the emergency suit locker beside the door and pulled out two of the ten helmets in the rack. Handing one to David, he reached into his own and pulled out the attached body stocking, shook it out, and stuck his feet into the legs. He reached behind him and stuck his arms into the arm holes, dropped the helmet over his head, and, wriggling his hands into the gloves, pulled the oversized zipper up from crotch to neck to seal himself in. The helmet itself was the air tank; as the zipper closed against the sensor, compressed air sprayed in around his neck and the suit stiffened with the slight overpressure. The air had the metallic tang of long storage.

The suits were strictly for emergency use. Without constant-volume joints at knees and elbows they were difficult to flex in complete vacuum, but they did at least supply a couple hours of air and enough mobility to let you get to a real suit in the event of a major air loss, and in full atmosphere they were excellent for sealing you off from your environment. They had only one radio channel and no plumbing or any of the other niceties of a full suit, but they were simple enough to allow keeping ten of them on either side of every pressure door, and that was their main advantage. They were there when you needed them, though this was the first time in his nineteen years on board that Ryan had actually put one on outside of a drill.

They were thin enough that he could still hear the fire alarm's rhythmic beeping through the helmet. "Ready?" he asked.

"Just a minute," came David's muffled reply. Ryan switched on his radio while David finished sealing himself in. David switched on his radio as well, pulled the fire extinguisher off the wall beside the suit locker, and nodded. "Ready." His voice came in clearly now.

The door had automatically returned to its emergency closed position while they were suiting up. Ryan palmed it open again and stepped through, then led off down the corridor into the smoke with a long, bouncing stride. The deck curved less and less as they moved away from the axis, but at the same time their weight increased proportionately, slowing their progress. It was another effect of having a rotating lifesystem under drive: the farther you got toward the outer wall the more spin-gravity you felt, even though you stayed on the same deck the entire way.

Ryan had grown up with the effect. When the gravity became too heavy for bouncing he switched to long, single-legged leaps, and when that became too difficult he broke into a jog. They followed the thickening smoke inward to its source, and when he saw which door the smoke billowed out from beneath, Ryan felt a peculiar mixture of alarm and amusement. Someone had finally decided to trash the chapel.

They'd overdone it, though, by the looks of it. Burning the chapel wouldn't do anybody any good if the fire took the rest of the ship with it.

The door swung open and three people staggered out, none of them wearing suits. They coughed and waved their arms in front of them to clear away the smoke, and as Ryan and David approached, one of them—Warren Terrill, Ryan saw—gasped something unintelligible and waved them inside. The door thumped shut behind them, leaving them in a gray swirling haze of smoke. The orange flickering light of open flame glowed at the far end of the room, near where the pulpit would be.

David charged straight ahead, fire extinguisher held in front of him like a shield. Ryan saw him disappear into the smoke, heard a thump and a curse, and followed more cautiously to find him kneeling over someone lying prone on the deck. It was Ryan's father, Ken, coughing weakly and gasping for breath.

Without stopping to think about it, Ryan grabbed Ken by the arms and dragged him to the door, kicked at it with his foot until Warren opened it for him, and dragged him on outside. The other two people there, Teigh Kuhlow and Michelle Dougan, took him from Ryan by his arms and legs and rushed off toward the hospital. Ryan watched them until they disappeared around the curve of corridor, wanting to follow them but knowing that as one of the only two people there in a P-suit he should stay to fight the fire.

He turned to Warren. "Was anybody else in there?" he shouted to be heard through the helmet.

"I think so," Warren said. He coughed as the thick smoke poured out of the chapel, added, "It smells like they're—" then suddenly he doubled over and vomited into the corner.

Ryan got the idea. He rushed back inside, trying not to retch at the thought himself. At least in the suit he didn't have to smell it.

The smoke was even thicker than before. Ryan had to crouch down as he searched in order to see the floor, and even so he could only see a circle about as wide as his outstretched arms. Over the insistently beeping alarm he could hear the hiss of the fire extinguisher as David sprayed it on the flames, but only when he was certain that nobody else had collapsed anywhere else in the room did he come up beside David to see what had been burning. He was expecting to see a charred body among the ashes, but the true situation was even stranger.

The whereabouts of his tree branch was no longer a mystery. It had been cut into lengths and piled up beneath a grating supported between two chairs, upon which sizzled the remains of one of the ship's milk goats. Beside the fire a portable air recycler howled in overloaded frustration.

Ken had been alone here, and he had started the fire himself. On purpose. That realization came all at once, but it still didn't explain the situation. "What the hell was he doing?" Ryan asked.

"Making a sacrifice, I'd say, by the looks of it," David answered.

"Making a sacrifice," Ryan echoed. "Sure. Why not?" As he looked at the remains of the goat, his concern for his father rose to a new level. There'd been some strange goings-on in the church over the years, but this was a whole quantum level stranger than anything Ken had tried before. Ryan nudged the pile of wood with his toe, jumping back when it suddenly collapsed and scattered sparks across the floor. David sprayed the last of the extinguisher charge over the sparks.

"We need an airtight container for this," David said.

"Right." Ryan went back out into the corridor and said to Warren, "We're going to need a sealable garbage can or something."

Warren looked like he was going to throw up again, but he swallowed hard and asked, "Who was it?"

"Nobody. It was a goat."

"A goat?" Warren asked.

"That's right. The idiot was sacrificing a goat!"

Warren hesitated, not knowing how to respond. At last he said, "I'll go get a barrel." He turned away and jogged off down the corridor.

David came through the door and closed it behind him. "The recycler should take care of it in a few minutes," he said. "Though I don't know how it's going to like Inerton." He waved the empty extinguisher in his left hand.

Ryan had a thought. "Why didn't the automatic system take care of it?"

"He disconnected the sensor."

"Oh. Sure, he would." Despite his eccentricities, Ken wasn't an idiot. Misguided maybe, but not so stupid he'd forget to disconnect the smoke detector if he wanted to start a fire. And the portable recycler said something for his degree of preparation. Evidently he just hadn't figured on getting so much smoke.

How much smoke *had* he gotten? "I'm going to go check on—" he started to say, but before he could finish he heard the clatter of more people approaching and Captain Van Cleeve came jogging into the corridor, leading two more crewmembers, all three of them P-suited and armed with fire extinguishers and carrying extra helmets. The captain stopped in front of Ryan and David and asked, "What's the situation?"

Ryan let David do the talking, but after David had described the scene in the chapel the captain turned to Ryan and asked, "You're sure he was alone in there?"

"Pretty sure," Ryan said.

The captain turned to the two people who had come with him: Bob Thorpe and Kristy Crawford. "Did either of you two know about this?" he asked.

"No, sir," Bob said.

Kristy mumbled something nobody could hear through their helmets. The captain reached out and flipped her radio switch.

"Try again."

Kristy's voice was still faint. "I said yes, sir, I knew. But I didn't know it was going to be like this."

"Hmm." That was all, just, "Hmm." He didn't ask what Ken had been praying for, and nobody bothered to state the obvious, but Ryan suddenly remembered what David had shown him in the axis. A cold, irrational fear enveloped him at the thought of his father down here sacrificing a goat while David was up in the astronomy module discovering a habitable planet. For a moment the coincidence seemed too great to be just that. For a moment Ryan felt the chill guiding hand of the Lord of Creation around him, and he suddenly realized why the ancients had always spoken of their fear of the Lord. Any god whose influence could be bought by scorching a goat was definitely a god to fear.

But the absurdity of the whole idea was too great to support Ryan's terror for more than a moment. He started to laugh, but stopped as another thought struck him. There was still going to be trouble.

And Bob and Kristy—regulars at Ken's services—were going to be part of it.

"Uh, captain, can we talk to you in private a minute?"

Van Cleeve frowned. Clearly, he thought that this was hardly the time for a private talk, but Ryan held his gaze until at last the captain nodded. Ryan led the way back into the chapel, and when David hesitated at the door he waved him in as well.

"You too, Dave."

Bob and Kristy didn't like the idea of a closed conference either, but Ryan gave them a big smile and said, "We'll just be a second, sorry," and closed the door on them anyway.

Ryan led David and the captain away from the door, in case the two outside tried listening through it. Smoke still filled the room, but it made no difference inside the suits. When they reached the still-smoldering goat the captain looked it over thoughtfully, then flipped off his radio, folded his arms, and cocked his head to the side, waiting. Ryan and David flipped off their radios as well and leaned in close. "Maybe you'd better tell him what you discovered before the fire," Ryan said.

"Before the—oh! Of course. I. . .damn." David reached for his breast pocket, but he had sealed the spectra printout inside his suit. Through the clear plastic, Ryan could see the paper sticking out of his pocket, but David evidently didn't think it was worth breathing smoke to retrieve it. He shrugged and said, "I have discovered what appears to be a breathable atmosphere around Centauri A-3."

The captain's eyes widened in surprise. "You have?"

"Yes. And a methane signature."

"That's. . .that's incredible!" The captain knew what methane signified.

"It's also incredibly bad timing," Ryan said. "Right after Ken did this—" he waved an arm at the sacrificial pyre "—is not the time to be finding habitable planets."

There was a long silence while David and the captain both realized the implications. The captain broke it at last.

"Vacuum," he swore.

Chapter Two

The Church

It had been a long nineteen years. To Ryan, the trip to Alpha Centauri had been his whole life. He had been eight years old when they left, but his memory of life on Earth and the year on Spacehome before the trip started had all but disappeared for lack of shipboard reminders. He had grown up on the ship; he liked it there; the immense void between stars was part of his life—but other people weren't so lucky.

There was no way to tell from Earth, or even from the telescopes in Earth orbit, whether or not the bodies that astronomers had detected in the habitable zones of the twin Centauri suns were truly habitable planets or not. Indeed, like Schiaparelli's Martian canals in the late 19th century, their very existence was a matter of debate. They were too close to the limit of observability to be more than statistical anomalies in the data. Only a closer look would provide any answers, but to some of the crew, the long years spent traveling toward a destination that no one knew even existed was more than they could handle. They had been selected for their level-headedness and for their dedication to the mission, but nobody really knew what the tremendous isolation would do to them over the course of years. The planners had made the ship as much like a small orbital colony as possible, balancing speed against the need to send along as complete and stable a society as they could send, but fear of the unknown had still taken its toll. Three of the original hundred-member crew had suicided just after turnaround, with the prospect of another ten years of travel ahead of them. Another had gradually drifted into catatonia. And Ken—Ken had Got Religion.

Like the rest of the crew, he had started off the trip agnostic. The mission planners had carefully screened the applicants for their religious beliefs, not so much to populate the ship with agnostics as to eliminate fanatics on either side of the issue. Even Ryan, at the age of eight, had been asked the basis of his personal beliefs, not just in religion but in other areas of thought as well. It had been a scary moment, that first search into the irrational layers of his being, and it was the first time he had seriously worried about being allowed on the trip, but his answers had evidently pleased the planners. Ken and Alice and Ryan Hughes had been one of the ten complete families picked from among thousands of applicants.

But even with their questioning, the planners hadn't considered the nature of agnosticism in a crisis. An agnostic doesn't believe that the nature or even the existence of God can be determined, but almost by definition he believes in the *possibility* of His existence. And in a crisis, well, it can't *hurt* anything to pray. . .

After about five years of staring off into the unknown, Ken had decided that it couldn't hurt to pray for a habitable planet at the end of the trip. He started doing it regularly. After a while he overcame his embarrassment and spoke about it to the rest of the crew, and discovered that some of them were doing it, too. It seemed only logical to get together when they prayed, under the assumption that any kind of telepathic link to God would be stronger with more people in the circuit, and with that thought came the logical conclusion that they should get the whole ship in on it.

It was a good excuse to get together once a week. The prayer meetings generally turned into a low-key party, and it seemed like bad taste to go to the party without going to the meeting first. And besides, it couldn't *hurt* anything. . .

For a couple of years that was as far as it went, but Ken, ever logical, began wondering if there might be methods to improve their chances of being heard On High. He began researching the old religions, running statistical analyses of prayer methods and their reported results, and he eventually came up with one thing common to almost every system of belief.

The church lost all but four of its members—including Ryan's mother—when Ken announced that people should stop having sex on Sundays. Ken was upset by their lack of faith, but he knew that he was onto something. Every religion had regulated sex in some way; it had to be significant. And it was better, he said, to have four faithful followers than a shipful of half-hearted participants.

Ken and his four disciples continued to pray for a habitable planet, and they continued their search for more certain methods of prayer. And, as the voyage grew longer and the distance from Earth stretched from two to three to four light years, their church began to pick up members again.

They were still agnostic. They had no assurance that their prayers were going anywhere, but in their helplessness they were doing the only thing that they could think of that might make a difference. Rather, they were doing *everything* they could think of, and that was the problem. They tried baptism, fasting, sensory deprivation, drugs, even self-flagellation, all in their attempt to open a communication channel with God.

As his father's behavior became more and more bizarre, Ryan had long talks with both the captain and with Bob Thorpe, the ship's psychologist. They were in agreement; attempting to stifle the church would merely drive it underground, where the attraction of things forbidden would actually lend it impetus in the long run. Also, Bob had argued, it *did* help those crewmembers who were feeling the effects of isolation most severely. Better to have them acting a little strange than going completely insane.

Not long after their talk, Bob joined the church. Ryan wondered how useful his advice had been, but he had to admit that the man's logic still seemed sound. Ryan had done his own research into religion; it seemed to be a natural human reaction to facing the unknown. Trying to change that almost instinctive behavior probably *would* cause more harm than good.

Now, almost at the end of the voyage, he watched the captain realize the flaw in that reasoning, just as he had realized it himself moments before. Perhaps they had never really believed that there could be a habitable planet at the end of the trip, or perhaps they had simply not thought it all the way through, but the simple truth was that Ken was going to take credit for it.

Not the discovery; that was David's uncontested achievement. No, Ken was going to take credit for the planet itself. In God's name, of course, but he would take credit, because he would suddenly be sure that his prayers had been answered. Worse, with this almost impossible coincidence he would be sure that the method of prayer was as much responsible as the prayer itself.

Ken's religious behavior had been annoying enough when he was agnostic; Ryan didn't want to think what he would be like if he became a believer.

The captain evidently shared his sentiment. "There are a lot of things I never thought would happen on this voyage," he said, "but I never thought I'd regret finding a habitable planet." He stared off through the smoke—thinning now that the recycler was catching up with it—and shook his head. "Well, I refuse to let Ken's excesses affect the mission. We're a colony ship and we've found a likely prospect, so by God—or whoever—we're going to act like it! Release your information, Mr. Bonham."

David nodded. He hesitated a moment, swallowed hard, then said, "Maybe we could lessen the damage somewhat if I said I'd discovered it a couple days ago. Ken will no doubt still claim it as a victory for prayer, but that would at least invalidate this latest method."

Van Cleeve frowned. "How do we explain your waiting until now to report it? You're not usually shy about your findings."

"I'll say I didn't want to get anybody's hopes up until I was sure."

"Someone is bound to look up your observation records. They'll find the discrepancy."

"Not if I alter the dates."

The captain nodded slowly. "No, I suppose not. Hmm. Mr. Hughes, what do you think?"

It took Ryan a minute to realize that the captain wasn't addressing his father. Mr. Hughes was *him*. And the captain was asking him how he felt about lying to the crew.

How did he feel about it? Well, he didn't like it, but the alternative was worse.

And thus do we write history, he thought. He took a deep breath and said, "I—sure. For all I know, maybe he *did* find out a couple days ago. If it'll keep Ken from going further out into space, then make it last week."

"Good. Then let's get this cleaned up and get to celebrating."

Ryan turned to the door to go see if Warren had returned with the garbage can yet, then remembered Bob and Kristy outside. Both churchgoers. "What about them?" he asked, nodding toward the door.

"Hmm," the captain said. "There's no hiding what happened here. They're in P-suits; let them get in on the cleanup. Maybe it'll make them think about the consequences next time one of them comes up with a bright idea."

David said, "Then if you'll excuse me, I have data to fudge."

With two other people to help clean up, Ryan could see no reason to stick around either. He said, "And I'd like to check on my father, if I'm not needed here anymore."

"Go ahead," the captain said. "I think we've got this under control now. And Ryan..."

"Yes?"

"Thanks."

Ryan stood for a moment, trying to think of a proper response, but at last he just shrugged and opened the door. What could he say? He was just doing what he had to do.

Like Ken? Wasn't Ken doing what he thought he had to do, too?

Without a word, Ryan walked past the two waiting outside and headed down the corridor toward the hospital. When he got to the cross-corridor he began to run.

The hospital was down a deck from the chapel. Down a deck and aft along the curve toward the axis, which put it in a lower-weight region despite being "down." Ryan took the stairs three at a time, tugging at his suit zipper as he descended, and nearly crashed into Teigh and Michelle getting into suits of their own on the lower landing.

He grabbed the handrail and pulled himself to a stop beside them. "You don't need those," he said.

Michelle paused with one sleeve on. "We don't?" she asked. She looked pointedly up at the speaker over the door, still sounding the alarm.

"Not now. We've got it under control."

"Oh."

Teigh looked skeptical. "Nobody else got hurt?"

"Just Ken. How is he?"

"All right, I think. Holly was giving him oxygen when we left, but he was breathing okay. You're sure nobody else got hurt? It smelled like somebody did."

Ryan pulled off his helmet, then remembered that it didn't come off at the neck like a regular suit helmet did. He held it awkwardly behind his head for a moment before letting it fall against his back. The fabric over his shoulders tightened with the weight.

"Yeah, I'm sure," he said. He thought about telling them what had been on fire, but suddenly he didn't want to be spreading it around. The story would spread soon enough without Ryan's help.

The fire alarm cut off in mid-beep. Michelle sighed with relief, then asked, "How much damage did it do?"

Lots, Ryan thought, but he didn't feel like saying that, either. He shook his head and said, "We don't know yet." That much was true enough. They wouldn't know how much damage had been done until they saw what new direction Ken took his church in the wake of David's discovery.

But they would know that soon enough. Ryan opened the door, then turned back and said, "I'll probably see you at the party tonight."

"Party?" Teigh asked.

Ryan forced a grin. "Just a hunch," he said, "but I bet the captain throws one." He stepped through before they could ask him anything more, and walked on down to the hospital.

Ken lay on his back on a table in one of the hospital's three exam rooms. Holly sat on a stool beside him, pressing the flat face of some sort of diagnostic instrument against his bare chest and looking into a monitor on a cart beside the table. She looked up when Ryan entered, nodded, and said, "Come on in." To Ken she said, "Don't talk. Just keep breathing normally." She reached across him and pressed the sensor against the skin beside his left nipple, then looked into the monitor again.

Her blonde hair was a cascade of curls hiding the monitor from Ryan's view. He stepped around her to the other side of the bed and looked down at his father, who met his eyes with an intense stare that had Ryan looking away in only a few seconds. The fire hadn't affected that, anyway.

He looked at the screen, visible from this angle but displaying a shifting pattern of grainy specks and streaks that meant nothing to Ryan. Just as he realized that he must be seeing into Ken's left lung,

Holly removed the sensor and the screen went blank.

"There's a little edema from the irritation," she said. "It doesn't look serious, so I'm going to let you breathe room air, but I'm going to put an oximeter on your finger to monitor the oxygen content of your blood." Ken obediently held up his hand while Holly took what looked like a miniature blood pressure cuff with a flexible display printed on it off her cart and snugged it around his forearm, then slid its ring-shaped sensor over the tip of his index finger. She tapped the display on and watched the numbers flicker on it until they steadied out, then, pressing hard on his wrist, she waited until the cuff began to beep.

She let up on his wrist and the beeping stopped as fresh blood rushed back into his hand. "Good," she said. "But don't wait for this thing to tell me if you're in trouble. If you have any problem breathing, let me know immediately, okay?"

"Okay." Ken's voice was hoarse from the smoke.

Holly smiled up at Ryan, a white, perfect smile that raised the oxygen content of his blood by half. "I think he'll live," she said.

Ryan looked back down at Ken. Ken stared back, that same fanatical intensity in his eyes, and suddenly, seeing the contrast between Holly's open friendliness and Ken's soul-searing challenge, Ryan had enough. Without looking away, he said, "I'd like to talk to him alone for a minute if I could."

In his peripheral vision he saw Holly nod. "Okay," she said, "but keep it short." She got up and moved away.

Ryan waited until she was in the next room, then said softly, "I'll keep it short, all right. Just short enough to tell you what a vac-head you are. Do you—"

"Ryan."

"Ryan what? Do you realize you could have killed us all? If that fire had spread—"

"Ryan, be silent!"

"No, *you* be silent for a change. Damn it, it's time somebody woke you up and told you the program around here. This is a starship, remember? Closed environment, remember? Everybody's got to earn their keep, remember? Well you're a liability. Your value as a farmer and a father wasn't high enough to pay for the damage you were doing *before* this, but now you're nothing but a menace. Do you have any idea what—"

"That is *enough*." The force of Ken's outburst set him to coughing. He brought it under control, looked warily at the oximeter for a few seconds, then looked up at Ryan again.

"You're a fine one to talk about earning your keep. What have you done with your life? It's been nearly twenty years and you still don't have a single skill that somebody else on the ship can't do better than you."

Despite being an old taunt, that stung. Ryan *hadn't* specialized, and now as they were nearing the end of the trip it was bothering him more and more, and his dad knew it. But he wasn't going to let Ken change the subject that easily. He said, "We can talk about me later; right now we're talking about you. I just want to make sure you realize that there are people on this ship who think we'd be better off using you for reaction mass."

"I appreciate your concern," Ken said dryly. "I know I have enemies."

"Well you don't know who they are, or you'd be more worried about it. The captain saw what you did, and he's mad enough to toss you out the airlock himself. Which he has the authority as well as the ability to do, you know."

Ken didn't respond, other than with his slight smile and his intense stare.

"Are you listening? *I'm* about ready to toss you out the lock, and I'm your own son. Doesn't that mean anything to you? Doesn't that make you wonder if maybe you're pushing this prayer business a little too far?"

"Religious leaders have always suffered persecution at the hands of those they are attempting to help. It's part of the job."

"Part of the job! Since when is burning down the ship part of the job? Or using up half of our breathing air in the process? Or killing one of our milk goats, or cutting a limb off the Tree? I could space you for that alone!"

"The Tree is going to die anyway."

That had come out of nowhere. Ryan stopped in mid rave. "What?" he asked.

Holly had stuck her head back around the door at Ryan's outburst, but she withdrew again as Ken said calmly, "The Tree is going to die as soon as we get to Alpha Centauri."

"Says who?"

"Says God. Or evolution, if you'd rather. A complex plant like a lodgepole pine needs gravity to help transport its growth hormones; when we shut down the drive it'll die. So cutting that limb off it won't make a bit of difference in the long run."

Ken was the chief farmer on board; if zero-gee would kill a tree then he'd be the one to know. He could be lying about it, but Ryan didn't think he was. He had that smug, matter-of-fact air of someone who had the facts on his side and knew it. No, Ken wasn't lying, and that, plus his obvious satisfaction in delivering the news, knocked the last prop out from under Ryan's self-restraint.

"No difference? You cut a limb off the Tree because it didn't make any difference? You stupid son of a bitch, I'll show you how much difference it makes!" Ryan balled his right hand into a fist and pulled back to strike, but a shout from the doorway stopped him.

"Ryan!" Holly ran into the room and grabbed his arm. Red with anger herself, she pulled him back away from Ken's bed and shouted, "What do you think you're doing? Get out of here! Go on, get out of my hospital!"

Ryan let his fist relax, and gently pulled his arm free of Holly's grip. He had to hold his breath for a moment to get enough control over it to say, "I'm sorry."

Holly was breathing hard, too. Her voice quavered as she said, "Well so am I, but you've got no business coming in here and disturbing my patients, no matter what the provocation. Now go on."

Ryan glanced over to Ken, then back to Holly. Things were screwed up enough without having her mad at him. He tried to think of something to say or do that might redeem him in her eyes, but after a moment he realized that the best thing would be to simply do as she had told him and leave. He took another deep breath, nodded to her, and walked to the door, being careful not to stomp.

He waited until he was halfway around the ship before he whirled and smashed his fist into the wall.

CHAPTER THREE

FRIENDS

NOVA HAD DISAPPEARED, gone wherever cats go when there's too much excitement for them, but Ryan's guitar was still lying where he had left it. He'd stopped for it on his way back home after recharging and putting away his emergency suit, but now instead of picking it up he sat down beside it with his back to the Tree and closed his eyes. He didn't want to go back to his room. What he wanted was to go to sleep. It would feel good to relax and drift completely away from the ship for a time, away from Ken and burnt goats and Holly's anger and everything else that bothered him. It would feel good, but at the same time it wouldn't, because sleep was one of the things that bothered him, too.

It seemed like sleep was just about all he ever did anymore. It was one of his little guilty pleasures, yet one he still indulged in whenever he got the chance. Every time he ran up against something he didn't want to deal with, or even when there was simply nothing much else to do, off he'd go into dreamland. He always told himself that he'd just take a nap and wake up refreshed and more ready to get busy with the rest of his day, but in truth it was escape, nothing more. He usually woke up feeling worse than he had before, and guilty about wasting the time.

All the same, he could feel it tugging at him even now. While he was asleep he felt great; the guilt came later. Sleep itself was bliss, and his dreams were almost always pleasant, too, sometimes of the barely-remembered Earth or of the Spacehome colony which built and launched *Daedalus,* but most often of the ship as a kind of timeless universe all to itself, a universe in which Ryan had specialized, in which he made a difference. Sometimes he was a doctor, or a farmer like his father, or an engineer, or even a musician. Sometimes Holly figured prominently and sometimes not, but Ryan could count on the dreams to be good either way.

But he could also count on feeling guilty about it when he woke up.

"Jeez, you're a weenie!" he shouted up into the branches of the Tree. He jumped up and grabbed his guitar and for a brief moment felt the impulse to slam it into the trunk, but instead, after taking a deep breath and holding it long enough to count to about fourteen, he sat back down and set the guitar in his lap and began to practice chord progressions, this time strumming them loud.

Laura Morrison was the oldest person on the ship, a position she held by a margin of nearly thirty years. She was also the easiest person on board to talk to, and the one in whom everybody wound up confiding at one time or another. So she didn't look surprised when Ryan showed up at her door nearly an hour later, fingers sore from playing all that time, but his attitude little better for the experience.

"Teigh told me about Ken," she said, leading the way back into the kitchen where she was baking cookies.

"Did he tell you Ken was sacrificing a goat?"

"No, he didn't mention that."

Ryan swung a chair out from under the table and straddled it, resting his arms on the back. "That's what he was doing," he said.

"That's. . .too bad," Laura said.

Ryan laughed. "Yeah. Want to know the real joke?"

"What?"

"While he was doing that, David found a habitable planet around Centauri A."

Laura rolled a ball of cookie dough around in the bowl of cinnamon sugar, placed it on the next-to-last spot on the pan, and pulled another gob of dough loose from the main lump. "That's pretty good, all right," she said, rolling the dough between her palms to make another ball. "He really found one?"

"That's what he says. Breathable atmosphere, anyway, and signs of life."

"Wow." Laura rolled the dough ball in the cinnamon sugar and put it in the last place on the pan, looked in the oven to check on the panful already baking, then cleaned the dough off her hands and sat down at the table beside Ryan. "That's. . .wow. Hah. I—"

She turned suddenly and looked out the window, out at the vegetable garden and the flowers and the plot of grass she kept under a pair of full-spectrum floodlights. Ryan looked out and saw Nova stalking another cat among the flowers: either Star or Shadow, he couldn't tell which from behind.

"So how did Ken take it?" Laura asked.

"He doesn't know yet. David's probably going to announce it here in a few hours, but he's, uh, well, he's changing the records first so it'll look like he found it a couple days ago."

She looked back in at Ryan, surprised. "David Bonham is doing that?"

Ryan felt himself blushing. "Yeah. We thought it might help keep Ken from burning any more goats. I don't know, maybe we're overreacting. What do you think? Do you think there's any chance that he'll just drop it? I mean, he's got what he wanted from God now, so he doesn't need to keep doing this anymore, does he?"

"Hah," Laura said with a snort. "That's not the way religion works. Ken may be telling himself that he's praying for a habitable planet, but what he really wants is assurance that somebody's looking out for him. He wants to know that somebody's watching over him, making sure that his life has meaning. Getting what he's been praying for is just going to encourage that."

"That's what I thought."

The oven timer pinged, and Laura got up and pulled out the pan of baked cookies, put the next pan in, and scooped the hot ones onto a cooling rack. She set the hot pan down on top of the oven and started making more dough balls.

"I wish they'd never invented religion," Ryan said.

Laura laughed. "You're not alone. It's done plenty of damage in its day. But really, it's not religion to blame so much as dogmatism."

"Dogmatism?"

"Belief in the official opinion. Asserting that your viewpoint is the absolute truth without regard to the facts."

"There's a difference?"

"Oh, sure. Religion's not always like this. A lot of times it's just good people believing in God and going on about their own business."

Ryan looked back outside just in time to see Star and Nova speed off through the flowers in a blur of gray. Wincing as a daffodil lost its head in the rush, he said, "That's kind of hard to believe."

"Well, it would be for you. You've never seen it work that way. But the ship is just one small society. Back on Earth and in the colonies, religion isn't anything like what it is here. It used to be, but it's not anymore."

"What changed it?"

Laura cocked her head to the side, thinking, while she rolled another couple dough balls. At last she said, "They bit off more than they could chew. There's always been an uneasy relationship between church and state, but back around the turn of the century, when I was growing up, religion had taken over quite a few governments. They were the most repressive nations in history, but that didn't seem to stop other people from trying it."

Laura was frowning now as she remembered. "You'd think that would have shown people how dangerous religion can be when you mix it with government, but to a true believer, the answer is never less religion. Even secular countries like the United States had evangelists who wanted to break down the boundary between church and state. They were a lot less tolerant of non-believers than your dad, too. When they built up enough of a following to influence elections, they started pushing their own particular beliefs on everybody, passing laws against anything they didn't like. Pornography, cohabitation, rock music. . .you know, they even banned teaching evolution in schools? That's when I gave up wanting to be a teacher."

"What's cohabitation?" Ryan asked. "I mean, besides living together."

"That's it."

"They banned living together?"

"What they were really after was men and women living together without being married."

"You mean like you and Teigh?"

Laura whooped with laughter. "Oh boy, would they have had fun with us! An old white woman and a young black man sharing a house and a bed—in some parts of the country I'd have been stoned for it and Teigh would have been burned on a cross."

"Stoned?" Ryan asked somewhat reluctantly.

"Throw rocks at until dead," Laura said with a grin. "The faithful would all get together in a mob and pitch pavement, then after they'd committed holy murder they'd go off and have a big picnic somewhere and congratulate each other for defending family values. Some of the networks would even broadcast it for the people at home so nobody missed out."

Ryan felt like he was adrift in zero-gee without a handhold. "People let them get away with that?"

"For a while." Laura sobered somewhat and began rolling dough balls again. "But the pendulum swings both ways, and it doesn't stop in the middle. After a few years of repression, people start missing their freedoms, and they start overthrowing governments. The

separation of church and state suddenly starts looking pretty good."
She brushed a strand of gray hair out of her eyes. "It took longer in
some countries than others, but by the time I was forty or so,
religion was pretty much a matter of personal belief again. The
world economy bounced back, too, and that's how we got
Spacehome."

She chuckled. "I remember when David—my·husband David,
not Bonham—designed the application form for immigration. For a
joke he put in a line asking the applicant's religion, but it just had
boxes for 'agnostic' and 'other' on it. Nobody complained."

Ryan had heard about David Morrison. Laura's husband had
been the driving force behind Spacehome from the start. He had
designed the immense cylindrical colony and overseen its
construction, and he and Laura had been two of its first inhabitants.
He had died in an accident before the colony was finished, but Laura
had continued to live there for another thirty years before joining
the Alpha Centauri mission.

She finished filling the cookie pan and sat down again at the
table. "Nothing lasts forever," she said. "Ken's started up
dogmatism—or maybe you'd call it fundamentalism—again, but it'll
die out sooner or later. Probably sooner, with the planet to explore
and colonize. We'll all be too busy to pay much attention to Ken."

"Yeah." Ryan said. "I suppose so." He drummed his fingers
lightly on the table, then added, "Still, he's right about one thing."

"What's that?"

"I'm even less of an asset on this trip than he is."

Laura looked at him quizzically. "What makes you think there's
any truth in that?"

Ryan shrugged. "It seems pretty obvious. I've blown the whole
trip without learning how to do anything vital to the colony. I'm
using up food and breathing air and space without giving anything
back."

"Wrong," Laura said with finality. "If you're useless, then what about me? Why do you suppose I'm here? Remember, they brought me along on purpose."

Ryan hardly hesitated. "You're a teacher. That, and you've lived through a lot. You've seen humanity move from Earth to the space colonies and now to another star. You've got a unique viewpoint."

"Hah. Sounds good, but it ain't so. The library's got more history than we need, and more viewpoints, too. And there are better teachers than me. No, I'm here because I make a good mother figure. People can talk to me, and I listen. I've got homey bits of advice backed up by the authority of years, and I'm not afraid to hand it out. Worth what it costs you, of course." She grinned. "It took me a while to realize it, but that's why they brought me along. I'm a likeable old coot."

"What does that have to do with me?"

"You're a likeable young coot, of course. Who else do you know on this ship who gets along with everybody as well as you do? Who else gets invited to all the parties? You're easily the most popular guy on the ship, Ryan."

"What, you're saying my purpose in life is to go to parties?"

"Maybe, if going to parties makes other people happy. That's your real job. Don't laugh; it's important." Laura blushed. "I know it sounds funny just saying it like that. It's like Macho; you're not supposed to talk about it. You're just supposed to do it naturally, but it's true. The biggest problem in a small society is keeping people happy, and we're one of the ways that job gets done." She got up just as the timer went off again, switched pans and scooped the hot cookies onto the rack while she said, "I'm not saying we're the only thing keeping people from suicide, but I *am* saying that you don't have to be a technical person to be valuable to the ship. Here, have a cookie." She handed him one of the still-warm ones from the first panful.

Ryan took a bite. As the flavor and aroma of freshly-baked snickerdoodle filled his senses, he couldn't help thinking that Laura was right. Not that he believed for a second that he shared any of her skills, but she, at least, certainly knew how to make a person feel loved.

He went to the party anyway, of course. A shipwide party was not a thing to miss. The park—a wide, high-ceilinged bowl of grass and trees and small hills at the three-quarter-gee level of the ship— was already filling with people by the time he got there, twenty minutes after David and the captain made their announcement over the intercom. Most of the people were gathered around the three kegs of beer that Laney Terrill, Holly's mother and the ship's dietician, had released from the stores.

Ryan advanced on the kegs to find his sister, Methany, pouring the beer. There was a burst of laughter from the group as he approached, and as Methany looked up and saw him standing in front of her she blushed a deep red.

Sean Little Bear, his dark braided hair hanging in front of his bead-encrusted leather vest, handed him an empty mug, saying, "Step right up, Ryan, but be prepared to pay the price. The lady here is demanding a kiss from every male who wants a drink."

Methany was ten, and she'd only recently discovered boys. Ryan looked at her in wonder, thinking that he'd been eighteen when he kissed a girl for the first time, and here in the space of twenty minutes his sister had come up with a plan to kiss every man on the ship inside a couple of hours. But she obviously hadn't figured her brother into her plan. "You don't—" she began, but she stopped, realizing that unless she wanted to argue every case there could be no exceptions in her game, not even for him. She stammered for the right thing to say, but Ryan swooped down and planted a loud smack straight on her lips before either of them could be embarrassed any further. Now there was applause mixed in with the laughter.

"Bravely done," Sean admitted. "She's bit three of us already."

Methany filled Ryan's mug and handed it back to him with a warning look that said clear as words: *Drink it slow*. He winked at her and said, "Ad astra!" lifting the mug high as he pronounced the old toast.

"Ad astra per inebrium!" Sean replied, draining the last of his own. He turned to Methany and held out the empty, puckering his lips at the same time. With a giggle, Methany kissed him and filled his mug.

As they walked away from the growing crowd around the kegs, Sean said, "That one's going to wind up running the colony or I'm a Cherokee."

Sean, Ryan knew from countless reminders, was Crow. Or Absaroka, to use the true tribal name. He'd been born in Los Angeles to parents who cared less about their Native American heritage than most whites did, but he'd grown up fascinated with his ancestors' way of life. He'd gone back to live on the reservation for a time before joining the Centauri expedition, eager to try his skills in the wild on a totally new, alien planet.

Ryan wished him luck. Twenty years of waiting to camp out in the dirt seemed like a lot of waiting for nothing, but he supposed somebody had to do the exploring. *Better Sean than me,* he thought. Aloud, he said, "I always thought you'd be the one running the colony."

"Me?" Sean asked in mock horror. "Not a chance. Van Cleeve's got me looking after the farm while your dad's in the hospital, and I'm already screwing it up. Give me the whole colony and I'd probably kill us all inside a week. Besides, I'm going to be too busy having fun to worry about administration. Your sister can have it."

They passed by a knot of people talking. Ryan overheard Mariko Paulsen, the biologist, say, "I don't know, maybe he thought he could get God's attention with the smell."

Ryan grinned. He looked over at Sean, who shook his head and said simply, "A memorable day, that's for sure. Let's go whack

Bonham on the back a time or two." He nodded toward an even bigger group around the astronomer.

Holly was there, her face aglow as she listened to David talk about his discovery. Ryan and Sean merged into the crowd, and David nodded to them without breaking stride. "The beautiful thing about it is the position of the orbit," he was saying. "We knew the Centauri system was edge-on to us when we left Earth, so we knew if we timed our arrival just right we could catch Alpha just as it hit the descending node and save a lot of delta vee, but we couldn't be sure that the planets would be in the right position when we got here because we didn't know their orbital parameters that closely. The way it looks, though, we'll be coming up on A-3 at just about the optimum configuration for a capture orbit. We can even shut down the drive early and coast the last few million kilometers before our final deceleration. I figure that'll cut two weeks off the trip time."

There was a prolonged cheer at that news. Two weeks out of a twenty-year trip was hardly significant, but two weeks earlier was still two weeks less waiting.

Ryan didn't cheer. He was thinking about the Tree. Any time cut off the trip was also time cut off the Tree's life. He wondered how long it would take to die in zero gee.

Holly saw him standing there with a frown on his face and pushed her way through the crowd until she stood beside him. "Hey, are you still mad at me?"

He shook his head. "I never was mad at you. You were right to kick me out of the hospital."

"Then what's the matter? *Ken* still bugging you?" She nodded toward a grassy mound near the wall and led the way over to it.

"Something he said," Ryan admitted, and told her about the Tree.

"Oh," she said. They sat down on the mound, leaning back on their elbows, and Holly looked out at the park around them; roughly thirty meters square and anywhere from six to ten high depending on where you stood. "I don't suppose we could transplant it down here, could we? We'll still have spin gravity even after we shut down the drive."

Ryan set his beer mug down beside him. "I don't think so," he said. "The farm's right overhead, and we'd have to move that to get enough room. And maybe the machine shop above that, too. The Tree's *big*."

"Hmm. We could do it, though."

They could, Ryan knew, but they wouldn't. When they'd had years of time ahead of them and nothing really to do but survive until the end of it, changing the layout of the ship had been one of the crew's favorite pastimes. When Teigh designed the lifesystem he had designed it with just that mutability in mind, making all the pieces modular so people could shift them around to meet their evolving needs, but now that they were so close to the end of the trip Ryan knew there would be no more rebuilding. There would be plenty of dismantling as most of the housing modules went down to the planet's surface to start the colony, but the farms and shop would stay in the ship, which would by then no longer be so much a ship as a space station. With all their effort going into the colony, they just wouldn't have time for saving the Tree. He said as much to Holly.

She nodded in agreement. "You're probably right."

They sat for a few minutes, looking out over the park and the people celebrating there, and finally Ryan said, "I'm sorry I bled all over your good time. That wasn't very nice."

"Don't worry about it," she said. "That's what friends are for, to listen when you feel like talking about something."

"Among other things," Ryan said.

He had been very conscious of Holly's hand right beside his on the grass since they sat down. Whenever he was with Holly he wanted to hold her, kiss her, make love with her. He'd wanted to since he was about Methany's age, but he still hadn't found the nerve to even touch her. Despite Ken's efforts to halt any "Godless licentiousness," as he put it, Ryan had had his share of other romances—but that didn't seem to make any difference with Holly. The longer he waited with her the harder it had become, until now he was nearly paralyzed at the thought of actually making a move. He wouldn't have done anything this time, either, if it hadn't been for Methany. His ten-year-old sister had more nerve than he did, and that embarrassing truth finally pushed him to do what his will alone couldn't.

He reached out and took Holly's hand in his. She stiffened at his touch, and he hoped it was simply surprise, but when he leaned forward and it became obvious that he was going to kiss her, she was still sending all the wrong signals. She was bracing herself the way Methany had when she had realized it was inevitable.

Ryan pulled back and let go of her hand. "What's wrong?" he asked.

"It doesn't feel right," Holly said.

"How do you know? We haven't even done it yet."

That brought a smile. "I mean, we're not that kind of friends. Don't get me wrong; I like you a lot. I love you. I really do. We grew up together, and we've shared just about everything, but that's the problem. We know each other too well. It would feel like kissing my brother."

"I just kissed my sister a while ago. It was okay."

"You did?"

"Yeah." Ryan recounted how he had gotten his beer. He couldn't believe how easy it was to tell her about it. Before, he would have gotten all tongue-tied trying to talk to Holly about kissing anybody, but now that he had at least made the attempt with her, it was suddenly easy.

Holly grinned at his story, but she shook her head and said, "It's not the same. When you kiss Methany you're both treating it like brother and sister, but if it was you and me then I'd be kissing you like a brother and you'd be kissing me like a lover. Wouldn't you?"

"I'd like to," Ryan admitted.

"And that's why it wouldn't feel right."

"Hmm."

Holly shifted uncomfortably. "I'm glad you, well, I'm glad you brought it up, though. I knew how you felt about me, and I've been trying to work up the nerve to say something to you for a long time, but it's really hard to broach the subject, you know?"

"Tell me about it."

"You're not mad?"

Ryan looked away for a moment, trying to decide if he was or not. At last he looked back into her eyes—they were even darker brown than he had remembered—and said, "Maybe a little, but not at you. I'm more mad at myself, I guess, for waiting so long. If I'd been more adventurous a few years ago, maybe you'd have still felt the same way I do."

"I don't. . .I don't know. Maybe. We can still be friends, can't we?"

"Of course we can still be friends. Just don't expect me to change the way I feel about you right away."

"I won't," Holly said.

"All right." There was a silence that threatened to grow longer. There really wasn't much more to say, was there?

Ryan sat forward and picked up his beer mug. "Hey," he said, "we're supposed to be whooping it up tonight. Come on." He stood and offered her a hand up. They walked back to the rest of the party, and within minutes were laughing and talking as if nothing had ever happened.

But Ryan left early all the same. Somehow he didn't feel like getting another beer, and he didn't feel like waiting around to see who Holly would leave with, either.

CHAPTER FOUR

A WOMB WITH A VIEW

THE INTERCOM WOKE HIM out of a dream. He started violently at the first chime, mistaking it for the predatory growl of some alien beast off in a forest of impossibly tall trees—all of which looked suspiciously like the one in the ship's axis—but the dream was already fading by the second chime. Ryan sat up and rubbed his eyes. The window—not a real one like Laura's, but a pretty good imitation—was projecting early afternoon light across his bed. He cleared his throat and practiced saying, "Hello, hello, hello," a few times to work the sleep out of his voice while he ran his fingers through his hair, then turned on the com and said it again. "Hello?"

"Did I wake you up?" It was Michelle. She smiled as he yawned.

His was a standard reply by now: "Yeah, but that's okay. I should have been up already. What's happening?"

"Nothing much. I'd like to get together for lunch if you feel up to it."

Lunch. It took a second for the concept to sink in, but when it did, Ryan said, "Sure. Give me a half hour, okay?"

"Okay. I'll meet you at Laney's."

Michelle winked out and Ryan dragged himself out of bed, showered, shaved, and headed upship, wondering why she had called. He had a pretty good suspicion. Michelle was the psychologist—one of two, actually, but Ryan wouldn't trust Thorpe with the punch line of a dirty joke since his conversion to Ken's church—and she had an uncanny knack for knowing when it was time for one of her "routine checkups." But then again, she was only a couple years younger than Ryan, and she had shown more than a professional interest in him before. Maybe she just wanted his company for lunch. With Michelle it was hard to tell.

She was waiting under the cafeteria sign. It was one of Sean's carvings, a half-meter plank with knife and fork surrounding raised letters that said "Laney's Eatery. Finest dining for___light-years." The blank was a square of white plastic with a number written on it in grease pencil. Someone had changed the number from 4.2 to 4.3 since Ryan had last looked.

"I missed you at the party," Michelle said, leading him inside and picking up a tray.

Between the plants that grew throughout the eatery Ryan could see a couple dozen other people sitting at scattered tables. That was only about a quarter of the crew; evidently a lot of people had partied until the wee hours. "I left early," he answered. He took a tray of his own and filled it with a lettuce salad and a couple slices of pizza, poured himself a glass of orange juice from a jug in one of the refrigerators, and headed to a fern-surrounded table near the wall.

They sat across from each other, talking about Centauri A-3 and their arrival there in just a few months, and Ryan was still not sure why Michelle had asked him to lunch until she asked, "So how do you feel about the end of the trip?"

"How do I feel about it?"

"Yeah. I mean, are you excited, or depressed, or indifferent, or what? All three maybe? It's a big change in our lifestyles coming up, and that sort of thing affects people in a lot of different ways. I want to find out how everyone's taking it, especially now that we've got a good hope of finding what we came out here for."

Ryan washed a bite of pizza down with a big swallow of orange juice and said, "Honest response? I'm not sure if I like it or not. I guess I'm glad there really is something out there, but like you say, it's going to be a big change in my lifestyle. I don't think I'm ready for it."

"I thought you might feel that way. You're one of the few people who's adapted almost perfectly to life on board."

"Beg your pardon?"

Michelle smiled. With her short brown hair and green eyes in a narrow, almost angular face, it was a smile very different from Holly's, but Ryan felt himself warm to it just the same. "I said you've adapted almost perfectly to life on board," she repeated. "It's no wonder you're less than enthusiastic about it ending."

"I wouldn't say I'm all that well-adapted," Ryan said. "In fact, I'd have said just about the opposite."

"What makes you think that?"

Ryan took another bite of pizza and chewed on it a while before he swallowed and said, "I feel like I've been wasting time. I've spent all my time reading or sleeping when I should have been training for planetfall. Everyone else either came on board with a trade or picked one in their first few years, but here I am with nothing to show for all my time here."

"You're worried about being valuable to the colony?" Michelle asked. "You shouldn't be. We really don't have any idea what skills we're going to need until we've been there a while. You're in good health with an open mind and no particularly bizarre hang-ups; you'll find a place, or a place will find you."

Ryan shrugged. "Laura says I'm going to be the colony nice guy."

"Nice guy?"

"Go to parties, listen to people's problems, give them homey bits of advice." He grinned at the obvious absurdity of it all. "That's what she said."

Comprehension lit up Michelle's face. "Ah, the nurturer. Laura told you about nurturers?"

"She didn't call it that, but yeah, I guess that's what she was talking about."

"She's definitely onto something, you know. The nurturer is one of the most important roles in any human society. Without one you don't even *have* a society, in the real sense."

"How do you figure that?"

Michelle leaned back in her chair and steepled her fingers on the edge of the table. "From studies of the early space missions, and from some of the even earlier long-range explorations on Earth. There were two very obvious ways a mission could come out; either the crew achieved what they intended to do and came back proud and happy and usually in just as good or better health than when they left, or else you'd have people wasting away and getting more and more irritable until things just fell apart and they had to abandon the mission. A few fell in the middle somewhere, but there was a real hole in the curve, and nobody could figure out why until somebody pointed out that every mission that worked had somebody who acted as a nurturer. Usually it was the cook, but sometimes it was a doctor or even an engineer. On one of the space stations it was the shuttle pilot who flew in their supplies. Ground control thought it was just the new supplies that boosted morale after he was there, but when they switched pilots there was practically a mutiny."

She leaned forward again. "The point is that you've got to have somebody in the group who makes life worth living. It can be as simple as having somebody along who's enjoying himself, but you've got to have at least one or you have trouble."

Ryan frowned. "You and Laura are both telling me all I've got to do is kick back and do nothing and everything will be all right. I don't *want* to kick back and do nothing. I've been doing too much of that as it is."

"You don't have to do nothing. In fact, you can do just about anything you want. If you're really a nurturer, you're going to be one no matter what else you do. What Laura and I are saying is that you shouldn't worry about whether you're earning your keep, because you already are."

"I don't feel like it."

"So do something about it."

"Like what?"

Michelle paused, thinking it over. "Well, let's look at it logically. You've got a self-esteem problem, which is getting worse because of an impending change in your lifestyle. I'd suggest trying to solve both at once by using the change as an opportunity to prove your worth."

Ryan finished his pizza and began nervously pushing his empty juice glass around on his tray. He hated being the topic of discussion. "And how do I do that?" he asked.

"I can think of one thing that's definitely going to need doing when we get there, and so far we've only got one qualified volunteer." Michelle waited until Ryan looked up at her before she said, "Exploring."

"Exploring."

"Right. So far Sean is the only explorer we've got."

"You're kidding. I thought just about everybody would be fighting for the chance to be the first to set foot on an alien planet."

"First to set foot on it, yes, but nobody wants to do any real exploring. I'm talking about walking around with a pack on your back, living in a tent, and trying not to get eaten by wild animals."

Ryan laughed. "The way you put it, no wonder there aren't any volunteers."

"I don't want anybody to think it's going to be easy. To hear Sean talk about it—and he's the expert on the subject—it's going to be a hard, dirty job. But it'd definitely give you something useful to do."

"I suppose it would." Ryan picked up his fork and chased a piece of lettuce around the inside of his salad bowl. The idea of being one of the first people to land *was* kind of exciting, but the thought of actually leaving the ship filled him with dread. And the idea of encountering wild animals didn't exactly appeal to him, either. "I don't know," he said. "I'm not sure I'd make much of an explorer."

"Why not?"

"I don't know. I just. . ." Ryan shrugged.

Michelle steepled her fingers in front of her again and said, "You know what a Freudian would say about all this, don't you?"

"No, what would a Freudian say?"

"A Freudian would say that the ship represents a womb, and you're resisting birth. A perfectly understandable reaction, mind you, since birth means leaving a comfortable environment for a world full of uncertainty, but it's hard to live a complete life without being born."

Ryan set down his fork. "A Freudian would say that? What about you?"

Michelle smiled. "I'd say that you have to be careful when you cite Freud, but he sometimes offers valid insight into a situation. Every child does have to leave the womb eventually."

"So you think I should go out there and hike around in the dirt for a while so I can feel like I'm accomplishing something?"

"I'm not offering you a placebo, Ryan. Exploring is a real job that needs doing. But I'm not pushing you to do something you don't want to do, either. I just want you to think about it. You *are* comfortable living here, and it *is* going to come to an end in another three months, and you *are* going to have trouble accepting it unless you openly embrace the change. Exploring is one way to do that."

Ryan nodded. "Well then, thanks for the suggestion, I guess. I'll think about it."

"Talk to Sean about it, too."

"Okay, I will."

"And don't worry about trying to prove your worth to anybody but yourself. You're the only one who even sees a problem."

"Besides Ken," Ryan said.

"Don't worry about what Ken thinks, either. Fathers never think their sons are doing enough with their lives. If you try to live your life to please *him*, then you really are going to need my help."

Ryan laughed. "True enough," he admitted.

Michelle laughed too. "And so saying, I've got to go talk to him. I really am collecting people's reactions to David's news, and he wasn't at the party last night either."

"Get ready for a sermon," Ryan said. They both got up from the table, and Ryan gathered their trays and put them in the recycler on the way out.

Michelle paused at the door. "Hey, let's get together one of these evenings for a movie," she said. "I hear we got another transmission from Spacehome a couple days ago."

"We did? Great!" Ryan said. "How about tonight?"

"Okay. Your place?"

"Sure."

"See you tonight, then." Michelle winked and turned away.

Ryan watched her until she had disappeared beyond the curve of the corridor. More psychology? Was she just boosting his ego, or did she really want to spend an evening watching a movie with him? Both, he decided. There was no reason why Michelle couldn't enjoy her work, was there? But the rest of what she'd said. . .he wasn't so sure what to think about that. Hanging his hide out in an alien environment just to prove he was worth his biomass didn't really strike him as the best idea he'd ever heard.

Out of habit, he turned and began walking aft along the curve toward the axis and the Tree. He would have to sleep on that idea a while.

Yeah, sleep on it, a tiny voice whispered in his head.

A minute later he was striding back the way he had come, heading for the farm to talk to Sean.

CHAPTER FIVE

SECOND CHANCES, SECOND THOUGHTS

"THIS IS GOING TO protect us from wild animals?" Ryan asked, dubiously eyeing the bright yellow nylon hemisphere he had just helped erect on the grass in the park. Helped "pitch," rather. Sean had been quite adamant about it: you erected buildings, maybe, but you pitched tents.

Now he surveyed Ryan's handiwork and said with a grin, "That's right, pilgrim. This great hulking edifice here is proof against one of the most voracious predators ever to plague a pack trip; the meanest, nastiest, ugliest varmint to ever suck the blood out of a weary traveler: the oft-swatted but never exterminated female mosquito."

Ryan said the same thing he'd been saying all afternoon to Sean's familiarization lecture: "Right."

Sean shook out the last piece of nylon from the tent bag, adding, "And once you get the fly on it, it's proof against rain, too."

"The fly?"

"That's what you call the rain cover."

"Any special reason?"

"Nope. Just file that along with 'carabiner' and 'clevis pin.'"

Ryan sighed. More jargon to remember. In the week since he'd signed up to be an explorer, learning the silly names for equipment was proving to be the most difficult part of training for the job. Dutifully, using the memory system he'd been taught before he even learned to read, he pictured a gigantic fly perched atop the tent, compound eyes glistening in the overhead lights. There; he'd be unlikely to forget that one, anyway.

He was just about to ask Sean what other fierce creatures the tent might repel when the public address system clicked on and Mac, the ship's Monitor and Control program, said, "All hands, prepare for a general bulletin from the captain. All hands, prepare for a—"

There was a crackle, then, "Van Cleeve here, and I've got good news. If you can stand another party so soon after the last one, I think we ought to gather in the park again tonight to celebrate Mr. Bonham's discovery of a second life-bearing planet in the Centauri system. That's right, David's just confirmed it: B-2 also shows a spectral signature consistent with life. Looks like we've suddenly got a choice, folks. See you at seven. Van Cleeve out."

Sean threw the tent fly into the air with a whoop and leaped upward after it, doing a full somersault in the low gravity before he landed again. "All right!" he shouted. "Twice the fun!"

Ryan grabbed the tent frame for support. Twice the fun? More like twice the exploration, and twice the chance to get himself eaten by the natives. What had he gotten himself into?

Methany was once again serving the beer, but this time she exacted no toll from her customers. She didn't need to; most of the men approached her with lips puckered already. Ryan forwent that bit of ritual, and as a consequence found himself making up for the last party by refilling his mug often.

Ken had made it this time. David's second discovery hadn't coincided with any bizarre prayer rituals, so the jury was still out as to whether God had had anything to do with either of them, but Ken was campaigning vigorously for Him nonetheless. As Ryan wandered away from the keg after his fourth or fifth refill, he heard Ken's voice rise over the general din: "Luck had nothing to do with it, I tell you! Luck is an illusion, an invention used to explain away an improperly understood universe. To say we had nothing to do with the creation of those worlds would be to deny our existence as functioning parts of the universal order."

"The existence of God, you mean," a quiet voice said, and as Ryan drew closer he realized it was David. Ken was preaching to David? *That ought to be fun to watch,* he thought, making a place for himself beside Warren Terrill in the circle surrounding the two.

Ken and David stood at opposite sides of the circle, like boxers about to leap into the center of the ring and slug it out, but theirs was not a physical battle. Ken's eyes still flashed hellfire, but the grin he wore below them defused some of their unnerving intensity. He had been making up for missing the last party, too.

"All right, I call it God, but you can call it whatever you like," he said in reply to David's comment. "I'm just saying we have a place in the universe. Our actions make a difference. Specifically, our prayers—"

"Did not create two planets out of nothing," David interrupted. "I refuse to believe that."

"I'm not asking you to believe that. I'm asking you to believe that our prayers influenced God—" Ken held up his hand to forestall David's outburst "—all right, influenced the structure of the universe in such a way that those planets were there for us. Choose any theory you like to account for it; maybe we affected some quantum event that threw us into a universe where the planets were there all along, or maybe we have some sort of control over our past, and we affected *this* universe to where the planets were there all along, or—"

"Or they really were there all along. What's wrong with that interpretation?"

Ryan raised his mug to David in acknowledgement of a point scored, and drank.

Ken shook his head. "It's cold, heartless, mechanical, and the universe doesn't work that way; that's what's wrong with it. The observer always influences the experiment. You know that. At the fundamental level, we're inextricably tied to the very structure of space and time. We can influence it. We *do* influence it, all the time, with the things we think and the things we do. Our attitudes matter. I'm convinced if we had done nothing, if we had just come here blindly accepting whatever we found, our chances of finding a habitable planet would have been far less."

To Ryan's surprise, David said, "I'll buy all but that last statement. Sure we affect the universe, probably in ways we don't yet understand, but you can't just blithely extrapolate from the quantum level to the cosmic level like that. We don't know whether the observer affects anything macroscopic. There's never been one shred of evidence for it."

Ken took a sip of his own beer, then said, "Why do you suppose we found out about the planets now, and not while we were still on Earth?"

"Because they're beyond the limit of observability from Earth. And now that we're maneuvering for final approach is the first time the drive flame hasn't been pointing right at them, which is why I was able to get a look at them."

Ken nodded as if he'd scored the point. "Awfully convenient, isn't it, that Earth is just a little bit too far away to tell for sure? And that the constraints of the only method of travel available to us made it impossible to tell what we were heading for until we were almost there. Almost like someone or something was testing our faith, isn't it?"

"That's just the way the universe is set up. You don't—"

"Exactly my point. That's just the way the universe is set up. But don't you wonder why? Out of all the possible configurations, don't you wonder why this one? I think it's obvious that God was testing us. He wanted to see if we'd prove ourselves worthy before he—"

"Stop, stop. No. Suddenly you're postulating a divine

consciousness directing all this. There's no evidence for that. None."

Ken smiled. "It's all around you, once you've made the leap of faith. There's the Bible, the Koran—all manner of holy works."

"That's the problem!" David swung his arms wide, nearly spilling his beer but bringing it under control and lowering the level in the mug before he said, "Religious faith means you have to take someone else's word on it. Not *God's* word, but some other person's, and that person may be lying, or at best deluded by others. If I'm going to believe in something, I need proof positive."

Ken shook his head sadly. "Oh ye of little faith. You're so afraid of it, and for no reason. Faith doesn't mean giving up rationality; it just means adding to it." He cocked his head as if listening to an inner voice, and when he spoke again it was obvious he was quoting. "'Now faith is the substance of things hoped for, the evidence of things not seen. . . Through faith we understand that the worlds were framed by the word of God, so that things which are seen were not made of things which do appear. . .'" In his own voice he said, "Sounds a little like particle physics to me," then went on quoting: "'By faith Abraham, when he was called to go out into a place which he should after receive for an inheritance, obeyed; and he went out, not knowing whither he went.' Sounds a little like us, doesn't it?"

Ryan found himself blushing. Having scripture quoted at him always did that to him. He wasn't sure if it was embarrassment for the person doing the quoting or just the embarrassment of being quoted to, but the result was the same. It always sounded so out of context, so mindlessly authoritarian; he felt himself immediately rejecting the argument, no longer wishing to even listen to it.

He suddenly realized he didn't have to, and turned away. David wasn't so lucky, but as he walked off, Ryan heard him saying, "You can find a quote that'll apply to almost any situation in any sufficiently complex piece of literature. I bet I could find quotes in a refrigerator repair manual that would apply just as well. The point is, once you accept an illogical foundation for your system of belief, you're open to all sorts of misinterpretations, and that's the problem with faith. There aren't any negative feedback loops. You can believe anything you want to without. . ."

Whatever else he and Ken said to each other was lost in the distance.

Life settled down to a semblance of normal in the following months, but as the ship backed deeper and deeper into the Centauri system, its path slowly curving into a closed orbit under the pull of the twin suns, the undercurrent of excitement among the crew became hard to miss. Everyone began readying for the impending move to one or another of the planets; packing their personal belongings, unpacking and servicing the tools for the colony, making plans and contingency plans and fallback contingency plans to account for every conceivable possibility.

Ryan tried to get caught up in the excitement, but for him anxiety was the stronger emotion. He found himself sleeping less, though not for lack of trying. He just couldn't relax with all the thoughts running around in his head. At the same time his stomach began to hurt and his appetite dwindled, enough so that Laney grew concerned about her cooking. Ryan talked with Michelle about it and got some suggestions for dealing with stress, but no amount of relaxation tapes or enforced diet could erase the certainty that his quiet, comfortable life was about to change forever.

As the actual moment grew closer, Ryan and Sean found themselves swamped with volunteers for exploring duty, but aside from training replacements in case one of them were injured, they kept the honor for themselves. Ryan had spent a long afternoon under the Tree considering whether or not he should give up his spot to someone who actually wanted it more, but in the end he had decided not to. He was as well qualified to be an explorer as anyone on board, save for Sean; this seemed his only chance to prove his worth to himself as well as to the rest of the ship. If he didn't go through with it, then Ken's assessment of him *would* be right.

And despite Michelle's advice to ignore what he thought, Ryan would do almost anything to prevent that.

CHAPTER SIX

FIRST CONTACT

THE SHUTTLE LOOKED LIKE a teardrop frozen in mid-fall. Its entire hull, windows included, was one smooth lifting body, broken only by two tiny vertical stabilizers and the two fusion engines in the rear. Waiting there on the other side of the airlock at the end of the docking port, sunlight glinting off it as it turned with the starship under the unfamiliar light of Alpha Centauri A, it looked sleek and fast and sexy, and for the first time since he'd agreed to this crazy business Ryan felt glad he was going.

It seemed as if the entire crew had turned out to see Sean and him off. The observation deck was packed with people drifting at all angles, and loud with shouts of encouragement and last-minute advice. Even Ken had come to wish them well, and Ryan felt an unexpected lump in his throat at the sight of him and Alice and Methany floating arm in arm near the window and looking proud. For the first time in years, they looked like a family.

Ryan reeled as another congratulatory whack on the back propelled him headlong into a hug and a kiss from Laura, who handed him off to Michelle for another, and so on in a frenzy of well-wishing that left Ryan dazed and even had Sean a shade redder than usual. There was enough kissing going on to start an epidemic, but with the stuff Holly had given the two explorers to boost their immune systems Ryan doubted if a bug could live in the same room with either of them.

Holly was there, too—right by the airlock door, in fact—and as momentum carried Ryan toward her he realized that she was going to kiss him as well. He hesitated as he pulled himself to a stop beside her, their talk at the first discovery party echoing in his mind, but her smile was genuine and so was her kiss.

It was a sisterly kiss, to be sure, but Ryan was glad he was facing away from the rest of the crew just the same. He could feel a bubble of surprise and exhilaration about to burst in his chest, and at that moment he was sure that the entire core of his being lay exposed for anybody to see. He looked into Holly's eyes—he didn't care if *she* saw into his soul—and she looked back with pride and admiration. It was threatening to become a Moment, but with effort he turned away and pulled himself into the airlock.

Sean came in feet first, waving a last goodbye. Ken had drifted up beside Holly; he stuck his head in after them and said, "Go with God."

Ryan's first impulse was to say, "He didn't volunteer," but he swallowed that and said instead, "Right, Dad. Thanks. Don't let Mom worry, okay?"

"I won't," Ken promised. He looked as if he were groping for more words, but if so he never came up with them. After a moment he grasped Ryan once again in a hug, let him go, and pushed himself back out of the airlock. He and Holly swung the inner door closed, leaving Sean and Ryan in sudden silence.

Sean grabbed the rim of the outer doorway and swung through into the shuttle's own airlock. Ryan followed on his heels and closed the ship's outer door, then the shuttle's outer door next to that. With a grin and a shake of his head Sean pulled an emergency suit out of the rack and tossed it to Ryan, saying, "Well, now we go out and earn all that attention."

Ryan felt a shiver run up his spine at Sean's comment, and the now-constant gnawing in his stomach gave him a new lurch of pain. Besides the inoculations, there had been one other pre-launch medical procedure that still gave Ryan the shakes when he thought about the implications: sperm samples, to preserve the colony's gene pool in case the explorers didn't come back.

He banished the thought to a deep corner of his mind and began pulling on the suit, and when he strapped the last item of explorer's gear—a .45 caliber automatic pistol—around his waist, he felt a little better. It made no sense, since going into a situation where he might need a gun almost by definition meant going into danger, but he had watched enough adventure movies to absorb at least a little of their macho man-with-a-gun aura of invincibility. A .45 was a primitive weapon, but it was loud and dependable—qualities which Sean maintained were more important than technological sophistication.

A few minutes later, suited and strapped into the two form-fit arm chairs before the controls, they blew the airlock coupling and Sean fired the topside attitude jets to shove them away from the starship. Through the windshield they could see people smiling and waving behind the observation port. Ryan waved back and gave them the thumbs up.

The ship receded, revealing the three other shuttles and two enormous cargo landers clinging to the rotating wall. Tracks led away from the central docking hub to their parking places. Like the shuttle they now flew, each would be winched into place over the airlock when needed.

The ship dwindled from a shuttle- and instrument-studded wall to a cylinder gleaming in space, a cylinder small enough to hide with an outstretched hand. A knobby sphere butted up against the far end was the drive, its ten-kilometer tether reeled in now that it was no longer in use. For the first time since he was eight years old, Ryan saw the ship for what it was: not the all-encompassing world he had lived in for nearly twenty years, but rather a small bubble of life in an enormous universe. It was a little scary to see his world dwindle so, but somehow exhilarating at the same time. He had needed to expand his scope.

Sean tilted the shuttle's nose away from the ship and there, rising up to take its place in the windows, was the planet. It was still "the planet," or, if someone needed to refer to it by name, "A-3." Laney had installed a box in the eatery for name suggestions, but they wouldn't open it and vote until after the explorers had returned with first-hand information on what it was really like. As Laura had put it, "We don't want to rush into this and have to live with a name like 'Earth' for the rest of our lives, now do we?"

Actually, they weren't even sure "the planet" would be their final destination anyway. They had two planets to explore before they made their choice. They had gone to A-3 first because it was easier to reach from their angle of approach and because, of the two stars, Centauri A was much more like the Sun, but unless it checked out perfectly from the start, they would be exploring Centauri B's system as well.

Let it be perfect, Ryan thought.

It was beginning to look like that might be the case. The planet below them was a swirling mass of blue and white, flecked with brown and green where land showed through the clouds. Except for the outlines of the continents, it looked just like pictures of Earth. *Daedalus* had been in orbit for nearly two weeks, its crew spending the entire time mapping and looking for signs of civilization and arguing over where the first landing ought to be, but even in that time Ryan hadn't grown tired of looking at it. It was beautiful.

But Earth's moon was beautiful from orbit, too, and that didn't make it habitable. Ryan knew he was being pessimistic, but he couldn't shake the feeling that he and Sean would find something wrong here, that they would have to explore both planets before the colony found a home.

He heard Sean muttering something beside him, flinched as Sean reached straight for his neck, then blushed when he heard a click and Sean's voice saying, "—to turn on your radio, that's it! Can you hear me now?"

"Yeah," Ryan said, adjusting the volume.

"I thought you were being kind of quiet there. So, you ready for some action?"

At one time Ryan would have said, "I guess so," but a couple of months of training with Sean had taught him to be a little more assertive unless he wanted to get ribbed for being a paleface. "Yeah," he said. "Let's do it."

David Bonham was monitoring from the observatory. His face looked out at them from the shuttle's tiny intercom screen. "Entry window coming up in three minutes," he said. "Engines armed?"

Sean flipped a pair of toggle switches. Above each of them, an LED glowed bright green. "Engines armed, green light."

"Attitude?"

"All wrong." Sean pulled back on the control stick and the nose of the shuttle rose up again, obscuring the planet. "There goes the view," he said. He used the pitch and yaw and roll thrusters in turn to line up the attitude indicator—a ghostly heads-up display of shaded lines—until the red and blue and green axes superimposed in all three planes, doing the whole maneuver with a minimum of motions that had Ryan envious. Ryan had practiced with the controls in simulation mode and gotten to where he could land the shuttle with most of the instruments on automatic, but Sean flew completely on manual. He had been a shuttle pilot for a few years back on Earth before he'd quit to live on the reservation, and he hadn't lost his touch in the years since.

They waited out the last few minutes, Ryan trying not to babble. The tension threatened to loosen his tongue, but at the same time he knew that they were recording. Four years and a few months from now, everyone in the solar system would be listening to what he said, and that made him consider every word. Sean was having no problem with that; he talked as if he were at a party, which, Ryan supposed, he probably felt he was.

Sean counted down the last seconds, then with a "Here we go!"

he pushed the firing button. Thrust built up in the next few seconds from none at all to a full gee and beyond. They rode it for four long minutes, killing nearly half of their orbital velocity before Sean shut off the drive and turned them around to face the direction of travel again. They touched atmosphere only a few minutes later, and the gee force began to build even higher—this time pulling them forward—as they braked. The radio hissed and crackled as the ionized air from the heat of their passage blocked the signal, but that only lasted a few minutes before they slowed to gliding speed and the hull began to cool again.

Sean dropped the nose back down until it was aimed along their flight path, and there they were, screaming along at about mach ten over the site they had picked for their first landing. They had chosen a rolling plain at about thirty degrees south latitude in the middle of a vaguely bird-shaped continent, a spot where, they hoped, they would find a relatively simple ecosystem to study until they learned some of the rules of life there.

Ryan felt a moment of panic as they dropped through the scattered cumulus clouds above the plain; at their speed and shallow angle of descent there was no way to miss going through at least one. He imagined it exploding in their wake, but he had no rear window to look through and see.

The clouds left dark patches of shadow on the greenish amber ground, but off to the right Ryan saw another black patch that wasn't shadow. He pointed it out to Sean, and Sean banked around to fly past it. As they flashed by they saw that it was a herd of animals feeding on the grass. There were too many to count—a couple hundred, at least, Ryan guessed.

"How many legs did they have?" Sean asked.

"We're too high to tell," Ryan said.

"Let's make another pass." Sean banked the other way and pulled them around in a circle, at the same time toggling the switches that opened the ports for the atmospheric engines. They came to life with a shriek and the shuttle drew downward with the new drag on the underside, but when its airspeed dropped to below sonic speed Sean leveled it out again under power and they continued to fly.

The herd had begun to scatter from the sonic boom. Dust rose behind the individual animals as they ran. Sean brought the shuttle past them a second time at only a couple hundred meters altitude, and as they went by Ryan picked out an animal that had been separated from the rest and watched until it disappeared beneath them.

"Four legs," he said. "One head, one tail. Looks like they might have horns, or maybe just big ears."

"I think they were horns," Sean said. He laughed. "They looked like buffalo. Thick shoulders, shaggy coat, and all." He banked around for another pass, kept the bank this time and circled once around the galloping herd. "Definitely look like buffalo," he pronounced. "You getting all this up there?"

The ship was in low orbit; it wouldn't stay within direct radio range of any one spot on the ground for more than a few minutes at a time, but they had put a communications satellite in stationary orbit over their chosen landing site so that the explorers could stay in contact continuously. David's voice came through the link as well as if they were talking by intercom on the ship. "Clear picture."

Mariko Paulsen, the ship's primary biologist, was monitoring their signal as well. Actually, everybody was probably listening in, but David and Mariko were the official mission directors. Mariko said, "They look like buffalo to me, too. Their horns are longer, but the resemblance is incredible."

"Do you think they really could *be* buffalo?" Ryan asked.

"No," Mariko answered. "More likely parallel evolution."

"Why do you say that?"

"Because if it's not, we've got to come up with a good explanation why we've got real buffalo four light-years from Earth."

"I can answer that easily enough." It was Ken.

"I'm sure you can," Mariko said, "but why don't we all wait until we have some data to base our theories on?"

Ken didn't reply.

"I'd like a tissue sample if you can get it," Mariko went on. "That'd answer a lot of questions right there."

Sean said, "Let's look around some more before we land."

"You're the pilot."

Sean leveled the shuttle and they flew east across the plain toward a low mountain range, encountering more herds of the same buffalo-like animals along the way, some a couple thousand strong. They found other animals as well, some like antelope, others like deer, and one particular herd of what looked like camouflage-painted horses running along the slope of a sparsely forested ridge. The trees on the ridge looked like pines. On the other side of the same ridge something like a mountain lion stood on a rock outcrop and lashed its tail as they circled around it. Overhead, riding the thermals along the ridgeline, soared a bird that might have been an eagle.

"This is getting kind of eerie," Ryan said at last. "It looks too much like Earth."

"Let's go ahead and land," said Sean. "Check out the small stuff for a while. Get Mariko her tissue samples."

"Sounds like a plan to me."

Ryan was proud of his self-control. His voice sounded calm and even, but he felt anything but calm. His stomach churned, and he felt beads of sweat standing out on his forehead. They were going to land. He was going to be one of the first two people to set foot on an extrasolar planet. He had trained for months for this moment, but now that it was about to happen he wondered if he would be able to maintain his cool.

Please, God, he thought, *don't let me throw up.*

CHAPTER SEVEN

THERE'S NO PLACE LIKE HOME

SEAN TOOK THEM BACK out into the plain, picking a spot a couple kilometers from a herd of buffalo. He angled the engines for vertical thrust and slowed the lander to a hover over the grass, then gradually lowered the thrust until they settled onto the ground. Ryan waited with his finger poised over the switch that would spray flame retardant on any fires the engines set, but the grass was green enough and the engine blast cool enough that he didn't need to use it.

Sean cut the engines entirely, and in the sudden silence he and Ryan looked at each other through their pressure suit helmets, both clearly wondering who was going to speak the first words from the surface of the new planet.

Ryan wasn't about to take the honor away from Sean. This was Sean's moment in the spotlight; Ryan was the sidekick on this trip and he had no desire to have it otherwise.

Sean nodded sagely, unbuckled his seat harness, and said, "Last one out the airlock is a paleface!"

He was already in motion as he spoke, his pressure suit hardly slowing him at all. Ryan felt his tension drain away in an instant; he slapped the release button on his seat harness and with a whoop leaped after him. They both crowded in the airlock and Ryan pulled the inner door closed, gave the handle a half turn to lock it, and as soon as the safety interlock disconnected the other door Sean pulled it open. It unsealed with a thump of inrushing air—the outside pressure was higher than on board the ship—and then despite Sean's words inside they just stood there looking out through the open doorway at the endless kilometers of waving grass. At last Sean pulled another lever beside the door and a collapsible stairway folded out from the hull beneath the door.

"After you," Ryan said.

Sean didn't argue. He simply said, "Okay," and strode down the three steps to the ground. The grass came up to his knees; he ran his gloved hand over the tops of it, took another couple of steps through it, and raised his hands out before him as if embracing the entire planet. When he spoke, his voice in the suit radio was firm and carefully enunciated. He was speaking for the record. "As the first human being to set foot upon this world's surface, I make a solemn promise on behalf of my entire race. We will live here in peace and in harmony with the way of this world, or we will not live here at all. This promise I guard with my life, and I charge everyone who comes here after me to guard it equally. *We will not mess it up.* In the name of humanity, Sean Little Bear has spoken."

Sean lowered his arms, but he didn't turn around. Ryan, his throat suddenly dry, realized that he was back on the spot. Sean had given him the chance to make a speech of his own if he wanted. He had rehearsed the landing in his mind a hundred times before, sometimes even with himself making the historic first step, but he had never come up with any satisfactory words to speak. Certainly nothing to match what Sean had just said. He had thought of making a joke of it, stepping down and saying "I claim this world for the bug creatures of Betelgeuse Seven," or some such silliness, but in the wake of Sean's speech he realized how inappropriate that would have been.

He set his foot on the first step, then the second, thinking frantically for something to say. With the third step he felt panic taking over; he fought it away and put his foot down in the grass. It was uneven underfoot, bumpy from the stalks growing in clumps a couple of inches apart. He took a couple steps through it until he stood beside Sean, and somehow found voice enough to say, "I make the same promise. We will not mess it up."

Sean nodded, and his solemn expression gave way to his familiar grin. "Good enough," he said. "Now let's see just what it is we'll be living in harmony *with*."

In the next few hours they began to find out. They stayed near the lander where the remote-controlled cameras could keep them in sight, but even so they had plenty to keep them busy. Some exploring, Ryan discovered, was less a matter of fighting off wild animals than of simply keeping your eyes open while you bagged specimens of the flora and fauna for detailed analysis back on the ship.

There was excitement enough without wild animals. David had already analyzed the air from orbit and pronounced it breathable, and they tested it again on the ground with a portable gas chromatograph and a plate of rapid-growth media Mariko called "Biogoo," but all the same when it actually came time to doff their pressure suits and take a breath, both Ryan and Sean felt their pulse rates quicken. They hesitated before unzipping their suits, laughing nervously at their hesitation, but feeling real fear just the same. Nobody had ever breathed an alien atmosphere before; they couldn't know, not with absolute certainty, that the chromatograph and the Biogoo hadn't missed something that would turn out to be poisonous. They were sure it hadn't, were sure enough that they hadn't even brought along a test animal to breathe the air first, but there was that last-minute fear just the same.

They decided to do it one at a time, just in case, and since Sean had gotten to take the first step, Ryan got the honor of drawing the first breath of otherworldly air.

Standing in the grass with his fingers on the suit zipper, he realized that some things had to be taken on faith. You could design the proper instruments and the proper tests to use them in, but the machinery by itself wasn't enough. Somewhere along the line you had to have faith. Faith in the people making the instruments, faith in the people designing the tests, faith in your ability to understand the results and apply them to the situation at hand—if you didn't have that faith then you were just wasting your time. You might as well go back to voodoo and save the development costs.

It was a sobering thought, knowing that everything you did depended in some degree or other upon faith. The biggest difference between world-views, even between world-views as disparate as his and Ken's, was not that one had faith and the other didn't, but rather in where that faith lay. Ryan had always put his faith in science, in the basic comprehensibility of the universe and in man's ability to control it, while Ken put his in God. If Ken were standing in Ryan's place with his finger on the zipper he would be praying to God that the air was good, while Ryan was hoping that the chromatograph was working right, and that he and Sean and David and everybody else really understood the human body's needs and tolerances as well as they thought they did.

This was Ryan's test. Did he truly believe in all this scientific gimmickry? Enough to trust his life to it? When he thought of it that way, it was hardly a question. Here he was over four light-years from Earth and scientific gimmickry was the only thing that had gotten him there—of course he believed in it. All the same, he took a deep breath of the suit's air before he pulled the zipper down and ducked his head through the opening. He exhaled halfway, inhaled cautiously, and only when he'd held that breath a few seconds did he take a full breath of the new planet's air.

He expected it to be anticlimactic, and it was. There were odors in it that weren't on the ship, but nothing different enough to be definably alien. More than anything else it smelled of dirt and grass.

Fifteen minutes later, when Ryan still showed no ill effects, Sean unzipped his own suit. He took the same cautious sniff Ryan had, but followed it a moment later with a throaty laugh that brought a reflexive smile to Ryan's face as well.

"Smells like prairie," Sean said as he stripped off his suit and tossed it in the airlock. He laughed again. "Hell, we've come all this way just to rediscover Montana."

Ryan had never been to Montana, but he felt the truth in Sean's statement. This world was so Earthlike it was scary.

Once they started collecting samples they began to find differences, which relaxed everyone a bit, but the differences were so minor that they hardly mattered. The grass wasn't any species of Earth grass, but it still looked like grass, with tufts of tiny seeds like undomesticated cereal grains on the ends of the stalks. The insects looked like insects, if you didn't mind the extra body segment on the ants or the butterflies with single undulating wings like tiny rippling paragliders, and though the birds looked more like bats than birds, even they weren't strange enough to look truly alien.

It was almost a relief when they discovered the rodents. At least the little creatures acted like rodents, squeaking in high-pitched voices and popping in and out of holes in the ground, but they looked like nothing you would find on an Earth prairie. They looked more like hand-sized octopuses with dark brown stripes running down the length of their light brown arms, only Mariko's arm count from a freeze-frame revealed that they should more properly be called "hexopuses." They moved in a graceful flowing walk on the ends of those six tentacles, sometimes stopping and standing on the hind four while they waved the front ones in front of them toward Ryan or Sean as if testing the air in their direction. Front seemed an arbitrary direction; they could turn their heads almost completely around. When startled they could move at least as fast as any field mouse, disappearing with almost magical speed among the grasses.

"Try communicating with one," Sean said.

"What?"

"Try talking to one. To see if it's intelligent."

"Uh...huh." Ryan looked up at the top of the lander, where the camera was following his and Sean's every move. This reeked of a setup.

Sean caught his glance. "No, I'm serious. It's in the contact protocols. We have no idea what might be intelligent here, and we have to find out before we move in."

"We do."

"Yep."

"And what if they are?"

Sean grimaced. "Then we decide whether or not we can live with them."

Ryan thought about that for a moment. "Shouldn't that be their choice, rather than ours?"

"Good man!" Sean's grimace morphed into a smile. "You pass the test. Go ahead, see if they want to talk."

Ryan felt stupid doing it, but he crouched down and waited until one of the hexopuses came within a meter or so and stretched out its arms toward him. He slowly imitated its gesture and said, "Hello, little thing. My name's Ryan. Do you have a name?"

The hexopus squeaked back at him. For a second Ryan felt a shiver rush down his spine, but before he could try to repeat the sound the creature had made, it darted off into the weeds, and though he waited a full ten minutes for it to return, it didn't show up again. He tried again with another one, but it only looked at him, squeaked, and ran away too.

He stood up and brushed the dirt off his knees. "I think they're just funny-looking field mice after all," he said to Sean.

"More like prairie dogs, but yeah, I think you're right," Sean said. He shaded his eyes and looked out toward the buffalo herd, just visible as a dark line against the horizon. "I feel like walking a while. Why don't we go see if those guys can tell us anything?"

"You get to do the talking this time."

"Deal."

They closed up the lander and headed out across the open plain, taking with them a telecam and a day pack for carrying back anything interesting they might find along the way. It took Ryan a ways to get used to walking on the uneven ground. His hiking boots were an unfamiliar weight on his feet, after years of soft shoes or going barefoot. His pistol slapped against his thigh until he slid the holster around to the back a little, and even then it bounced along uncomfortably against his right buttock. *Exploring is a pain in the ass*, he thought, but the notion made him smile. It hadn't been a pain in anything so far, not really. Now that they were actually *doing* it, even his stomach had quit hurting.

He heard the rhythmic swish-swish of his and Sean's legs cutting through the grass, looked up at the clouds drifting in puffy patches overhead, and for the first time really realized that he was on the surface of a planet. He was on the outer edge of something that was open to space, and only gravity kept him and the air he breathed from drifting away. He felt the ground against his feet and thought: *This is gravity. This planet is pulling on me, not pushing like the decks of the ship do. It feels the same as centrifugal force, but it's a completely different phenomenon.*

He wondered if the whole planet was like that somehow. It looked like Earth, felt like it, acted like it, but underneath it could be completely different. All the proteins and sugars could be stereoisomers of the earthly ones and the colonists might not be able to digest any of them, or what looked like grass could turn out to be a skyscraper city for intelligent microbes and he and Sean had already destroyed a complete civilization.

Or maybe he was buying trouble where there wasn't any. Maybe it looked like Earth because it was like Earth.

"You're awful quiet there, Pilgrim."

Ryan looked over at Sean, saw the big grin on his face, and said, "I'm trying to imagine all the awful things that can happen to us down here."

"Hah. Did you remember tornadoes?"

"I hadn't gotten to that yet," Ryan admitted.

"What about meteor strikes? Just because we're on a planet doesn't mean we can quit worrying about meteor strikes, you know."

"Oh." Ryan thought about that a minute, then asked, "How do you patch a planet?"

"With seeds. Heads up, they've noticed us." Sean pointed toward the buffalo herd, where some of the members had raised their heads and were looking toward the approaching humans.

"They don't look too excited, do they?" Ryan said. He pointed the telecam at them and pressed the transmit button.

"Not yet. They've probably never seen anything like us before, so they're not sure what to do. If we act like predators—and if they act like buffalo—then they'll probably tighten up into groups with the females and calves in the middle and the males facing out, but if we don't look like anything threatening they'd probably let us get right in there with them if we wanted to."

"Do we want to?"

"Not really. If we get in close and then they decide they don't like us, we're in trouble. Don't let their size fool you into thinking they're slow. Or friendly. We used to lose a couple dozen tourists a year to the buffalo herd on the reservation when the tourists tried to get close enough to take pictures."

"So what do we do?"

"We call from here to see if maybe they're not what they seem." Sean stopped about twenty-five meters away from the nearest animal and, cupping his hands around his mouth, shouted, "Hello over there! Can you understand me? Three point one four one five nine two six whatever it is. Take me to your leader! We come in peace! That's one small step for a man, one giant leap for mankind! Hello!"

The buffalo milled around uncertainly, and one old, grizzled bull took a couple steps toward them. His massive shoulders were about as high as Ryan's head and his horns curved out and around until the forward-facing points were about a meter apart. Ryan's laughter dwindled as the bull cocked his head in a very human gesture of curiosity, straightened it, then stretched his neck out and let out a loud bellow.

"*Marrrooo*," Sean repeated, only half joking now. "Pleased to meet you. I'm Sean Little Bear, and this is Ryan Hughes. Can you understand me?"

The bull lowered his head and snorted.

Sean made a passable attempt at snorting like the bull, and lowered his own head. To Ryan he muttered, "This might be like hollering 'Your mama' at him, so get ready to run."

"Run where?"

"Away. No, scratch that. Wait until he gets close and then run to the side."

"To the side," Ryan echoed. Well, sure, that did make more sense than running directly away from a half-ton alien. But it still sounded far from foolproof. "We should have brought the rover," he said. The shuttle's tiny cargo bay held a small four-wheeled all-terrain vehicle for just such encounters as this.

"Probably," said Sean. "Next time we will."

Other members of the herd were coming up beside the bull, all staring at Sean and Ryan, but none of them made a threatening move. Even the bull remained still.

Ryan panned with the telecam, noticing how the grass was eaten and trampled where the herd stood. It was trampled off beyond the herd, too, but not on the side where he and Sean stood. The creatures were evidently eating their way toward where they'd landed the shuttle. "Mariko, what do you think?" Ryan asked the telecam.

"Not enough data." Mariko's voice sounded tinny in the telecam's built-in speaker. "It looks like standard herd animal behavior, but that might be deceptive. Intelligent herd animals might act the same way."

"I'm going to—" Sean began, but Ryan never got a chance to find out what he was going to do, because the bull lowered his head again, sighted down his horns, and charged.

"No I won't," Sean said as he backpedaled a few steps until he was even with Ryan. He looked to both sides and said, "Get ready to jump...ready...ready...*now!*"

Ryan didn't need to be told. As soon as the buffalo got within a few meters of him he leaped to the side and kept running, but when he looked over his shoulder he saw that the buffalo had skidded to a stop and had turned on him again. He could smell the thing now, a hot, musky sort of odor that awakened something primitive in him. The bull rushed him again, and almost instinctively Ryan threw the telecam at it with all his strength and leaped aside again, drawing his gun in the same motion.

"No, don't shoot it!" Sean shouted.

"I don't...plan on it," Ryan shouted back, gasping for the breath that had been scared out of him. The buffalo turned again, lowered his head, and at the same time Ryan shouted, *"Stop!"*

He pulled the slide back and let go, jacking a bullet into the chamber, and fired the gun into the air. The report was far louder than the pounding of hooves, and both Ryan and the bull flinched, but Ryan had to shift his weight and jump to the other side as the bull suddenly veered the direction he had planned to go. He fired another shot into the air as it passed, this time headed back into the herd, then he turned and ran in the other direction.

Sean caught up with him and they sprinted back toward the shuttle, checking over their shoulders all the while. "That was the...stupidest thing you could...have possibly done!" Sean puffed as they ran.

"Not so," Ryan said. He stumbled in a hexopus hole, recovered and looked over his shoulder again, then slowed to a walk. "It's stopped. And no, it wasn't stupid." He popped the magazine out of his pistol and put the pistol back in its holster, took three bullets out of his pants pocket and refilled the magazine, leaving the one in the chamber, then slid the magazine back into the grip. He said, "I remembered how the other herd scattered from the sonic boom when we flew over, so it seemed a good bet that they don't like loud noises. Besides, I wanted to give it a chance to realize *we* were intelligent. Showing it I had a weapon was the only thing I could think of at the time."

"You ever heard of a stampede?" Sean asked.

"No," Ryan said, truthfully. "What's that?"

Sean looked back to where the buffalo had already returned to grazing. "Forget it," he said.

"Damn!" Ryan said, smacking himself on the forehead. "The telecam's still back there."

"Forget that, too. Let Mariko and David try to talk to them for a while." Sean started walking back to the lander. He was obviously mad about something.

"Hey, I'm sorry," Ryan said, not quite sure what he was sorry about, other than that Sean was mad.

"Not your fault," Sean said. "You did the right thing. I was so busy trying to talk to it I forgot there are other ways to communicate." He turned to Ryan and a grin slowly spread across his face. "I bet those guys on the ship tipped over backward when they got a faceful of buffalo on their screens."

"Ha, I bet."

After they'd walked a while more, Sean said, "You know, I think we've been going about this all wrong. We've been looking for intelligence in anything that moves, when what we ought to be looking for is *signs* of intelligence first."

"What kind of signs?"

"Well, guns, for instance, or even sticks. Any kind of tools. Clothing. Some kind of sign that what we're looking at manipulates its environment. We carry all sorts of stuff around with us; it's reasonable to assume that other intelligent beings would too."

"What if we stumble across a bunch of nudists?"

"Then we look for opposable thumbs."

"How do you figure?"

"If something's going to manipulate its environment, then it's got to have something to manipulate it *with*. An animal without opposable thumbs is going to have a hard time holding onto anything, so it's not going to get very far along the evolutionary road toward intelligence."

That argument had bothered Ryan the first time he heard it, and it still bothered him now. "What do we know about alien intelligence?" he asked.

"Nothing at all," Sean replied. "Which is why we're trying to talk to prairie octopuses and buffalo. But until we learn something about it, we've got to use our own criteria, or we're going to get chased off by every territorial animal on the planet while we're trying to talk to it."

Ryan could see the sense in that. "So what should we do now?" he asked.

Sean had evidently been waiting for that question. He said, "I vote we go find us some mountains and do some real exploring. Fill our backpacks and walk up a river valley for a few days. What do you say?"

"I say fine, let's go."

Sean looked surprised at Ryan's enthusiasm, and in truth, Ryan was a little surprised as well, but he was still high from his encounter with the buffalo. It had given him confidence. He had proven that he could take care of himself, and now something inside of him was pushing to test it again. It felt almost instinctive, that urge to pit himself against the wilderness, but it was real, and he wasn't going to suppress it. Not now. For the first time in his life, he felt as if he were doing something worthwhile.

CHAPTER EIGHT

CUSTOMS AGENTS

THE VALLEY THEY PICKED was one of several leading down out of the craggy, snow-capped mountain range that formed the backbone of the continent. Its river had cut deep into the heart of the mountains, leaving a wide flood plain which they could follow inward through half a dozen ecosystems on their way to its source.

They parked the shuttle at the mouth of the valley, where the river left the mountains to flow lazily through a few kilometers of rolling foothills and on into the lowlands beyond. The valley floor was flat and green with grass and bushes, while the sides were covered with trees. Even from the air they could see that the trees hung heavy with bright yellow and red fruit.

"This could be the place," Sean had remarked as he circled around it once before landing, and now as they walked through it, their backpacks squeaking and shifting and settling onto their backs, he said again, "This really could be it. It'd be perfect for farming, and we've got the mountains right there for timber, and I bet those fruit trees turn out to be apples or oranges or something like them. I bet we won't even have to plant our own. I wonder how the fishing is."

"The fish are probably ugly green things with knobby antennae and eyes on stalks," Ryan said good-naturedly.

Sean's enthusiasm couldn't be dimmed. "Who cares, as long as they take a fly," he said. "Look, there's a deer."

Ryan looked where Sean pointed. At first he couldn't make out anything but bushes, but then one of the shadows moved and he suddenly realized that he'd been looking right at it. It wasn't quite a deer—the horns were too straight, and it was stockier than an Earth deer—but it was close. Close enough to call it a deer, anyway.

He took a picture of it. They'd gone back and retrieved the telecam after all, hovering in the shuttle to scare the buffalo away, but Ryan's throw had broken it and they had decided to keep exploring rather than go back to the ship for another one. They still had a regular camera for photos and a radio to keep in touch with, and that, Sean insisted, would be good enough. David and Mariko and the rest of the crew would just have to wait for photographs.

They had the samples from the first landing site to play with, anyway. Ryan had packed them into a retrieval probe and launched them into orbit before they had left. He had even included a hexopus—caught in a live trap after a ten-minute wait with a piece of cheddar cheese for bait—and a tissue sample from the buffalo as well. Ryan hoped Mariko could make do with hair caught in the telecam's lens, because that was all she was likely to get.

The day was shorter than Earth's, a little over twenty-one hours, so the sun was already setting by the time they worked their way a couple kilometers into the mountains. West was behind the peaks, so the mountain shadow quickened the dusk even more. Sean had been breaking trail all afternoon, but when the sun disappeared behind the mountains he stopped at a broad grassy field on the inside of a bend in the river and said, "Time to set up camp."

Ryan was in no mood to argue. He was hot, his pack had been digging into his shoulders for the last hour, and his feet hurt. Gravity was less than a full gee here, but with another twenty-five kilos on his back he figured it was like walking in one and a third gee anyway. He slid out of his pack and leaned it up against Sean's so they were both standing upright, then went over to the riverbank and splashed water on his face. A silvery flash of motion caught his eye, but whatever had made it was gone before he could get more than a glimpse of it. He supposed it was a fish, though. Everything else Earthlike was here.

They had seen more wildlife than Ryan had imagined could exist in one river valley. He had already filled five photochips for the camera, taking pictures of everything from tiny wildflowers to an enormous antlered buffalo that Sean insisted should be called a moose. He had taken pictures of the trees, their apple- and orange- and nut-like like fruits, granite rocks, Sean holding a blue and violet butterfly on his outstretched palm—everything. They had ceased commenting on how Earthlike it all was. They'd grown tired of repeating themselves.

They made a short foray into the trees to gather firewood, then pitched their tent while the sky darkened and the stars began to come out. Ryan got out the radio and made their report to the ship, then after dinner—rehydrated with stream water from which they had filtered everything larger than a water molecule—they sat by the fire while Sean told stories about his days on the reservation.

Ryan was listening with one ear, the other tuned to the unfamiliar night sounds around them, but he shifted his attention back to the campfire when Sean said, "It was doomed from the start, of course."

"What was?"

"The whole reservation idea. Clear back in the eighteen hundreds when they set it up, it was doomed."

"What do you mean? If reservations have been around that long, it doesn't sound like they're doomed to me."

"It does if you're Native." Sean cracked a stick in half against his knee and tossed it on the fire, sending swirls of sparks up into the night. The sudden flare of red light accentuated his already-red skin and the intense shadows sharpened the angle of his nose and eyebrows until he was almost a caricature of himself. He didn't see Ryan's eyes go wide; he was staring into the fire and saying, "The whole idea behind the reservations was to give us a place where we could live our own way while the palefaces lived theirs, but that was impossible from the day we met."

"Why?" Ryan asked.

"Because there was only one direction for us to develop. We were okay as long as we stayed in our tepees and didn't try to change, but stagnation isn't a lifestyle and we knew it. We needed to change and to grow just like everybody else, but with the white man's example sitting right there in front of us, any development at all was bound to take us that same way. We tried to force another direction when we closed the borders to whites in forty-four, but that was doomed too." He looked up at Ryan, who had by then looked back down at the fire. "I mean, the whole idea of a border. It's like a nudist colony, only we're an Indian colony. A little enclave of different behavior, but it's not a real civilization. Not with that enormous technological empire surrounding us."

Ryan looked up again, and their eyes met. "So that's why you came here." It wasn't quite a question.

Sean laughed. "I came here because I got nailed for fishing without a license. It's true! It made me so mad I sent in my application that same day. I wanted, just once in my life, to be able to walk all day and not have to worry about who's land I was on, or whose fish I was catching. I never really thought they'd pick me, but it was worth a shot." He looked out into the night and laughed again. "Looks like it paid off, eh?"

Ryan looked outward too, and there, just beyond the fire's circle of illumination, were half a dozen soft points of light. As he watched, one of them blinked.

"Sean," he said softly. "We've got company."

"Where—oh."

"Flashlight?" Ryan asked.

"Camera," Sean replied.

"Right." Ryan reached behind him and fumbled for it in his pack. As he turned it on and aimed at the glowing eyes, he heard

Sean draw his pistol and cock the hammer.

"Ready?" Ryan asked.

"Ready."

Ryan pressed the shutter button. He looked up past the camera as he did, and in the sudden light from the flash he saw three enormous hexopuses watching them from about ten meters away. They each looked to be about a meter tall, with a head like a balloon on top of a mass of tentacles as thick as Ryan's legs. In the harsh light he couldn't discern their color.

They shrieked in surprise, and Ryan fired the flash again. This time they were twice as tall, fleeing full-tilt on the tips of their tentacles. Ryan heard a shriek and a thud and he fired the camera again to see two of them down in a tangle of legs. More shrieks from the night, and suddenly a splash as the third landed in the river.

He was laughing too hard to hold the camera steady any more. He held it overhead and fired another shot anyway, but the two who had collided were already up and out of sight. Ryan could hear the third one splashing its way across the river.

Sean lowered the hammer on his pistol with exaggerated caution and put it back in its holster. Then he seemed to melt, collapsing back in the grass in soundless mirth and lying on his back, twitching.

"Fa—" he said, then erupted into giggles. "Fierce—" and more giggles. At last he took a full breath and managed to say, "Fierce monsters in the night!" before the giggles took him again.

Morning dawned far too early. They had gone to bed shortly after chasing off the tentacled creatures, but even with a motion detector clipped to the top of the tent and the camera within easy reach, Ryan slept poorly. There were too many sounds out there, and he couldn't convince himself that they all belonged to creatures as easily scared as the first. Sean slept like Ryan had used to on the ship, which didn't help Ryan's confidence any, either. And then on top of that was the twenty-one hour day bringing daylight just as fatigue won out over fear and he had begun to drift off.

Sean let him sleep while he cooked breakfast, but they were still up and traveling before he had fully awakened. The exercise and the cool morning air began to revive him, though, until by the time the open meadows near the river gave way to forest he was awake enough to appreciate it. There were more trees than he could have imagined possible in any of his dreams under the ship's single lodge pole pine, and more varieties, too. None of them were quite like the ship's Tree, but again nature had kept the same basic shapes here as she had used on Earth.

"The ecosystems blend together more than I'd expect," Sean said as he picked a bright yellow fruit from a low-hanging branch and examined it closely. He took out his knife, cut it in half, and after a cautious sniff said "Lemon peach. Leach. No, that doesn't sound good at all. Pemon, maybe. But whatever it is, I wouldn't expect to see it growing among evergreens." He held the fruit in his hand, clearly wishing he could take a bite, but he finally tossed it onto the forest floor and wiped his hand on his pants. He picked another whole one and sealed it in a sample bag, which he put in Ryan's pack. They were taking turns carrying the samples, and it was easier to reach in each other's packs than into their own.

Ryan photographed the tree. "I wish we knew what was edible and what's not," he said. "All this fresh fruit is starting to make my mouth water."

"Something's been eating them," Sean said, pointing at a litter of peel scraps lying on the ground below a thick, horizontal branch.

Ryan looked at the peels, then looked among the trees for signs of the animal that had left them, but other than a few flies and a tiny paraglider butterfly, the forest was still. He could hear something chattering excitedly farther upstream, but whatever was doing it was still out of sight.

It had been like that all morning. Where yesterday they had seen wildlife all over, today they walked through a world practically empty of animals. Something had scared them all away. The most obvious somethings were the two humans tromping through their territory, but if that was the case then why hadn't they gotten the same reaction yesterday? It was almost as if another animal were running along ahead of them and scaring everything into hiding before they got there.

Ryan shrugged. There didn't seem to be much they could do about it, and in the meantime there was plenty else to look at.

The forest thickened as they pushed deeper into it, the treetops merging in places to form a canopy overhead and the flora becoming more and more exotic all the while. It wasn't rain forest, not quite, but it was thicker than anything they'd seen so far.

They had just stopped to pick a sample of another fruit, this one a grape-sized sphere that glistened like polished silver, rows of them studding the undersides of its tree's branches like light bulbs, when their isolation suddenly ended. From a tree a few meters in front of them came a piercing howl, and answering howls erupted from other trees all around. Ryan dropped the silver grape in surprise, looked up into the trees for the source of the noise, and saw them: the same sort of creatures they had scared away from their campfire the previous night. Mostly tentacles, they were hard to spot among the branches, but they were making up for that difficulty by swinging from branch to branch and screaming.

They were working each other into a frenzy. Ryan could see about a dozen of them, but it sounded as if there were more. As he watched, the ones he could see began to edge closer.

"Are we being attacked?" He had to raise his voice to be heard over the din.

"I'm not sure," Sean shouted back. He drew his pistol, but he didn't point it at anything yet. Ryan drew his too, and together they watched the creatures approach. They seemed to be driving one of their number ahead of the rest; it howled and hesitated until they practically threw it from a neighboring tree into the silver grape tree, then, very cautiously, it wrapped a tentacle around a branch and dropped like a spider on a thread until it hung just in front of Sean and Ryan. The others' hooting and screeching diminished until the forest was silent again.

In the daylight—even the dim light filtering down through the trees—they could see more than the simple outlines they had seen in the flash the night before. The creature was mostly arms, covered in short brown fur down to a forearm's width or so from the tips, where it looked to have dry, leathery skin much calloused from holding onto branches. The arm from which it dangled seemed to have stretched like elastic until it was at least three times the length of the others. Its body was shaggier than its arms, but more of a greenish brown, and its head—an oblong connected the squat way with the long axis running front to back and without benefit of a neck—was the shaggiest of all and completely green. Two powder-blue eyes, their pupils split in six radiating spokes like the rays in a star sapphire, stared at the humans from near the top of the head. It had to have ears, judging from the racket it and its companions had been making just a moment before, but just where they might be under the fur was anybody's guess.

The mouth was easy to spot: an oval opening about where it ought to be but bearing another couple of tentacles at either corner. At least it didn't have fangs, Ryan thought. That was obvious enough; the thing had its lips pulled back in a grimace that had to be painful, showing off big, square, not-too-clean teeth. It didn't move, just dangled there in front of them, its one greatly elongated tentacle reaching up into the branches overhead while the other five hung loosely below it. Ryan slowly unclipped the camera, focused for a close-up of the thing's face, and tripped the shutter.

Of course it flashed in the dim light. The creature screeched and bobbed upward a meter on its stretchy tentacle, but the others started their chorus again and rattled branches until it descended to face Ryan once more. They stood watching one another for another few seconds until finally, breathing a soft sigh as if in resignation, the creature lifted one of its free tentacles and reached out with it toward Ryan's face.

This time Ryan did the flinching. The creature screeched and pulled itself upward again, but once again the others drove it back down with their hooting.

"Let it touch you this time," Sean said.

"That's easy for you to say," Ryan muttered, but he handed Sean the camera and held his ground when the thing reached out for him again. The tip of its tentacle was cool against his cheek, and not as rough as he'd expected it to be. Its skin was more like the pads on a cat's feet; tough but still soft to the touch. It ran its tentacle over his face, down to his shoulder, then felt along his left arm until it came to his fingers. Ryan wiggled them obligingly for it, earning a hoot of surprise and answering hoots from the spectators all around.

Ryan heard the beep and saw the flash as Sean took another picture. The creature jerked away from Ryan, but didn't try to escape this time. "What do you think?" Ryan asked. "Do tentacles count as opposable thumbs or not?"

"We'll have to see what it can do with them," Sean said. "I don't see any sign of tools or clothing."

"True enough."

"Do you have a name?" Sean asked the creature. He thumped himself on the chest and said, "Sean." Pointing at Ryan, he said, "Ryan." He pointed at the alien and waited for a response, but it gave him none. After a moment it shifted its attention to Ryan's backpack, reaching over his shoulder and running its tentacles over it, finally pulling him around so it could get a better look. Ryan tried looking over his shoulder, but he couldn't see what it was doing. He heard, though, when it pulled loose the Velcro holding the flap, and he decided that was enough. "No," he told it, turning back around and taking a tentacle gently in either hand and pushing the creature away.

He might as well have dismembered it for the reaction he got. It shrieked in rage or alarm or some alien emotion, bouncing up and down on its tether and waving its other five tentacles in the air. That set the others off again, and they wouldn't shut up until Ryan turned back around and let their spokesman fish around in his pack.

Ryan heard things hitting the ground by his feet. He thought he recognized some of the sounds. "What's it doing?" he asked Sean.

Sean was laughing quietly. He was still covering the creature with his pistol, still snapping pictures with the camera in his other hand, but he was obviously enjoying the sight. "Trashing your pack," he said.

"What?" Ryan turned around again and saw the creature holding a sample bag between two of its tentacles, while with a third and a fourth it tried to figure out how to open it. The bag held the lemon-peach that Sean had picked earlier. Ryan's cook stove, water bottle, spare clothing, and the rest of the contents of his pack lay scattered on the ground beneath the creature.

It finally managed to tear the bag open. Dropping the bag on the ground, it hooted once and rose back into the tree with the fruit, which it began to eat. The rest of the troop gathered around it, chittering and hooting in much quieter voices now, while it ate the fruit and dropped the peels on Ryan, who began reloading his pack.

When the creature had finished eating, the others began howling at it again, but this time it howled back at them just as loudly. Finally it turned away and began to climb back up into the forest canopy, and the others followed it, their cries diminishing into the distance.

"What the hell were they?" Ryan asked when they were gone.

"Customs agents," Sean said.

CHAPTER NINE

FISHING FOR CLUES

THE NAME STUCK. Twice more that day groups of the creatures stopped them, digging in Sean's pack once and Ryan's once again. The third time they tried it the humans attempted to fend them off and continue walking, but the whole troop became more and more boisterous with each step until finally they found themselves retreating from a hail of sticks and nuts. Even when they fired their pistols in the air the creatures wouldn't let up with their bombardment for more than a few seconds. Only when they let the inspector frisk them and go through their packs would the troop let them past.

"So what do you think, have we found intelligent life?" Ryan asked when he called the ship with their report from camp that evening.

Mariko made noncommittal humming sounds. "It's hard to say. It's obviously territorial behavior, but that alone isn't enough to judge their intelligence. Most animals are territorial to one degree or another. If we knew *why* they stopped you we'd have more to go on, but I don't see any obvious answer to that. Or to why they let you go after a search. If they're intelligent, I'd have expected them to either try to drive you away or try to take you prisoner, but if they were just protecting their young or their food supply, I don't think they'd let you through at all. Especially not when they found you carrying something they could eat."

"How about simple curiosity?" Ryan suggested. "Maybe they

just want to see who we are." He was leaning up against his pack with the radio in his lap. The sun was already down and the sky was darkening toward night, but he and Sean were both too tired from the day's hike to even think about setting up camp yet.

Mariko thought about Ryan's suggestion for a moment before saying, "Possibly. I'd think that behavior pattern would be counter-evolutionary, though. Dropping down in front of a predator, for instance, wouldn't be a good idea."

Sean was sitting beside Ryan, munching on a handful of home-made cookies from the goodie bag Laura had given them. He took the microphone from Ryan and asked around a mouthful of crumbs, "How often do unfamiliar predators come by? Maybe it's worth it to lose a member of the troop once in a while to find out for sure if something's violent. Remember, the one who does the searching definitely doesn't want to be doing it."

"That's what intrigues me," Mariko admitted. "If the others are forcing one of their number to approach you, then that implies communication. You're sure they didn't try to say anything to you?"

"Not verbally. They said 'stop' clear enough with sticks, though."

"Did any of them carry their sticks with them?"

"No, it looked like they just threw whatever was handy."

"How about excrement?"

"What?"

"Chimpanzees sometimes, ah, bomb intruders with excrement. Your 'customs agents' sound a little like chimpanzees the way they scream from the treetops, so I wondered if they had some of their other habits as well."

Sean laughed nervously. "Not that one, they didn't."

"Hmm. I wish I could see them. When are you coming back?"

"I figure we'll go another day or two before we turn around. We'll probably make better time on the way back, so call it, oh, four or five days."

"Do you think you can bring one back with you?"

Sean laughed. "Not unless it comes willingly."

"I was afraid of that. Well, I'll have to be content with your reports, I guess."

Ryan took the microphone again. "What did you find out about the buffalo?" he asked.

"It's completely different," Mariko said, relief evident in her voice. "They have more in common with the hexopus you sent than with any terrestrial organism. Of course they both have more in common with us than they have any right to, but I'm sure it's simply a matter of evolution following the same general principles here as there." She paused, then went on. "Ken has another explanation, of course."

"I'm sure he does," Ryan said. "God made it look like Earth so we'd feel at home, or something like that, right?"

"Worse than that," said Mariko. "He's decided we've found Eden. The real thing."

"Oh." Ryan felt a sinking sensation in the pit of his stomach. He'd hoped Ken would relax and get on with the job of colonization once the planet was proven habitable, but it sounded as if he was going off on another tangent instead. "Well," he said, trying to make a joke of it, "Tell him we haven't found any apples yet."

Mariko chuckled. "I'll do that."

Ryan signed off, and he and Sean began setting up camp. Sean had searched out another clearing in the forest for it, even though it meant walking an extra couple of kilometers and losing his chance to go fishing before dark. He'd spent the last twenty years sleeping in a closed-in environment, he'd said, and he wanted wide open spaces now that he had the chance. Camping there also ensured that anything approaching them would have to do it on the ground, putting the customs agents, at least, at a disadvantage. They didn't expect that to discourage them entirely, but it would keep them from dropping straight in from above.

Ryan could feel them watching him as he collected wood for the campfire. The forest was getting dim by then and he couldn't actually see them up above him in the trees, but he knew they were there by the prickling at the back of his neck. He retreated with an armload of branches and broke them into sections, stacking some of the smaller twigs in the fire ring that Sean had made while he gathered the wood. He rummaged around in his pack until he found the matches in their waterproof container, took one out and lit it on a rock, then lit the fire. When he had the flames crackling good and high, their light driving back the twilight, he felt a little better, but he could still feel the agents' eyes watching him.

They showed up again just after dark, and this time they drew close enough to be illuminated by the flames. To Ryan they looked like a surrealist's idea of a wood sprite, hunkered down on the ground on all six tentacles, their glowing eyes never leaving the fire. At last he grew tired of their staring and scared them off with the flash, but this time they didn't stay away for long. The motion detector's alarm did a better job, but they came back in the middle of the night and again just before dawn, triggering the siren both times.

Morning again came too early. The twenty-one hour day was going to be hard to adjust to. Ryan and Sean dragged themselves out of the tent well after sunrise, packed their packs, and continued their journey upstream, but they took it easy that day and only made a few kilometers before stopping again, exhausted, in mid-afternoon. They crossed three more of the customs agents' territorial borders during the day, but after the searcher at the first one had trashed Ryan's pack once again they had learned a trick to let them pass unmolested: they carried a piece of fruit from the previous territory and handed it to the inspector first thing, then continued on while it ate.

Bribery, Sean had explained, was evidently a universal custom.

"So what do you think?" Ryan asked him now as he helped pitch the tent for their third night on the trail. "Does accepting a bribe indicate intelligence?" They still hadn't decided how high along the road to sapience the customs agents were.

"It never did back on Earth," Sean replied. He pounded in a stake pinning the nylon dome to the grass, then tossed his pounding rock to Ryan. "Hard to say what it means here. I'm still not sure about these guys. Some of the things they do make me think they're intelligent, but then next time I look at them I just don't know. They don't use tools as far as I can tell, they don't wear clothes, and they haven't really tried to communicate, either. Except to tell us to stop, but a dog can do that just as convincingly."

Ryan anchored his side of the tent, tossed the rock toward the fire ring, and pulled his sleeping bag out of its compartment in his pack so it could fluff up in the tent a little before he slept in it. From inside the tent he said, "I've been trying to think up a good test that'd determine just how smart they are, like a puzzle for them to solve or something, but I haven't been able to come up with one that'd prove anything."

Sean laughed. "Maybe they're testing *us*. Maybe they're waiting to see what we come up with before they decide whether they want to talk with us or not." He tossed his own sleeping bag into the tent, then began digging in his pack for something else. "But I doubt it. I think if they were intelligent, they'd have made it clear by now."

Ryan backed out of the tent again and saw Sean fitting together a four-piece fishing pole. "You're going fishing?" he asked in the voice of one who expected to get a long night's sleep, starting with an afternoon nap.

"Good guess," Sean said. He smiled to show he hadn't meant to be sarcastic and added, "It gets dark so quick around here I didn't have a chance before, but now that I've got a couple hours, well, this is what I came here for." He reached into his tackle bag for the reel and clamped it to the handle, ran the leader up through the eyes and pulled it tight to stretch the curl out of it, then squatted down to tie on a fly.

Ryan wasn't all that excited about fishing, but all of a sudden he wasn't nearly as eager as he had been to go to sleep, either. He knew he had sufficient reason to, and he didn't imagine Sean would say— or even think—anything untoward about it if he did, but *he* would, and that was reason enough to stay awake, at least a little while longer. Since volunteering to be an explorer he had broken his lifetime habit of afternoon naps, but it had been a painful process. It had been like breaking a drug addiction, and as with any addiction he knew it wouldn't take much of a push to send him right back into it again. One guilt-ridden afternoon nap might be all it would take.

So he hunkered down beside Sean and watched him tie the fly to the end of the leader. It was a colorful one, with brown fuzz in front of white wings, an iridescent, fluffy green body with a red band around the middle of it, and an orange tail with a black tip. Sean noticed his attention and said, "Royal Coachman. I always try a Coachman first when I don't know the water. I usually have good luck with 'em. 'Course, whether or not it'll work here is another question, but you've got to start somewhere." He bit off the loose end of leader, then took a pair of small pliers out of his bag and with a grimace mashed the barb flat so that the hook ended in a simple point.

"Hate doing that to a good fly," he said, "but there's no sense in catching something permanently until we know we can eat it." He stood up, slung his tackle bag over his shoulder, and said, "Better bring the camera. I hear a twenty pound Brown calling my name."

"Twenty pound Green, more likely," Ryan said, but he picked up the camera and followed Sean to the river bank.

Sean began stripping line out of the reel, waving the pole back and forth all the while until he had enough line in the air to stretch three-quarters of the way across the river. A little over halfway across and a little way upstream from where they stood, a submerged rock split the current and formed a pool; Sean took aim and with a careful cast dropped the fly just shy of it. The current swirled it underwater immediately, and he pulled it out with a gentle tug. A second cast overshot the pool, and Sean shook his head in disgust.

"Damn, I'm out of practice."

"Wonder why." Ryan backed up to give Sean more room to cast, and to get the pool as well as the fisherman in the camera's field of view.

Sean cast again, this time slapping the fly hard into the head of the pool, where it stayed for a second before the current grabbed the line and dragged the fly across the surface and under again.

"All right," Sean said, taking in line and casting again but this time for the lower end of the pool. "I guess I'd better start with the simple stuff and—hah!" The fly touched down lightly, immediately disappeared in a swirl of silver, and the fishing pole bent into an arc. Sean gave it a tug and the fish—at least it looked like a fish amidst all the spray—broke clear of the water and thrashed against the line before splashing back in and making a run for the submerged rock.

"Oh no you don't!" Sean shouted, pulling on the line and raising the pole, a move that prevented the fish from reaching cover but renewed its fury at the same time. It broke the surface again, and this time Ryan was ready with the camera, snapping the picture while the fish was still in the air, Sean still tugging on the line with a look of pure astonishment on his face. The fish splashed down again and immediately changed direction, rushing straight back toward Sean, who backpedaled and pulled in line furiously until the fish suddenly swerved again and made another run for the rock.

Sean snubbed the line and the fish broke water again, then changed direction as soon as it hit, now rushing for the bank. Sean kept the line tight but he couldn't prevent the fish from going in under the bank, where it seemed to grow roots. No amount of tugging on the line would budge it, not even when Sean reeled in until he stood just over it and pulled straight out with the pole toward the middle of the river.

"This bugger is smarter than any customs agent," Sean said, his astonishment giving way to a smile more expressive than Ryan had ever seen on his face before. "Let's just try something here." He let out a little line, kept it tight by pulling it away from the pole in his left hand while raising the pole in his right, then in a quick move he stamped on the ground and tugged downstream at the same time. The fish shot out from under the bank at the sound, raced off downstream for a moment, changed direction again, and headed once again for its spot under the bank. Sean waited until it was about a meter from the edge then tugged hard on the line, pulling the fish free of the water and adding enough momentum to its forward motion to carry it onward to land flapping in the grass at his feet.

"Got you," he said, his breath coming a little ragged now. The fish thrashed for a moment longer, then gave up and lay quietly on its side, two rows of shark-like gill slits opening and closing along the side of its head. Its body was mostly silver, with stripes of brown and red along its sides, and the top of its head had a puzzle-pattern of yellow lines across it. It had more fins than a normal fish, each with a red tip. Sean laid his pole beside it, the butt even with its tail, then with his thumb marked how high its head reached on the scale above the handle.

"Seventeen and a half inches," he said with pride.

"Inches?" Ryan asked.

"Fish are always measured in inches."

"Oh."

Ryan took a picture of it there on the grass, then Sean took a pair of clippers out of his tackle bag and nipped off the end of a fin. He did the same with a gill, put the pieces in a tiny sample bottle, then gently lowered the fish back into the water, where it took a moment to orient itself before it disappeared in a flash of silver. Sean examined his Royal Coachman, which had popped loose the moment he'd let the line go slack. It looked a bit ragged now. Sean held it in his fingers, looking out over the water, obviously debating whether to cast it out again, then finally shook his head and said, "No, one like that's enough. Come on, let's call it a day."

As they walked back toward the tent he said softly, "You know, I think your dad might be right."

"Right about what?"

"Eden."

"Oh. Yeah." There were certainly arguments in his favor, Ryan thought. The planet seemed tailor-made for humanity. If a person had to leave the ship and spend the rest of his life on a planet, he couldn't imagine a better one to spend it on. One with a longer day, maybe, but that was really a minor problem. He was sure he could get used to short days, given time.

Not all at once, though, and evidently neither could Sean. Despite his success at fishing, he was soon fighting off the yawns himself. They didn't even bother with a fire, but cooked dinner over a portable stove, made their report to the ship while they ate it, then set the motion detector and crawled into their sleeping bags just as the sun dropped behind the mountains. Fatigue caught up with them and they were out in minutes, but shortly after dark an insistent beeping woke them again. It took them a moment to realize that it was not the siren this time, but the radio.

"This had better be important," Sean said when he found the microphone.

"It is," replied David. "I've been doing infrared scanning to see if I can track these customs agents of yours by night, and I've found a whole group of them around your last camp site. You didn't forget to put out your fire, did you?"

"No," Sean said with the quiet venom of someone accused of a heinous crime. "We didn't forget to put out our fire. Why?"

"Because there's a hell of a hot spot down there, and if it's not your fire then it's theirs."

CHAPTER TEN

PLAYING WITH FIRE

THE FOREST AT NIGHT was a vastly different forest than the same collection of trees had been during daylight. During the day it had seemed fairly open beneath the canopy, with the trees spaced widely apart and paths through the underbrush easy to find, but at night it was a tangle of vines and roots and branches that clawed at arms and legs and pack frames and made progress nearly impossible. Fatigue didn't help matters any, either; Ryan found himself staggering even on the few level stretches of trail.

A branch scraped across Sean's pack, whipped free, and slapped Ryan across a hastily-raised arm. It was hard to decide which was worse, following close and dodging branches or hanging back and missing Sean's warnings about rocks and deadfall. They were almost impossible to see; without a moon and with Centauri B on the day side of the planet, the only light came from diffuse starlight filtered through the forest canopy. It was just enough to let Ryan distinguish tree trunks before smashing into them, but not enough to give any meaning to the shadows on the ground.

Ryan had clicked on his flashlight when they started out, but Sean had put a stop to that immediately. They would need their night vision when they got where they were going, he had explained, and it would take at least half an hour for their eyes to recover from exposure to bright light.

"Besides," he had said, "if these guys are attracted to light, we don't want to be drawing them to us. We want to go to them and see what they're doing with our campfire."

So they stumbled along as best they could in the dark. The forest was quiet save for their own cursing and panting. No customs agents stopped them at territorial borders. What nocturnal creatures there might have been were either naturally silent or scared into silence by the humans crashing through their territory. Ryan could hear the river spilling over rocks off to his left, but Sean kept them far enough from it that the sound was little more than a sigh like a breeze through the tops of the trees. The forest was more open, easier to navigate, up here away from the water.

They'd been traveling for a couple of hours when the radio crackled softly and David Bonham's voice said, "You're a kilometer away now."

Ryan had put the radio in one of his pack's side pockets, passing the cord out the opening and clipping the microphone to the frame where he could get to it without taking off his pack. He unhooked it now and spoke quietly into it. "One kilometer, thanks. What's the situation ahead of us?"

"Still burning. A couple of hot spots have moved away from the fire a few hundred meters and back again; I assume they're carrying flaming branches."

"Ask him if they've got fires going anywhere else," Sean said from ahead in the darkness. He was still walking.

"Have you spotted any other fires?" Ryan asked, trying to keep up.

"I've got a search going. So far I've found two, one of them just a few kilometers to the north of you, but I'm pretty sure they're both natural lightning fires. Both of them are in the paths of thunderstorms, and neither one shows any sign of being tended."

"How far have you searched?"

"The search covers the whole continent."

"Two fires on the whole *continent*?"

"Three."

"Three, right." Two or three, it wasn't the answer Ryan had expected. "How sensitive is your detector? Maybe it's missing small campfires under the forest canopy."

"This is the same detector I was using to track animals by their heat," David said. "It wouldn't miss a campfire in a cave."

"You sure? Caves might be exactly where they keep their campfires."

"Even fires in caves put out smoke, as you may recall from personal experience, so unless they want to choke to death on it they're going to have to vent the smoke outside, where I'd still see the heat signature. No, they simply aren't using fires, except for the one right in front of you."

"So what are we supposed to deduce from that?"

"I've got two theories," David said. "One, that they know all about fire and just don't use it except for special occasions—"

"Like cooking interstellar explorers," Sean put in.

"—or the other," David went on without pause, since Ryan hadn't keyed the microphone, "that you didn't get your fire put out all the way last night and when it flared back up today their natural curiosity led them to check it out."

"We did too—" Sean began to say, but Ryan sensed too late that Sean had stopped walking. He crashed into Sean's back, dropping the microphone, and staggered backward to regain his balance. He felt a crunch underfoot.

"Uh oh."

"That wasn't what I think it was, was it?"

"I think it was." Ryan felt for the cord dangling from his pack and reeled in the microphone, or what was left of it. Sharp bits of plastic scratched at his palm. He couldn't find the transmit button.

"Give me some light here," he said.

Sean flicked on his flashlight, hiding most of its light behind his hand, but even in its diminished glow they could both see the obvious: the microphone was smashed beyond repair. Ryan had stepped directly on it, crushing the case and driving shards of plastic into the electronics. He found what was left of the transmit button and pushed it anyway, saying, "David? Can you hear me?"

Silence. There should at least have been the soft hiss of an open channel when he let off the button, but even that was gone.

"Maybe it's shorted into transmit mode," Sean said. "Here." He turned Ryan around so he could get into his pack and removed the radio, then unplugged the microphone.

David's voice commenced in mid-word. "—eat, I lost your signal. Ryan, Sean, do you copy?"

Sean plugged the microphone cord back in. "Okay, try it again."

"This is Ryan. I stepped on the microphone, and I'm afraid it's busted. Can you hear me?"

Sean unplugged it again, and they heard static for a few more moments, then, "This is David Bonham calling the exploration party. Come in, exploration party. Do you copy, over?"

Sean plugged the microphone cord in again, unplugged it, plugged it in, unplugged it, back and forth half a dozen times. "Maybe he'll at least pick up the carrier wave," he said.

But after a few seconds more, David called again, "This is David Bonham calling the exploration party. Come in, exploration party. Do you copy, over?"

"We copy just fine, damn it," Ryan said. "Much good does it do us. I'm sorry, Sean."

"Don't worry about it. Could have happened to anybody."

"Yeah, but this is twice now it's happened to me. The video camera, and now the radio."

"Twice is coincidence. I'll wait three times before I call you a real screw-up."

Ryan could hear Sean's grin in the tone of his voice. Sean truly wasn't angry. Ryan wondered how he could take so calmly being cut off from the ship, then realized that was precisely what he *wanted*.

Sean liked the idea of exploring on his own, without a bunch of control-chair kibitzers nagging at him and accusing him of not putting out his campfire. He had probably been hoping for just such an accident for days. Ryan shook his head, a grin of his own spreading across his face. "Thanks. So now what?"

Sean put the radio back in Ryan's side pocket. "Well," he said, "We know he can see us. Let's see if we can communicate visually, at least long enough to let him know we're okay." He pointed the flashlight skyward and clicked it on and off half a dozen times. Where it hit the undersides of leaves overhead, it looked like the camera flash going off.

The radio still spoke softly within its pocket. "This is David Bonham calling the exploration party. Come in, exploration party. Do you copy, over?"

"Look at the monitor, idiot," Sean growled.

"This is David Bonham calling the exploration party. Come in, exploration party. Do you copy, over?"

Sean kept trying for another minute or more, but David gave no sign of seeing his signal. His messages kept getting more and more urgent.

"Maybe the trees are blocking the light," Ryan suggested.

"There's not much we can do about that," Sean said. "The only place without trees around here is in the middle of the river, and I'm not going to wade out there just to calm David down. He's following us by our body heat; he'll know where we are even without the radio." Sean paused for a moment in thought, then went on, "He'll know we're okay if we continue on the way we were going, right?"

Ryan tried to decide what David would do. There weren't any other large animals in the area—he would have warned them if there were—so he could rule out an attack by anything bigger than a cat. If they kept moving. . . "I guess so," Ryan said.

"So let's get going before he decides we've both had fatal heart attacks or something."

Sean led off into the night again, his flashlight once more turned off. Ryan reached around into the side pocket of his pack and turned off the radio as well. The whole idea had been to sneak in close and watch what the customs agents were doing without being detected; he didn't want to get within hearing distance and then have David give them away with another transmission. Ryan hoped that the business with the radio and the flashlight hadn't given them away already.

The customs agents were far too engrossed in the fire to pay any attention to noises or lights in the forest. Sean spotted the firelight after walking only a few hundred meters more. It was not the soft flickering of quiet flames, but an ominous red glow reaching deep into the forest all around them. They could hear it roaring and crackling even from half a kilometer away, and over the fire they could hear the hoots and whistles of the creatures tending it.

They advanced cautiously from tree to tree until they stood at the edge of the clearing in which the fire burned. The sight confronting them was a scene from a deranged artist's vision of Hell: around an enormous bonfire, dozens of six-tentacled monsters cavorted in orgiastic frenzy. Some carried flaming branches, others tossed sticks and even whole logs onto the fire, but most simply leaped about and added their screams to the cacophony of confusion around the blaze.

And in their midst, dancing and howling with even less restraint than the others, one of the creatures held aloft a gleaming stainless steel cylinder that could only be a backpacker's waterproof match container.

"How the hell did he get *that*?" Ryan asked, then immediately answered himself. "When they searched our packs, of course. But how did they know how to use them?"

"By watching us," Sean said. Neither of them whispered. There was no point in whispering; indeed, over the roar of the fire a whisper wouldn't have been audible a foot away.

Ryan nodded. "I guess that explains why they haven't got fires going anywhere else."

Sean slid his pack down off his shoulders and leaned it up against the tree they were hiding behind. Ryan took off his own and stacked it beside Sean's. He took the camera from his pack, switched off the flash, and took a couple shots of the fire by its own light, then simply stood watching the aliens cavorting around it. Neither he nor Sean spoke for a time. Sean leaned his forehead against the tree for a moment, raised up and looked back at the fire and the dancing customs agents, then said, "We *really* screwed up."

"Yeah, I guess we did," Ryan replied. How badly was just now soaking in. "Can we do anything about it?"

"I sure hope so. Cover me."

"What are you going to do?"

"Take our matches back and put out the fire."

With those words, Sean stepped out from behind the tree. Moving from nighttime shadow into the fire's glare, he must have seemed to appear from nowhere. The customs agents stopped their dancing in mid-step, and suddenly the only noise was the crackle of the flames.

Sean advanced upon the one with the matches, holding his right hand out in front of him, palm up, as he walked steadily closer. "I don't think you ought to be playing with those," he said in a strong, confident voice. "Not for another thousand years or so at least. Come on, give them here."

The creature seemed almost to understand him. Ryan, watching from the shadows with pistol drawn and cocked, supposed that Sean's intentions were clear enough for any thinking being to comprehend even if his words were not, but whether or not the customs agent would comply with them was another question.

Evidently the shock of having an alien walking purposefully toward it was enough to settle the issue. The creature hardly moved as Sean walked straight up to it, reached out, and took the match container as gently as if he were picking a piece of fruit from a tree. He put it in his pocket and then said, loud enough to be heard all around the fire, "Now let's show you how to put one of these out."

He began untying his bandana from around his neck, evidently to use as a makeshift bucket to carry water from the river, but something in the sky caught his attention, drawing Ryan's and the customs agents eyes upward with his own to where a pillar of violet flame drifted toward them from down the valley.

It was their shuttle, David flying it to the rescue by remote control. Why he was using the fusion drive rather than the atmospheric engines was a mystery, but it had to be their shuttle. They couldn't have launched another one from the ship so quickly, not even if David had panicked and called for a rescue the moment the radio went dead.

"He couldn't stand being left out," Sean said scornfully. "Well, that pretty much wraps up this party."

The customs agents quickly came to the same decision. As the shuttle moved overhead, its drive flame roaring and illuminating the forest with a noise and light far greater than even the bonfire's, they craned their oblong heads skyward, front tentacles raised in alarm or supplication or some other alien gesture, then as one organism they dropped down on all sixes and rushed for the trees.

The shuttle's drive flame winked out, to be replaced by an equally powerful landing light. The roar of flame diminished by half, the bonfire still supplying noise of its own, but the shrill whine of the shuttle's atmospheric engines grew louder as it descended. David at least had the presence of mind not to land on a grassy field with the main drive.

The shuttle touched down next to the fire, and the external speaker boomed, "Sean, Ryan, get on board!"

"Not until we put this thing out!" Sean shouted back. He headed for the river. Ryan carried the packs over to the airlock door, then dug into his until he found his cook pot and followed after Sean. Together they poured water on the blaze until it hissed and steamed its way down to a puddle of dirty water full of half-burnt sticks. They tossed the sticks and the rocks making up the fire ring into the river, smoothed over the ground as well as they could, then carried their packs inside the shuttle and lifted off.

"So whose dumb idea was it to come after us?" Sean was at the controls, but there was really little to do there but ride out the high-gee thrust into orbit. Ryan was looking out the side window and watching the planet drop away from them. It had started as a flat wall of blackness, changing to a curve with a thin line of back-lit atmosphere as they rose into space. The simplicity of the sight, coupled with the thunder of the fusion rocket at their backs, was somehow as exciting as the descent had been.

"Mine," a voice said over the radio. It took Ryan a few seconds to realize that it was the captain's.

Sean looked over at Ryan and cocked an eyebrow, then grinned. "Brilliant idea, sir," he said. "My mistake."

"Cut the crap, Little Bear. I wasn't thrilled about you approaching that fire anyway, but when we lost your radio signal I decided that risking my exploration crew wasn't worth what little scientific gain we might get so I ordered Bonham to pull you out of there. My decision. I didn't expect you to like it, but that's tough. There'll be other chances to make contact."

"I'm not sure that's such a good idea, sir."

"Not sure if it's a good idea? Why not?"

"Because that fire of theirs was a direct result of their meeting with us, not a part of their natural development."

The captain was silent a moment before he said, "I'm not sure I follow you. What are you talking about?"

"I'm talking about showing an alien race how to use fire."

"You did that?" the captain asked incredulously.

"We did. Not on purpose, but they learned it from us nonetheless. I might have stopped the idea from spreading when I took the matches back from them, but I doubt it. They've seen that they can build one; that's not a concept they're likely to forget."

"What matches? Are you *sure*?"

"*Our* matches, the ones they stole from us, and yes I'm sure."

"Maybe you'd better back up a ways. Just how did you teach them to use fire?"

"By example. They watched us build a campfire two nights in a row, and they evidently got the idea from that. This morning they took the matches from one of our packs when we crossed one of their territorial borders, and they used them to start a fire of their own."

"You're saying they knew how to use matches after simply *watching* you?"

"That's what it looks like."

"I think you're jumping to conclusions."

"I wish I were. I hope I am. But David says they aren't using fires anywhere else, so I don't see any other explanation."

The captain *hmm*ed a moment. They could hear him talking with someone else out of microphone range, then he came back on and said, "I don't know. You may be right, but then again there may be another perfectly reasonable explanation. We'll discuss it further when you get back on board. Van Cleeve out."

Ryan turned to Sean and asked, "What other perfectly reasonable explanation could there be?"

Sean reached out and pulled back on the throttle, lowering the engines' thrust by a gee or so. "I don't know," was all he said. He tilted the shuttle over with the attitude jets and let them build up orbital velocity now that they were out of the atmosphere, varying their thrust with constant attention to the starship's position as represented by a blinking dot on the attitude indicator.

Ryan looked out the front windows for the ship itself. Presently it came into view, first just a distant speck of light moving against the background stars, but growing swiftly into a machinery-studded cylinder again. In the excitement of exploring, Ryan hadn't realized how much he'd missed it until now. Seeing his home of the last twenty years gleaming brightly in the sunlight brought a catch to his throat and a tightness to his chest. He thought of the people waiting to welcome them back: his parents, Methany, Michelle, Teigh, Laura, Holly—everyone—and suddenly he didn't care what news he and Sean brought with them. They were going home, and that was enough to think about for now.

Sean braked to match orbits and maneuvered the shuttle into place with a minimum of thruster burns. The docking collar latched to the airlock with a clang, and they were once again part of the starship.

Holly's voice came in over the intercom: "Green light on the seal. We're ready on this side with the isolation box."

"Let us get suited up," Ryan replied.

They were taking no chances with alien infection. The procedure had been decided upon clear back in Earth orbit: anything brought on board the ship from the planet—including the exploration party—had to go into an isolation chamber, and none of the air they breathed would be recirculated into the ship. Ryan and Sean donned their pressure suits again, closed the airlock and vented it to space, turned on the wide-spectrum sterilizing lights to kill anything that might otherwise survive in vacuum, and only then did they open the shuttle's outer airlock door.

Beyond the airlock was an even smaller isolation chamber, a steel box with small windows set in three sides. A face peered in each window: Holly, Doctor Kaplan—the original ship's doctor—and Teigh. Evidently he had been drafted to help push the chamber through the hallways to the hospital. It was in free-fall up here in the docking bay, but it wouldn't be so easy to maneuver deeper in the ship.

Ryan opened the lock and he and Sean pushed themselves into the box, closed the box's inner door, and waited while the medical team purged the airlock and used the lights again to cleanse the outer surface of the door. At last they uncoupled the box from the lock and began pushing it through the corridors to the hospital.

Once beyond the airlock area the isolation chamber was mobbed with well-wishers. Ryan and Sean each took a window and waved and smiled at the people on the other side of the glass on the way, but the sealed chamber and their spacesuit helmets muffled sound to the point that they couldn't hear or be heard.

Holly shooed the crowd away when they reached the hospital, allowing only the medical staff to accompany the isolation chamber inside. They pushed it up against the quarantine room's airlock and sealed it in.

The quarantine room was small, barely big enough for two beds against the walls, a clothing locker at the head of each, and a small table with two chairs at the foot of the right-hand bed. The airlock took up the space at the foot of the left one, and at their heads, between the clothing lockers, a doorway led into the bathroom. It might have been a room in a college dormitory, except that the entire wall at the foot of the beds was transparent, and through that wall near the table protruded a pair of isolation gloves and a small specimen airlock. On the wall beside that hung a video intercom, with a remote keyboard and pointer so Sean and Ryan could use it as a computer terminal.

Sean opened the door, peeled off his suit as he stepped through, tossed it onto the right-hand bed and disappeared into the bathroom without a word. The hiss of the shower drifted out the open door.

Ryan had hardly noticed the lack of showers on the planet, not with so much else to think about, but now that he was back on board the ship he realized that for the first time in his life he'd gone more than a day without one. His skin felt like the inside of a recycling tank, and his hair was matted and sticking out at all angles. He looked a mess, and there was Holly standing on the other side of the quarantine room's glass wall and watching him.

For a moment he felt like running for the bathroom as well and fighting Sean for the shower, but then another thought struck him and he arrested that motion. For twenty years he had always been freshly bathed and unmussed, and in that time Holly had come to see him as all too familiar; maybe he should let himself look like an explorer for a while more. With a wry grin he peeled out of his pressure suit, shook his hair out, and walked over to stand across the glass from her. Doctor Kaplan and Teigh were standing beside her; he smiled and waved at the three of them.

"Welcome back," Holly said simply. A speaker overhead brought her words into the room.

"It's good to be back," Ryan replied. He sat down in one of the chairs beside the table. "It's been a wild night."

"Night?" Holly looked puzzled, then sudden comprehension lit her face. "Oh, of course. You're ten or eleven hours ahead of us by now. It's three in the afternoon here."

"Oh. Yeah, I forgot that it would be." In the few days that they had been gone, the planet's shorter day had put them almost directly opposite ship's normal time.

"You must be tired."

Ryan nodded.

"Well I'm glad you had the sense not to shower right away. I need to get samples from your skin and hair and clothing to check for parasites, and I want to run some blood and urine tests, too."

"Make you a deal," Ryan said. "I'll give the skin and urine samples, but you get the blood from Sean."

Ryan hated needles and Holly knew it. Still, she shook her head and said, "Sorry. The more samples we get, the sooner we'll know whether or not it's safe down there. Don't worry; I'll be careful and quick and it won't hurt much at all."

"Famous last words," Ryan said, but he held out his arm and let Holly reach through the gloves to feel for a vein. She swabbed the skin and inserted the needle with swift, practiced motions, and before he knew it she had three tubes of blood and was pressing a cotton ball against the needle prick in his elbow.

"Here, hold this tight," she said, and while he held the cotton ball she put the swabs and the tubes of blood into a sample cabinet, ran it through the airlock beside the gloves, sterilizing the outside of the cabinet with ultraviolet light on the way through, then took it with her into another part of the lab where her analyzing machinery waited.

Doctor Kaplan and Teigh had been eyeing Ryan critically while Holly took the blood sample. Suddenly Dr. Kaplan's frown relaxed and he nodded sagely. "Ah, suntan," he said.

"Suntan?" asked Ryan.

"Your skin is darker than normal. You didn't use the U.V. blocking cream?"

Ryan had smeared some on his arms and face the first couple of days, but after that he had forgotten. He said so.

"You're lucky you were under the trees or you'd have been burned," the doctor said.

"Then you'd look like me," Teigh said with a grin.

"You get a paunch from sunburn?" Sean said, stepping out of the bathroom with a towel wrapped around his waist and a Bible in his hand.

"Touché." Teigh nodded toward the Bible. "You taking up theology?"

Sean grinned. "Ken strikes," he said, holding it aloft. "Inspiring reading while on the john." He saw Ryan holding the cotton swab to his arm and said, "Hey, did I miss all the fun?"

"Hardly," said Ryan. "We decided to let you donate the pound of flesh." He got up from the chair and, still holding his arm, went into the bathroom to take his shower.

When he emerged, feeling fresh and clean and with his hair frizzed into a halo from drying it with the towel which he now wore around his waist, he saw his parents waiting on the other side of the glass. "Hi Mom, hi Dad," he said, turning toward the locker at the head of the left bunk and opening it to find some of his own clothing there. Most of it he had placed there himself before they left, but a new pull-over shirt had to be a present from his mother. Ryan took it off the hanger and held it out. "Thanks," he said.

Alice smiled. "You're welcome."

Ryan took a pair of pants off the hanger, briefly considered taking pants and shirt into the bathroom to change into, but decided against it. Sean, lying back on the right bunk, hadn't used the bathroom to dress in; why should Ryan? He unwound his towel and pulled on his pants.

Ken rolled a lab stool out from under a counter for Alice to sit on, then got another for himself. "So," he said, "you have been to Eden and returned to tell the tale. Tell me, then, what was it like?"

Ryan chose to let the name "Eden" pass. He didn't feel like getting into an argument over it. He stuck his arms into his shirt and drew it on over his head, winked at his mother, and said, "A lot like Earth, actually."

"Of course it would be, at least physically," Ken said. "God intends us to live there, after all. But I meant, what did it *feel* like? Could you sense the Holy Spirit at work there?"

Ryan shook his head and sat down on the edge of the bed facing his parents. He opened one of the drawers in his locker, took out a pair of socks, and began to pull them on. "No, sorry. All I felt was excitement the whole time I was there. I was happy to find it livable—still am—but I didn't feel any moving religious experience."

Ken's smile was completely unexpected. "I'm not surprised," he said. "Evidently the Lord still chooses not to reveal Himself to us directly." Ryan could hear the capital letters in Ken's speech—Ken had been preaching long enough to get the emphasis just right. He went on to say, "I'm happy for you all the same, for you have been judged and found acceptable, or you would never have been permitted to land."

There was a silence while Ryan tried to think of a polite way to answer that. He looked to Sean, but Sean was either asleep or faking it. He looked back to Ken, and was about to say something that started with, "Look, Dad . . ." when his mother smiled sweetly and said, "So how did you like camping out in the wild? Your father and I used to do it all the time, you know. Did your shoulders get used to the weight of the backpack? Did you eat well?"

CHAPTER ELEVEN

FAITH AND REASON

RYAN WOKE IN DARKNESS. It felt good to wake in a bed again, but the unfamiliar surroundings left him disoriented for a moment just the same. Then he looked through the glass wall and saw the pale glow from the various lab instruments, and he remembered where he was. His internal clock told him it was midday, but the glowing numbers on the stand by the bed read 3:48 a.m.

He realized what had awakened him when he heard the toilet flush just through the wall at his head. A moment later the door opened and Sean stepped back to his bed, but instead of sliding in he just sat on top of it, leaning back against the clothing locker and looking out through the glass wall into the hospital.

"You awake or just sleepwalking?" Ryan asked softly.

"Slept out," Sean replied.

"Me too." They had both taken the afternoon nap to end all afternoon naps, sacking out shortly after Ryan's parents had left and catching up on three nights of lost sleep, but now it was at least twelve hours later and that, Ryan discovered happily, was about as long as he could sleep.

"I've been thinking," Sean said.

"Thought I smelled smoke."

"Ha, paleface make-um joke."

Ryan raised up and shoved his pillow all the way forward against his locker, then turned around and leaned back against it with his legs still under the covers. "All right, so what have you been thinking about?"

"What do you think I've been thinking about?"

"The customs agents?"

"Damn right the customs agents. I just hope that we didn't mess them up as bad as I think we did."

"How bad do you think we messed them up?"

Sean exhaled noisily. "Just changed the entire course of their evolution, that's all."

"How do you figure?"

"You remember when I was telling you about Native Americans and what happened to them when the Europeans showed up? The white man brought all sorts of tools that we had never thought of; wagons, guns, plows, you name it. It wasn't long before we were using them all too, and it wasn't long after that that our whole way of life came to a halt. Well that's what's going to happen here if the idea of fire catches on."

Ryan thought about that a moment. "But fire is so basic! Any civilization is bound to use fire. We may have given them the idea, but any intelligent race would have to figure it out sooner or later, wouldn't they?"

"Who's to say? How do we know that fire is the only way to start a civilization? That's how we did it, but there could be a dozen other paths. Nobody knows, and that's my whole point; now we'll *never* know. They've got the concept, and they're locked into that course of history forever. We've destroyed any chance they ever had to try it a different way."

"Are you sure it's that bad? I mean, we took away their matches and put out the fire; they've got no more idea how to start one on their own than they did before. Eventually they'll forget about it and they'll be right back where they started."

"Maybe," Sean said in the voice of one not convinced. "We can hope."

They held the ship's meeting that afternoon. Sean and Ryan and the few crewmembers who had to remain at their posts attended electronically through intercoms, but the rest gathered in the auditorium and watched the narrated slide show the two explorers presented.

Just a day after being there, Ryan already felt as if the pictures were of someone else's trip. Even the ones with him in them seemed more like a special effect made on a computer than an actual photo of him on an alien world. He wondered if everyone else saw them that way as well, if the pictures gave them anything like the sensation he got from actually being there. He doubted it.

The shots of the customs agents fleeing from the camera on their first night out made everyone laugh, as did the one of the agent rooting through Ryan's pack the next day. They applauded the shots of Sean landing the first fish caught on the new world. But when Sean flashed the last photo in the presentation, the one of the agents dancing around the bonfire, they laughed at it as well.

"I wish it were funny," Sean said when the laughter died down, "but the fact is, it's tragic. According to David there are only two other fires on the whole continent, and both are from natural causes. It's pretty obvious these guys learned how to start this one from us, and that tells me they're already a long ways up the evolutionary ladder toward intelligence. And if that's the case, then I don't think we have any business living on their world, or even visiting it again." He used the slideshow controls to bring up the lights in the auditorium, but left the picture on the screen.

There was a stunned silence, slowly giving way to the murmur of whispered conversations, growing to a babble of voices, punctuated at last by Mariko's outspoken, "Of course we have to visit them again. They represent a wonderful opportunity to study an emerging civilization."

"And destroy that very civilization in the process," Sean said, raising his own voice to be heard. He set the slideshow program to display his intercom image on the screen alongside the picture of the customs agents so the people in the auditorium could see him. "They learned how to use fire from us. What's next? Clothing? Houses? Radio? Spaceships? If we keep showing them examples of our technology, they'll never develop anything of their own."

"That's not so," Mariko argued. "There are established methods for limiting the observer's influence on a population under study."

"Sure, limiting. That's like a limited hull breach. We still lose irreplaceable resources, and so would they. They'd lose their imaginations. They'd wind up copying us in every way they could. The only thing your studies would tell you would be how long it takes them to figure out each step along the way. It's not worth destroying their chance at developing their own independent culture just for that."

Ken's sermonizing voice cut into their argument. "You miss the point," he said, standing to be recognized. When he had everyone's attention, he repeated himself. "You miss the point, though I can't understand how you could. The similarities between this planet and Earth are too great for coincidence. It's obvious that God has recreated Eden for us, and that he intends for us to live there. If it already contains intelligent creatures, then it seems equally obvious that they're here for us to teach, to fill with the word of the Lord, to enlighten and bring up in innocence and to—"

"Like the missionaries 'taught' my ancestors?" Sean asked. "That's just another name for conquest. See what I'm talking about, Mariko? Maybe *you* wouldn't influence them, but what about people like Ken? How can you keep idiots from trying to change them on purpose?"

"I resent—" Ken began, but Sean cut him off.

"The only way to do that is to eliminate the possibility. I say we should leave the inhabitants of this planet alone and go to Centauri B. Now. Our presence in their night *sky* could be screwing with their natural development. And as for teaching them the word of the Lord, Ken, you even attempt it and I'll stick this Bible—" he waved the copy Ken had left in the quarantine room's bathroom in front of the intercom pickup "—so far down your throat you can read it through another orifice. I made a vow that we wouldn't screw up this planet, and I intend to keep it. You go back there over my dead body."

Ken ignored the threat. "How can you even consider spurning God's gift?" he demanded. "He has allowed us to re-enter the Garden of Eden, and at the same time he has given us a mission to perform. Our duty is clear. We face the embodiment of evil, the force that led mankind to be expelled from the garden; we must now redeem the serpent!" He extended his right arm toward the screen, which still showed the band of customs agents dancing on multiple tentacles before the fire. "There!" he shouted. "There are the sons and daughters of Satan, waiting for redemption at our hands."

"Ken," Mariko said, "That's no more a snake than you're a theologian."

Bob Thorpe shouted, "Ken's right! If you're too blind to see the truth—"

"Oh, shut up, Thorpe," someone else shouted. "We've put up with you for—"

Another voice joined the rising tide. "Revelation, chapter twenty-one, verse one: 'And I saw a new heaven and a new earth, for the first heaven and the first earth were passed away—"

The pandemonium that followed was highly entertaining to watch over the intercom. It seemed as if it might go on all night, but finally the captain sounded the emergency siren, and in the sudden silence that followed he said quietly, "The next person to speak out of turn cleans the air scrubbers for a year. Is that clear? Okay, then, now that everybody's gotten that out of their systems, maybe we can start thinking with our brains instead of our adrenal glands. Any objection to that? Good. Mariko, you have the floor."

"Thank you." Mariko was already standing; she waited for the others to sit back down before saying, "I think Sean has a legitimate point. We're in a position to do inconceivable damage to an alien species just as it takes its first steps toward civilization. That is, *if* these creatures are actually intelligent and aren't just accomplished mimics. We don't know that. We need to study them more just to establish which it is. But if they *are* intelligent, then we still need to study them. Sean worries about contamination, but I don't think it's inevitable. We *can* study them if we're careful, and the insight we gain into the nature and the development of intelligence will be priceless. We have the chance to witness a race's first use of fire, the first step that launched our own species on the road to the stars!"

"They were pushed," Sean growled, but not loud enough to be picked up by the intercom. The captain's threat had been enough even for him.

Mariko was still speaking. "This is the first time humanity has encountered an alien intellect; we can't just run away from it. But neither can we convert it to Christianity, or any other system of belief. Think for a minute, Ken. What was the original sin all about? Eating from the tree of knowledge, wasn't it? But what are you proposing, if not playing the serpent ourselves and forcing them to do the same thing? By your own standards, you should be against contaminating them with our ideas. This is *their* Eden, not ours.

"Therefore, I propose that we study them, but carefully. Set up our colony outside their territory, and limit our growth so that we never interfere with their normal development. Or possibly set up our colony on Centauri B-2, if we find it to be equally habitable, and use the starship as a base for studying this planet. But to deliberately turn our backs on this opportunity to study an emerging intelligence would be the worst thing we could possibly do."

Sean pushed the intercom's call button. On the auditorium screen, his image blinked.

"You have a comment, Sean?" the captain asked.

"Yeah. Worst thing for who, us or them?" Sean asked. "I think Mariko and Ken are both full of—ah, are both considering only *our* side of the question. What about the customs agents? I think it's obvious the best thing for them would be if we just left them alone. Once they make it into space on their own—*if that's what they choose to do with their civilization*—then maybe we can contact them, but until then we should keep our stupid noses out of their business and off their planet."

Several people raised their hands.

"Warren?" the captain said, pointing at Holly's father.

"That's easy for Sean to say." Warren faced Sean's screen image and said, "You've already been there. You've already hit dirt; you've caught your big fish. What about the rest of us? We've waited just as long as you have to stand on a planet again, and now you say we should fire up the drive again and go somewhere else. Well maybe you're right about these 'customs agents' of yours and maybe you're not, but I say we ought to at least take a few months on the ground before we go gallivanting off through the cosmos again. Find us someplace out of the way like Mariko suggested. Take a few months of shore leave. Take the time to learn what we've *really* got facing us here, and then decide what we want to do."

He began to sit down again, but the applause from the rest of the crew caught him by surprise. He stood again, blushing, then with a nod to everyone sat back down.

Holly stood next. When the captain nodded at her, she said, "We have to wait at least until the quarantine period is over. We won't know for sure that it's safe down there until then."

"It's safe," Ken said. "I am certain of that, just as I am certain that—"

"Air scrubbers, Ken. Last warning." The captain scowled at him, and Ken shut up. Turning back to Holly, he said, "Thank you, Holly. We'll remember the quarantine. Warren, I'll take your suggestion under consideration as well. I'm just as eager to get off the ship as you are, as long as I'm sure doing so won't harm the natives. Sean, I'm not going to take your concerns lightly either. We've got two weeks to wait before we can go down there again anyway; we'll use that time to make the best decision we can. And it'll be a decision based on the *facts*, not feelings, and not privileged communications from some higher power. Until then, let's try to keep the rhetoric to a minimum and the thinking to a maximum. Okay? Okay. Meeting adjourned."

For the next few days, Ryan and Sean spent their time watching the planet from the satellite over their landing site. The customs agents were moving around quite a bit through the forest, entire "bureaus" (a name Mariko had coined for a group of the creatures) of them moving kilometers in a day, but no one on the ship could know if that was natural behavior or not. Mariko theorized that it was not, that the behavior they were witnessing would have taxed the "stop and search" system of territorial boundaries to the breaking point long ago if it were the normal pattern, but she was the first to admit that her theory rested on incomplete evidence. She used that as an argument in favor of visiting the planet again, pointing out that observations from above simply couldn't provide the sort of information she needed in order to understand an alien species' social systems.

Sean continued to argue that they should leave the planet alone, but nobody other than Ryan wanted to hear it. Besides, after the initial few days of stirred-up activity, the customs agents began to slow down in their movements, and it began to look as if no permanent damage had been done. They had started no more fires, anyway. More and more people raised the question of whether they were really intelligent after all.

Ken, of course, argued along a different tack. He claimed that further delay would anger God, that it would seem as if they were spurning His gift. He and his core group of followers pushed for immediate landing and colonization, and for once he had over half the crew on his side.

"We're losing the battle, Kemosabe," Sean said during a break in the latest round of discussion. "I wonder if I can fake a good alien disease."

"I thought about that," Ryan replied, "but Holly'd be onto you in a minute. You can't change your blood chemistry, and without that all you could do is claim a stomach-ache."

"True," Sean admitted.

"So we lose this battle. But one battle isn't the war."

"You've got a plan?"

"Maybe. It's obvious we aren't going to keep people off the planet, so all we can really do is try to minimize their impact. Why not put down on an island?"

Sean cocked his head, considering.

"We can argue it from the safety standpoint," Ryan went on. "An island would be easier to guard from predators. And from our viewpoint, whatever we do there will be isolated, less chance to spread."

"An island without customs agents on it," Sean replied, nodding. "Mariko can go to the mainland to do her studying, and one of us can go along to keep her honest, but the rest of the crew stays put. And if Mariko finds that the agents are intelligent, then we've got a stronger argument to leave them alone. I like it."

The captain liked it too, when they called and put their proposal to him. Within the week they began ferrying people down to their chosen island.

CHAPTER TWELVE

BABES IN THE WOODS

"FREE AGAIN!" SEAN STOOD on a beach of white sand, a row of almost-palm trees on one side and the ocean sparkling and stretching out to the horizon on the other. He tilted his head back and howled a two-pitch howl, pounding his fists on his chest to produce a sort of staccato punctuation.

Ryan laughed. "What was that?"

Sean peered at him beneath lowered brows. "Don't you know a Tarzan yell when you hear one?"

Ryan shook his head.

"I tell you, the things you don't know are a constant revelation." Sean howled and pounded his chest again. "Try it. Clears the sinuses, the lungs, the stuffiness from your step—it's a universal remedy for going buggy in a damned quarantine chamber."

Blushing at the thought of yelling so uninhibitedly, Ryan shook his head and looked toward the lander, parked on a hill just above the beach. It was a much bigger craft than the one he and Sean had taken on their first trip down; this was one of the two main colony landers, designed to carry fifty people at a time. A little over half that many—the third of the crew that the captain would allow on the planet at any one time—streamed in and out of it, carrying rolled-up tents, portable cook-stoves, chemical latrines, a tiny fusion-electric generator, and a hundred other essentials for living in the wilds. Ryan had helped with the moving for a while, but when he had seen

Sean standing on the beach he had gone down to see what he was up to.

"I can certainly understand their eagerness to set up," Sean went on, talking through a smile that seemed a permanent fixture in the hours since he had piloted the first wave of people down for shore leave. He had picked an island about fifty kilometers from the coast, an isolated seamount that reared out of the ocean to a height of almost a kilometer at the peak, from which a fresh water stream ran back down through lush forest to a blindingly white beach scattered with shells. Out in the water a few hundred meters a reef surrounded most of the island.

"Too bad you're not sticking around to enjoy it," Ryan said. They had brought an airplane with them in the lander's cargo hold; in the morning Sean would be flying Mariko back into the area where they had encountered the customs agents.

"Too crowded here anyway," Sean replied.

"Yeah."

"Going to climb the peak while I'm gone?"

Ryan shrugged. "Thinking about it. Don't know what I'll name it if I do, though."

Sean nodded. "Yeah, that's the trouble with new mountains. Every time you climb one you have to name the bugger."

The crew had decided that naming features on the new planet would be done by the explorers or discoverers of the particular feature being named, with the crew either ratifying or vetoing the names with a two-thirds vote. Surprisingly, a "bureau" of "customs agents" passed unanimously at the first meeting after the ruling. The name for the planet hadn't been voted on, but "Eden" seemed to be winning by default.

They watched the waves roll in for a time. The surf was a meter or so high out in the open ocean, but it lost its energy against the reef and what waves made it to the shore were hardly more than ripples. Sean reached down and picked up a flat stone, curled his forefinger around it, and sent it spinning out over the water. It hit and skipped, skipped again, again, and disappeared with a splash.

"Hey, that's neat. How'd you do that?"

Sean looked at Ryan in open astonishment. "Skipping stones?" he asked. "You don't know how to skip stones either?"

"Where would I learn?"

Sean turned to look at the lander, at the people setting up camp beside it, and back to Ryan. "Babes in the woods," he said softly, shaking his head. He picked up another stone, fitted it to his forefinger, and sent it skipping out to sea. "Babes in the woods," he repeated, laughing.

Sean's description of the colonists seemed particularly apt during the next few days, but gradually people discovered how to deal with the alien environment of a planet's surface. The environment itself was instrumental in their success; a more perfectly suited place for humanity was hard to imagine. Trees of all descriptions covered the island, the fruits from which Holly pronounced edible after a battery of lab tests. The bay provided fish that were also edible and almost as easy to gather as the fruit. A species of flightless bird living on the mountainside could have been mistaken for turkeys at first glance, and some experimental digging near the stream turned up half a dozen edible root vegetables. A little exploring also revealed berry plants and some natural grains growing in a meadow not far from camp. There seemed to be no stinging insects at all. The island had predators—jungle cats and a species of wolf—but they fled whenever a human came near.

Ken was quick to point out the parallels between Eden the planet and the biblical garden. He was hard to refute; indeed, no one seemed to be trying. Even David Bonham began speaking civilly to Ken, and what was more alarming, began speaking as if he believed the Eden hypotheses himself.

"I'm considering it, yes," he admitted to Ryan when Ryan asked him about it one afternoon as they gathered fruit for Laney. "I'm not convinced, but at this point I think it's just about as believable an explanation for all this as parallel evolution."

Ryan, up in the tree and tossing its crisp, yellow "snapples" down to David, pressed him for his reasoning. "Why do you say that? What's wrong with parallel evolution as an explanation?"

"The life forms are too similar. There's no reason for things to be this close to what we have at home. Think about it; Australia has stranger animals than this island does. And the difference in genetic code between what we have here and the Earthly counterparts seems to rule out the theory that someone seeded both Eden and Earth millennia ago. Ken's theory that God created it for us is actually the only one that fits the facts as we know them so far."

"But why wouldn't God use the same genetic code here as he did on Earth?" Ryan asked.

David shrugged. "I don't know. Maybe so we *wouldn't* attribute it to an interstellar seeding expedition."

Ryan had no argument to refute him with, save that it seemed silly to invoke God rather than try to solve the mystery by scientific means. To see David invoking God as the explanation seemed even sillier, but evidently only to Ryan. Ken's church had gained an enormous amount of credibility when David began attending services.

Ryan tossed down another handful of snapples, one at a time. David held them in a fold of his shirt as he caught them, then knelt down to transfer them into the basket. Neither he nor Ryan noticed Holly approaching until she was right below the tree, and she didn't notice Ryan at first, either.

"Hey," she said. "I was just heading out for a walk. Want to come along?"

David straightened, a snapple in either hand. "Sure," he said. He tossed the snapples playfully, just bouncing them off his palms, then handed her one.

She looked it over, smiling, found the seam that gave it its name, and twisted it open with a pop. "Here," she said, handing a half back to him.

"Thanks." David took a bite. Swallowing, he looked up into the tree and said, "One more armload and we're done."

Ryan breathed out the breath he'd been holding. "Right," he said.

Holly looked upward. "Oh, Ryan! Hi. I didn't see you up there. Want to go for a walk, too?"

He considered it for all of a second. "No, thanks," he said. "I've got stuff I should do back at camp."

"Sure?"

"Yeah, I'm sure." He had nothing else to do, either in camp or anywhere else, but he didn't feel like playing chaperon for David and Holly. It would be too obvious what he was doing, and if there was truly any interest between them then his presence would probably only make it worse.

He pulled down a snapple-laden branch and began tossing fruit down to both David and Holly, resisting the urge to send one down the fast way to David's head. That wouldn't make a good impression, either.

Over the next couple of days he again and again questioned his decision to stay out of their way, as they sat together at dinner, went swimming together, or just smiled at one another in passing. Each time it happened he felt a hot stab of jealousy, but each time there seemed to be nothing he could do to change anything, either. He tried talking with Holly, tried letting her know that he existed as well, and she was kind and nice to him as ever, but there was no spark of romantic interest there and he knew it.

When the frustration built up to the point where he felt he could no longer stand it, he decided to climb the mountain. It wasn't much of a climb; he could have done it in an afternoon without a pack, but he decided to take his time and camp overnight on the summit. After backpacking with Sean he realized that he liked the sense of solitude. He wanted to do it again, but since the first group of people on the ground was scheduled to go back to the ship in just a couple more days so that another group could come down, this would be his last chance at it for weeks to come.

He followed the stream upward to where it emerged from the mountainside in a spring. He filled his water bottle there and headed on up, bushwhacking straight up the slope, figuring he couldn't miss finding the top that way. It was a steep climb at first, but after half an hour of it he found himself atop a ridge line that led more gradually to the peak.

He reached it by evening. The sun still had an hour or more to go before it would touch the horizon. The peak was rocky and windswept, giving him a clear view of the island spread out below him on all sides. The mountain shadow was a long triangle with the point reaching almost out to the reef on the north-eastern side. The inside of that triangle was too dark to let him make out much detail, but the rest of the island was still well-lit. Ryan could see the lander and the camp around it at the mouth of the stream. Specks of white in the water were probably people swimming.

He took a pemon from his pack and sat on a rock to eat it and to think of a name. Here he was, first person to climb a mountain on the planet, and without a name to give it. He'd considered quite a few on the way up, but none of them seemed really right. He didn't feel like naming it after himself, and it seemed presumptuous to name it after Sean, who would probably rather have a bigger mountain named after him anyway. He'd thought of a few more generic names, like "Triangle Mountain" or simply "First Peak," but in the end, sitting up there on the top of it and looking back at the camp, he decided to call it "Holly Mountain." She was why he'd climbed it, after all.

He heard the bell that Ken used to call his service to order ringing faintly through the distance. He looked up into the sky. *You up there, God? Do you hear Ken's bell too?*

He recited his own prayer, the one he'd decided upon a few days ago in case God really was listening. *Dear God, if you're up there, don't let us screw this place up. Amen.* He smiled, then added a postscript. *And I wouldn't mind it if Holly paid a little more attention to me, either.*

The sky didn't split with lightning or thunder. Nothing much happened that Ryan could sense, save that he felt a little embarrassed. A guy shouldn't have to ask for help in getting a girl.

The sight that greeted him when he walked back into camp early the next afternoon was almost too strange to believe. He was again following the stream, watching the water birds fluttering along ahead of him, when he rounded the corner and surprised Laney Terrill, Holly's mother, reaching into the stream to scoop out a pot of water—in the nude.

There was a moment of startled silence.

"I—I'm sorry. Didn't mean to catch you at your bath," Ryan said, seizing the only explanation that came to mind, though it seemed strange that she would be bathing this close to camp. He turned to go around her, his eyes averted, when he saw his father striding across camp, also without a thread of clothing on. Ken disappeared into the eatery tent, holding the flap for Bob Thorpe and David Bonham as they strolled out, also in the nude. No, not quite; David was wearing sandals.

Ryan turned back to Laney. "I think I missed something here," he managed to say.

Laney smiled and straightened up with her pot of water. She was blushing a little, and Ryan couldn't help noticing that a woman—even a woman as round as Laney—blushes in more places than just her face. "We, well, we decided last night to drop the nudity taboo," she explained. "It just seemed kind of silly to be wearing clothes in paradise, so we decided to try going without for a while."

"I see," Ryan said.

"No pun intended," Laney said through a grin.

"Huh? Oh. Ha." Ryan shook his head. He was blushing deep red, he knew, far deeper than Laney.

"I wasn't sure about it either, at first," she said. "I'm afraid I eat too much of my own cooking to have much to show off, you know. But you get used to it pretty fast, and it's sure a whole lot cooler cooking this way, so long as you wear an apron."

Ryan looked away again. Laney was a bit on the heavy side, that was true, but that was hardly relevant. This was Laney Terrill, Everymom, standing before him with no clothes on.

"I, uh, I guess an apron would be kind of important, wouldn't it?"

She laughed, and it was the same loud, jovial peal that she'd always had. "You know it, buster. Something's got to keep these things out of the soup."

Ryan couldn't look. He found that he couldn't *not* look, either, but Laney was simply standing there with her water bucket, wearing only a smile.

"Come on," she said. "You must be hungry. I bet you haven't had lunch yet, have you?"

"Uh, well, no, now that you mention it." Ryan fell into step beside her and they walked into camp. He felt eyes watching him.

"Did everybody...?"

"Nope. You don't have to if you don't want to, and there are a couple of people who don't. Your mom, for one. Nobody else cares one way or the other. We just decided it'd be nice to have the option."

Ryan felt relieved that he wouldn't have to be averting his eyes from his own mother. Doing it with Laney was bad enough. But he didn't have to be doing it with Laney, or with anybody else, he reminded himself. How come he was acting like such a prude?

Because he had a whole lifetime of conditioning, he supposed. But so did everybody else, and they'd evidently gotten over it. Aloud he said, "I guess I'll probably give it a try. It's kind of a shock, though, to come back down off the mountain and find a whole social convention gone."

"That's right, you climbed the mountain! Warren saw you up on top with the telescope."

"He did?"

"Yes. He took a picture of you. You look very handsome in it. So what did you name it?"

Ryan blushed again, but he told her.

"I think that's wonderful. You'll have to tell her yourself."

"Is she...?"

"Naked as a jaybird, except when she's working."

Ryan resolved to visit her in the hospital, then, but instantly changed his mind. How long had he wanted to see Holly without her clothes? Forever? About that long. He would visit her in her tent.

Provided David wasn't there.

"Why don't you ask her swimming?" Laney suggested, as if reading his thoughts. "That's how we all got used to the idea yesterday. Sort of move into it gradually, if you know what I mean, and if you start to get embarrassed you can dive back into the water."

Ryan laughed self-consciously. "The term 'embarrassed' takes on a whole new meaning now."

"Ha. I suppose it does." They reached the eatery tent. Laney paused at the door and said, "Why don't you go take off your pack and whatever else you feel comfortable with and come back for some lunch?"

"Okay," Ryan said. He turned to go, then looked back around. "Thanks, Laney."

Laney laughed. "Any time. And smile, you'll enjoy it."

Ryan discovered that Laney was right on both counts: he did get used to it quickly and he learned to enjoy it even before that. Having a table to conceal his reaction when Kristy Crawford walked into the eatery helped with the former, and having her sit across from him and matter-of-factly eat her lunch while she asked him about his night on the mountain helped with the latter. Kristy was quite a bit younger than he was, fifteen or sixteen, he supposed, and though he had never really developed much of an interest in her on the ship—she being one of Ken's most devout followers—he certainly didn't disapprove of any of her physical attributes. She sat before him with an air of perfect innocence that must have come from her conviction that she was forgiven for original sin, that humanity was truly redeemed and she was in fact in Eden. She was so unselfconscious about her nakedness that by the time they were done eating Ryan felt confident enough to stand up and walk outside the tent with her, then take his leave and go visit Holly.

He found her in the hospital after all. The hospital was simply a four-bunk tent with a medical kit in it, at this point more of a central location for dispensing sun-screen than anything else, but it was one of the first tents to be set up and it was there in case anybody needed it. Ryan knocked on the hollow gourd that Holly had hung at the door for the purpose, and she turned around from peering into a microscope to see him standing there in the doorway. She evidently didn't consider peering into microscopes to be work, because she was wearing no more clothing than her mother or Kristy, or for that matter Ryan himself. And she was beautiful.

"I named the mountain after you," Ryan blurted.

She looked properly stunned. "You did?"

"I did."

"Why?"

"Because I love you."

"I—I'm flattered. I don't know what to say."

Say that you love me and will live with me forever and name our first son after me, Ryan thought, but he couldn't bring himself to speak the words.

"You don't have to say anything," he said instead.

"I want to say something. I just don't know what it is yet." She sat down on one of the cots. A tiny breeze blowing through the door caught a wisp of her hair and dropped it into her eyes. She reached up to brush it aside, the motion raising her right breast along with her arm, and Ryan felt his enforced calm shatter. The involuntary response he had been desperately trying to avoid began to rise.

Holly looked up, saw his embarrassment and the reason for it, and smiled reassuringly. "You know, just because I want you for a friend instead of a lover doesn't mean I never wanted to get the clothes off you."

"Academic curiosity?"

"A little more than that."

Ryan moved into the tent, feeling more awkward than simple nudity in front of Holly could account for. How *did* she feel?

"Isn't it incredible how important clothing is to the way we look at someone?" she asked.

He tried a joke: "Well, it certainly changes *what* you look at."

Holly looked down to her breasts, then back up at Ryan. "I don't mind," she said. "I really don't. When Ken suggested we do this I didn't think I'd like having people stare at me, but you know, when we all took off our clothes we all stared at each other together, and then after a while we just didn't stare anymore. I think I'd be uncomfortable if you were wearing clothes and I wasn't, but if you don't mind me looking at you then I don't mind you looking at me."

"'You show me yours and I'll show you mine,'" Ryan said. "Remember how we used to do that in the park at night?" They had been about eight and nine years old, just after the voyage began.

Holly nodded. "Just like old times." She stood up and did a slow pirouette. "What do you think? Have I changed all that much since then?"

"You've, uh, filled out some."

"Yeah, isn't it disgraceful?" She pinched her waist and managed with effort to get a roll of flesh between thumb and forefinger. She looked up and grinned. "You've filled out some as well."

"Equally disgraceful," Ryan said, looking down at himself. "Or so my father would probably say."

"Not so. He was very adamant about that. It's just going to happen until we get used to looking at people this way. Don't worry about it."

"I won't worry about it if you won't. But I don't know; you've got a naked man professing his love for you, and there are beds all around. . ." He waved his arm around the tent.

"I'm not worried with you. You want love, not just...sex." Holly lost some of her smile with that statement. "Oh, why is it so difficult between friends? We've known each other forever; we've seen each other naked a dozen times when we were kids, and we've always been able to talk about anything but love. Ryan, I—I love you just as much as you love me. More, maybe. I love you so much that I never want to lose you and that's what happens when people bring sex into a love like ours. The friendship dies."

Ryan sat down on the cot across from her. "It doesn't have to."

"It doesn't have to, but it does. Ours would."

"How do you know?"

"I just do. I can feel it. You're someone I can come to and talk with about anything, and I know the moment we had sex that would change. And Ryan, talking with you, feeling that kinship with you; that's more important to me than sex. It always will be."

Ryan looked at the wall of the tent. He focused on a tiny square of the ripstop nylon surface, staring intently at it until it blurred and lost whatever attraction it had held. He looked back at Holly. Holly Terrill, gorgeous blonde with the wide-open, forever-astonished brown eyes and wonderful smile and smooth, full, perfect breasts and slender waist and long, graceful legs, beautiful feet, delicate toes: every bit of her perfect. Never to be his, but his forever if only he didn't touch.

Welcome to Eden, he thought.

CHAPTER THIRTEEN

TEMPTATION

THE SOUND OF A BACKPACK falling noisily to the sand jarred Ryan out of a sound sleep. He opened his eyes, closed them against the sudden intense sunlight, then opened them again more cautiously. Sean was standing across the tent from him, an amused expression on his face.

"Caught you with your pants down, I see."

Ryan levered himself up onto an elbow. "What?"

"Joke. I just got back. Looks like you've been enjoying yourself."

Ryan shook the sleep out of his head and sat up. Sean's words filtered in, finally. "Oh. Ha. I wish. What time is it?"

"About one o'clock." With the twenty-one-plus hour day, one o'clock was about mid-afternoon. When they started the colony in earnest they would probably restructure the hour so that there were twenty-four of them again, but for now they were simply lopping off the day at nine-seventeen p.m. and starting over with midnight.

"Oh." Ryan ran a hand through his hair. He hadn't been out of bed since last night. "No wonder I feel so lousy. So how was your trip?"

"Good and bad." Sean sat down on his cot and began taking off his boots. "Mostly bad. We found the customs agents again. Everything looked fine; they wouldn't talk to us, acted just like before—Mariko had just about decided they weren't any more intelligent than monkeys—but then two nights ago Teigh spotted another campfire from the ship. There was that lightning fire just north of where we were, and evidently the agents finally figured out they could get a light from that. Now there are campfires all over the place."

"Damn."

"Just so. Mariko and I snuck up on one and watched for a while. You'll never guess what they were doing."

"Roasting hot dogs?"

Sean tossed a boot to the sand. "Give them a few days and they probably will be. No, these guys had two fires going, and they were practicing at lighting one and putting it out and lighting it and putting it out, over and over again. And all the while more customs agents were streaming in to watch and leaving with flaming branches of their own."

"You're kidding."

"I wish I were." The other boot hit the sand.

"I guess that kills the mimic theory."

"Sort of does, doesn't it?"

"So what did you do?"

Sean looked at him with narrowed eyes. "Do? What *could* we do? They've figured it out. The idea's spread. Maybe if we'd killed them all that first night we could have stopped it, but there's no way now short of nuking the whole mountain range."

"That seems a little extreme," Ryan said.

"I'm not sure it wouldn't be justified. Mariko keeps telling me it's not as bad as I think, that if they're so smart they would have figured it out soon anyway, but I don't buy that. These guys are alien! Mariko couldn't even see that they were intelligent until night before last; how does she know what they would or wouldn't do?" Sean threw a sock toward his boots and missed.

Ryan stood up and went to the tent door. "But she does agree they're intelligent?"

"Oh yeah. No question about that."

"Then we can't stay here. Not even on this island. If we stay anywhere on the planet, eventually my dad or somebody like him will decide to meddle even further."

"That's obvious to you and me, bucko, but not to anybody else." The other sock hit the boots.

"Have you told the captain about it yet?"

"Yeah. He's not sure what to think. He's going to call another meeting in a few days, after he and the rest of the crew have had a chance to hit dirt for a while and see what the planet's like first hand. He says we'll decide what to do after everybody's seen it."

"I'll have to catch it from the ship, then," Ryan said. "I'm going back up to help make room for the others."

"Good. That puts one of us in both places, because I'm staying here. It's my turn to vacation in paradise." Sean collapsed back on his cot. "Ah, that feels good. We walked out of the mountains this morning and then stiffened up in the plane on the way back." He closed his eyes, opened them again, and said, "Hey, long as you're up, slip over to Laney's and get me something cold to drink, would you? I'd do it myself, but I don't have anything clean to wear in public."

"Ryan?"

He was sitting in the sand under a short, round-topped tree, watching the ocean. He'd gone walking, bored after running Sean's errand and showering and shaving and doing all his other waking-up rituals, and he'd wound up here, part way around the curve of the bay. He turned to see who had spoken.

It was Kristy Crawford.

"I saw you going for a walk, and I followed you. I hope you don't mind."

She was standing a few steps away, uncertainty written into her face and her stance. With the beach for a backdrop and a slight breeze blowing in from the ocean to waft her brown hair gently to the side, she looked so slender and young and fragile and beautiful all at once that Ryan could hardly speak.

"No," he managed, then with still more effort, "not at all."

"I want to talk to you."

"Uh, sure."

She took the last few steps toward him and sat down beside him in the shade of the tree. The shadow from its round ball of leaves was only a couple meters across; Ryan scooted over to give her room. He couldn't help looking at her as she sat in profile beside him. She was a thin girl, willowy thin, and her breasts were proportionately small. They were almost conical, without the weight to pull them into roundness. Her nipples were red raspberries sticking straight out from their centers.

"Uh, what did you want to talk about?" he asked, knowing already.

She confirmed his guess. "Sex," she said.

"Sex," he echoed. "Uh, what about sex?"

"I've never done it," she said simply. "And I want to."

"Oh. With me?"

"Yes."

Ryan looked back out at the ocean. "Can I ask why?"

"Because you're a kind and caring person."

It was out of his mouth before he'd even considered the words: "I knew it would pay off someday."

She giggled nervously. "Then you'll show me how?"

"I—" He stopped. "I—" he started again, and stopped again. At last he got out, "Why now? I mean, I thought you were pretty religious." He looked back at her.

"I still am," she said, smiling. "But sex isn't a sin anymore."

"It's not?"

"Ken says we've been forgiven for original sin. That means sex is okay again."

Ryan could hardly believe his ears. "Ken said that?"

"Yes."

"So that's why...?"

"I've always been curious, and I figured you know how. You never were particularly religious. So now that it's all right, and you've evidently been forgiven too, I thought you'd be a good teacher."

Ryan felt suddenly mired in contradictions. Kristy was right; he knew how. The ship's population was small, but not so small that the opportunity to experiment had never presented itself. And Ryan had never believed that sex before marriage was a sin. So why did he feel so strongly that sex with Kristy right now would be? Because Ken had okayed it? No, it was much deeper than that, much more primal.

He couldn't help thinking of Holly trying to tell him that she didn't love him, at least not sexually. She'd said she loved him as a friend, and sex would change that. Was this how she had felt?

"You don't love me, do you?" he asked Kristy.

"I love everyone."

"Ah. Right. But not me in particular, more than everyone else."

Kristy frowned. "Nnn—no. Does it matter?"

"I'm not sure."

She was obviously confused by all this. Why didn't he just show her how it was done? Why indeed?

Ryan took her hand. He looked into her eyes and saw the trust there. "Kristy, I'm flattered that you'd want me to teach you. I really am. It's a very important thing, choosing who you share it with first. But it's just as important to understand why, and I'm not at all sure that simple curiosity is a good enough reason."

"You're saying I should love you first? More than I love everyone else?"

"No," Ryan said instantly, for as soon as she asked, he knew that wasn't his reason. It might have been *a* reason, but it wasn't his. Something else bothered him, besides having a girl he hardly knew asking him for sex. Was it this girl in particular? Did Kristy turn him off somehow? Was he afraid of virgins? Or was it just the way she had asked?

No, it was the *why*. Simple curiosity.

He smiled. He had it. Now how to tell her gently?

He began: "You've heard the news about the customs agents that Sean and I found, haven't you?"

"Yes?" It was a question. Why are you talking about them now? Trying to change the subject?

"You know they watched us build a fire, and learned how to do it themselves. Sean thinks—and I believe him—that we messed with their development by doing that. They weren't ready for fire yet, wouldn't have discovered it for centuries, if ever. But now they've got it. They'll never forget how it works or what it's like, and that's going to affect the way they do things forever. Sex is like that, too. You—"

"You're saying I'm not ready for it." Kristy was innocent, but she wasn't dumb.

"Right. Now don't get mad; let me explain why I say that. Having sex is like the customs agents discovering fire. It's going to change you, permanently. You'll have to take my word for it, but it will."

"I won't get pregnant. I've taken care of that."

"I'm not talking about getting pregnant. I'm just talking about sex. It'll change you. It'll change you because, if it's done right the first time, you're going to like it. It's going to be the best thing that's ever happened to you. You're going to want to do it again. You're going to think about it all the time and it's going to color everything you do. You're going to start forgetting things because you're too busy thinking about sex, and it'll be months before you learn to quit thinking about it, even for a little while."

Kristy shivered. Her nipples were even more prominent now. "You make it sound like a drug."

"It *is* a drug. The most addictive one there is. It sends a jolt straight to the pleasure of your brain every time you do it, and that's why it's important to be ready for it."

She breathed in, her eyes wide. "So that's why it was considered a sin. But Ken said it's okay now. That must not happen when you have sex anymore."

"That's exactly what I'm afraid of."

"What?"

"That's exactly what I'm afraid of. If we had sex right now, I don't think that would happen, and that's the problem. It's *supposed* to be that way."

"It is? You *want* to be addicted?"

"That's right."

"I don't understand."

"That's why you're not ready for it."

She looked as if she was about to cry. Ryan knew how she felt: anger and frustration and, most of all, confusion. He'd just felt it himself not even a day ago, and it tore at him to see her going through it now. Had Holly felt this way, turning him down? Probably. But he had one advantage that Holly didn't have; he wasn't afraid of destroying a friendship.

He reached out and drew Kristy into his arms. She looked up into his face through a veil of her own wind-tossed hair, blinking her eyes to keep them from brimming over with tears. Carefully, gently, Ryan brushed her hair aside and kissed her.

He was glad he'd just heard a lecture on addiction. Kristy's lips were half melted already, and when she realized what was happening she brought her hands up to touch him, at first hesitantly on his chest, then, more confidently, she slipped her arms around him and pulled him against her, melting completely.

There was a moment in which time ceased to have meaning.

"I understand now," she whispered.

He shook his head, at the moment the only motion in their world. "No you don't. Not yet. But you're learning. When someone makes you feel that way just by *thinking* about them, then you'll understand."

He found Ken in the lander, arguing with the captain over the intercom.

"I don't see the need for the delay," Ken was saying. "We know it's habitable; it was made with us in mind. Why ship people back up when we're all going to live here eventually anyway?"

The captain was frowning as he spoke, obviously angry but just as obviously not willing to let Ken push him over the line into shouting. "Because that's the way we're going to do it," he said. "We're not going to throw caution to the winds just because the planet appears benign. We're going to follow the mission directives to the letter, and that means we explore it thoroughly before we even address the question of colonization."

"How can there be any question?" Ken demanded indignantly. "Of *course* we'll colonize it."

"That remains to be seen. In the meantime, we've got another rotation of crew eager to go down and they can't unless somebody comes back up to help run the ship. So I've posted a duty roster, and those people on it are to return tomorrow."

"You're asking people to leave Eden!" Ken said. "The theological implications of that could be—"

"You want to test it first hand?" the captain asked. "I've left your name off the return list, but I could easily add it. One more word of insubordination from you, and I will. Is that clear?"

Ken sighed. Evidently he wasn't quite ready to defy orders yet. "Clear enough," he said, and he signed off. He turned around in the control chair and saw Ryan standing in the doorway. "The captain insists you go back to the ship," he said.

"I heard." Ryan went on inside and sat in one of the frontmost passenger seats. "That's no problem; I'm ready to go anyway."

"You are?"

"Yeah. I'm not sure I like it down here."

Ken started as if he'd been slapped. He had evidently not even considered such a thought. "But—but this is Eden!"

"I know. I just got propositioned by one of the beautiful naked ladies. I want to talk to you about that."

"You're uncomfortable with nudity?"

"Not that. I never thought it was that useful a taboo anyway. But I *am* uncomfortable when a very mixed up young girl comes to me asking for sex because you told her it's okay."

"Who did that?"

"Who isn't important. What matters is that you told her she couldn't sin anymore."

"Well she can't. Not that way. Not in Eden."

"You're saying that what was once supposed to be a mortal sin is now perfectly okay just because we're *here*?"

Ken crossed his arms across his chest and frowned. "You're the last one I'd expect to be defending chastity. You're the one who made me realize what living here would mean, you know."

Ryan narrowed his eyes. "What?"

"On the ship, after you came back from your explorations. The first time I saw you, you stood before your mother and me without clothing and without shame. That was when I knew what God had planned for us."

Ryan had to think a minute before he could remember the incident that Ken was referring to. "I was just out of the shower, Dad."

"It didn't matter. I knew when I saw you that God had freed you of inhibitions, and that we should all be free as well. That includes sexual inhibitions."

"Look, forget God for a minute. We're talking about sex. You say we shouldn't be inhibited, and I can agree with that, but you forgot to warn people that the opposite of inhibited isn't necessarily casual."

Ken tilted his head in thought, trying to make sense of Ryan's statement. "I don't follow you."

Ryan stood, began pacing the aisle between rows of seats. "I can't believe I'm having this conversation with my father. Look, I'm talking about tenderness. Love. The things that make sex special. You're telling people they can have sex instead of saying hello."

Ken waved his hands in the air. "That's exactly the point! It *should* be casual. It's only when we're completely casual about it that we can get away from its sinful aspects. Lust and envy and obsession and—"

"You think that's worth killing the joy?"

"The what?"

Ryan whirled around to face Ken again. "The joy! The reason for doing it in the first place, dammit! You're trying to pervert it into something it was never intended to be."

"I'm trying to do nothing of the sort. I am merely following the will of God."

"God told you to do this, did he? Did he speak to you? Write you a letter? What exactly did he say to you?"

"I interpret His intentions by the way He manifests himself to me in the world."

"Meaning you guess."

Ken had been uncomfortable with the direction the discussion was heading, but now that Ryan had turned it around to the familiar attack on his *a priori* reasoning he smiled, shaking his head as he did. "Not at all. I am certain of His intentions. He has made them obvious to anyone who wishes to know. Look at the facts: We're the best that humanity has to offer. We left behind all our diseases, both physical and mental, when we left Earth. We purified ourselves for the journey, finally becoming on our own what God intended us to be all along. In return he has given us back Eden. That much should be obvious even to you. The rest follows directly."

"This is Eden. The biblical Eden. You really believe that?"

"I believe it with all my heart."

That's the problem, Ryan thought. *You should be using your brain.* But he didn't say it aloud. Getting Ken mad wouldn't do any good. Nothing else would, either, but he had to try. Calmly, he said, "Has it ever occurred to you that maybe God created it for the customs agents, and not for us? That it's a test, to see if we've learned how to live and let live? Maybe this is just one last temptation, not redemption."

Ken shook his head sadly. "No. This is Eden. I'm sure of it."

"And you really think the customs agents are here to preach Christianity to. You plan to do that, to screw them up just like the Spanish missionaries screwed—"

"I fail to see how bringing them the word of God would screw them up."

Ryan sighed. "No, I don't suppose you would."

Ken drew himself up indignantly to deliver fire and brimstone, but Ryan cut him off. "Save it," he said. "I didn't mean it as an insult; I just meant that this argument's pointless. I'm not going to convince you and you're not going to convince me, so why don't we just drop it? We've both got better things to do."

He held Ken's gaze, neither challenging nor submitting but rather just holding his gaze and waiting to see if Ken could still see the reason in *any* argument.

Evidently he could. At last he nodded and said, "You're right, of course. God will enlighten you in his own time."

"Or you," Ryan replied. He turned away and strode out of the lander, conscious of the image his departing backside presented. Well it was Ken's own doing if people mooned him when they left his presence. He grinned at the thought, but it was a short-lived grin. In his religious zeal, Ken would no doubt miss that point, too.

The ride up in the lander wasn't nearly as crowded as the ride down had been. Ryan sat at the controls, monitoring the autopilot and hoping nothing would go wrong that would require him to actually fly the thing. Behind him, spread out among fifty seats, sat the two dozen people who had either been recalled or had decided on their own to come back, and behind them the cargo compartment carried only a few sealed canisters of native fruits and vegetables. The rest of the equipment it had held would remain on the ground.

Sean had stayed down on the planet, as had Ken. Ryan's mother had not. Ryan hadn't talked with her since before they had gone down, but he could tell just by looking at her that she was furious about something, and he could guess easily enough what it was. She wasn't the only person wearing clothes—most of the others, Ryan included, had decided that they would continue to wear them when on the ship—but she was the only one who seemed actually repulsed by the few such as Kristy who still went without. This latest proclamation of Ken's, and the crew's reaction to it, had evidently been the final straw in the load that had broken her patience.

Just how far it had broken Ryan didn't realize until they had docked with the ship and he offered to help carry her luggage back to her apartment.

"I don't know where to take it yet," she said. "I'll have to check with Teigh."

"With Teigh?" Ryan asked naively, then the implication behind her statement hit him. As the ship's architect, Teigh coordinated the distribution of living quarters.

"You're moving out?"

"I am. More precisely, I am divorcing him, though he tells me that divorce has no meaning now because neither has marriage." She turned to Ryan and the murderous look in her eye sent a chill through him. "Can you imagine that man saying such a thing, after all these years I spent with him for no other reason than because I was married to him?"

"He said marriage has no meaning?"

"That's right. That's contrary to the Bible, but I think he's

146

making it up as he goes along now. Claims that we're all in a 'state of grace' so we can't sin no matter who we fornicate with, which means that the marriage vows can't be binding. Fine, then. I'm no longer bound." She started walking toward the residence decks.

Ryan, carrying her largest duffel bag as well as his own pack, shuffled along beside her in shock. He had always wondered why his mom hadn't divorced his dad years ago, whether it was because Methany was still growing up or whether Alice didn't want to have the first divorce on the ship, but even though he had wondered why she hadn't, he realized now that he never really expected it, either. He was hardly what he could call close to either of them, hadn't been since he'd moved out of their home and separated himself as much as possible from Ken over ten years ago, but somehow the idea of having his parents no longer married still came as a blow.

"I'm sorry," he said. "I'm sorry it came to this."

"So am I." His mother's voice softened. "I loved your father. He was a very competent, very tender, caring man. I knew it was fear that drove him into religion, fear of the unknown, and I wanted to help him through it however I could. I kept telling myself that once we got here, once we found a place to start a colony, he wouldn't be afraid anymore and we could go back to living the way we were before. But it was just too much for him. It consumed him. The man I married no longer exists."

Ryan didn't know what to say, except, again, "I'm sorry."

They reached the door. His mother had led them home, to her and Ken's apartment. Evidently she had decided not to bother Teigh until later. She had time, after all, with Ken still on Eden.

She opened the door and stepped through. Ryan slid out of his pack and propped it in the hallway, then carried her duffel inside. She was standing in the center of the living room, her back toward him, but when he stepped up beside her she turned around and he could see that she was crying.

"Hold me," she said. "I need someone strong to hold me."

CHAPTER FOURTEEN

TROUBLE IN PARADISE

LATER, AFTER ALICE AND RYAN had both had a good cry and she had assured him that she just needed some time alone now and yes, she would be fine, Ryan went to see Laura. He felt somehow guilty doing it, even though he had the excuse of arranging things with Teigh while he was there, for the real reason was that *he* needed someone strong as well, if not to hold, then at least to talk with, and Laura was that someone.

"It's open!" she shouted at his knock.

He let himself in. A bag just like the one he had carried for his mother lay in the middle of the room, and Laura was poking a towel into a corner of it.

"Oh, good," she said when she saw who it was. "You can tell me what I need to take with me."

"Not a whole lot of clothing," said Ryan, wondering how Laura would take to the new custom below.

"I heard," she said simply. She must have realized then that he was curious, because she went on to say, "If you think something as simple as nudity is going to fluster a ninety-year-old woman, then you've got another think coming. What *I'm* scared of is the whole idea of setting foot on a planet again. Do you realize it's been forty-nine years since I've done it?"

"Forty-nine years?" Ryan asked incredulously. He scooped Nova out of the overstuffed chair where she'd been sleeping and sat down with her in his lap. She gnawed on his knuckle for a moment—her way of saying hello—then began to purr.

"That's right. Moved to Spacehome when it was still under construction, and never went back down. Afraid to, at first, but mostly just didn't want to, I guess. But now I want to and I'm afraid again."

"Nothing to worry about," Ryan said. "I've done it twice now, and loved it both times. It's beautiful."

Laura yanked the zipper across the top of the bag and stood up. Even in her nineties, doing so wasn't much of an effort for her. "Well," she said, "scared or not, I'm looking forward to it."

From down the hall came Teigh's voice. "You talking to yourself again, woman, or is somebody there?"

"Ryan's back," she answered.

"Oh. Hi Ryan! Be right out." They heard zipping sounds, and in a moment Teigh appeared with his own duffel bag. He dropped it beside Laura's and held out his hand. It took Ryan a moment to realize that he was offering it to shake. That custom had all but died out on the trip. He shook hands without getting up from the chair.

"The traveler returns," said Teigh. "So tell us, what do we need to watch out for down there?"

"Ken, mostly," Ryan said. "He's really going out the lock."

"You mean more so than usual?"

"Teigh!" Laura scowled at him.

"Sorry."

"No apology necessary," Ryan said with a wry grin. "I feel the same way about him. But yeah, he's getting worse. Just before I came up he told everybody God didn't care who they had sex with, as long as they didn't enjoy it. And he's still gung-ho on preaching to the natives."

"Uh oh."

"Uh oh is right. And he also told Mom their marriage vows don't mean anything anymore. So Mom's moving out. She wants you to assign her an apartment to herself before you go down."

Teigh and Laura both looked at him in surprise.

Laura spoke first. "I'm sorry," she said simply.

Somehow the words that had seemed so inadequate when he said them to his mother seemed more than adequate now, coming from Laura. To know that someone else understood, that she was at least aware of his inner feelings whether she could do anything about them or not, was the one thing he needed most.

"Tell her she can have her pick," Teigh said. "Any apartment on any level she wants. I'll kick the captain out of his quarters for her if she wants them, after what she's put up with for us."

"I'm sure a regular apartment will do," Ryan said. "She just wants someplace that doesn't remind her of him."

"Right. I'll fix it up." Teigh went back into one of the back rooms, no doubt to check the database for vacant space.

Laura sat down on the arm of Ryan's chair and put her arm around him. "It's hard to watch your parents go through this," she said. It was a statement of fact, not a question.

"Yeah." He rubbed Nova beneath her chin while he tried to gather his thoughts. "You know," he said at last, "I want to be mad at Ken, but I can't. He's the one who's lost everything."

Laura nodded. "I'm glad you see that. He's going to need your love now more than ever."

"I...I'd love to love him. That sounds dumb, I know, but that's how I feel. I *want* to love him. I want to help him. That's what Mom wanted to do too, but she couldn't find a way, and I don't know any way either. What can we do for him? He's so deep into religion that he's not even rational anymore. He thinks every crazy notion he gets is planted in his mind straight from God. How can we deal with that? He won't even consider any interpretation of events but his own."

"You can't fight religion with logic. Religion is an emotion, just like love or fear. If you want to compete with it, you have to use emotion yourself. Fight fire with fire. You still love him; use that to bring him around."

"How?"

She squeezed his shoulder. "Let him know you still love him, but let him know you love him even more when he's rational. He needs love too; if anything can affect him, that will."

"That's what Mom thought, but it didn't seem to do any good when she tried it."

"Who can say what good it did? We made it here alive, didn't we? If she hadn't loved him as much as she did, he might have become even more dangerous than he is."

Ryan looked up from the cat in his lap to meet Laura's eyes. He shrugged. "Who knows? You're saying it's my job now to keep him from becoming dangerous?"

Laura shook her head. "It's not your job, or anybody else's. But if you want to help him, that's how to go about it."

The intercom rang, saving Ryan from the necessity of a response. Laura got up to answer it. When she pushed the accept button, the captain's image blossomed onto the screen, and he said, "Hi, Laura. Is Ryan there, by chance?"

"Right here," she answered. She turned her head. "Ryan?"

The captain, calling for *him*? Ryan got up and walked into view, wondering what kind of trouble he was in now. "Hello?"

The captain's expression didn't look like trouble, exactly, but he wasn't smiling, either. With Captain Van Cleeve, that didn't mean a whole lot one way or another. He said, "Thought I'd find you there. I need to talk to you on the bridge."

"Yes, sir. I'll be right up."

"Good." The captain reached toward the screen and the intercom went dead.

Ryan looked toward Laura with eyebrows raised.

"Better scoot," she said.

"I guess."

"You take care of your mom, too. Ken's not the only one who's lost something, you know."

"Right. And you have fun down on the surface."

"I plan on it." She held out her arms and gave Ryan a big hug.

Teigh came back into the room, saying, "I leave the room for a minute and she's in another man's arms. Can you believe that woman?" He grinned and changed the subject before either Ryan or Laura could respond. "I found four different empty storage rooms that can be converted into apartments. I emailed their descriptions directly to your mom. She can have her choice. You know how to use the modular wall sections, so go ahead and build whatever she wants. I've already okayed the withdrawal from stores."

"Thanks."

"Any time. And hey, don't look so glum. Maybe this'll be what it takes to wake Ken up a little. I've seen it happen before."

"I'll remember that." Ryan gave Teigh a hug as well, said his goodbyes, and went to see what the captain wanted.

"I want you to take command of the ship while I'm down on the planet."

The bridge was all the way forward in the ship's central axis. In orbit around Centauri A-3, with the drive shut off and reeled in close to the living section, there was no thrust to provide even the twentieth of a gee that Ryan was used to there. He had been uncomfortable before the captain's statement, but now he felt even more so.

"Command?" he echoed stupidly. "Me? I thought David and Warren were our reserve captains."

Van Cleeve nodded. He was floating free above one of the three control chairs, holding himself in place with one hand on the chair back. "They are, if the job becomes vacant suddenly. Otherwise it's my decision, and right now you seem to be the most logical choice."

"Uh, may I ask why you think so?"

"Because I think you've got sense enough to handle the job. And because you have the trust and the respect of the crew. That's the most important thing a captain can have on a civilian ship. If you order something done, they'll do it first and ask questions later."

Ryan could hardly believe his ears. The crew respected him? Ryan Hughes, the guy who wasted a twenty-year opportunity to make something of himself? If it hadn't been the captain telling him so, he would have laughed out loud.

But it *was* the captain telling him so, and Laura had said essentially the same thing once before, and so had Michelle, for that matter. And Kristy, too, if not in so many words.

Maybe they did respect him, then, but did that necessarily mean he'd make a good captain? "I wouldn't know what to do," he said. "What orders to give."

"You probably won't have to give any. Being captain mostly means you worry about potential problems and sign the log every day."

"But if something happens—"

"If something happens that requires your immediate action, then yes, you're in charge. You know the ship as well as anybody, so what to do in an emergency shouldn't be a problem. If it is, you can always call me, and if I think my presence is required I can always come back up. I'll be taking one of the small shuttles down just in case. But your only likely source of trouble is going to be people, so I'll give you the same advice I got when I first took command: Don't order anyone to do something they don't already want to do."

Ryan didn't need to speak his question; his puzzled look was enough.

"That's right," Van Cleeve said with a grin. "Except when you're right and they're wrong, of course, but even then you'd better be able to prove it to 'em damned fast. A captain can't afford to have his crew resent his authority, because if they do it won't be long before they want it for themselves."

Ryan tried to sort through the implications of the captain's advice. "Is that why you let the landing party go nude?" he asked at last.

"Dead on. Once Ken got everybody to agree to it, there was nothing I could do to stop it. We'll have to wait until they get tired of it or somebody gets hurt before we can change it now. Until then it's not important enough to force the issue."

"Then you can't order Ken to leave the customs agents alone?"

Van Cleeve sighed. "I doubt it. Ken's just about to mutiny as it is, and he's got followers. That's part of why I'm going down there; to see if there's any way I can patch things together instead of splitting the crew further apart. If I just order him to leave them alone, he'll mutiny and take part of the crew with him, but if I can convince everyone else it's best, then he'll have to go along with it. He knows the rules as well as I do."

"What about leaving for B-2?" The other possibly habitable planet hadn't yet received even an informal name; they were still using its parent star's letter and orbital position. Ryan chose not to use Ken's name for the planet below them, either, saying instead, "If we leave A-3 entirely, we solve the customs agent problem by default. Except for what we've already done, of course."

Van Cleeve nodded. "That's another course we may take. We might convince the crew to let their curiosity send them on one more trip before we settle down for good. But after seeing what we've got here, it would take some doing."

Ryan could practically hear the whoosh of misconceptions going out the airlock. "I thought the captain had absolute power over the ship and the crew," he whispered.

"Absolute *authority*," Van Cleeve corrected him. "The authority comes with the position, but the power comes from the crew. They give you the power or not; their choice, not yours."

"That explains a lot of things."

"Doesn't it, though? And now that you've learned the deep, dark secret to the profession, I officially pass control of the ship over to you until my return. Mac, log the transfer."

The Monitor and Control program's synthetic voice said, "Transfer of helm logged. Ryan Hughes is now acting captain until your return."

Van Cleeve held out his hand. "Keep 'er running smoothly."

Ryan barely hesitated this time. He took the captain's hand in his own and shook it, the motion setting him adrift until the captain guided him back to the deck.

Van Cleeve turned away toward the door, but stopped and turned back around when Ryan said, "Uh, Captain?"

"Yes, Ryan?"

"What you just told me—there's a hidden assumption in there. You're implying that I want to be captain."

Van Cleeve's eyes sparkled in amusement. "Don't you?"

Of course not! Ryan nearly shouted, but the captain's expression stopped him. He seemed so sure. Could he be right? *Did* Ryan want to be captain?

He'd never even considered it as a possibility before, not even in his daydreams. His self-image had been too low. But now, after the fact, how did he feel about it? Really feel. Did he like it?

"Guilty," he said finally, a sheepish grin spreading across his face.

"Thought so. Enjoy yourself. But remember your responsibility. Now if you'll excuse me, Captain, I have a shuttle to catch."

"Yes sir."

Ryan watched Van Cleeve drift out the door and pull himself out of sight by a handhold. A moment later the pressure door to the central axis thumped closed, leaving Ryan alone in the bridge. He turned once around, slowly, as if seeing the three control couches, the banks of switches and gauges and monitors, the racks of instruments—all for the first time.

"Mine, all mine," he whispered, but the words rang hollow in the empty room.

The captain didn't necessarily need to spend much time on the bridge anyway. Even with his new status, Ryan found himself spending most of his time in the outer decks, helping to prepare the colonization equipment while at the same time campaigning for taking the ship to Centauri B and exploring the planet there. He surprised himself in his eagerness to hang his hide out in an alien environment again, but really, he supposed, he had been worrying about nothing all along. Exploring might be dangerous under the wrong circumstances, but if the explorer took the right precautions then there really wasn't that much to it.

His campaigning seemed to be having little effect among the people who had already set their hearts on starting the colony on "Eden," but about half the crew at least listened to him, and seemed genuinely concerned over the fate of the customs agents at the hands of humanity. Predictably, the split followed almost exactly the line of religious involvement, the notable exceptions being Mariko, who was neither religious nor eager to leave Eden, and Kristy, who was both.

Ryan wondered at her unique nonconformance with the party line, but he hadn't worked up the nerve to ask her about it. He hadn't worked up the nerve to say more than hello to her since the afternoon she'd propositioned him, even though she seemed to be making no particular effort to avoid him.

He wasn't really avoiding her either, but he was paying more attention to Michelle, and that kept him out of circulation for most of his free hours.

He was watching a movie with Michelle in her room when Mariko's call came in. The monitor froze in the middle of an air-car chase—not surprising since the mindless plot seemed to be *mostly* air-car chase—and the Monitor and Control program's voice said, "Communication for Captain Hughes."

"Who?" Ryan asked automatically, but he caught himself before Mac could respond and said, "Oh. Go ahead."

The frozen image of two air-cars ducking a walkway remained on the screen, but Mariko's voice said over it, "Hello, Ryan?"

"Yes, Mariko."

"I need to use your eyes."

"My eyes?"

"That's right. I haven't got a video transceiver, but I need an orbital view of the forest around me. Could I get you to have a peek and tell me what you see?"

"Sure," Ryan said. "What do you want me to look for?"

"Fires, what else? I've been chasing smoke all day, but I can't seem to locate the source of it. I think the customs agents are learning to hide from me."

"Not surprising," Ryan said. "Hold on just a minute, and I'll tell you where they are. Mac, give us an orbital view of the area Mariko's in."

The frozen air-car chase changed to the by-now familiar image of planetary landscape seen from above, relayed from the stationary satellite orbiting over the continent and artificially enhanced to show the terrain. The mountain range with the customs agents in its foothills cut a diagonal through the picture, and a ripple of orographically-induced clouds paralleled it out on the plain.

"You still there, Mariko?" Ryan asked.

"Still here."

"Okay, we've got our sights on you. Mac, search for hot spots in her immediate area."

A couple dozen red dots appeared in the lower section of the image, as well as a large splotch of the same color above them. An isolated cloud coincided with the latter.

"What's that?" Michelle asked, reaching out to touch the screen over the spot.

"A large heat source," Mac responded. "Surface area five square kilometers and expanding. Preliminary diagnosis: forest fire."

"Forest fire?" Ryan asked. "You mean the whole—"

"How close?" Mariko cut in.

"The closest point is one point one kilometers to the northwest of your position."

"Which direction is it going?"

"It is moving eastward. Toward you."

"Space! That's why I couldn't find the damned fire; I was smelling smoke from kilometers away! How fast is it coming toward me?"

"Rough estimate, one kilometer per hour. A few minutes' monitoring will be necessary to refine that figure."

"Display Mariko's position," Ryan commanded, and a blinking blue dot appeared in a valley to the lower right of the red patch.

"Give us a north arrow," Michelle added.

A thin arrow appeared out in the plain, pointing up and to the right. That meant that the leading edge of the forest fire was coming at Mariko in a wide front rather than reaching toward her with a thin finger. And if the distance from her to the fire was one point one kilometers, then the front looked to be at least five kilometers long. She was closer to the southern edge, but not by enough to matter. She wasn't going to be able to get out of its path on foot, not through forest as thick as what she was in.

"How'd you get over from the island?" Ryan asked. "Shuttle or airplane?" Captain Van Cleeve had taken a shuttle down; if he had let Mariko use it, then her problems were solved.

"Airplane. I left it down at the base of the mountains."

"Damn." Rescuing her with the airplane was out of the question. The plane had an autopilot, but without vertical takeoff and landing capability it wouldn't be able to land in anything but a large clearing to pick her up, and there were none of those close to Mariko.

"Mac, what's the strategy for escaping a forest fire on foot?" Ryan asked.

There was a pause while the Monitor and Control program accessed the appropriate files, then it replied, "Move downhill if that is consistent with moving away from the fire. Fires burn faster uphill than down. Stay near water if possible, keeping the water between yourself and the fire. If the fire overtakes you, submerge yourself in the water and breathe through a hollow tube if one is available, or surface momentarily to breathe if not. Hold your breath while the fire passes over you. If possible, protect yourself from falling trees by hiding in the shelter of a large rock or previously fallen log."

"You get that?" Ryan asked.

"Got it," Mariko replied.

"All right, then, head for the river," Ryan said. "Leave everything but your radio and run for it. I'm going to send Sean after you in the shuttle, but if he doesn't make it in time I want you under water as soon as you hear flame."

"Got it," Mariko said again.

"Mac, keep tracking her. Contact the island."

A moment later the screen split to show the orbital view of the burning forest on one side and the interior of the main fifty-passenger lander on the other. Through the intercom Ryan and Michelle could hear the alarm announcing their incoming call, and a moment later they saw Ken enter through the open airlock and advance to the screen.

"Hello, son," he said, smiling. "Or should I say, 'Captain son?'"

Ryan wasted no time answering. "Dad, Mariko's in trouble. Sean's got to fly the captain's shuttle out to get her."

Ken's smile faded. "Sean left this morning for the other side of the island. On foot."

Ryan felt a lump grow in his throat. Not there? He had to be there. "Great," he said. "Well *somebody's* got to go after her. She's right in the path of a forest fire."

"I'll go," Ken said.

"You don't know how to fly a shuttle."

"How difficult is it? The autopilot does the actual flying, doesn't it?"

It did, but Ryan would rather have had just about anybody else on board while it was doing so. He didn't want Ken within a thousand kilometers of the customs agents. Somebody ought to ride along, though, just in case Mariko needed help getting on board once the shuttle arrived, and Ryan couldn't think of a good excuse to tell Ken to get someone else.

"All right," he said. "You go. But tell somebody where you're going first, and see if you can find another body or two to go along in case we need them. Don't waste time at it, though; speed is more important than manpower."

Ken nodded in agreement. "Roger, Captain," he said, and as he wheeled around and rushed out of the lander, Ryan got the feeling his father wasn't being facetious. Maybe he *was* acting like a captain should act at that.

But if so, then he would be glad when Van Cleeve took the job back from him. He hadn't bargained on suddenly being responsible for another person's life.

Wait a minute. He *wasn't* responsible. Ryan was in charge of the starship, but not necessarily the crew on the ground. He should have told Ken to get Van Cleeve. Too late. Unless the captain came back with Ken, it *was* his responsibility, because they couldn't afford the time to go back and find him.

Still, there was the intercom in the shuttle, and probably half a dozen other hand-held radios as well. Ryan said, "Mac, call the shuttle and all the portable radios. Try to find Captain Van Cleeve."

"Acknowledged."

What else wasn't he doing that he should be? There had to be more he could do than just ordering someone else to take care of the situation. He thought about flying a shuttle himself from the ship, but it would take time to winch it up to the dock, more time to power it up, and still longer to drop out of orbit onto Mariko's location. The situation would be decided long before he could get there.

But the thought did remind him of one more thing he could do. "Mac," he ordered, "begin engine warm-up on the shuttle Ken will be flying."

"Acknowledged."

The video image switched to the interior of the much smaller shuttle, and Ryan and Michelle could hear the atmospheric engines whine to life. Moments later, Ken rushed into view, David Bonham in tow. David slapped the airlock closed behind them, they strapped into the pilot's and copilot's chairs, and within seconds they lifted off.

Once in the air and away from the island, the autopilot got Mariko's longitude and latitude from the starship's Mac, calculated a ballistic trajectory to that point, and fired the fusion drive for a few minutes to send them on their way. For better or worse, it was going to be Ken and David to the rescue.

CHAPTER FIFTEEN

RESPONSIBILITY

"HOW LONG WILL IT TAKE them to get there?" Ryan asked, and Mac answered, "Twenty-two minutes."

"Twenty-two minutes, Mariko. Can you hold on that long?"

Mariko was panting now. "You tell me. How fast is that damned...fire moving?"

Ryan waited for the program to respond, but evidently it didn't recognize the question in Mariko's voice. Either that or the multiple radio conversations as it tried to find the captain were distracting it. "Mac?" Ryan asked. "How fast is the fire approaching Mariko?"

"I clock it at nearly three kilometers per hour now. It has begun burning in the canopy, and is now being pushed eastward by surface winds. Mariko's pace is roughly zero point eight. Both she and the fire are moving uphill."

"Mariko, go downhill!" Ryan ordered.

"Downhill is back toward the fire," Mariko panted. "If I can top this ridge before it catches up, then downhill puts me in the river."

"All right, but hurry. You don't have that big a lead on it." Ryan made the same calculation in his head that Mariko was no doubt doing in hers: the fire was about a kilometer away by now, catching up with her at two point two per hour; that gave her just under half an hour. The shuttle should be there by then, but it would be tight.

Where was Van Cleeve? Even if Mac hadn't been able to find him right away, by now he should be frantically trying to call Ryan, or the shuttle, to find out who had left in it without warning.

Mac expanded the scale on the monitor and Ryan and Michelle watched as the dot that was the shuttle advanced toward the dot that was Mariko and the fire. "Is there anything else we can be doing?" Ryan asked.

"Pray for rain," Mariko said, just as Ken said simply, "Pray."

Ryan looked to Michelle. She rolled her eyes, but a moment later she shrugged. Ryan got her meaning. It couldn't hurt, could it? Other than the acute embarrassment at the prospect of invoking an imaginary friend in front of a real one. But if there was even a chance that it might actually help, then he'd endure the embarrassment. *God,* he thought, keeping his eyes on the monitor, *if you exist, and if you're watching this, and if you care at all about Mariko, please slow down that fire. And send rain.*

Nothing much seemed to happen. Ryan hadn't expected anything. He felt silly for having even tried, but damn it, he didn't *know* there was nothing to it, and when a person's life hung in the balance you tried whatever you could think of that might help. He wondered if this was the sort of situation that had started religion in the first place; someone watching helplessly while a person they cared about was in trouble. They couldn't do anything directly, but maybe, just maybe, they could do something indirectly. . .

It might have started that way. That's how Ken's fascination with it had started, anyway.

"Situation update," Mac announced. "Mariko has stopped."

"Mariko, what's wrong?"

"Tripped on a log. No big—ouch!"

"What happened?"

"I twisted my damned ankle. Let's see if I can still—ouch! I said pray for *rain,* not *pain.*"

"Can you walk on it?"

"Yeah, but I'm not going to be setting any speed records."

"Situation update," Mac said again. "High-sensitivity scanning reveals a cluster of heat sources rapidly approaching Mariko's position. Preliminary analysis: they are probably animals fleeing the fire. Mariko, you should prepare to take shelter in case they overrun you."

"How far away are they?" Mariko shouted.

"One hundred meters." Mac was silent a moment, then began counting down, "Fifty meters. Forty-five. Forty. Thirty-five."

"I don't see anyth—wait. They're up in the trees. Customs agents." Ryan and Michelle heard her panting, then, "They're stopping. Great, they're going to demand tribute. Yep, here comes one—no, two of them. They're stretching down toward me. Look, I'm going to give them the radio and get the hell out of here. You can track me via infrared."

"Negative," Mac replied. "Your signal is lost amidst theirs."

"Well I've got to give them somethi—what are you doing? Hey!"

"Mariko?"

Silence.

"Mariko, what's happening?"

Silence.

"Dad, see if the autopilot can get you there any faster."

"Roger. Autopilot, you heard the captain. Faster."

The same voice as Mac's came through the radio link. "I am already on a maximum-speed trajectory. Anything faster would put us in orbit."

"What if you use the engines to keep us down?" David asked.

"That maneuver exceeds my capability."

Of course it would. Sean could probably do it, but Sean was off skipping stones somewhere. Damn.

"Mariko, can you hear me?"

"I'm—all right." Mariko sounded anything but all right; her voice was a high-pitched squeak.

"What's happening."

"They're giving me a lift. Literally. Trouble is, customs agents travel...with their heads down when they swing, so they've...got me by the legs. I wouldn't...recommend it right after lunch, but it does...seem to be working. We're about to the top of the—watch it!" There was a moment of silence, then, "Branch broke. Good thing they've got extra arms, or I'd have a headache on top of a sprained ankle. How fast are we going?"

Mac understood her question this time. "Four kilometers per hour. You are outrunning the fire."

"Good enough. We're over the top and starting down now. The ride's a little smoother this way, too. You oughta see these guys work; they're practically falling down the slope. Five arms working at once. I'd hate to wrestle with one of 'em."

"Ten minutes until the shuttle arrives," Mac announced.

"Good."

"Receiving communication from Captain Van Cleeve," Mac added.

Ryan breathed a sigh of relief. "Put him on," he said.

The monitor image didn't change. Evidently the captain only had a radio, not a video intercom. Better than nothing. Ryan quickly filled him in on the situation, finishing with, "I'm sorry I couldn't check with you first, sir. Do you want to take it from here?"

"Not on your life. You're doing fine. You're *all* doing fine. I'll stay on the line here, but unless you need me for something I'll shut up and let you do your jobs. Van Cleeve out."

His responsibility hadn't changed a bit, but somehow Ryan felt immensely better knowing that Van Cleeve was watching over his shoulder. He thought about his half-hearted prayer, wondering if truly believing in God would have given him the same feeling. Was this how Ken felt, believing that God watched over him? If so, that would explain why religion was so addictive. Having a higher power backing him up was a wonderful feeling, one he would be reluctant to give up.

A few minutes later the shuttle began braking thrust and a few minutes after that the atmospheric engines brought it to a stop in a clearing near the river bank.

"They definitely heard that," Mariko announced. "Changing course toward it. I think I see it through the trees. Yeah! Home free. Come on, you guys, let me return the favor. Ken, open the door."

"Mac, give us external video from the shuttle," Michelle said, and the monitor obediently flicked to the scene at the river bank. They were looking westward; over the tops of the trees just ahead of them they could see a billowing cloud of smoke, shot through with flickering red pillars of flame as the fire cleared the top of the ridge and began advancing down toward the river. Closer in, Mariko was emerging from the trees, on foot again but still red-faced from the blood that had rushed to her head during her ride. Beside her walked—if walked could be the word to describe their sinuous six-legged gait—over a dozen customs agents, two of them supporting her like comrades in battle. Three others carried young customs agents on their backs, the young ones holding on tight with all six tentacles around their parents' necks. One of the adults carried a backpack—Mariko's that she had left behind—uncertainly in its grasp.

"Mariko, don't let them have that pack," Ryan ordered.

"I don't plan on it," Mariko replied.

"I don't think it's wise to give them a ride, either," David said.

"Moot point," Mariko said. "I think this is as far as they're going to go."

Her escort had stopped moving, and when she took another step forward, they stayed put. "All right, I guess they can take care of themselves, anyway." She turned back to the customs agents and retrieved her pack, then stood facing them for a moment, obviously trying to think of an appropriate way to take her leave. Finally she reached out toward them with an open hand. One of the two who had carried her reached out tentatively with a tentacle and wrapped it around her offered hand. "Thanks, friend," Mariko said, still holding the radio's transmit button down with her other hand. "I owe you one." She grasped the other customs agent's tentacle too, then took a step back and waved to the others, but they didn't return her gesture. With a shrug, she pointed toward the river and said, "Go on, get across. Wait it out on the other side."

They seemed to understand. As one creature, they slid gracefully through the grass, slipped into the water, and swam across. They stood on the opposite bank and watched as Mariko walked to the shuttle and climbed aboard, then moments later the shuttle lifted off and left them leaning backward, watching it disappear into the sky.

"What next, Ryan?"

David had asked the question, but all three passengers in the shuttle waited for Ryan's reply. It was a good question. What *should* they do next?

"How about the fire?" he asked, eyeing the aerial view. The fire had burned halfway down the ridge already, and showed no sign of slowing. "Is the river going to stop it, or should we be trying to put it out?"

"A crown fire such as this one, with the wind behind it, could possibly jump the river," Mac said. "I would suggest starting a back fire."

"What's a back fire?"

"A back fire is one started intentionally ahead of an advancing flame front, using the main fire's natural updraft to draw the back fire toward it and exhaust the fuel in the larger, fire's path. The technique requires the establishment of a previously-cleared zone to keep the back fire from burning on in advance of the fire you wish to suppress. The river would be ideal for that purpose."

Ryan had heard the phrase, "Fight fire with fire," before, but he'd never really stopped to consider how it would work. It sounded inherently ridiculous, but he supposed Mac must know what it was talking about. "So what do we do, hover with the fusion drive?" he asked.

"That would be the simplest method."

"Dad, David, what do you think? Does it look like that'd be possible?"

Ken nodded. "Theoretically, it should work. In practice, who knows? We could just make it worse."

"How worse could it get?" David asked. "If the one we set gets out of hand, then it burns across the river a little earlier than it would anyway, that's all."

"Good point," Ryan said. "All right, then, let's try it. Mac, are the customs agents out of range?"

"They are moving up the eastern ridge forming the river valley. I will monitor their position, but they seem to be well out of range."

"Captain, you want to veto this?"

"Not at all. It sounds like you're doing the right thing."

"Okay. Let's go ahead and do it."

Ryan and Michelle watched on the monitor as Ken directed the shuttle to use the fusion drive on the west bank of the river. Timing was critical, Mac warned; if they started the back fire too soon then the draft from the main fire wouldn't be strong enough to draw it in, but if they waited too long it would just add to the main fire and the heightened flame front would be sure to jump the river. The fire wasn't approaching the river in an even line, either; they had to rush upstream and down to set small fires when it reached the right distance.

"Give us a magnified overhead view," Ryan ordered, and the monitor split to show the satellite image on the left and the shuttle's view on the right. On the left, the forest fire was a wavy line of red throwing a billowing cloud of smoke up high into the atmosphere. In front of the cloud a tiny, straight jet of flame pulsed on and off as the fusion drive set its own fires. Just as predicted, the updraft drew the back fires inward, the two flame fronts roaring toward one another faster and faster until they met with an almost explosive swirl of flame hundreds of meters high.

Ryan found himself holding his breath, waiting to see if any of that inferno would cross the river and continue eastward, but after a few minutes of furious burning the flames began to die down to a still-impressive but no longer advancing fire.

"The customs agents have reached the ridge top," Mac announced. "They have stopped there."

"They're watching us," Ryan said. "Let's hope they learn something this time too."

"Do you think they started it?" Michelle asked.

"That's my guess. Mariko, what do you think?"

"That's the way I read it too."

Mac said, "Review of stored satellite data indicates that to be the correct analysis. The source was a campfire lit two days ago and tended until early this morning, when it apparently spread to the surrounding forest."

David said, "I bet there's going to be a lot of that until they learn how to handle it better."

"We should teach them," Ken said.

Ryan shook his head, but the gesture was lost on all but Michelle. He said, "We don't have that right."

"Son, you just said you hoped they'd learn from watching us. Which do you want?"

"I want to keep them from killing themselves off with what they've already learned from us. If they learn how to set a back fire from one example, that's one thing, but if we go in and hold seminars on fire management, that's something else entirely. The best way to keep a fire safe is probably in a stove, isn't it? So are we going to teach them about that? But if we do, then from there it's only a small step to putting a house around it, and once you've got a house you can't move with the food supply anymore so you've got to start planting vegetables and keeping livestock, and then you get into commerce, and from there you get governments to regulate it, and where does it stop?"

"He's got a point." It was Mariko. "These creatures are intelligent. Much more so than chimpanzees. Maybe even more so than our own ancestors when they discovered fire. I think they *could* learn to run a government. They've already got the concept of a border down cold. After watching them in action, I think they could probably even learn to fly this shuttle, but I don't necessarily think that would be a good idea. Without all the experience that leads up to something like a spaceship, they have no need for one, and no business having one. The same goes for houses and agriculture, and probably for religion as well, Ken."

"Religion is primal," said Ken. "No preparation is necessary."

"I think you're wrong."

"You're free to think so, but that doesn't make you right."

Ryan said, "But if we leave them alone and Mariko's wrong, we do far less harm than if we mess with them and you're wrong."

"Leaving an intelligent species in spiritual ignorance would be the greatest evil we could possibly do," Ken replied with certainty. "Particularly this one. God has made his will clear on the matter."

"Again, I think you're wrong," Mariko said. "I don't think anything is clear here."

"That's because you haven't made the leap of faith necessary to see clearly. Ask David how much clearer things become when you look to God for guidance."

"David? You buy all this hocus-pocus?"

He cleared his throat with a loud harrumph. "I wouldn't put it in quite those words. Let's say I just admit that certain evidence does fit Ken's scenario better than any other. But as far as setting up missions and bringing enlightenment to the heathens, I'm on Ryan's side. Sorry, Ken, but I just don't see the evidence to support your argument there. Every time a religion has tried to convert people who don't have the background for it, it ends in disaster."

"It won't happen that way here."

"Offer me proof. Until then I can't buy it."

Ryan said, "Uh, guys, how about the fire?" The shuttle was still hovering a kilometer or so above the river, Mac monitoring the dying fire through its cameras.

"Right," David said. "Looks to be contained, at least on the river boundary. I don't know how we're going to stop it to the north and south, though."

"That will probably not be necessary," Mac said. "To the north the natural bend in the river will act as containment, and to the south the fire will run out of fuel as the forest becomes less dense. The only dangerous direction of movement was eastward."

"Well, let's stick around and watch it for a while anyway. I don't want it to start back up again if we can prevent it." A thought that had been tickling the back of Ryan's brain suddenly came to the surface. "Hey, how come that other fire, the natural one the customs agents got their second light from; how come that one didn't take off like this?"

"That fire was in a younger section of forest," Mac replied. "One that had already burned recently. The canopy was not as well established, nor was there as much undergrowth to act as a bridge between forest floor and the canopy. This section, by comparison, had not burned in many years. It was the long-term accumulation of fuel that allowed the fire to grow to the magnitude you witnessed."

"Is that natural for a forest, or do you think the customs agents were putting out the fires around here before we showed up?"

"That assessment would require a correlation between known customs agent habitat and forest type. I will initiate such a search if you wish."

"I wish," Mariko said.

"Acknowledged. Results may take a few hours."

"Bet you they were putting them out," Mariko said. "They probably thought fires were like any other deadly beast; to be killed whenever possible. Until we came along and showed them a use for them."

"Until I showed them," Ryan said. "Sean and I started all this."

"Don't be too hard on yourself. They'd have learned it from anybody."

"Yeah. I still wish it hadn't been me. And I don't want to be responsible for anything else like it, either. I think we should get out of here before we do any more damage. At least *look* at B-2. It could be every bit as nice as this place, without customs agents."

"If it doesn't have forest fires, I'm ready to go," Mariko said.

David added, "From a purely scientific standpoint, I'd like to see what else there is in this system before we settle down to farming and raising families. It makes sense to go now, before we rob the starship of most of its long-term life support capability to start a colony."

"And I say if we leave here we'll never be allowed back."

Ryan's ears perked up at Ken's proclamation. This was a new one. "Never be allowed back?" he asked.

"Surely you remember what happened the last time humanity left the Garden of Eden."

Ryan snorted. "Assuming for the sake of discussion that wasn't just a story; we were kicked out. We're leaving here of our own free will, and we can come back any time we want."

"That's not the case," Ken said. "God doesn't make an offer like this twice. If we reject His gift, we won't be offered it again."

"Oh come on, Ken. What's 'He' going to do, put a force field around it?" Mariko asked, sarcasm heavy in her voice.

"He could."

"He could turn us all into toads, too, if He wanted to. If He exists at all, which I doubt."

"Don't mock Him!"

"Ken, you can't mock someone who doesn't exist. You on the other hand. . ."

"I saved your life just now. I'd think you'd at least be grateful."

"The customs agents saved my life, Ken. The same guys you want to teach about guilt and original sin. I *am* grateful, to them, and I'm going to do everything I can to prevent you from—"

"And I'm going to do the work of God no matter what—"

"Hey!" Ryan shouted. "Enough of that. It's hot enough *outside* the shuttle without you guys starting fires inside as well. Is the situation stable below you?"

"Holding steady," David said, a trace of amusement in his voice.

"All right, then. We'll keep Mac watching it, but you might as well go home. We can get you back to the fire again quick enough if anything flares up. Mariko, can you fly your plane back with that sprained ankle?"

"Yeah."

"Good enough. Do it."

On the left side of the monitor, in the satellite view, the speck that was the shuttle drifted to the south, away from the fire and out of the mountains, to stop in the clearing where Mariko had left her airplane. On the right side, in the view from the shuttle's cameras, Ryan and Michelle watched her hobble over to the plane, climb inside, and moments later take off and bank sharply around toward home. The shuttle rose to a few kilometers altitude, then lit the fusion drive and streaked off after her.

"Mac, keep an eye on the fire," Ryan said. "Alert me if anything happens that I should know about."

"Acknowledged."

"Captain, are you still there?"

"Still here and getting ready for an earful when those two hotheads get back," Van Cleeve replied. "You stirred that situation up nicely."

"Sorry," Ryan said, the heat rising in his face.

The captain laughed. "Don't be. I'd rather we get it out in the open and argue about it than sit on it and stew and plot against each other. This way we'll talk it out in a meeting and get it solved democratically."

But what if the majority of people want to stay? Ryan wondered. Just having everyone want it that way wouldn't make it right. What would he do then?

He supposed he'd worry about it when the time came, that's what. Until then he could continue to campaign for what he thought was right.

The captain said, "You did a good job today, Ryan. I'm glad I've got you running things up there. Keep up the good work. Van Cleeve out."

Cleared of communications, the monitor went back to the movie Ryan and Michelle had been watching earlier. Two air cars swooped beneath a walkway with a roar, scattering pedestrians like leaves in their wake, then banked sharply to miss a hover bike coming the other way and shot off down an urban canyon toward what looked like an impossible snarl of ramps, walkways, floating buildings, and streams of traffic.

Ryan reached out and tapped it off. To Michelle he said, "It was a dull movie anyway."

CHAPTER SIXTEEN

DIVINE INTERVENTION

"FINAL TALLY, FIFTY-NINE FOR, thirty-seven against, eight abstaining. The motion to explore Centauri B-2 carries." Captain Van Cleeve paused to allow the ragged cheer to die down. "Preparation for departure will begin immediately. The third and final rotation of crew to the island will be moved ahead of schedule so everybody can have a chance to dig their toes in the sand before we break orbit. Second rotation will stay on the island to gather food to supplement the ship's stores. All first rotation personnel still on the ground will return to the ship and help prepare it for the crossing. Any discussion?" Van Cleeve's tone made it clear he didn't want any, but the formal meeting procedure called for closing statements after a vote and he obviously didn't want to violate procedure on this one.

Ryan, presiding over the shipboard side of the meeting in the auditorium, watched the monitor link to the island for his father's reaction. Ken had argued passionately against leaving; first reciting scripture, then switching to manifest destiny and the crew's duty to establish the most viable extra-Solar colony possible, then trying an appeal to the basic laziness inherent in human nature by describing at length the many virtues of Eden that they would be giving up forever if they left. Ryan had begun to worry when he tried that last tack, but Ken couldn't resist turning his argument into a sermon about God and His Infinitely Mysterious Ways, and in the end he wound up alienating more people than he converted. Ryan suspected that quite a few of the people who had voted in favor of the trip were voting against Ken rather than for another few months in the starship, but he was glad to have their support for whatever reason.

Now, after the vote, he expected Ken to jump up and hotly denounce them all as sinners and tools of the devil, but his father merely sat there in his chair in the front row of the meeting, a look of resignation on his face. And without his lead, no one else seemed compelled to speak either. Van Cleeve saw his opportunity and said, "Very well, then, meeting adjourned."

"Meeting adjourned," Ryan echoed in the auditorium, and then a babble of voices erupted around him, but he didn't even try to listen. What people said now didn't matter anyway. It was official: they were going, and that was that.

He felt a slow warmth spread through him at the realization. He—and Sean and Mariko on the island—had argued their case and won it fair and square. The crew had listened to them. Their opinions counted for something.

It was a heady feeling, somehow more fulfilling than being chosen acting captain in Van Cleeve's absence. He wondered if it was addictive. Probably. Most enjoyable things were.

The next day he went to greet the few remaining first-wave crewmembers coming up on the lander from the island, and to say goodbye to the last wave on their way down. It was a less happy occasion than the previous arrivals and departures. Despite the vote—no, *because* of the vote—there were hard feelings, and certain people avoided certain other people as they passed in the observation deck. Ken, Bob Thorpe, and half a dozen others formed a tight knot of rejection, but Ryan braved their hostile stares and went over to them.

"Welcome aboard," he said.

His father just looked at him a moment, then said, grudgingly,

"Thank you."

They both fumbled for something else to say, but though it quickly became evident that they were doomed to failure, neither of them could turn away. At last Bob broke their deadlock. "Come on," he said to no one in particular. "We've got some unpacking to do."

"Right," said Ken. He turned away, then, as if finally thinking of what he had wanted to say all along, he turned back to Ryan, but instead of speaking he grasped him in a tight hug that forced Ryan's breath out of him in a whoof. Ryan could feel his father's fingers pressing into him with such intensity that they trembled. Bewildered, Ryan hugged him back. Finally Ken pushed himself away and, without explanation, turned around again and went on into the ship.

What was that all about? Ryan wondered. Was that Ken's way of saying he forgave him?

He was still puzzling over it nearly an hour later while he floated in the bridge and monitored the lander's final descent down to the island. Everything was going normally. There was no reason to believe it wouldn't, but he felt better being in the bridge where he could watch all the lander's vital signs and coordinate things most easily in case of a mishap. He supposed his brief tenure as captain was teaching him how to worry constructively.

The lander made its final braking turns out over the ocean, engaged its atmospheric engines, and flew to a gentle touchdown on the island. "Landing completed," the autopilot informed him. "Engine shutdown commencing. Right engine off. Left engine off. Full stop."

"Very good, thank you," Ryan replied. "Cease reporting." The tracking monitor became a swirl of static, the digital readouts of altitude, velocity, heading, and so forth below it blinking back to zero. Ryan tapped it off and turned to leave the bridge, but his eye caught red lights blinking in another monitor station and he hesitated, curious. The activity was in the main drive section.

Someone—almost certainly Warren Terrill—was evidently running the main engines through a diagnostic check to make sure they were ready for the trip.

Except that the blinking lights were over such legends as "FUEL PRESSURE REGULATOR," and "FUEL FEED RATE REGULATOR." As Ryan watched, another red light blinked on over the label, "AUTOMATIC IGNITION SEQUENCER."

Someone was shutting off the safeties.

Maybe it was all part of the normal drive diagnostic procedure, but somehow Ryan doubted it. With the safeties disconnected, the drive was little more than a bomb ready to go off at the first wrong move. And with its cable reeled in the way it was, the blast could take the entire ship with it.

"Mac, give me one-way visual into the drive section control room."

The intercom monitor lit to show a wall covered with racks of machinery and festooned with wiring conduit.

"Widen the view."

The wall seemed to recede. An airlock, its inner door open and a crumpled emergency pressure suit lying half in, half out, came into the picture. On the opposite side of the frame, a face moved out of eclipse.

Ken. He was sweating profusely, the drops beading on his skin in zero gee. He reached toward something off screen, and another light began blinking on the console in front of Ryan.

No alarm sounded, though, and it should have. No doubt Ken had disarmed that circuit first thing. Ryan searched for the proper switch to re-arm it, flipped the toggle, but nothing happened. Ken had evidently done more than just switch off the alarms. Ryan tried toggling the safeties back on as well, but that was equally ineffective.

So this was why the hug. Ken had been saying goodbye.

Damn it, Ryan thought, not sure if he was angrier at Ken or at the ship's designers. It shouldn't have been possible for one person to destroy an entire starship. There should have been more safeties, more protection on critical systems like the drive, more—

More weight. The safeties already in place had probably added months to the travel time. And more idiot-proofing would only have made Ken's job harder, not impossible. No amount of protection could stop sabotage; a starship was just too complex. Too many fragile systems had to work perfectly all the time just to keep it going. If a determined person could stop any one of them, he could shut it all down, and there was no way to protect every subsystem on the ship. Ken had just chosen the quickest method, that was all.

"Open—" Ryan said, but his voice cracked and he started over. "Open two-way communication with Ken."

He watched Ken jerk in surprise when the screen lit in front of him. "Ryan!" he breathed.

"Ken. *Dad.* What are you doing?"

"That should be obvious. I'm going to prevent you from leaving Eden."

"By blowing us into atoms? That's what's going to happen if you keep up what you're doing there."

"I know what I'm doing. I've been preparing for this since I realized it was going to be necessary. But I don't intend to blow up anybody but myself. Two thirds of the crew are already on the ground, and as long as nobody tries to stop me, I plan to give you and everybody else who's still on board time to take another lander and get away from here before I set it off."

Ryan took a deep breath. "You don't want to do this."

"I do and I am. Now don't argue with me. I want you to get a lander into position for launch, then make a ship wide announcement that everyone should meet in the shuttle bay immediately. Don't tell them why. If you do, I blow the drive now."

Ryan looked at the controls in front of him. The fuel pressure was still at zero and the reaction chamber was still unprimed; it would take Ken at least ten minutes to carry out his threat. Not a lot of time, but maybe enough if Ryan used it properly.

He gripped a chair back for support. "Dad, listen. You don't know we're going to leave here forever. We could find that Centauri B's planet isn't even habitable and we'll have to come back. If living here is really what God has planned for us, then don't you think that's what'll happen?"

Ken glanced up at the monitor and shook his head, then bent back to his work. Another light glowed on Ryan's console. "I can't take that risk."

"It's not a risk. If you're right, that's what'll happen. God will make it happen. Trust in Him, Dad."

"I do trust in Him, Ryan. I trust that He's guided me to do this. He's given us Eden, but in order to stay, it's evidently going to take one more sacrifice. I'm willing to make that sacrifice so the rest of you can stay."

Ryan snorted. "We don't *want* to stay."

"Such is my shame. Had I been a better spiritual guide, you would have. But without the ship it won't make any difference. You'll be there, and future generations will grow up in innocence."

"There won't *be* any future generations if you blow up the ship. All of our colonization gear is still on board."

Another warning light blinked on. "You don't need it. This is Eden. You can live here without tools."

They probably could, Ryan thought, but it wouldn't be much of a life. He looked around him at the bridge, at the banks of meters and controls on all sides. There had to be something he could do from here to stop Ken from blowing up the ship. But what? Think.

And keep trying to convince him not to try it in the first place. "We don't want to live there," he repeated. "It's our choice, not yours. Not even God's. He gave us free will, and we're using it, for better or worse. It's not your decision."

Ken consulted a pocket note pad, then flipped another switch. "It is. One of the duties of religion is to protect people from themselves. You'll thank me for this later."

Ryan gripped the edge of the control console to keep from waving a fist at Ken. "No we won't. We'll curse your name. If you do this we'll remember you along with Hitler and Bush and—" Ryan couldn't think of another historical figure in their league, but another name suggested itself and he went with it instinctively. "—and Satan himself. Think about what you're doing here. You're talking about killing a third of the crew and—"

"I won't kill anybody if you do what I tell you."

Ryan's eyes found a caged, doubly interlocked combination switch marked "EMERGENCY DRIVE DISENGAGE" that looked promising, until he realized it was used to shut off the drive once it was running, not before. By the time that circuit became active, assuming Ken hadn't already disabled it anyway, they would all be a radioactive cloud.

He glanced back at Ken, who was still methodically flipping switches on his side of the screen. Maybe he could be scared into stopping. But what kind of a scare would a man about to sacrifice himself respond to? Only one. He said, "Even if you let us all get away, there's one person you'll still be killing, and that's yourself. That's suicide. Isn't that a mortal sin? Won't that send you straight to Hell? I don't think that's quite what you have in mind, is it?" He paused just long enough to let that soak in, then said, "Now listen; you and I are the only ones who know about this so far. Let's keep it that way. Undo what you've done over there, come back to the ship, and we'll forget it completely. I promise. I won't put it in the log and I won't tell anybody and it'll just be between you and me. Okay?"

Ken grinned a sickly, scared grin. "Nice try, but no. Martyrdom in the service of God isn't a sin. My duty is clear, and so is yours. Get the crew on the lander and get out of here."

No, Ryan thought. *My duty is to the ship, as well as the crew.* But time was running out. Ken had already started the fuel pre-heating sequence. As soon as it developed enough pressure to flow into the reaction chamber, he could blow them up anytime he wanted.

Ryan studied the drive controls once more for a way to defuse the bomb Ken was rapidly turning it into, at the same time searching frantically for anything he could say that would reach him. There had to be something he would listen to. Reason hadn't worked, and scaring him with eternal damnation hadn't worked; what else was there?

There was love. Laura had told him that. "Let him know you still love him," she'd said. "If anything can affect him, that will."

It was worth a try. If he could just say it. "Dad," he began. "Dad, I—I know it looks like I've fought you every step of the way, but you've got to understand why I did it. I did it because...I did it because I love you. Because you're my father. I don't want to see you hurt yourself, and that's what you're doing. I want to help you. Do you understand that?"

Ken looked up at the monitor, at Ryan's face, and his own expression softened. "Yes, son, I do understand that. I understand perfectly, because that's exactly the reason why I'm doing this for you; because I love you. I don't want to see you hurt by your own ignorance."

"It's going to hurt me just as much this way. Can you imagine how I'm going to feel if I get on that lander and leave you alone up here? I don't think I could live with that."

"You'll learn to."

"I don't think so."

"You will. Your mother's already halfway there."

His mother. Space. She had moved out of the apartment just this morning, anticipating Ken's return. "Is that why you're doing this?"

"I'm not going to blow up the ship because your mother divorced me, if that's what you're asking. I've told you why I'm doing it."

"But you're mad at her. I can hear it in your voice. You think she moved out because she doesn't love you any more. Well that's not so. She loves you too. She was hoping she could get your attention, make you see how hard you were making things for yourself as well as for her. She wants to help you."

"I don't need help."

"Ask Michelle about that. Ask Bob Thorpe. Dammit, Dad, you're about to destroy everything we've spent twenty years of our lives to achieve and you don't think you need help?"

Ryan could see the worry lines crease Ken's face. Could he actually be considering what Ryan said? "You trust Bob Thorpe, don't you? He's on your side. Will you talk to him, ask him if he thinks you need help? For me, Dad? Because I love you?"

Ken closed his eyes. He was trembling. *I'm getting to him,* Ryan thought.

Ken shook his head furiously, as if trying to shake the confusion out of it, and when he opened his eyes again, they once more burned with fanatical zeal. "No!" he shouted. "No. It's too late for that. I'm doing what I have to do. I mean it, now, get off the ship."

"Dad, listen—"

"Don't talk to me anymore! I don't want to hear it. Leave, now, and don't try anything or I'll blow the drive with you still on board. Goodbye." Ken reached forward, and his image disappeared from the screen.

"Mac, give me one-way visual again," Ryan said, and the screen lit up with the same scene as before. Ken was once again working busily to turn the drive into a bomb, and there didn't seem to be anything Ryan could do to stop him.

Was the crew actually going to have to abandon ship and let Ken blow it up? It certainly looked that way. Ryan glanced around the control room again, hoping for sudden inspiration, but it was all just a maze of switches and dials to him now. He was too rattled to think straight.

He felt like a complete idiot. He should have been able to do *something*. All the heroes he'd ever heard of would have. He'd had his chance, too, but he'd blown it. If he'd gone after Ken the moment he'd seen what he was doing, he might have been able to physically drag him out of the drive module, but it was far too late for that now.

No, that wouldn't have worked anyway. Now that he thought about it he realized what the pressure suit lying in the path of the inner door signified. Ken had effectively locked the outer door that way, since the airlock safeties wouldn't allow it to open unless the inner door was sealed tight.

Unless of course Ryan could have bypassed the safeties somehow, the way Ken was bypassing the ones controlling the drive.

It was a moot point. He didn't have the time.

But Ken didn't have a suit on, either.

Ryan felt the hair on his neck rise at the thought that had just occurred to him. There was one way to bypass the entire airlock door. He could do it. He could save the ship. All it would take would be for him to kill his father.

He looked at the fuel pressure gauge. It was beginning to climb.

He looked at Ken, sweat flying away from him now in fat globules as he worked frantically to finish his preparations before Ryan thought of a way to stop him. Would he really give the people on the ship the time they needed to get into a lander and out of range of the blast? Watching him work, Ryan didn't think so. Ken was too scared. The moment he got the opportunity, he would push the button.

"Mac," Ryan said. "Arm the explosive bolts on the drive module airlock."

He held his breath, expecting the control program to require Captain Van Cleeve's authorization, but evidently his temporary authority was enough.

"Explosive bolts armed," Mac responded.

"Prepare to blow the bolts at my command."

"Prepared to blow."

Ryan took a deep breath, then let it out in a long sigh. He couldn't do it. Not like this. He had to at least give his father one more chance.

"Reestablish two-way communication with Ken."

"Established."

"Dad."

Ken didn't look up, but his flinch told Ryan he had heard him.

"Dad, I've figured out how to stop you. You've got one chance and only one to live through it. Put your hands up where I can see them, right now."

"You're bluffing."

"I am not, Dad. Put you hands up in front of you."

Ken looked up at the monitor, locked eyes with Ryan, and said, "You cannot thwart the will of God."

"Maybe *this* is the will of God, then, because I *can* stop you, and I will. I'm giving you a chance to live through it, is all. Now get your hands up where I can see them."

"No." Ken looked down and reached forward toward the control board again.

Ryan couldn't know what he was reaching for. It could have been just the video cutoff again, or it could have been the main throttle control. He couldn't afford to wait any longer.

"Mac, blow the bolts."

Ryan closed his eyes. He couldn't close his ears, though; over the intercom he heard a thump and a whoosh and a startled cry of alarm from Ken, rapidly fading to nothing. When he opened his eyes again, the drive control room was empty. The inner airlock door remained open; the outer one was missing entirely. A tiny flash of motion that might have been Ken or might have been the empty pressure suit winked at him from the blackness of space as it tumbled away from the ship.

CHAPTER SEVENTEEN

BETWEEN STARS

"I FEEL RIDICULOUS on this couch."

"Humor me."

Out of the corner of his eye, Ryan could see Michelle sitting in her chair beside his head, her left leg crossed primly over her right, her hands toying with a note pad held against her knee.

Ryan slapped the couch beside him. "At least sit over here beside me. Better yet, lie down. You want pillow talk, let's do real pillow talk." He tilted his head back to see her expression.

She was smiling, and blushing a little as well. They had made pillow talk a time or two under different circumstances. But this time she shook her head and said, "Not this time, Ryan. This has to be official, by the book. If you want to be certified sane and healthy, we've got to follow standard procedure, and that means you on the couch and me in the chair."

Ryan looked back down at his feet. When he'd first returned to the ship he'd continued to wear his hiking boots, but he'd eventually grown tired of their mass working against him in low-gee and he'd switched back to his shipboard slippers again. Now he noticed he was wearing a hole in the toe of his right one.

"I don't know if I want to be certified sane," he said. "A guy who kills his father isn't necessarily all straight in the head, you know?"

"That's why we're doing this; to find out how you're dealing with it."

"Badly."

"What makes you think so?"

Ryan couldn't help grinning sardonically. "And they're off and running," he said, mimicking a sportscaster's voice. When Michelle didn't respond, he said, "All right, what makes me think I'm dealing with it badly? Well, for starters, I've gone back to sleeping a lot again. And feeling guilty about it."

"What do you think the significance of that is?"

"I don't know. Loss of self-respect, maybe. Or maybe I'm trying to give myself an obvious, everyday reason for feeling so lousy so I won't have to think about Ken all the time."

Ryan heard the tap of Michelle's fingers on her notepad. "How long have you been oversleeping?"

"You mean hours per day or when did it start?

"When did it start?"

Ryan tried to remember. The first few days after he had...taken care of Ken were all jumbled together in his mind, but he didn't think he'd slept much at all. He'd been afraid of the nightmares he was sure would haunt him. Exhaustion had finally caught up with him about the third day or so and he'd slept a night and half the following day, but that one instance wasn't the beginning of the pattern. He'd had quite a few normal days after that, helping set up for the trip they were already a week into.

And that, he supposed, was the trigger. So many normal days. "I guess it started when I realized I wasn't going to have nightmares about it after all."

"And you felt you should?"

"Shouldn't I?"

"Not necessarily. If you've already integrated what happened into your world-view, then there's no reason why you should be dwelling on it, either consciously or unconsciously."

"You're saying I should just go on about my business as if nothing ever happened?"

If he turned his head just a little to the left, he could see Michelle in his peripheral vision. She leaned back in her chair and said, "That would be one way of dealing with it. If you'd hit on that one from the start I would've been worried, but you didn't. You went through a pretty normal grieving process, considering the situation."

"But now it's time to forget about it?"

"That's for you to decide. I'm just wondering if you aren't manufacturing a guilt association to cover for the one you think you should be feeling."

Ryan looked back at his feet. It was possible, he supposed. The fact was, he didn't think about Ken much at all unless he made a point of it. Maybe he was sleeping in just to make himself feel guilty in the first place. It was certainly working, if that was the case.

"How come nobody else expects me to feel guilty?" he asked suddenly. "I mean, everybody acts like I'm some kind of hero. Even Mom."

"The video is pretty clear," said Michelle. "You did everything you could to resolve the situation peacefully, and everyone knows it. Ken would have died no matter what, but because of you, we've still got a starship."

"I could have changed the air mix," Ryan said. "If I'd thought of it soon enough I could have changed what he was breathing to pure nitrogen and knocked him out without him suspecting a thing."

"Twenty-twenty hindsight," Michelle said. "If I'd paid more attention to him instead of hoping he'd cure himself, I could have stopped him last *year*. Captain Van Cleeve could have figured he was dangerous and put him in the brig until we were on our way. We all could have done something different, but we didn't. We did what we though was necessary at the time, and now we live with the consequences."

"Except Ken."

"Ken suffered the consequences of his own actions."

"And mine."

"You're manufacturing guilt again."

Ryan shrugged. Maybe he was. Michelle tapped some more on her note pad, then said, "Let's leave that for now. What else is bothering you?"

"The memorial ceremony," Ryan said without pause.

"What about it?"

"That it happened at all. Appealing to God to take his soul and all that. Assuming God even exists, then He either did or He didn't; I don't see any reason to believe our pleading would make a bit of difference."

"The ceremony is for the people left behind. You know that."

"Yeah." After a moment, Ryan said, "Okay, what really got me was David running the show. David, talking about God and Eden as if he believed every word Ken ever said."

"You're angry that David believes in God? Or that he talks about it out loud now?"

Ryan hadn't thought about it that way before. Michelle had a point. "Maybe I'm just mad at him for going public with it. For talking about it as if he's *sure*. He's helping keep alive the organized insanity that killed my father."

"He's presenting a much more moderate approach than Ken did."

"I wish he weren't approaching it at all." Ryan felt a blush steal over him at an associated thought, quickly buried the thought, then something—maybe just the reminder of where he was—brought it out again and he said, "And I wish he weren't approaching Holly quite so successfully, either."

More tapping on the notepad. "Let's talk about Holly for a while. You're still in love with her, aren't you?"

Ryan cursed himself silently. Why the hell had he brought that up, anyway? He—why didn't he ask? "Why did I bring that up? You're more girlfriend than she ever was."

"I'm a different girlfriend. Right now I'm your psychologist, and that's why you mentioned it. And I don't mind talking about her. If it bothers you that she and David are seeing one another romantically, then we should talk about it."

Ryan folded his arms over his chest, decided that was probably a defensive gesture, and laid them back at his sides again. "All right, if you want to. Yeah, it bugs me. It bugs me that she thinks we're too close to get physical. That doesn't make any sense to me."

"What doesn't make sense about it? That she thinks that way, or the thought itself?"

"Both. How can you be too close to get physical? It's an oxymoron."

"Why do you think so?"

The question caught Ryan by surprise. "Wha—how am I supposed to answer that? I think so because that's the way it is. The more you like someone, the closer you get, physically as well as emotionally."

"With everyone?"

"You're baiting me. Next you're going to say, 'How about your sister? How about Sean? How about Laura?' Well for each one of them there's an obvious reason: I'm not into incest, I'm not gay, and Laura's in her nineties and she has Teigh anyway."

Michelle laughed softly. "Funny you should mention Laura. She's the perfect example of what we're talking about here. Let's just pose a hypothetical question: If Laura were thirty instead of ninety, how would you feel about her then? Would you be sexually attracted to her?"

Ryan thought about it. If Laura were young, what would his feelings about her be? Intelligent, vivacious, loving—she'd be his dream come true. "Of course," he answered.

Now Michelle laughed outright. "Ryan, Ryan. That's not what you were supposed to say." He tilted his head and gave her a questioning look, and she waved her arm in dismissal. "No, you're not a pervert. But you *are* a rare kind of person. You and Teigh are probably the only two people on the ship with the self-confidence to love someone like Laura as a woman."

"I don't think she bites."

"Ah, no, but she does love everyone on the ship. That's kind of hard for most men to understand. Maybe hard even for you, if you're truly jealous about Holly. But what's more to the point is the idea of being the only person on the ship she *didn't* love. That would be even harder to take, wouldn't it? But people who get physically involved fall back out of love all the time, and they usually wind up with less affection than they started out with. Most people don't want to take that kind of risk with someone like Laura. Or with someone like you. But you don't see it as a risk, because you've never had any problem getting people to like you."

Ryan looked back down at his feet. "So we're back to that, hmm? Holly doesn't want me because I'm the ship's nice guy?"

"That's essentially what I think's going on, yes. Most people don't want to risk losing their nurturer. They'd rather not have a lover than not have a nurturer. It's usually not even a conscious decision, but almost everybody makes it."

Ryan could see a hole in her argument. "Not long ago a girl who'll remain nameless asked me to have sex with her *because* I was a nice guy."

Michelle laughed. "Without trying to guess her identity, I'd bet she's young, inexperienced; that was maybe even her first time. She didn't know what to expect. Am I right?"

"Dead on," said Ryan, impressed.

"Thought so. She didn't know yet how easily sex can complicate a relationship."

"But you do. So why...?"

In his peripheral vision he saw her set her notebook on her lap. "Why don't I worry about what it'll do to my relationship with the ship's nice guy? Maybe I do worry. But I know what I'm worrying about, so I can make a conscious decision to ignore it if I want."

All this talk about being a "nice guy" and a "nurturer" was embarrassing. Ryan didn't think he was so special; why did everyone else seem to think so? He let out a deep breath and said, "I feel like I'm somehow deceiving everybody. They all think I'm so great, and really I'm just a lazy, mixed up kid who dwells on his own problems most of the time. Every time you tell me how popular I am, I want to say no, you've got me confused with somebody else."

"Good."

Michelle was smiling when he turned to look. "Beg your pardon?" he asked.

"I said 'Good.' That's the way it should be. If *you* thought you were great then nobody'd be able to stand you."

Ryan could see the truth in that. He could also see the paradox inherent in it, but rather than getting angry about it, he found himself laughing. "I love it," he said. "It's a built-in negative feedback system. I didn't think people's personalities had them."

"Some do, some don't," Michelle said. "You're one of the lucky ones."

"And Ken was one of the unlucky ones, wasn't he? He didn't have any nifty feedback mechanism to tone him down when he started to get a little too strange."

Michelle nodded. "That's a pretty straightforward interpretation of the situation, yes." She tapped at her note pad for a minute or so without speaking. Ryan waited for her to finish, and at last she said, "As far as I'm concerned you're healthy, sane, and behaving normally for someone who's undergone the trauma you have. That's my official evaluation for the record. Off the record I think you're coping just fine, too."

"Thanks, I guess," Ryan said, though he actually felt let down. "I was kind of hoping you'd be able to tell me how to deal with it better," he confessed.

Setting the note pad on her desk, Michelle said, "All I can suggest is that you stay busy. Keep your mind on other things. The death of a parent, no matter how it happens, isn't something you consciously accept. Acceptance happens on a deeper level, and it happens faster if you don't dwell on it." She paused, then said, "As for what to do about Holly, I don't know what to tell you."

Ryan sat up and looked directly at Michelle. "That's just as well. I shouldn't have brought her up in the first place."

With a playful shake of her head, Michelle said, "Sure you should have. I have an interest in your love life, you know." She got up from her chair and sat down beside Ryan on the couch. "This comes just from me, not from your psychologist. I know how you feel about Holly, and I want you to know that it doesn't bother me. I understand relationships like yours. Not from experience, but I know what's happening and I think it's probably harder on you than it is on either Holly or me."

"You're not jealous?" he asked incredulously.

"Not enough to worry about."

"That's—I don't know. That's hard to understand. When I see David and Holly together I get so jealous I can hardly think." He shook his head and added, "That kind of shoots holes in the theory that I'm a 'nurturer,' doesn't it? Laura doesn't get jealous every time someone smiles at Teigh, does she?"

Michelle shrugged. "She might. Nurturers love everybody around them, but they usually have a favorite, and there's nothing in the contract that says they have to share their favorite with anybody else. Laura could be intensely jealous for all I know, but the opportunity for her to show it has just never come up."

"Good point." Teigh and Laura had lived together for as long as Ryan could remember, even before they started the trip. They weren't married, but they might as well have been.

Michelle said, "Even if she doesn't feel jealousy, the point to remember is that you're both basically normal human beings. Psychologists love to talk about personality types, but everyone is unique. You're going to have your own behavioral inconsistencies and your own individual reactions to things no matter what niche I or anybody else puts you in, and that's nothing to be ashamed of. That's what makes you *you*."

That's what makes me such a jerk, Ryan thought. Here he sat with a girl he liked, one who liked him as well—maybe even loved him—and all he could think about was Holly. What was wrong with him that he couldn't accept the situation for what it was and get on with his life? He wished he could answer that, but the one person who might be able to help him understand it didn't seem to see anything wrong.

Or maybe she did. After an uncomfortable silence, she said, "I don't want to make it sound like jealousy is necessarily okay, either, you know. If it doesn't go away on its own pretty soon, we should talk about it again. There are methods of treating it."

"You make it sound like a disease."

"It can become one." Michelle was serious. "If you're not careful, it can do to you just what religion did to Ken. In my profession we call that a disease." She smiled. "But don't worry about it just yet. What you've got is a pretty mild case, and I'm betting you'll get over it without help."

Michelle stood up, and Ryan—taking that as a sign the interview was over—stood up with her. He hesitated, thinking he should say something to change the subject before he left, but he knew now would be an inappropriate time to ask for a date and he couldn't think of anything else to say. He looked into her eyes, saw in them only fondness and caring and not a trace of the jealousy he would have been feeling if he were in her place, and felt himself melting from the inside out. She was too good for him. He didn't deserve her.

But he wasn't going to drive her away. He took her in his arms and wrapped her in a hug and said, "Thank you. You've given me a lot to think about."

She hugged back, rubbing his tight muscles. "That's what I'm here for."

Ryan tried to heed Michelle's advice and keep himself busy. With the starship again under acceleration, the central axis and its tree once again became a favorite place to while away the hours, but Ryan was careful to keep those hours productive. The colony was going to need carpenters, and even though some of the crewmembers already claimed that skill, he supposed they could always use another hand at it, so he spent a lot of his time reading up on the profession.

When his head filled with mortises and tenons and rafters and trusses, he turned to his guitar and practiced with that until he developed both calluses on his fingers and the ability to play at least one song all the way through, and when he could stand neither carpentry nor guitar, he went looking for odd jobs to do. With Ken gone he could almost always find something that needed doing in the farm, and after the month spent paying more attention to Eden than to the ship there was plenty of cleaning and maintenance to be done elsewhere as well.

The trip between the two main Centauri suns was mercifully short, measured in weeks rather than the years from Sol. The crew didn't have time to get bored in the confines of the ship again, nor did they have the uncertainty of whether or not they would find a place to live. Centauri B's second planet might or might not provide that place, but if it didn't, they had already found Eden; and now that Ken was out of the picture, living there didn't seem quite as unlikely as it had before. Without his fanatical brand of religious zealotry to contend with, they might actually be able to live there without disrupting the customs agents. As a fallback position, at least, its existence was a great reassurance.

With that frame of mind, the atmosphere on board ship was as joyous as it had ever been. Parties and dances sprang up at a moment's notice, and Ryan went to his share of them, but so did

Holly and David, and every time he saw them together he felt as if someone had kicked him in the stomach. They both acted open and friendly and Holly even danced a time or two with Ryan, but he knew there was nothing more than friendship involved. He surprised himself when he realized that he was glad people had taken to wearing clothes again on the ship. He didn't think he could bear to see Holly unclothed any more, and especially not beside David.

He knew he should probably talk with Michelle about it again, but despite her assurance that she understood, he didn't want to subject her to the feelings of rejection he was sure she would have if he confessed that his jealousy was getting worse instead of better. He tried talking to Laura about it, but for the first time in his life she was unable to comfort him either. Her advice to accept Holly's decision wasn't what he wanted to hear.

At least he had the upcoming exploration to keep his mind off her part of the time. Now, after doing it once, his earlier reluctance to explore seemed silly to him. Exploring was fun, it was exciting, and what was more, his experience had convinced him he was good at it. He looked forward to the chance to show off his skill once again to the entire human race. More, he looked forward to taking the first step on what would eventually be humanity's second home.

He didn't know why he was so sure that would be the case, but he was. If he'd been Ken he would have said God had told him so, but as it was he could only call it a hunch. He felt good about it. As they drew closer and David's observations showed it to be every bit as beautiful as Eden, he began thinking of names for it, names like *Home* and *Perfection* and even—to upstage the naming-by-default of Eden—*Heaven*.

His eagerness to explore lasted right up until the moment when David asked to be part of the team. When Sean told him the astronomer wanted to join them, he could hardly believe it, but when the captain okayed the request he found that he not only had to believe it, but worse, he had to pretend he liked it. He had no valid reason to oppose David's presence; if he objected it would look petty.

Then Mariko, remembering her frustration in waiting for samples sent up by rocket, also volunteered, and they were four.

Chapter Eighteen

Hostile Natives

THERE WERE DIFFERENCES. Even from orbit, Alpha Centauri B-2 was visibly unlike either Earth or Eden. It was a smaller planet, circling closer around a smaller, dimmer star, but that was only the beginning. Only a quarter of its surface was water, and that mostly in lakes and small seas. The planet's slow rotation rate of nearly 35 hours reduced the Coriolis effect, which made for fewer major storms, but general atmospheric circulation and local topography evidently made up for the loss. The curving arms of the few frontal systems that did develop swept around the planet in slow motion, merging in collision with smaller, more localized disturbances to create a chaotic cloud pattern covering the entire globe in a mosaic of storms and clear skies.

Learning from past experience, the exploration party picked an island for their first landing site. There weren't as many to choose from as there had been on Eden, but after identifying the likely candidates they settled on one about fifty kilometers long by thirty wide and about a hundred kilometers from the edge of the second-largest sea. It would be big enough to support a complete ecosystem and close enough to the mainland that its flora and fauna were likely to be close to the norm for the rest of the planet, yet far enough away to keep it isolated in the event of another mishap like the one with the customs agents.

Sitting in the shuttle's copilot seat, watching for the second time an unfamiliar planet swell in the windows as they dropped toward it, Ryan swore silently that they wouldn't repeat that mistake.

He didn't know just how they were going to avoid it, though. Aside from the two extra people, this expedition had been set up just like the previous one. All four of them wore emergency pressure suits which they would remove once the air checked out, after which they would begin collecting specimens and ranging farther and farther afield. They would refrain from camping out until they were certain no intelligent natives lived on the island, but even so there would be plenty of opportunity for idea contamination before they realized it if there were. Depending on the natives' degree of development, the initial few moments of contact could impart anything from the idea of walking upright to the idea of space flight.

It was Ryan's fervent hope that there simply wouldn't be intelligent natives in the first place.

Once in the atmosphere, Sean flew them in a slowly descending spiral around the island, hoping to get a good look at what they might be encountering once they reached the ground, but the island was mostly forest. The few clearings they found seemed devoid of animals, either naturally so or, more likely, just scared away by the shuttle's noise. The shoreline held seabirds, but after the first pass even they disappeared into the trees.

"They're a little spookier than on Eden, aren't they?" Sean asked. He banked around for another run up the island's long axis.

"Seem to be," Ryan admitted. His attention was divided between what he was seeing and the speech he was trying to remember. Ever since the four explorers had agreed he would have the honor of being first out the airlock, he had tried to come up with something that carried the same sentiment as what Sean had said on Eden, but without repeating Sean's speech word for word. He had practiced it over and over again until he was sure he could say it in his sleep, but he still worried that he would forget it under the pressure of the actual moment.

"I guess we'll just have to set down and check it out on foot. You guys ready?" Sean turned in his seat to look over his shoulder at David and Mariko, strapped into acceleration chairs behind Sean and Ryan.

"Ready," said David.

"Any time you are," said Mariko. "I can't see a damn thing from back here anyway."

"How 'bout you guys upstairs?"

"You're go for landing whenever you want," Warren replied. With David already on the ship, he had inherited the communicator position.

"Down we go, then. How about there?" Sean pointed toward a small clearing in the forest as it rushed by on their left.

Ryan eyed it critically, but there was little to see besides a brown patch. "Looks as good as any other."

Sean banked the shuttle around, circled the clearing once, then brought them in for a smooth touchdown in the center of it. Turning to Ryan, he said, "It's your ball game, kid."

Ryan unstrapped and sidled past David and Mariko to the airlock. He wondered why they weren't getting up as well, then he suddenly realized they intended to let him cycle through the airlock alone as well as take the first step beyond it. He didn't need that much honor. "Come on," he said, "we can all crowd in together."

It was a tight squeeze, but Sean managed to get the door closed behind them. When the safety interlock gave him control, Ryan pulled the handle on the outer door and swung it open.

The rush of anticipation was just as strong as the first time, moreso because this was his planet. He had fought for it, had prevented the sabotage that would have denied them the chance to come here, and now he was only a moment away from taking the first human step on its surface.

It looked wonderful. His eyes had already adjusted to the dimmer, more orange light of Centauri B; it seemed just as bright and white as "normal" sunlight, and in it the grasses and low bushes growing just beyond the airlock looked as green and lush as anywhere. A small, fast, orange-and-green bird, a little bigger than a hummingbird but with the same quick flight characteristics, darted in and out among the bushes. Ryan was surprised to see animal life so soon after they had landed; he would have expected the noise to have scared them away for longer than that. Especially a bird as small and apparently vulnerable as this one. There had to be a reason why it wasn't afraid of loud noises, but Ryan couldn't think of one right off.

They would learn. They had a whole planet full of new mysteries to solve, starting with the first step.

Taking a deep breath, he pulled the handle that unfolded the stairway, waited for it to extend and lock in place, then walked down the three steps to the ground. It felt about the same as Eden's ground had felt underfoot: uneven and slightly springy. A bush about knee high stood just beyond his reach; he resisted the urge to take a second step and run his hand over it. First things first.

The bird noticed him and buzzed past in an orange blur. Ryan flinched, then grinned and shook his head. His first word wasn't going to be "Yeow!" if he could help it.

He opened his mouth to begin his speech, but he never completed the motion. He saw a flicker of movement out of the corner of his eye, but before he even had time to flinch again, something kicked him in the back of the head and sent him flying into the bush in front of him.

Through the ringing in his ears he heard the explosion echoing off the wall of trees surrounding the clearing. He also heard a babble of voices over his suit radio, but none of them made any sense. His body seemed to be tingling all over, or more like itching. He raised up and got his right arm under him, pushed himself to his knees, and only then did he notice the blood staining the inside of the transparent plastic suit. The suit was shredded, and so was his clothing and the skin underneath.

The words came automatically. They had become a cliché, the phrase of choice in any similar situation ever since their first use in a spaceflight accident over a century before. Swallowing the squeak he was afraid would come first, Ryan cleared his throat and said as calmly as he could, "Houston, we've got a problem here."

Inside the shuttle again, his three companions stripped off the remains of his suit and clothing as gently as they could and began treating his wounds. A spray from the medkit stopped the bleeding and killed his pain, but there was surprisingly little of that to begin with. Ryan was sure most of it was psychosomatic from seeing blood everywhere. The cuts were so clean, so surgically smooth, that he hadn't even known he'd gotten them until he'd seen the blood.

Whatever had cut him—something in the bush, he supposed— had only reached his front side. But how he had been thrown into the bush in the first place remained a mystery. "What happened?" he asked. "What blew up?"

"The bird did," said Mariko. "It swooped down at you like a hawk and when it hit your helmet it blew up."

"Good thing you were wearing the suit," said David. "It probably saved your life." David and Mariko and Sean were still wearing theirs, Ryan noticed.

"The *bird* blew up?" he asked, incredulous.

"That's what it looked like," Sean answered. "Sounded like a quarter stick of dynamite or so."

Mariko added, "It's a wonder it didn't break your neck."

"Tell me about it." Ryan watched Sean spray clear sticky stuff on his legs, then asked again, "The *bird*? How could a bird blow up?"

"I'd like to hear an answer to that myself," said Mariko. She was examining one of the cuts on Ryan's chest. Ryan watched her tease it open, nod knowingly, then close it and hold it together until the adhesive spray knitted the edges again. "I think you're going to live," she said. "The cuts are mostly superficial, and the ones that aren't look like they'll heal clean."

David had been examining the remains of Ryan's suit. Suddenly he shouted, "Ouch, dammit!" and dropped it, grabbing his left thumb.

"What happened?"

"It cut me." He held out his thumb for all to see. His glove had a slice in it, and a bright red diagonal line swelled across the flesh beneath it.

Sean asked, "What cut you? Ryan's suit?"

"No, there's a leaf stuck to it. The leaf cut me." David stuck his thumb out through the gash in his suit, held it for Sean to spray with the sealant, then pulled it back inside and held the suit together while Mariko patched it with tape from the medkit. Satisfied he would live, he picked up Ryan's suit again and carefully removed the leaf.

It looked like a leaf. Green, round on the stem end and tapering to a point on the other, about four centimeters long and half as wide. It looked fairly stiff, but David held it gingerly between thumb and forefinger the flat way, the way a person would hold a sheet of paper. Holding up Ryan's suit by one glove, he drew the edge of the leaf along the forearm like a scalpel blade. It sliced cleanly at first, then dragged to a stop. He turned it a bit and made another cut with a new edge, again getting only a centimeter or two before it dulled as well.

He held it up close to his faceplate and squinted at it a moment. "There's a translucent ring around the edge, a millimeter wide or so. Looks like glass." He pushed the leaf sideways against the suit fabric as if to break off the tip, but it bent softly like a normal leaf. Examining the edge again, David said, "The glassy part broke, and so did the outer couple millimeters of the leaf, but the middle is more flexible."

"Let me see that." Mariko held out her hand, carefully took the leaf from David, and examined it closely. "Hmmm," was all she said.

Ryan was getting tired of being flat on his back. He started to raise up, but Sean stopped him. "Stay still for a while. You're not glued tight yet."

"Great." He let out a sigh. "Good thing my little speech was going to be about proceeding with caution, huh? I'd hate to think what might have happened if I'd been careless."

Ryan heard a tinny voice coming from all four suit helmets; that had to be Warren speaking from the ship. He couldn't hear what Warren said, but Sean replied, "I don't think so. Let's give him a few hours and see how he heals first."

More talk over the radio, then, "There's that possibility, all right, but so far there's no sign of it."

David looked at his thumb again while Mariko said, "This is pure speculation, but I'd be willing to bet a plant with a defense like this wouldn't need to be poisonous too." She listened a moment, then, "Good point. I'll do an assay and see." She was still holding the leaf; she took it to the instrument rack against the aft wall and began turning on equipment.

"Did I hear someone mention poison?" Ryan asked as calmly as he could.

Sean nodded. "Not to worry, though. If the leaves were poisonous, I bet you'd already be feeling it."

Suddenly Ryan was sure he *was* feeling it, but he knew that was only from the suggestion. He felt fine, actually, for someone who had just been bombed and knifed. He wondered about infection from alien organisms or subtle poisons in either the leaves or the air, but his immune system was already on red alert with the accelerator Holly had given all the explorers, and he probably hadn't breathed enough of the air to matter even if it did test out dangerous.

He lay on his back, waiting for the antiseptic glue to knit his skin together, waiting for Mariko to find out what the leaf was made of, and wondering why he had ever wanted to be an explorer. It had suddenly ceased being fun.

"Silicon dioxide," Mariko announced a few minutes later. "A little boron, some phosphorus. Glass, basically. The leaf evidently secretes the stuff on its edge. Wonder how it does that?"

A few minutes more and she had her answer. "Hydrofluoric acid. Dilute, but enough to dissolve glass. There's a separate vascular system just for the acid." One of her instruments beeped and she consulted its screen. "The leaf itself is a little more normal. It's mostly carbon, hydrogen and oxygen in about the same proportion as you'd expect for proteins. A few familiar amino acids, but quite a few unfamiliar ones. Hmmm." She consulted another instrument. "That's our green pigment molecule, but it doesn't look much like chlorophyll, and it's not in chloroplasts, either. It's just free-floating in the cell. Hmmm."

"That's all very interesting," Ryan said from his position on the deck, "but am I going to die or not?"

"That'd be not, I believe. No known poisons. No, I take that back. Hydrofluoric acid is poisonous, so don't eat any of the leaves."

"Thanks for the warning." Ryan raised up to a sitting position, and this time Sean let him.

Sean was grinning. "You look like the loser in a cat fight."

"I feel a little like one, too," Ryan said. "Vacuum. This hasn't been the most auspicious beginning, has it?"

"More exciting than the last time, that's for sure." Sean got up and went forward to the windows. "Looks peaceful out there now."

"See any more orange and green birds?"

"Nope."

"What kind of bird flies at your head and blows up, anyway?" Ryan asked. The tone in his voice said clear as words: *How was I supposed to know it would do that?*

"One that was very pissed off, I'd guess," Sean replied. "Blowing up has to be a last resort. We probably landed on its nest or something."

David had gone into the cargo hold; he returned wearing what looked like a baggy pair of white coveralls over his pressure suit. He was carrying another pair in either hand. "This ought to keep us safe from slicer-dicers," he said, handing one each to Sean and Mariko.

They were heat- and radiation- and abrasion-resistant oversuits, designed for use while working on heavy machinery in space. Made of Kevlar, they would stop bullets if necessary. Glass-edged leaves would present no problem at all to a person wearing one.

"Slicer-dicer," Mariko said, taking one of the suits from David and starting to pull it on over her own pressure suit. "I like that. Genus and species names both. Slicer-dicer it is."

"You're kidding, right?"

"Not at all. The taxonomic system we used on Earth was a hopeless mess. Why use Latin when nobody understands it anymore? We speak English, so our names for things ought to be in English too."

"What're you going to call the blow-up bird?" Ryan asked.

"Well, actually, both the bush and the bird ought to be your choice. You discovered them, after all."

Ryan laughed. He stopped suddenly and looked down at his chest, but when he saw that none of the cuts had opened he laughed again. "Slicer-dicer's fine. And as for the bird, I'm open to suggestion."

"Kamikaze," said Sean.

"Kamikaze?"

"Suicide pilot. Crashes into things and blows up on purpose."

Ryan remembered an old movie. "Oh, right. Well, yeah, that certainly describes the little bugger."

"It'll be a good warning word, too," David pointed out. "It's all K's and stressed vowels."

"Good point," said Mariko. "We may have to shout it a lot if those guys turn out to be common. What do you say, Ryan?"

"Sounds good to me."

"So be it, then. We can worry about the genus later, when we know more about them. So what do you say; should we go out for another attempt at collecting specimens?"

Sean zipped his coverall up to the neck. "We should at least get an air sample," he said. "We've only got an hour or so left in these suits before we need to recharge."

Ryan, wearing only the spray-on adhesive, realized he wasn't going to be going out this time. "I could keep an eye out for kamikazes from up here," he said. "Maybe even shoot them down with the com laser."

"Hell of an idea," Sean said. "Good thinking."

David nodded. "Even so, do you think it's smart for all of us to go out?"

"We'll do it in stages," Sean replied. "I'll go first, get an air sample and pass it back to you in the airlock, and you'll pass it on in to Mariko for testing. If nothing attacks me by then, you can come out, and if nothing threatening happens by the time you get the sample tested, Mariko can come on out too. No matter what you find out about the air, we stay suited this first time. Sound like a plan?"

"Sounds good."

"All right, then. Let's give it another shot. No pun intended."

Ryan, dressed once again in regular pants and a pullover shirt from his backpack, watched from the pilot's chair while Sean stepped outside. They had instructed the autopilot to scan for kamikazes or anything that looked similar and target them with the com laser, but the section of ground immediately beneath the shuttle was out of the laser's reach. Ryan watched that space, ready to shout a warning if he saw any sign of motion, but Sean was the only thing moving out there at the moment.

Sean opened a sample vial, waved it around in the air, then sealed it and handed it back into the airlock. He turned back to face away from the ship, and his voice came in over the intercom. "Ryan was interrupted before he got a chance to make the pledge, but I make it now. Despite what happened, I still charge every person who comes here to live in harmony with the way of this world, or not live here at all. I charge us all to do everything we can to protect this world and its life forms from our own ignorance and folly. We come here to learn, and, we hope, to live, but not to conquer. We will not mess this one up either. Sean Little Bear has spoken."

When Sean was done, the airlock door opened and David passed the vial of air inside to Mariko, then closed it again. A moment later he stepped down the ladder to stand beside Sean and said, "I agree wholeheartedly. No conquerors need apply, here or anywhere else in the universe."

Ryan raised his eyebrows in silent surprise. He hadn't expected that of David, not since his conversion to the church.

While Sean and David took a few cautious steps away from the airlock, Mariko fed the sample vial to the chromatograph, and a minute or so later got the reading everyone expected. The on-site test was only an independent confirmation of what they had already determined from orbit. "Looks like we're free to breathe it," she announced. "Chemically, anyway. Let's just check it for bugs." She took the vial to another instrument that sucked its contents through a filter and passed the results under a microscope.

"Got a few," she said. "Let's try 'em on Biogoo." She used remote manipulators to set up a culture in a dish of the amber-colored medium, then headed for the airlock herself. With a cheery, "My turn," she left the shuttle to Ryan.

Ryan watched as his three companions moved slowly out into the clearing. Mariko was taking samples of everything she could find: dirt, grass, leaves, bugs—whatever she stumbled across. David helped her with the collections, but Sean kept his pistol drawn and his eyes on the forest. Even with Ryan and the autopilot covering for him, he was taking no chances.

They circumnavigated the clearing, taking a brief foray into the trees after they had made a complete circuit. Nothing much happened while they did all that, but on their way back to the shuttle another kamikaze suddenly flew up out of the ground between them and safety. Ryan barely had time to shout a warning before the autopilot lanced out with the laser and the kamikaze disappeared in a brilliant red flash and a loud *wham*. Mariko dropped her sample bag in surprise, bent over to retrieve it, and thus missed being the center of the second explosion. Kamikazes began flying out of holes all around them, circling angrily and darting in toward their heads. Sean fired into the swarm and may have hit one or two, but the autopilot accounted for at least a dozen in the same amount of time.

It sounded like a war going on. The three explorers retreated under a hail of fire, sprinting for the airlock while the autopilot finished off the kamikazes. Ryan heard the airlock cycling, then a hearty laugh over the intercom as the outer door sealed them off from danger. The inner door opened and the three of them burst into the shuttle, slapping one another on the back and howling in mirth.

"Whee-ooo!" Sean shouted, lowering the hammer on his pistol and dropping it back into its holster. "Now that's what I call a population explosion."

"Oof," Mariko groaned.

David, ignoring them, slumped down in one of the rear acceleration chairs. "I wonder what set them off. Ryan, did you see anything we might have done?"

"The autopilot—" he began, then realized what David was asking. "Oh. No, I didn't. You were walking back toward me, and just about when you got to that kind of matted-down area there they started flying up out of the ground."

"Kind of matted-down area?" Mariko asked. She sidled past David and looked out the window where Ryan pointed. "Aha. It's not so apparent from ground level. That could be our explanation right there; we probably violated their territorial boundary."

Sean and David squeezed forward to look, too. "Yep," Sean said, "I bet that's it. Ha. Learning all the time."

"Look at 'em," said David, his voice soft with wonder. Now that the explorers were safe inside, the shuttle had stopped firing, and the remaining kamikazes were swarming around like a hive full of angry bees. Big, fat, orange and green bees.

Mariko's eyes held a faraway look. "I wish I could get a close look at one of those things," she said. "I'd love to find out how they explode like that. Can you imagine the evolutionary pathway that could lead to something like them?"

"No," David said. "No, as a matter of fact, I can't."

"What's that supposed to mean?" Sean asked.

David looked over at him. "It simply means I find it hard to believe that evolution could create something like that. They were almost certainly made this way from the start."

Sean sighed. "You're not talking genetic engineering, are you?"

"Perhaps," said David. "In the most general sense."

Mariko looked pained. "Oh, come now. Creationism? I don't think we need to invoke that just yet. Exploding animals are odd, but not impossible."

"I didn't say they were impossible; I just said I find creation to be a more likely explanation for them. It requires fewer untestable hypotheses. Occam's razor dictates we assume it to be correct until we prove otherwise."

Mariko shook her head vehemently. "Not so! Creationism may require fewer untestable hypotheses, but the one it *does* require is too much for me to swallow. Sorry, David, but I stick by evolution. Evolution is a predictive science. Looking at those flying bombs out there, I can say with confidence that something else has evolved a defense against them, because if nothing had, these guys would be extinct. They would have wiped out every biological niche in the ecosystem, and then the system would have crashed."

"That argument can be just as effective in favor of creationism," David countered. "If random chance were behind all this, the ecosystem should have crashed long ago. But it obviously hasn't, nor has Eden's ecosystem, nor has Earth's. We've got three planets bearing life and they're all *full* of life; I say that implies a guiding hand keeping things from getting out of control."

"Or it implies that evolution is a sufficient system of checks and balances on its own," said Mariko. "Divine intervention is an unnecessary complication to a perfectly adequate theory."

"You're the one who said how hard it was to imagine the evolutionary pathway leading to kamikazes."

"Imagining God is even harder," Mariko snapped.

Sean looked over to Ryan and rolled his eyes. Ryan nodded in sympathy. Sean turned to the scientists and said, "Hey, guys, how about if we go looking for more evidence instead of arguing about it from in here? Wouldn't that be more fun?"

"How're we going to get past those things?" David asked, nodding toward the swarm of kamikazes.

"In a rover," Sean replied.

They hadn't used them on Eden, not with its benign environment encouraging them to explore on foot, but each of the shuttles and the main landers carried amphibious transport vehicles for exploration and cargo hauling. They would be perfect for warding off kamikaze attacks.

David nodded thoughtfully. "Right. Okay, let's go take a drive through Hell."

CHAPTER NINETEEN

THE FINAL STRAW

MARIKO FAVORED DAVID WITH a long stare, then turned away and said, "Let me check the Biogoo first." She moved off toward the instrument rack in the back, took the culture dish out of the incubator, and held it to the light. It was still the same amber color as it had been when she exposed it, indicating that the smaller organisms in the atmosphere, or at least those in the sample, were nothing their enhanced immune systems couldn't handle.

"We can breathe it," she announced, reaching up and tugging open her Kevlar oversuit zipper as she spoke. She peeled out of that and the pressure suit and scratched madly at her scalp and neck where the rigid helmet had made it impossible to scratch.

"What'll we do for head protection?" Ryan asked her as he put the oversuit back on without the pressure suit. "Those kamikaze's seem to go for the head, and I don't think a Kevlar hood'll be enough if one gets too close."

"We, Kemosabe?" Sean asked.

"We," Ryan answered firmly. "I'm okay, especially if we're going in a rover. But I don't want my head blown off the next time I go out on foot, either. We need helmets of one sort or another."

David was removing his own pressure suit. As he re-donned the coverall, he said, "Well, your pressure suit is already useless; you might as well use the helmet from it. We can do the same if the need arises."

"That ought to work," Ryan admitted. The helmet alone wouldn't provide air for long, but he supposed it could circulate up through the neck ring when the internal tank ran out. If it didn't, they could cut holes in it for ventilation.

Sean nodded. "All right, then, let's do it." He stepped closer to the intercom and said, "Warren, we're going out in a rover."

"You sure that's wise?" Warren asked.

"We're taking precautions."

Warren *hmm*ed a moment, then said, "Okay. But be careful."

"Always." Sean stripped out of his suit, wadded it up inside its helmet, and carried it with him back into the cargo hold. David and Mariko followed him.

Ryan picked up the remains of his suit and cut the fabric from the helmet with his pocket knife, leaving the shoulders and part of the back on it so the Kevlar oversuit would help hold it in place. He retrieved his pistol from the pile of discarded clothing and followed the others into the cargo hold where he got a set of the white protective coveralls for himself, then he carried it all with him into the rover.

The rover looked a little like the ground cars Ryan had seen in movies, save that it stood taller on bigger, fatter tires and wasn't nearly as aerodynamically shaped. It was built for rugged terrain, not speed. Inside, it had two individual seats in front and one large bench seat in back; Mariko had already taken the one in front beside Sean. Ryan climbed in back beside David and tossed his gear into the cargo section behind the seat.

When all four of them were strapped in and ready to go, Sean pressed the cargo door remote and released the latches holding the rover to the deck. It rolled forward a few centimeters, stopped until the door tilted out to become a ramp, then with a whine of electric motors, rolled over the edge and down onto the ground. The door rose up and sealed with a thump behind them.

"How about a close look at the kamikaze nest, as long as we're protected?" said Mariko.

"All right." Sean fed the motor power and the rover rolled smoothly over toward the area of different vegetation marking the nest. It looked like a matted-down clover patch with small holes in the ground between plants. A kamikaze flew up out of one of the holes, made a slow circuit around the rover, then flew back down into the nest.

"It evidently doesn't see the rover as a threat," David said.

"Or it knows it can't hurt something this big, threat or not," Mariko replied.

"Enough of them could," David said. "If they all went off at once." As he spoke, two more kamikazes flew up and circled the rover.

"True," said Sean, backing up and driving wide around the kamikaze nest. "Let's give them some time to calm down while we look at whatever else this planet has to offer."

He drove in a diagonal across the field, swerving occasionally to avoid a slicer-dicer. The puncture-proof tires could probably have taken it, but the sharp leaves would whittle away at their tread, and there was no sense in wearing them out unnecessarily.

"You have a particular destination in mind?" Ryan asked.

"There looked to be a game trail over this way when we made our walkaround. It'll probably be easier driving along an established trail than just heading out through the trees."

"Ah. Probably so."

As they drove along the edge of the forest in search of the trail, Ryan took the opportunity to look at the trees. The biggest ones were about thirty meters tall and grew a single trunk all the way up. From the shuttle they had looked a little like pines, but now that he was closer Ryan saw more differences than similarities. Their branches looked more like palm fronds or fern leaves: wide, symmetrical compound leaves on thick stalks spiraling up the trunks. They reminded him of spiral staircases, though a person would have to stoop over to keep from hitting his head on the next level even at the bottom, and at the top the spiral was too tight even for a child. A cat would have been able to climb one easily, though, if it could manage the jump up to the first branches.

Provided the branch didn't cut the cat in half on the first step. Ryan looked for signs of anything living in the trees, and as his eyes became accustomed to the peculiar growth pattern he was able to pick out anomalies that might have been bird nests or maybe even birds themselves, though none flew away or even moved while he watched.

Beneath the big trees stood smaller ones of different species, not all of which shared the spiral structure of the tall ones. Ryan wondered if he was seeing the equivalent of deciduous and evergreen trees here, or if their variation marked some other, more alien difference.

Sean found the trail he was looking for and turned into the woods. Ryan braced himself for a rough ride, but the rover continued to roll along smoothly, grass rustling past along its underside. There were a few tight squeezes between trees, but none actually barred the way.

"This is more like a road than a trail," Sean muttered after a few minutes of driving.

Mariko was busy taking pictures with the rover's top-mounted video camera, which relayed the transmission through the shuttle to the ship in real time. "Good," she said, not looking up from the monitor. "It's hardly jouncing the camera at all." Just as she spoke, the right front wheel jolted against something, throwing them all forward against their seatbelts. A second later the back wheel bounced over it as well.

"You were saying?" David asked.

"Rock," Sean said. "I didn't see it in the grass. But this does feel like a road. If the paths weren't weaving all over the place like they are, I'd swear it was."

Paths? Ryan raised up to look out the windshield. The trail looked like three trails, actually, weaving back and forth in the grass, drawing closer together and drifting farther apart seemingly at random. They never crossed, though, and all three seemed equally traveled.

He turned around and looked out the back window. They were leaving twin tracks of bent-over grass behind them, two stripes as parallel as the edges of a laser beam. Even where the rover had turned to follow a bend in the trail, the two tracks were the same distance apart. The obvious difference between tire tracks and the natural game trail calmed the fear he had felt at Sean's statement. They weren't on a road. The trail wasn't an artifact of intelligent life.

He looked over at David, wondering if he were considering the same question. Was he wishing that they *would* find intelligent life, so God's Plan As Revealed To Ken would once again come under consideration? And how would David twist that plan now that he had come to embrace Ken's demented vision? *Creationism*, Ryan thought, snorting aloud at the very idea. How could someone like David abandon the logical thinking of scientific inquiry so completely that he could embrace something like creationism?

And what could someone like Holly see in someone like David? She'd had even less use for Ken than she'd had for Ryan; why was David so different?

He looked away, back out his own window. Jealousy wasn't going to get him anywhere, not with Holly. He didn't know what would, but he knew jealousy wasn't it.

Away from the shuttle and the noise of the kamikaze attack, they began to see more evidence of animal life. Flickers of quick motion in the treetops and down among the leaves on the forest floor were all they saw with their own eyes, but they froze the video image to reveal dozens of different birds and a handful of small, ratlike rodents of various shapes. They saw nothing resembling deer or large game of any sort, but they knew they would find some eventually. They had seen herds of animals from orbit.

The rover entered another clearing like the one they had landed in, but it was empty save for grass and a few insects. Sean drove them around it once, then headed off into the trees again along another trail when the circuit failed to turn up anything interesting. This trail seemed less well traveled; rocks gave them a bouncy ride and fallen logs barred the way on occasion, but Sean was able to drive around most of them, and the rover's fat tires and high ground clearance let them drive over those he couldn't go around. They wound their way up a gradual incline, down the other side, and into another clearing.

"Stop!" Mariko shouted as they nosed out of the trees, but Sean had already hit the brakes. There, grazing on the grass in the middle of the clearing, stood four enormous gray animals. One of them raised a massive head and looked toward the rover with four tiny eyes set two to a side in its long snout. It finished chewing a mouthful of grass, then lowered its head again and took another bite.

All four were about the size of small elephants, armored with thick scales over their entire bodies, and even thicker plates of bone or horn or something similar covering their heads. Ryan doubted if a .45 bullet would even get their attention, much less penetrate their hides.

"They look like dinosaurs," he whispered.

David nodded. "Triceratops without the horns."

"There's your defense against kamikazes," Sean said to Mariko.

"Sure enough." Mariko zoomed the camera in on the group, then backed out again and panned around the clearing to get good documentation of their surroundings. "Let's try driving around them and see how they react," she said when she was done.

"All right." Sean drove the rover out from under the trees and turned right to begin the circuit. Two of the creatures raised their heads to watch, and one took a step backwards, right onto the head of one of the two still grazing. For a second they just stood that way, then the one with its head pinned to the ground let out a bellow that shook the air and wrenched itself loose. The one who had stood on it regarded the other without concern, then bent down and began to eat again. After a moment the other did so as well.

David laughed. "Doesn't look like they're much for intelligence, are they?"

"They don't need it, not with all that armor," Mariko said.

"I suppose not."

The rover bounced around the clearing, Sean taking care not to drive over any of the slicer-dicer bushes or kamikaze patches in their way. At Mariko's urging he closed the distance with the dinosaur-like creatures by half and made a second circle, but even when he swerved toward them still more to avoid a slicer-dicer they ignored the rover completely.

"They have absolutely no curiosity, do they?" Mariko asked.

"Let's try some noise," Sean said, pushing the horn button. A loud honk echoed around the trees.

All four armored heads came up.

"That got their attention."

Sean honked the horn again. One of the creatures stepped forward, but the rump of the one in front of it blocked its progress. It turned ponderously until it found a clear path, stepped around its companion, and stood staring at the rover with its head cocked slightly to one side. It blinked one eye, then two more. The fourth eye quivered slightly, but stayed open.

"Clumsies," Mariko said with a giggle. "Or no, just clums. I dub thee 'clums.'"

"Clums?" asked Ryan.

"Sure," Mariko said. "It's descriptive enough, isn't it?"

Sean laughed. "And a group of them can be called a 'stumble.'"

"Perfect!"

"So what's a group of kamikazes, then?" David asked.

Mariko wrinkled her brow in thought. "A 'flight?' No, that's too plain. So's a 'squadron.' Hmm, let me think."

"How about a 'blast?'" Ryan suggested.

"A blast! Sure. You recording this up there?"

"Of course," Warren's voice answered from the speaker in the instrument panel in front of Mariko.

The clum that had been watching them took a step forward. Sean shifted the rover into reverse, but didn't back up until the clum took two more ponderous steps toward them. The clum kept coming, and Sean kept backing slowly away from it, but the clum speeded up until it began gaining on them. When it got within a dozen meters or so Sean shook his head and said, "Okay, enough of this." He swerved around broadside to the clum and turned to drive away from it, but before he could shift into forward gear the clum put on a burst of speed and crashed head-on into the rover's side just behind Ryan.

The side caved inward with a loud metallic squeal and a shower of broken glass. Cursing, Sean jammed the shifter into forward and the rover lurched ahead, pulling the clum, whose head was now embedded in the deformed metal, with it. The clum roared and shook itself loose, then charged again with surprising speed, smashing in the back door the same way it had smashed the side. The impact threw the rover forward, and now under power they sped away toward the edge of the clearing. The clum trotted after them a few steps, then stopped and went back to the others.

"Are you guys all right?" Warren shouted.

"Yeah, we're fine," Sean growled.

A rasping noise was coming from the wheel just behind Ryan. Sean stopped the rover, and the rasping stopped. "But it sounds like the rover may not be," he added. "All right, gang, let's have a look." He started to open his door, closed it again, and said, "Helmets."

David and Ryan dug the one already-ruined and three complete pressure suits out of the back and handed two of them forward.

While the others cut their helmets free, Ryan struggled into his Kevlar oversuit, wincing as the stretching motions pulled at his not-yet-healed wounds. He strapped on his pistol, put his helmet on, tucked the flaps of pressure suit fabric down inside the oversuit, zipped the oversuit up to the neck, and pulled its hood up over the helmet. When everyone else had done the same, they opened the doors and got out to inspect the damage.

The source of the rasping noise was readily apparent. The clum had practically molded the fender over the top of the right rear tire, and its lugs were rubbing against the metal. While Ryan kept an eye out for kamikazes or another clum attack and Mariko began collecting more vegetation and dirt samples from the clearing, Sean and David braced themselves against the tire and pulled the fender out so the tire could turn freely again.

Shaking his head at the twisted metal and broken windows, Sean said, "Well, it isn't pretty anymore, but it should still work." The pressure suit's radio and power source was all part of the helmet; Sean's voice was louder through that than through the air. He went around to the back and tried to open the door, but it was stuck tight. "This, on the other hand, is scrap." He nodded over at Ryan. "It looks like your planet is a little harder on equipment than Eden."

"My planet?" Ryan asked innocently, but despite his protest, Sean's words rang true. It *did* feel like Ryan's planet, created to order just for him after his trial with Ken. But, he wondered now, was it reward or punishment?

He looked out at the four grazing clums—a 'stumble' of them, he reminded himself—and shook his head. It wasn't a reward and it wasn't a punishment, either. It was just a planet, and his to explore.

"Well," he said, "let's go see what other kinds of damage we can do, then."

They found out soon enough. They decided to take a different trail back toward the shuttle from the clums' clearing, but the one they chose was even thicker with rocks and fallen logs than the last one and they had to crawl over each obstacle with care. After a kilometer or so of that the rover began to make a loud howling noise in the differential, and though Sean drove it as gently as he could from then on, they only got another half kilometer before it gave a loud bang and stopped completely.

When they got out and looked under the rover, they found the differential in pieces beneath it. "Well, this looks like the end of the road, guys," Sean said, leaning back in and switching off the power to the motor.

"Can we fix it?" David asked.

"Not with what we've got with us."

"Oh."

"What do we do now, then?" Ryan asked. "Walk?"

Warren broke in from the ship. "Negative. Let me bring the shuttle in on remote."

Sean snorted. "Hah. And where would you land it? We're in the middle of a forest."

"I can blast a spot for it."

"And start a fire. No."

Warren mulled that over for a moment, then said, "There's another clearing about a kilometer farther along in the direction you're headed. I'll bring the shuttle in over your path to scare off anything around, then land there and wait for you."

"Hold on a minute," Sean said in a stern voice. "We don't need rescuing just yet. We know how to avoid kamikazes, and we won't be stupid enough to get near any more clums, and we're protected against the vegetation, so there's no reason why we can't just walk on back to the shuttle. It's only four or five kilometers away as it is."

"No reason until you meet the next hostile lifeform. That place is crawling with 'em."

"Three," Sean argued. "Only three so far, and none of them

dangerous unless you get too close."

"But the next one might be dangerous at any distance."

"How about this," said David. "We've got to walk the kilometer to the next clearing anyway; why not wait until we get there to decide? We'll know more by then, and you can still beat us there if it turns out we need it."

Warren had to concede that David's plan made sense. The four explorers gathered up what they could carry from the rover—pistols and cameras and binoculars and Mariko's samples and bags and jars for more—and set off down the trail on foot.

Ryan carried the video camera, and he kept it running constantly as they walked, providing both audio and video feed to the ship in the hope that it would keep Warren from panicking and coming after them without need. Why he wanted that wasn't completely clear to him—by all rights he should have been eager for rescue—but he supposed he wanted to hold off as long as possible before having to declare "his" world a failure.

That they eventually would, though, seemed a foregone conclusion. How could they live on a world populated with flying bombs and knife-edged bushes and dinosaurs with short tempers? He didn't see how, not unless they wanted to continue living in sealed environments as if they'd never left the starship. And if that was the case, then what was the point? Why not just stay on the ship and be done with it? Ryan wondered if he could convince the crew that that would be better than going back to Eden. From his present perspective, he couldn't help wondering if it *would* be better. Of the three places he'd seen: ship, Eden, and here, Eden was by far the most comfortable place to live.

The sharp crack of an explosion from up ahead knocked him out of his reverie. Pistols drawn, the four explorers advanced around a curve in the trail to find a dead animal, one about a third the size of a clum but not as well shielded, obviously killed by kamikazes. Its body was nearly covered with them, and as Ryan zoomed in on them with the camera he saw that they were feeding. Tiny, razor-sharp beaks ripped and tore at the creature's flesh, some slicing outward from the ragged wound in its neck toward the tougher hide of its back while others pulled at the flaps of skin, flaying the carcass like a hundred tiny butchers skinning a rabbit.

Mariko, watching through her binoculars, laughed aloud in glee. "That's why they do it!"

"Do what?" Sean asked.

"Blow up. It's their way of getting food."

Sean considered that a moment before saying, "I don't know. That assumes altruism on a grand scale, 'cause if you're right then one of them's got to die before the rest of them get a meal. That doesn't seem like a good survival tactic."

"Neither does a bee's sting killing the bee, but they still evolved that way. If their reproduction rate's high enough, then some of them are expendable."

"But one for every meal?" Sean peered off into the forest on either side of the trail, decided on a direction, and led the way around the kamikaze kill, watching carefully for the nest.

Mariko, following him, said, "Could be. Or maybe they don't always eat meat, or if they do they don't always have to blow up to kill it. Who knows? But this proves that they don't do it just for the hell of it. There's a reason, and it ties into the rest of the ecosystem." Mariko turned around to look pointedly at David as she spoke.

David shrugged his shoulders. "I don't argue with that. But if you want to re-open that subject, I'll point out that fitting into the ecosystem isn't sufficient evidence to deny creation. Even God would have to create an ecosystem that worked, unless He wanted to intervene continuously."

"And why wouldn't He?" Mariko asked, again following Sean. "If you postulate His presence—using the male pronoun only for convenience, of course—then why shouldn't He intervene all the time?"

"Maybe He does," said David, holding out his hands in a palms-up, who-knows sort of gesture. "Maybe the laws of physics as we understand them are just a statistical pattern behind divine intervention. Evidence of His preference in the outcome of otherwise chaotic events, if you will. And maybe the larger things—kamikazes, for instance—are His way of making statements, like saying we don't belong here."

The matter-of-fact way David said it hit Ryan like a jolt of electricity. "God God God God God!" he shouted. "Signs and portents! Where do you get off with all this God business? What happened to your scientific objectivity?"

David stopped walking and turned to face Ryan. He had reddened slightly, but whether from embarrassment or anger it was hard to tell. "Nothing's happened to my objectivity," he said in a gruff voice. "It's objectivity that's led me to believe in God in the first place." Ryan started to protest, but David cut him off. "You want to know why I believe in God? I'll tell you why. Remember when I first found evidence that Eden was habitable? I fudged the data so it wouldn't look so coincidental, but you know what else was going on at the same time. Ken was using an ancient prayer ritual to ask God for a habitable planet at the *very moment* I got the spectral readout. Think of the odds against that. Calling it coincidence is ignoring the truth."

David crossed his arms over his chest. "And then when we actually got there, what did we find? A perfect planet, even better suited to human life than Earth. Again, the odds for that happening by accident are incredibly slim, especially now when we see what sort of exotic creatures are possible. That's too much coincidence. I see clear evidence of purposeful action."

Ryan scowled. "And I see rational inquiry retreating for the comfort of easy answers. There are a million possible reasons why things worked out the way they did, but you wanted a quick explanation, so you just made something up. That's not objectivity;

that's self-delusion. Religion is an attempt to explain the universe without understanding it."

"It's a different way of *looking* at the universe," David replied. "A more holistic way."

"And that holistic way of looking at things makes you think this whole planet was created just to make us go back to Eden?"

"I don't know," David said. "That's a big assumption. Maybe it has a purpose of its own, a purpose completely unrelated to humanity. But it does seem reasonably clear we don't belong here."

Just a few minutes earlier Ryan's own thoughts had led him toward the same conclusion without the help of God, but now he said, "I'll believe that when we find intelligent life here as well. Not before."

"Or when something succeeds in killing one of us," David said.

Mariko had stopped just beyond David and was listening to their argument with an amused expression on her face. Sean had continued on a dozen or so paces away and was waiting for the others to catch up. He wasn't amused at all. "*I'm* going to kill somebody if you don't shut up and get moving. Come on. We can debate theology later; right now we've got a job to do."

Neither Ryan nor David wanted to drop it, but one look at Sean's face and they fell into line. Sean led them in a wide arc through the forest, rejoining the trail well beyond the feeding kamikazes. His threat, rhetorical as it was, carried weight; they were silent for long minutes at a time, and even then only broke it to point out interesting new vegetation or, more rarely, new birds or insects along the trail.

They rounded another bend in the trail, and ahead of them they could see the light between tree trunks that signified another clearing. Cautiously, Sean led them forward until they could hide behind the last few trees and peer around them into the meadow.

Something was out there. Half a dozen somethings, it looked like, and Ryan felt his subjective universe shudder under the blow as he made sense of what he was seeing. The creatures were definitely alien, looking more like horses than humans and not much like either, but the three-wheeled vehicles they rode were more proof than even opposable thumbs could have been: here was Ryan's intelligent life.

CHAPTER TWENTY

SIGNS AND PORTENTS

"So," RYAN SAID, "do we try to talk with them or do we just quietly steal away to the ship and go home?"

He wasn't sure if he was being facetious or not. All the way out from Earth, the thought of meeting a true tool-using intelligence had been one of the most exciting possibilities he'd considered, but now after seeing what kind of damage even a simple case of idea contamination could do, he wasn't sure they ought to let their presence be known to creatures who had already discovered the wheel.

Sean shook his head. "I don't know, but whatever you do, Warren, don't fly the shuttle in here."

"Roger," Warren said.

"What I'd like to know," said David, "is why we didn't hear anything on the radio spectrum. If they've got powered vehicles, they should have radio."

Mariko chuckled softly. "Maybe God didn't think to give it to them."

"Shut it," Sean warned. "Ryan, zoom in on them with the camera. See if you can see what they're using for a power source."

"Right." Bracing the camera against the side of the tree he was hiding behind—one of the tall, spirally growing ones, whose leaves weren't sharp after all—he pushed the telephoto button and watched the video image swell in the eyepiece. He stopped when one of the creatures filled the screen and panned with it as it rolled forward a few meters and lowered its head to the ground to eat.

The vehicle seemed almost part of its body, so smoothly did it blend in. It had two wheels in front and one in back, but no matter how hard Ryan looked for an engine or controls or even a seat for the rider, he couldn't see any of those features. It looked almost as if the creature—a sort of three-legged, yellowish-red llama seen through a distorting mirror—was simply standing on a set of wheels.

"Well?" Sean asked.

Ryan looked up from the camera. "Have you ever seen roller blades?"

"What?" Sean asked.

"Roller blades. Wheels you strap on your feet." Ryan had once spent a lazy afternoon in the library looking at a compilation of fads, and there had been video of people swooping around on a cement courtyard at some university.

"Why would anyone want to put wheels on their feet?" Sean asked. "You'd fall right over, wouldn't you?"

"Not the people I saw," Ryan said. "Anyway, these guys look like the original inspiration for them. I don't see any power source at all. Just a wheel at the end of each leg."

Sean looked out toward the creatures again. "There's got to be a power source. They're not pushing off like they'd have to if they were just wearing big wheels on their feet."

"I'm just reporting what I see." Ryan looked back into the eyepiece and zoomed in even closer on one of the wheels. "It's definitely leg all the way down," he reported. "Unless the framework is covered with hair for some reason. The legs don't split to hold the axle on either side like you'd expect for a metal frame, either. There's just one point of attachment and that's on the inside hub in front and on the left in back. I can't see how they're holding onto the axle; the leg just comes to a big round knob there. Looks like they tilt the wheel a little so their weight bears straight down on the rim.

The wheel itself looks kind of rough on the surface, more like tree bark than a regular tread pattern. Now that I think about it, the whole wheel looks like a section sliced out of a tree. It's solid, and I can see concentric rings in it."

"It does," Mariko said. She was looking with her binoculars. "It looks biological," she whispered. "It's all part of the animal. They grow their own wheels."

"Impossible," Warren said over the radio.

"You're getting the same picture," Mariko replied. "What do *you* make of it, then?"

"Give me a good steady image for a minute." Ryan obliged him, and after a long pause Warren said, "I don't know. It certainly *looks* natural, but how can it be? How could anything evolve a wheel?"

"How could something evolve an explosive? How could it evolve a leg, for that matter? Trial and error. Trial and error and lots of time."

"But wheels are terrible on uneven ground. How would they get over a fallen log?"

Mariko shrugged. "Maybe they can lock up the wheels and walk on them like hooves. Who knows?"

David cleared his throat and said, "Or maybe they were genetically engineered. They might have been made this way on purpose."

"By God?" Ryan asked sarcastically.

"By anyone with the capability, God included."

"Hah," Ryan grunted. "And where's the evidence for *them*?"

"Maybe we're looking at it."

Ryan had no answer to that. Maybe they were. He didn't know what to think.

Sean took the binoculars from Mariko, looked through them for a moment, then passed them to David. "That still doesn't answer the main question: are *these* guys intelligent or not?"

Mariko said, "I'd be willing to bet they're just animals. They've got no opposable thumbs."

"Neither do the customs agents," Ryan pointed out.

"Customs agents have tentacles. These things don't. All they've got are mouths and wheels."

Sean looked back around his tree at the creatures. "It looks that way from here, anyway. Hmm." He looked back to his three companions, cocked his head in thought, and finally came to a decision. "We've got to find out sometime, I suppose. But just in case things aren't what they seem, let's take the chicken approach. Ryan, you and David stay hidden and cover us while Mariko and I go have a closer look. Warren, get the shuttle ready for liftoff in case things get out of hand."

Some part of Ryan didn't like the idea of letting someone else do the exploring. He'd liked it better when it was just him and Sean doing everything together. But even so, he realized the wisdom of what Sean suggested. Somebody should cover from the trees, and it made sense that one of those somebodies be Ryan. He had already been wounded once today; the medkit spray held him together, but he wasn't healed yet. If he had to run suddenly or jump out of the way of a charging alien, he might do himself still more harm.

"Shuttle is ready," Warren said.

"All right, let's go." Sean stepped out from behind his tree and motioned Mariko to do the same. Together they walked along the trail into the clearing, their white oversuits glowing in the sun when they stepped out of the shade. Sean, his right hand hovering close to his pistol, looked like a gunfighter advancing on his adversary.

The wheeled aliens raised their heads and fixed their eyes on the approaching humans. Ryan saw only two eyes per head this time. The creature in front raised its left front wheel and stamped it down on the ground, and three of the others rolled around to flank it on either side. The two smallest ones stayed behind the others.

"Herd behavior," Mariko remarked. "Protecting the young from attack."

"Let's not get too close, then," Sean said. He stopped less than a third of the way toward the creatures and slowly reached up and took off his helmet. They backed up a meter or so at the sight, but didn't break their formation.

"Hello," Sean called to them. "Can you talk? Tell me, where did you get those crazy wheels?"

The leader of the group waved its head back and forth as if trying to see something hidden, but it didn't seem to be looking at Sean or Mariko. It didn't seem to be looking at the spot where Ryan and David waited, either, but farther to their right, off into the forest behind them. Suddenly it let out a squeal like a stepped-on squeeze toy and the entire herd turned and rolled away across the meadow faster than the rover could have gone under full power.

"What did you do?" Sean demanded, turning around to face Ryan and David.

"Nothing," they said in chorus. Ryan added, "They just spooked. I don't know what—"

A low growl from behind him coincided with the sharp crack of a branch, and a sudden weight smashed Ryan face first into his hiding-tree. He toppled onto his side and found himself staring into the open mouth of yet another alien creature, this one a blur of shaggy brown fur and yellow teeth and enormous, curved, sharp black claws. It roared and reached down to take a bite out of Ryan's head.

"Shoot it!" he shouted, scrambling frantically for his pistol, but he had fallen on it and the creature had him pinned. He could see David backing away, a look of fascinated horror on his face, but he wasn't drawing his gun. "Shoot it!" Ryan screamed again.

The beast's jaws looked just about big enough to enclose Ryan's entire head, pressure suit helmet and all. It seemed to be taking measurements, lowering and tilting first one way and then the other, drool dripping onto Ryan's faceplate all the while. It grunted a deep "Huh, huh, huh" while it tried to figure out where the vulnerable spot might be in its unusual prey.

Ryan could hear a babble of excited voices in his ears as Sean and Mariko and Warren all shouted to ask what was happening, but the person foremost in his mind was David, standing only a few steps away. Why didn't David shoot?

That was obvious. If a wild beast messily devoured Ryan on the first exploration trip, then the colony would almost certainly go back to Eden. David had as much as said so only a few minutes earlier. It would be a most convenient "act of God," and all David had to do was let it happen.

The beast came to a decision. "Shoot it, you son of a bitch!" Ryan screamed again as it extended its jaws as far as they could go and bit into his helmet. All he could see now were fangs and the dark, wet interior of its mouth.

Ryan kicked out with all the force he could muster, hoping to hit something sensitive on its underside, but even so, the effect on the creature was far more than he imagined possible. He heard a dull thud and felt the creature flinch, then with a scream of rage it let go of his head, whirled around to face David, and swiped out at him with a paw.

Without all the meat around his helmet dulling the sound, Ryan heard David's second shot clearly. The beast howled in agony and fell backward as a third shot ripped a furrow across its side. Ryan saw fur and bone explode outward from another shot to its head, another straight into its side, and another under the jaw before it collapsed across his legs and tried to curl up into a ball. Holding the pistol out at the end of a wildly shaking arm, David advanced until the barrel was only inches from one of the thing's eyes and fired his last shot. The beast quivered and lay still.

"Ryan, talk to me!" David's voice was a high-pitched squeak.

"Thanks," Ryan managed to grunt. He tried to raise up on his arms, but the one he had landed on didn't want to cooperate. He lay back down and said, "I was afraid you were going to let it get me."

"I—I froze for a minute. Christ, I'm sorry. I couldn't move. Are you okay?"

Sean and Mariko skidded to a stop beside them. "Are you okay?" Sean echoed. He was holding his helmet on with one hand while he holstered his pistol with the other.

Ryan hurt all over, but he'd hurt plenty before the attack. "I don't know," he said. "Why don't you get that thing off my legs and I'll see."

It took all three of them to drag it off him. He managed to sit up, and was relieved to find that his arm didn't feel broken, just twisted and bruised. He looked down at the beast that had attacked him, tilting his head sideways to see past the starred crack in his helmet from one of its teeth. The thing was monster enough for horror movies, with its shaggy brown fur matted with blood—red as regular blood, Ryan noted—and a long, toothy snout and claws the size of a man's fingers at the end of two oversized arms; but the effect was somehow spoiled by the wheels at the ends of its three legs.

"So, what do we call something like this?" he asked.

"Biker," Sean replied, and in answer to Ryan's questioning look, he added, "It's got long hair and a mean disposition."

"Oh."

A scream of engines drowned out further comment. They turned to watch the creatures in the meadow disappear into the trees on the far side, and moments later their shuttle settled to the ground in a swirl of dirt and grass.

"Think you can walk?" Sean asked.

"Let's give it a try." Ryan held out his hands to be pulled up, wobbled a minute on legs sore from supporting the weight of the 'biker,' but with Sean on one side and Mariko on the other to hold him up, he was able to make it to the shuttle and cycle through the airlock to collapse again in one of the acceleration chairs.

"Not yet," Sean said. He made him get back up and helped him off with his helmet and clothing one more time, then made him lie back on the floor while he went over him with the medkit again. Most of Ryan's cuts from the slicer-dicer bush had reopened, but now he also had the beginnings of big red bruises to keep them company.

Sean shook his head in dismay. "If you hadn't been wearing that oversuit, you'd be missing some parts, pilgrim."

"Tell me about it."

David had remained silent through the entire process, staring out the window, but now he spoke up to say, "I'm sorry I didn't shoot it sooner. I don't know what happened. I just froze."

"It happens," Sean said. "You got it in time anyway, so don't be so hard on yourself."

David looked down to Ryan, his face reflecting the same horror he had shown when the biker attacked. "You thought I was waiting on purpose, didn't you?" he whispered.

"The thought did cross my mind," Ryan admitted.

"You—you really thought I could do that?"

Ryan shrugged, and winced in pain. "I don't know what to expect from you anymore. I thought maybe you'd think it was a sign God wanted me dead, and let it happen."

"I couldn't—" David dropped his head into his hands and shook it back and forth. "No. That's not the way it works." He looked back over at Ryan. "If God wants to give me a sign, He'll have to make it clear. Absolutely clear, especially when somebody's life lies in the balance. If He wants you dead, then He'll have to make sure I can't prevent it."

"Like maybe by making you freeze up?"

"Hey, the guy saved your life," said Sean. "Lighten up."

Ryan looked away, embarrassed. "Sorry." He took a deep breath, looked back at David. "All right. I mean it, I'm sorry. I shouldn't have thought that of you, but I did and I'm sorry. But with all this talk about God and what He wants and doesn't want—all this unsubstantiated speculation accepted without question—and then seeing you stand there while I was being attacked, I just jumped to the wrong conclusion."

"I...guess that's understandable," said David. "After what Ken did."

Mariko, working on something in her instrument rack, said, "What about Ken? What about the rest of these 'signs' we were talking about? Does God have to make Himself perfectly clear about where we ought to colonize, too?"

"In order for it to affect the decision, yes."

"Then how come you're so hot to go back to Eden? That's far from being the obvious choice."

David's eyes widened in surprise. "Is it? You think we should stay here, on a planet where the hummingbirds can blow your head off and the bushes can cut you in two and hairy monsters jump you from behind?"

Mariko turned away from her instruments. Red and amber lights winked on the panel behind her as she advanced on David. "You think we should go back and finish the job we started with the customs agents? Take the easy route even if it kills off a developing race? Is that the way your God works?"

"We don't know everything about the customs agents. We could be mistaken about them."

"And we could be mistaken about God, too. Either one of us. But let's suppose for a minute He does exist, just for the sake of argument. Suppose He set all this up for us to find. Has it ever occurred to you that it might be a test?"

"A test?" David echoed.

"A test. To see what choice we'd make. That's a lot more in line with the way the biblical God works. He gives us free will, but it's up to us to use it wisely, and He's always testing to see if we're worthy. So what if He wants to see how humanity behaves when we go into space? What's He going to do? He's going to set up a test, give us a moral dilemma and see how we react. I couldn't think of a much better test than this. But if that's what it is, that changes the picture a little bit, doesn't it?"

Ryan remembered asking Ken the same thing once before, during their last argument on Eden, but Ken had brushed the question aside without even considering it. David at least considered it, but even so, the result was the same. "It would if the situation weren't already clear," he replied simply. "If this were a test, then there would *be* a choice." He looked out the window again and said, "But how in God's name could we choose this?"

CHAPTER TWENTY-ONE

A HERO'S WELCOME

"I WANT YOU BACK UP here immediately." The voice was Holly's, but Ryan didn't like the sound of it.

"I'm perfectly all right," he said. "Look." He held out his arms and did a muscle-man flex before the intercom camera. He was still nude, but that only seemed to be hurting his case. The spray adhesive had resealed his cuts, but his bruises were turning purple now, and even messing with the color balance on the intercom couldn't hide them from her.

"All right? Ryan, you've got the worst injuries I've ever *seen*, and that's just on the surface. What about internal bleeding? Have you checked your CBC? Liver enzymes? Creatinine? You could be bleeding to death and not know it."

"Mariko can check all that, can't you Mariko?"

Mariko was standing beside Ryan, but Holly didn't give her a chance to answer. "Mariko is not a doctor. *I'm* the doctor, and I want you up here where I can take care of you."

"I agree," Mariko said. Ryan turned to shoot her a look of betrayal, but she stared right back and said, "I don't want you cratering on *me*. Besides, we've learned plenty for our first foray. I'd like to take our biker body back to the ship and see what makes it tick. And roll."

"Sean?"

Ryan turned to his best friend, but Sean shook his head and

said, "They're right, paleface. Time to hit the showers and think this over before we try it again." He leaned down next to Ryan to get into the intercom view and said to Holly, "We'll be up as soon as we get the biker loaded."

"Good." She smiled. "Cheer up, Ryan. I'll have you put back together in no time."

Ryan scowled. Doctors. First they said you were about to die, and then they said you'd be fine. So which was it?

Ryan once again waited in the shuttle, monitoring the autopilot's com laser targeting while Sean and Mariko and David went out to collect the dead biker. Sean started to cut down a small tree with a hand saw to use as a carrying pole while Mariko and David went over to the biker to tie ropes to its arms and legs. They had just bent down over it when Mariko shouted, "Look out!" and jumped back. Ryan could see her waving her arms frantically while a dark speck darted in and out around her head.

The com laser lanced out toward the kamikaze, but instead of the explosion Ryan expected, it merely fell to the ground in a smoking lump.

"What the—" Mariko bent down and flipped the kamikaze over with a stick. "It didn't blow."

Sean, standing with saw in one hand and pistol in the other, asked, "But the autopilot hit it?"

"Dead on."

"Huh. Is it different from the others?"

"Not so's you'd notice, aside from being half burnt."

"Well, keep a lookout for more." Sean holstered his pistol and returned to his sawing, evidently confident that the autopilot could protect them from attack. He cut through the tree in four or five quick pulls, topped it and sawed off the branches, then dragged the pole over to the biker, where they tied it on and David and Sean lifted it to their shoulders.

Mariko reached out and gingerly picked up the kamikaze by its tail, holding it at arm's length. Neither Sean nor David complained about the division of labor.

Ryan dropped the cargo hatch for them when they reached the shuttle, then helped tie the biker to the latches that had previously held the rover while Mariko found a rigid sample canister for the dead kamikaze. She looked dubiously at the canister, then stripped off her oversuit and wrapped that around it. "That ought to contain the blast if he decides to go off after all," she said as she tied it to the floor beside the biker.

Sean pulled off his helmet and unzipped his own oversuit. Tossing the whole works into a locker, he went forward into the control section to warm up the engines for the ride back to the ship.

Holly was waiting for them when they arrived. She took all four of them straight to quarantine, but this time instead of sharing a room, Ryan's injuries earned him one to himself. It was a regular examination room fitted with an airlock, which Holly—wearing an emergency pressure suit—followed him through immediately upon his arrival. Inside he found a bed in one corner, an exam table in the middle of the room, and a cart full of medical instruments beside the exam table. Holly instructed him to strip and lie down on the table, then immediately began poking and prodding and taking blood pressure and blood samples, the suit hardly slowing her down a bit.

She kept up a running commentary as she worked, scolding him for continuing to explore despite his injuries, accusing him of hyperactive machismo glands, and threatening to give him a lobotomy for his own protection. When she had proven to her satisfaction that he wasn't in immediate danger of bleeding to death, she handed him a plastic cup with a lid and told him she wanted a urine specimen, "...to see if you've damaged your insides as thoroughly as you have your outside."

Ryan examined the cup without moving from the table. "I'm

glad to see you, too," he said without looking up.

Holly jerked back as if he'd slapped her. Turning away, she reached up as if to run her hands through her hair, but encountered the helmet instead.

"Damn it," she swore. "*Damn* it." She stood there for a moment with her hands on her helmet, then lowered them to neck level and with a quick downward motion, unzipped her suit. She peeled out of it in jerky, frustrated motions, threw it away from her to land helmet-first with a loud *clunk* by the airlock, and turned to face Ryan once again. The fire in her eyes would have scared even Ken.

Ryan tried to sit up, but she pinned him down with a stare. "Don't move," she growled. "You want glad to see you? I'll give you glad to see you." She took his shoulders in her hands, pushed him flat against the exam table, and bent down to plant a lip-bruising kiss full on his open, astonished mouth.

This was no sisterly kiss. Ryan had time to get over his shock, time to kiss back, time to put his arms around her and pull her down against him, time to feel the effect of her kiss in every neuron in his body.

It could have been an hour, for all he knew, before they finally came up for air. His time sense had stopped completely. Holly again pinned him to the table with the intensity of her stare as she whispered, "Is this what you want? Okay, I'm glad to see you. I'm glad you're alive. But don't you ever, *ever* scare me like that again, do you hear me?"

Ryan could only answer with a nod.

Holly stood and backed away, smoothing her lab coat while she fought to bring her breathing rate down to normal. "Now," she said, "I wasn't kidding when I said I wanted a urine sample. Clean catch. The instructions are on the bathroom door."

Ryan nodded again. He slid around to sitting position on the exam table, looked up into her eyes once more, and finally found his voice. Nodding toward her discarded pressure suit, he said, "You shouldn't have taken that off. I could have some horrible, communicable alien disease."

"Hah," she snorted. "I'm the doctor around here. I decide who's got alien diseases and who doesn't."

"Sure you do."

Holly pointed toward the bathroom. "Urine sample."

"All right." Ryan slid off the exam table and carried his plastic cup into the bathroom, but it was a good ten minutes before he could calm down enough to do the job.

Holly was wearing her isolation suit again when he stepped out with the filled cup in his hand. Neither of them said anything about either the suit or the time he had taken. She simply took the cup from him, set it on the tray alongside the blood tubes she had filled earlier, and told him to lie back down on the exam table. Quickly, with a minimum of words, she took skin scrapings from his hands and feet and smeared them on already-labeled microscope slides, ran a fine-toothed comb through his hair and put comb and all in a baggie, and made him stick his hands against a plate of growth medium. When she was done she said, "You can shower now, but be careful with your lacerations. The adhesive isn't water-soluble, but you could still pull it loose and there's a limit to how many times you can do that before you scar." Without waiting for a reply, she picked up her tray and carried it into the airlock, waited for the ultraviolet light to sterilize the outside of her suit, and cycled through.

She would have to keep wearing it now. By exposing herself to Ryan, she had become just as contaminated as he was. She apparently didn't think that was much of a risk, but he knew she wouldn't endanger the rest of the ship by opening her suit to the general environment.

He wondered where she would sleep.

The examination room didn't have the transparent wall his and Sean's earlier quarantine room had. Without it, when Holly left him he felt truly alone, with only his thoughts for company. They were small comfort, jumbled as they were. He got up and showered, dressed in a pair of pajamas he found in the clothing locker, and lay back on the bed. He amused himself for a few minutes with the Velcro seams in the pajamas, no doubt designed to allow a doctor easy access to any part of her patient she needed to reach without moving him. Ryan could think of other uses for such a pair of pajamas. He imagined Holly ripping them from him in a moment of lustful abandon, shedding her own clothing just as easily...

Get real, he thought. He'd already been naked as vacuum when she kissed him. She'd been as lustfully abandoned as he'd ever seen her, and she'd still kept her lab coat on the whole time. He certainly didn't feel disappointed—it had been an exciting enough moment as it was—but he had enough detachment to realize that they were still a long way from having sex on an examination table.

Still, they were undoubtedly closer than before. He closed his eyes and relived the moment again, a sardonic smile spreading slowly across his face. To think, all this time he'd been trying to impress her, when what he'd needed to do was get her worried instead. Worried and mad.

But how would she act toward him once she settled down? Would she be her normal, aloof self again, or was this a permanent change of heart?

His thoughts spiraled around and around the subject, looking at it from every angle he could think of, but there was simply no way to predict what would happen. He would just have to wait and see.

He needed a distraction, then, because every time he let his mind drift he came back to the same question. He looked around the room, but it was practically bare. Nobody had stocked it for his arrival like last time. He wondered why not, then realized that he'd been gone less than a day, and it was the middle of the night on board the ship.

Still, somebody should have at least called, shouldn't they? He got up and went over to the intercom on the wall. It was a mobile model, mounted on an arm, and sure enough, it was set to "do not disturb." He tapped the "on line" icon and asked, "Mac, do I have any messages?"

"You have three," control program responded. "Shall I play them for you?"

"Please."

He sat down in the chair beside the intercom and pulled the screen down to eye level. It flickered static for a second, then Ryan's mother smiled out at him. "Holly tells me you're going to live. I'm glad to hear it; you had me worried. Call me when you get out of the shower. Love you."

She winked out, to be replaced by Michelle with essentially the same message.

After Michelle came Laura. Her laugh wrinkles were scrunched up tight, and she said simply, "Welcome back. I predict interesting times ahead. Hang onto your hat." She winked out in the true sense of the word, one eye shuttered in the ancient gesture of conspiracy.

What in the world was she talking about? Could she have known what Holly would do? Just how good a judge of character was she, anyway?

The intercom chimed for attention. Ryan waited through the second ring, then pushed the accept button. Kristy Crawford smiled hesitantly out at him. "Hello, Ryan."

He felt a blush coming on, as he had every time he encountered her since their time together on Eden. "Uh, hi Kristy."

"Hi. I'm glad you're all right."

Holly must have made a ship wide announcement while he was in the shower, Ryan realized. "Thanks," he said. "So am I."

"I—I've been thinking about you a lot lately. I haven't said anything because I didn't want to seem pushy, especially after the way I, well, the way I propositioned you on Eden, but I've still been thinking about you a lot."

Ryan didn't know what to say. He'd been stupid; of course she would think about him, just as he was always thinking of Holly. He'd been so hung up on his own problems that he hadn't even considered what Kristy was going through.

"I, uh, well, I've thought about you a time or two myself," he told her, knowing there were two meanings to a line like that. He knew which way she would take it, too, but he couldn't bring himself to let her down, not now.

She nodded. "I've thought a lot about what you told me down there, too, about waiting until somebody, well, makes me feel the way you did just by thinking about them." She looked down at something off screen. Was she reading notes? Good grief, how long had she been struggling to say this?

She looked back up at him. "I asked Laura about it, and she said I ought to just come out with it. So here it is: Ryan, I feel that way about you. I can't get you off my mind, and I don't want to anyway. Maybe I don't know what love is, not really, but I think I'm in love with you."

So that was what Laura's cryptic warning had been about. Kristy had fallen for him, big time. He knew from experience that telling her it wasn't mutual wouldn't change that a bit, either. The more distant he got, the harder she would try.

He shook his head. "I don't know what to say. I guess I never really considered the possibility."

"*Will* you consider it?"

He watched her watching him expectantly, waiting for him to turn her down, and he just couldn't do it. Not like this, over the intercom, not after what she'd had to have gone through to call him in the first place. "Of course I will," he said. "But I'm not going to lie to you, either. It might not work out. And even if it does, you know Michelle and I already see each other a lot. And I've also got a crush of my own on Holly. That's not likely to change, no matter what happens between you and me."

Kristy smiled. This was evidently still more than she'd expected. "I can share," she said.

"Maybe. Think about it. You might be better off falling in love with someone else." The moment he said it, he realized how inane that advice was. He'd be a million times better off loving someone besides Holly, and had that mattered to him? Not a bit. But maybe Kristy was more logical than he was.

Somehow he doubted it. Love wasn't logical, not for anybody.

"Tell you what," he said. "We really don't know each other very well at all. When I get out of quarantine let's get together and just talk for a while, find out if we've got anything in common. Okay?"

"Okay."

"It's a date, then."

"All right."

Ryan hesitated. What did he say now? The moment was about to become awkward, but Kristy salvaged it by saying, "You won't regret it. 'Bye."

"'Bye," he echoed, and the screen swirled into static. He leaned back in his chair and closed his eyes. Had he done the right thing? He wanted to spare Kristy the torment he'd gone through with Holly, but he wondered if encouraging her now only to discourage her later would actually be worse in the long run. He didn't know.

Why do you want to discourage her, anyway? a tiny voice asked.

Why indeed? Monogamy was the custom aboard ship, not the rule. What was to keep him from seeing Kristy as well as Michelle and Holly? If all three liked him, why should he have to choose between them?

Because he wanted only one, that was why. If Holly's angry kiss had truly meant anything, then he wanted only her.

And if it didn't?

He didn't want to think about that. To take his mind off it, he returned his mother's call, and after a few minutes' thought he returned Michelle's call as well. He didn't tell her about Holly or Kristy. He felt a pang of guilt at what seemed too close to deception, but he wanted some time to think it over first. He had her feelings to consider, too.

His head hurt. Ryan thumbed the intercom to "do not disturb" again and padded back to the bed. He pulled the sheets down, crawled in, turned out the light, and stared into the darkness. Sleep was a long time coming, but the dreams were wild.

CHAPTER TWENTY-TWO

A MORAL DILEMMA

HE WOKE TO THE SOUND of the airlock cycling open. It was still dark in the room. He reached out for the light switch just as whoever it was in the airlock reached for the one by the door; there was a brief flash of brightness, then dark again. He flipped his switch the other way and there was another momentary flash of light. He decided to wait for his visitor to turn on the light, realized they were waiting for him, and flipped the switch again. Another flash as whoever it was came to the same conclusion.

"All right," Ryan said into the darkness. "You do it."

The light came on and stayed lit, revealing Holly, still in her pressure suit.

She smiled at him from beside the airlock, but she carried a plastic tray full of blood tubes, needles, a pressure cuff, and a few other instruments Ryan recognized from before.

"I should have known," he said, sitting up in bed and running a hand through his hair to get it out of his eyes.

"Good morning to you, too." Holly's smile dimmed a bit. She walked over to the bed, set down her tray on the night stand, and took a blood tube and a needle from it.

"Is this routine, or have I got an alien bug?" he asked.

"Routine," she said, tying the tourniquet around his upper arm, wiping the inside of his left elbow with an alcohol swab, and deftly going for the vein with the needle before Ryan had a chance to protest. She stuck a tube with a red stopper onto the needle.

He watched blood begin to fill the evacuated tube, then looked up at Holly's face. She kept her attention on her work, but he didn't need to see her eyes to know what she was thinking about.

"Sorry I made you mad yesterday," he said.

"No you're not." She didn't look up.

He laughed. "You're right, I'm not."

Blood continued to well up in the tube.

"Are you?" he asked.

"Sorry you made me mad, or sorry that I kissed you?"

"Either one."

She met his eyes for a moment, then looked back down. "I'm sorry you opened this whole can of worms."

Ryan had actually opened a can of worms once, to replenish a garden plot where they had died out. He blanked out the image and looked at Holly's face in profile inside the bubble helmet. Her eyelashes quivered ever so slightly.

"It needed opening," he said.

"No it didn't."

"I think what happened yesterday proved otherwise."

Holly pulled the nearly-full tube off the needle and replaced it with a purple-topped one. "You think we needed this? Ryan, we were doing fine before you went on this macho crusade to prove yourself."

"You're pairing with David. I don't call that fine."

"David's a good man."

"He's a religious wacko."

She glanced over at him again. "Is that what you think? That anyone who believes in God is a wacko?"

"Pretty much. But this isn't really about David, is it? Or religion. I want to talk about you and me."

"I don't." The blood flow had stopped. She pulled the needle outward a couple millimeters and it started up again. "I want to go back to the way it was before we got here. I want to have you for a friend, and I want the ship to be full of hope and dreams again, and I want—"

"You want to make sure you don't lose me. You'd rather not risk getting intimate because you don't want to risk *not* being intimate later on if it doesn't work." He hadn't really believed it when Michelle had told him that, but now it seemed more likely to be true.

Holly wasn't buying it. "Bullshit," she said.

"Then you won't object if I go back down to the surface again as soon as I'm healed?"

She looked up at him again. "Of course I would, but it has nothing to do with how I feel about you. As the person in charge of patching you up, I think it's ridiculous to risk your life on a planet that's obviously uninhabitable."

"Who says it's uninhabitable?"

"Who says—Ryan, the place nearly killed you in less than a day!"

"Aaaghhh! The needle."

Holly looked down, released the tourniquet, calmly pulled the needle and tube out of his arm, and gave him a cotton ball from her tray to hold against the wound. "Which reminds me," she said, uncapping a pen and labeling the tubes of blood, "Mariko's doing an autopsy on the biker. She told me to tell you when you got up."

"Oh. Thanks."

Holly picked up the tray and walked over to the airlock. She turned at the door. "Sorry I hurt you," she said.

Ryan wondered if she was talking about jiggling the needle or screwing with his head or not agreeing with him about the planet. Maybe all three. But there was one cure for all his hurts. "You could kiss it better."

She frowned. "Don't count on it."

She cycled through the airlock before he could think of a response.

Mariko was smiling. Ryan could see her grin even through the reflections from bright overhead lights on her isolation suit helmet. He could also see more than he really wanted to of the inside of an alien predator, but his fascination was just strong enough to keep revulsion at bay.

Mariko was taking no chances. Her entire lab had been sealed off from the rest of the ship, but she wore the suit anyway, just in case another nasty surprise awaited her inside the biker. Ryan sat alone in his quarantine room, wearing pajamas and watching Mariko via intercom. Quite a few others were no doubt watching as well.

The biker was a mess. Seven .45 caliber hollow points targeted more or less at random had left few unspoiled areas for investigation. Mariko hadn't been smiling when she opened its chest cavity and tried to identify the major organs, but now that job was over and she was working on what she'd wanted to examine all along: the wheels.

That they were part of the creature and not artifacts was obvious up close. The rings Ryan had seen earlier on the grazers' wheels were indeed growth rings, and the rough tread came from cracks formed by their annual expansion. How the hubs worked was still a mystery, but becoming less of one every minute. Mariko had flayed the skin off one and was working her way inward layer by layer, finding new arrangements for familiar structures at every turn.

"Look at the way the artery joins to the wheel," she pointed out to her electronic audience. "I thought the blood supply would have to go in through the axle somehow, but instead it attaches outside, like a cap over the bearing. This layer of cartilage evidently seals tight enough to keep it from leaking even when it's rolling." She lifted a flap of brownish material with a tweezer. "Sure, look here. This muscle running all the way around the edge squeezes down to seal it off." She turned the wheel over, examined the similar structure on the other side, and nodded. "The vein goes through the axle and does the same thing on the other side. Blood goes in one side, through the wheel, and out the other side, even while it's moving. Elegant. But that still doesn't tell us how the thing rotates in the first place. I think it's time to cut it open."

Ryan studied the wall while Mariko used a hand saw to open up the wheel, but when she said, "Hah, look at that," he turned back to the intercom. She had cut a chord deep into the circle, just missing the axle, and now held an unequal half in either hand. She held one of the freshly cut edges up to the camera, and Ryan saw that in the middle was a separate piece of bone or something similar that was free to move like a rotor in a disk brake, except when it was whole that part would be attached to the axle bone and would stay put while the wheel rotated around it. Mariko set half of the wheel down and used a finger to push on the rotor in the other half until it slid free with a wet slurp. It looked as if it had been fairly hard to move.

She held the inner piece, about half the diameter of the outer one, up to her faceplate and said, "The surface looks almost furry." A low-power microscopic examination confirmed her observation; she reported to her audience that both the surface of the rotor and the hollow interior of the wheel bristled with stubby appendages.

"Cirri!" she exclaimed suddenly. "Big, fat bundles of cilia. *That's* where the power comes from. And the brake. These biker guys can start and stop any time they want to. Which means they can also use the wheels for hooves and walk when they need to, just like we figured they could. And since they've got two regular arms with claws on the ends, they don't need weapons on their feet. It works out beautifully." She zoomed in on one of the cirri with the microscope and started babbling happily about microtubules and myofibrils and occasionally uttering a startled, "Hello, what's this?"

Ryan, deprived of the microscopic view, gave his attention to the entire creature. Something about it bothered him, something other than the blood and the internal organs that were no longer internal. It had started as a subtle nagging at the edge of perception when he'd first seen it draped across his legs, and had grown over the course of the night and the next day to a decidedly real feeling that something about it wasn't right. He looked at it again now, wondering if his feeling was just a phantom memory of the terror he'd felt during his first encounter or if he actually had a handle on something.

The bullet holes drew his attention. Something about the bullet holes. Ryan forced himself to look at one, really *look* at it, and slowly the association came to him. The bullet holes looked a lot like the kamikaze wounds he'd seen on the other creature, the one he'd seen killed and eaten. He'd have been willing to bet that a kamikaze had about the same destructive power as a .45 bullet.

If that was the case, then a kamikaze could kill a biker. A biker wasn't heavily armored like a clum, and even with its wheels it couldn't outrun one of the explosive hummingbirds. Yet it would offer a much bigger meal than the creature they *had* killed. Why hadn't the kamikazes gone for it instead, or for one of the other wheeled creatures in the meadow? They must have known they were there. And on a larger scale, what kept the kamikazes from driving the defenseless wheelies—Ryan supposed that would be a good enough name for the whole taxonomic family—what kept them from driving the wheelies into extinction?

Did they breed like rabbits? Was the planet covered with millions of bikers and worse, reproducing like mad to counter the attrition due to kamikazes? Ryan doubted it. He could believe it of an herbivore, but the biker was clearly a predator. Millions of bikers would need hundreds of millions of something else to feed *them*, and the planet just wasn't that populous. No, some other mechanism kept them from becoming kamikaze food.

No doubt Mariko had already figured it out. Ryan keyed the intercom to voice and asked, "Mariko, what keeps kamikazes from killing bikers?"

Mariko looked up to the intercom. "Good question," she said.

"I've been wondering that myself. So far I don't see any obvious reason."

"Oh."

"I'm sure there is one, but figuring out the food chain here could take years." Mariko grinned happily at the prospect. That kind of investigation—the meticulous study of an alien ecosystem—was just what she had signed up for. She was obviously even happier to find a bizarre ecosystem like this than she had been with Eden's relatively straightforward, Earthlike one.

Ryan was less pleased. He wanted a world they could live on, not just something to study from inside armored vehicles. But the universe didn't seem too concerned with what Ryan wanted.

He nodded toward the left side of the screen, knowing that to Mariko it would look as if he were indicating the biker, and said, "Well, have fun."

"I plan on it," Mariko replied, turning back to work.

Ryan switched off.

Mariko called back a couple hours later. "Then again," she said as soon as Ryan answered, "it could only take a few hours."

Ryan had been using the intercom to access the library, where he had found a century-old Soviet volume on bomb shelters. It took him a moment to switch mental gears. "What could only take a few hours?"

"I think I've figured out why kamikazes don't eat bikers."

"Oh! Why not?"

"There's an enzyme in the biker that neutralizes the kamikaze explosive, that's why not." Mariko held up a Petri dish in which a glob of brown jelly quivered. "Almost half the kamikaze's body mass is explosive, or was. Damndest nitrogen compound I've ever heard of. It's got all the nitrogen and oxygen you could ask for in an explosive, but it's bound up with enough fluorine atoms in key places to where it won't blow. I checked the biker tissue for fluorine and found the enzyme. The moment it touches the explosive, it binds with it and renders it inert. The way I figure it, kamikazes learn that they can't eat biker meat, so they leave them alone."

Ryan whistled appreciatively. "That's a pretty good trick."

"You bet it is."

"But that one was eating biker meat. Why?"

"I'm guessing, but I think the gunshot wounds confused it. It probably thought the biker'd been killed by other kamikazes, so it must have thought it was safe to eat. Either that or it was just young and didn't know what was safe and what wasn't. A few members of each generation probably have to test it out from time to time to refresh the racial memory. That's the way it works with birds and butterflies."

"Huh? What do birds and butterflies have to do with it?"

Mariko grinned. "Monarch butterflies use the same defense mechanism, that's what. Well, not exactly the same, but the same style. Monarchs evidently taste bad to birds. That's their defense. Trouble is, a few birds have to eat a few monarchs before they realize that, so not every monarch is safe. Same with the bikers. Every now and then a kamikaze has to eat a biker so the rest of them will realize they can't."

"Oh. Damn." For a moment Ryan had thought Mariko had solved the kamikaze problem—just duplicate the enzyme and use it as a repellent—but it was hardly a solution if it only worked on a percentage basis.

She was already ahead of him. "It won't work to drive them away, but we might be able to spray their nests with the stuff. If none of them can blow up, the whole nest will eventually starve. We could probably rid an island of them fairly easily if we wanted to. I'm synthesizing a batch so we can try it out next time we go down."

"But won't that upset the balance somehow?" asked Ryan. "Whatever they *do* eat would multiply unchecked."

"Not if we introduced our own replacement for kamikazes."

"What do you mean? What replacement?"

"I don't know for sure. I'll have to study the entire ecosystem before I can tell you, but I'd be willing to bet there's a perfectly good substitute from our own Earth stock for whatever niche the kamikaze fills. Maybe coyotes, or maybe bald eagles, or maybe coyotes *and* bald eagles. And maybe hummingbirds, too. The point is, I bet we can find something to replace kamikazes. Something we can still live with."

"Sean's not going to like that idea much," Ryan pointed out. "I don't think *I* like that idea much. We're supposed to adapt to the planet, not the other way around."

Mariko shrugged. "If we want to live here, we're going to have to adapt plenty, but the planet's going to have to give some, too. You've got to remember that *we're* part of our own ecosystem. Mankind can't exist all by itself. We're going to affect wherever we live; the only thing we can do to make it better is use our intelligence to determine what effect we have."

Ryan sighed. "Maybe we'd be better off staying in the ship, where the only environment we affect is our own."

"Maybe we'd be better off just staying on Earth, where we evolved." Mariko's tone of voice left no doubt she was being facetious.

Ryan said, "Okay, I get your point. But I hate the idea of wiping out an entire species just so we can live here."

"I don't particularly like it either, but that seems to be our choice. We wipe out the kamikazes if we stay here, or the customs agents if we stay on Eden. Take your pick."

"That's not a choice and you know it," Ryan said.

Mariko shook her head. "Try telling that to the rest of the crew."

Ryan tried doing just that. When Kristy called him a few hours later, unwilling to wait for him to get out of quarantine to talk with him again, he hardly waited for her to say "Hi" before he said, "Hey, did you hear the great news? Mariko's found a defense that'll work against kamikazes."

"Oh," she said. "You mean you're actually thinking about going back down there?"

"Of course. I think it could work out after all."

"What, you mean live there?"

"Yeah, that's the general idea."

Kristy couldn't find anything to say. She shook her head in disbelief, her eyes fixed on Ryan's through the intercom.

"It's not as crazy as it sounds," Ryan said. "Think of the Europeans who colonized America. They faced worse problems than we do."

"Sure they did."

"They did. Think about it. We have bikers, but they had grizzly bears, which were just as bad. We have kamikazes, but they had hostile natives, which from the Europeans' viewpoint were worse. And they didn't have as good a shelter as we have, or fusion generators for power, or—"

"Ryan, this isn't the Old West. This is a jungle."

"People live in jungles, too."

"Sure they do," Kristy said. "And they have a hard time of it even with modern technology to help them out. Does that mean *we* have to have a hard time of it, too?"

"Of course not. I'm just saying we do have a choice. It's a moral choice, between our own discomfort for a while—until we learn to live here comfortably—or screwing up someone else's world forever."

Kristy made an exasperated face. "It's more than discomfort, Ryan. Your planet could kill us all."

"No it couldn't! For one thing, we'll be careful. More careful than I was when I got hurt. For another, we won't start a colony until we know what to expect and how to deal with it. And for another, it's not *my* planet." He grinned when he said that, but he was serious.

Kristy grinned back. "Oh, but it is. Everybody I know is calling it 'Ryan's world.' It'll be about as easy to change as 'Eden' was."

Ryan's world. It would never be official. One of the expedition rules was explicit on that matter: geographical features could be named however the discoverers pleased, but entire worlds were not to be named after people. On the record books, then, the planet would probably be known as "Hell" or worse, but Kristy was no doubt right. Unofficially it would be "Ryan's world," and there was nothing he could do about it.

An entire planet named after him. It was Ryan's turn to be speechless. Kristy laughed and said, "You're so cute when you get embarrassed."

"Shush, girl."

"Won't."

"Then do me a favor."

"What?"

"If you're going to call it my world, then at least help me try to *make* it my world."

She shook her head. "I'm madly in love with you, but not that mad."

"At least think about it, okay?"

She hesitated, clearly not liking the idea, but at last she said, "Okay."

"Good."

"But for every minute I spend thinking about it, you've got to kiss me once when you get out."

"*What?*"

"You're manipulating me; I manipulate you. Take it or leave it."

Why had he ever thought Kristy was naive? She lacked experience, not intelligence. "I can't do that," he told her.

"Why not?"

Because I love Holly, he wanted to say, but he knew he couldn't.

And that wasn't any reason as far as Kristy was concerned, anyway. Or Holly, for that matter. She would be happy to see him pair off with Kristy.

Or would she? She talked like it, but would she really?

"All right," he said, "but once for every ten minutes."

"Five."

"Seven and a half."

"Six. Final offer."

"Six it is. Keep a log."

"What's the matter, don't you trust me?"

"Of course I trust you. I want to know what arguments you come up with."

"Oh. All right." She smiled seductively, said, "Start practicing your pucker," and winked out.

Once for every six minutes, eh? Ryan lay back on his bed, arms crossed behind his head, and smiled at the ceiling. Ah, the fringe benefits to being an explorer.

With a sudden start, he realized he'd been an idiot. He should have let her win at five.

The next few days in his private quarantine/hospital room nearly drove him crazy. The ship was abuzz with talk about "his" world—nearly everyone who came to visit or talked with him over the intercom had an opinion about it—but he couldn't participate in a tenth of the conversations he knew were going on. He knew the question of whether or not to colonize would be answered officially in a ship wide vote after an open meeting, but he still couldn't help feeling that the real decision was being made now, without him.

And it wasn't going well. The entire crew had watched Ryan get blown up and cut up within seconds after leaving the shuttle, and no amount of kamikaze repellent or Kevlar suits would make them feel secure in a world where that could happen. Ryan argued that there might be places naturally free of kamikazes, but David made infrared scans for the distinctive heat signature of their explosion and announced that there were only two areas on the entire world devoid of the creatures: the oceans and the polar ice caps.

Kristy was also true to her word: day after day she gave him dozens of arguments for leaving Ryan's world to the biologists and colonizing Eden, arguments including the redder sun's effect on plant growth, the smaller planet's greater susceptibility to global climate changes, and the shorter year's long-term effect on biorhythms.

Ryan refuted some of them right away, and some he refuted after a few hours of computer simulation, but others could only be addressed by overcoming them in action. On those, all he could offer for an immediate response was his own certainty that each of her objections *could* be overcome, but he quickly discovered that his own faith in the human ability to triumph over nature was far less contagious than Ken's form of faith had been.

Or worse, David's version of it. David was just as busy campaigning for his point of view as was Ryan, but David had a much more seductive pitch. He was more cautious in stating it than Ken had been, couching his phrases with "could be" and "maybe," but the essential message was strong enough: whether its existence was an act of God or simple chance, Ryan's world proved that humanity belonged on Eden. Even the not-particularly-religious found that message easy to accept.

"What about the customs agents?" Ryan asked during one open intercom debate. "Have you forgotten them completely?"

"What about intelligent life here? We haven't ruled that out," David replied. His was one of about a dozen faces on the screen, but the argument was between him and Ryan alone. Even Sean had stayed out of it so far, though he was one of the ones watching.

Ryan said, "We haven't found any, either. We *know* it exists on Eden."

David nodded as if conceding a point, but he said, "You have a curious blind spot when it comes to the issue of intelligent life. You ignore evolution entirely."

"What?" Ryan asked, taken by surprise. Evolution should have been one of *his* arguments, not David's.

But David put it to effective use in his own case, saying, "If evolution takes its course, we can assume intelligence will eventually come to exist here as well, whether it does now or not. If we settle here, we would disrupt that evolution. So you see, Ryan, your argument can be used both ways. It could even be argued that leaving this world alone is the more benevolent act, since the customs agents have already evolved intelligence."

"But—that's—according to that argument, we should only settle planets with intelligent life on them!"

"Or terraform completely dead worlds. Unfortunately, we don't have that option here."

Ryan knew better than to suggest staying on the ship, at least over an open channel. He was already in the minority; that kind of talk would just make it worse. All he could say was, "We do have the option of leaving an already-developed intelligence alone, and we should do it," but he had lost that argument and he knew it. He needed another approach.

One of the other faces on the screen was Laney Terrill's, and she spoke up when David seemed disinclined to. "Ryan," she said, shaking her head sadly, "I can't believe this is you saying these things. You're asking us to risk not only our own lives, but the lives of all the generations to come on a hostile world. I'm sorry, but if it comes down to a question of my children and grandchildren or a bunch of hairy octopuses, I'm going to protect my own."

Ryan felt as if he'd been kicked while he was already down. Laney influenced more on the ship than just people's appetites; if she came down against him, his cause was doomed. Carefully, remembering what Mariko had said to him earlier when he'd complained about the consequences of trying to fit into an alien environment, he said, "We can protect them here, Laney. Look around you. Right now we're living in one of the most hostile environments imaginable. The vacuum just beyond these walls could kill us all in a second if we lost our air. There's hard radiation out there as well, and inside we've got our own disasters constantly waiting to happen. We've got to recycle with almost perfect efficiency; we've got to limit our population growth; we've got to limit our intestinal *bacteria's* population growth—but we do it. We've solved every problem associated with living in space, solved them so well that we could send a ship on a twenty-year trip and expect it to get where it was going with its crew still alive. Think how much easier it'll be on a planet, even *this* planet, where we don't need to hold our air in and we don't have to—"

"You think we came all this way just to live in shelters for the rest of our lives?"

"No, that's not my point at all! I'm saying that learning how to live in space was incredibly tough to do, but we did it and we can use what we've learned to live comfortable lives wherever we want. Even here. Especially here. *That's* what we came all this way for—to find humanity's next frontier and learn to live in it, not just to find another cushy planet for the human race to fill up with bodies."

Laney wasn't convinced. "How many people do you think died learning how to live in space?" she asked.

"I don't know. Quite a few, I imagine. The point is—"

"Quite a few is right. There are exactly one hundred and seven people on this ship, Ryan. One hundred and seven people to start a new society. We can't afford to lose any of them."

There were thousands of frozen sperm samples and frozen ova in the gene bank, millions of possible combinations, but Ryan knew that wasn't what Laney was talking about. She was talking about people with names, friends who could be killed on a hostile world.

Sean saved Ryan from having to answer. "We're going to lose people no matter where we live, Laney," he said. "People get sick.

People fall off cliffs. People get hit on the head with coconuts. And people get bored and drink themselves to death. *That's* what I'd be worrying about if I were you. Not wild animals, not birds that blow up, not even ruining the development of a new race; I'd worry about what boredom's going to do to people if we pick the easy route."

"I think you're being a little melodramatic, aren't you Sean? You can't be seriously suggesting that boredom is more dangerous than wild animals."

"I am. Look at the Native Americans. We were doing just fine for thousands of years, living side by side with bears and mountain lions and poisonous snakes and you name it. We lost people from time to time, sure, but we had a healthy, stable society. Stable, hell; we were growing. Then the white men came and put us on reservations—put us on *welfare* on reservations, so we got the same living whether we worked or not—and suddenly the biggest killer of Native Americans became alcoholism. Two hundred years later it's *still* the number one cause of death. That's because we're bored. We're bored to death."

"That's very touching, Sean, but we're not going to be on a reservation."

"No? That whole planet is one big reservation. I mean, what was the first thing everybody did when they got there? Shucked their clothes and headed for the beach. Day after day after day, people picking fruit, going swimming, making love. Great fun, yeah, but is that any kind of a *life*? You know what I found when I got back after flying Mariko to the mainland? Ryan, sacked out in his tent in the middle of the afternoon, bored to tears. He looked like he was thinking about suicide already, and he'd only been there a few days. That's what we've got to look forward to if we go back to Eden. Every one of us is going to feel the same way inside of a month."

Ryan felt himself blush all the way to his toes. It hadn't been boredom that had made him look that way. But nobody knew that except Holly, and she wasn't on line.

It wouldn't have mattered even if she had been. Nobody bought Sean's argument anyway. "Sean," Laney said, "if you think you can convince me a hundred people on an entire unexplored planet are going to grow bored enough to drink themselves to death, then you're further out of touch than I thought you were."

"Maybe so," Sean said. "Maybe so. But then again maybe not, and I don't think we can afford to guess wrong."

"I don't either," Laney said, but it was plain she wasn't agreeing. It was equally plain that neither Sean nor Ryan was going to change anyone's mind by arguing about it.

"The problem is," Laura said when Ryan called her for advice, "you're trying to use faith to prove a logical argument. It's faith in technology and in the human spirit under fire, but that's faith nonetheless. That's fine; you can win arguments that way, but if you want people to follow you on the strength of your convictions, you've got to appeal to their emotions. Make it a matter of pride or honor or good old fashioned manifest destiny, but don't just tell people what they've got to believe."

"Wait a minute," Ryan protested. "I don't want to win the argument by emotion; I want to win it because I'm right."

"*Are* you right?"

Laura too? Ryan felt a lump growing in his throat. Having Laney against him was bad enough, but having Laura against him was a hundred times worse. He said, "I've got to be right. The alternative means wiping out an entire civilization."

"Does it? You think so, and I happen to think so too, but you haven't convinced everyone of that. And you haven't convinced *anyone* we can live here. All you've convinced us of is what you *want* to be right, but just because you want it doesn't make it so."

Her expression softened when she saw his helpless look. "I'm not saying you're wrong. I'm just saying you've got to prove it to the rest of the crew before we'll believe you. And if you want to prove it logically, you've got to prove it so well that we'll give up what *we* want to be right in order to believe you. That's how you win a logical argument."

"I see."

Laura nodded. "Cheer up. Not everybody likes a logical decision, but I think we're all smart enough to make one if the choice is clear enough."

"I hope so," Ryan said, but he knew Laura was right. Well, that was a relief. Instead of trying to prove a particular point of view, all he had to do was dig up enough facts to make the truth obvious to everyone. Simple.

CHAPTER TWENTY-THREE

A LOGICAL DECISION

"NO. I WON'T RISK ANOTHER landing party until we know more about the life forms down there. Mariko is still making discoveries in her lab, some of which may provide more insight into survival techniques." Captain Van Cleeve glared sternly at Ryan out of his half of the intercom screen. On the other half of the screen, Sean glared just as sternly back, but from Ryan's point of view it looked as if both men were angry with *him*.

"I don't think we can afford the time for Mariko to figure out the ecosystem from up here, sir," Ryan said. "The longer we wait, the more people are going to decide the place is too hostile to live on. If a clear majority of the crew decides that's the case, they can call for a vote and force a decision based on incomplete data. I don't think you want that any more than we do."

"Of course I don't. But I don't want two of my most valuable crewmembers killed trying to prove a point, either."

"We won't be killed," Sean said. "That's the point we want to prove."

Van Cleeve shook his head. "I recognize that. I recognize it all too well, dammit! Trouble is, I don't believe you yet, either."

"You can't have it both ways, Captain. If we want the facts, somebody's going to have to go get them."

"We're getting facts from Mariko's lab. Maybe not as fast as you'd like, but that's how fast they're coming in, and nobody's life's at risk in getting them. So, for the last time, no. Not yet. Soon, yes, but not yet." The captain glared at them a moment longer, then winked out.

Sean's intercom image widened to give him the whole screen. "I guess he told us," Ryan said.

"I don't think he realizes how close we are to a vote," said Sean.

"How long do you figure we've got?"

"Maybe two days, unless something happens to delay it."

Ryan felt his pulse quicken. "Unless something happens to delay it. Are you thinking what I think you're thinking?"

"I'm thinking there's only one sure way to prove it's possible to live there."

"But if we get killed, they're sure to vote for Eden."

"They're sure to vote for it now."

Ryan tried to find a center of calm from which to look at the situation objectively. Were he and Sean right? He was certain of it. But right enough to disobey direct orders to prove it? That wasn't as easy to answer.

He tried looking at it from the other side. Was his duty to obey the captain stronger than his duty to protect an entire intelligent race? When asked that way, the answer was obvious.

"So, what do we need to take with us?" he asked.

The empty shuttle loading bay echoed with the whine of the winch, conducted through the metal skin of the ship as it hauled the shuttle up to docking position. Herding the net bag containing their tools ahead of him with one hand and holding the pressure cylinder of synthesized biker enzyme with the other, Ryan kept a wary eye on the door leading back into the ship, but so far they had gotten away clean.

Clean in more than one sense. Both he and Sean wore pressure suits, and had been wearing them since sneaking out of their quarters. Their time in quarantine was only half over; they had no desire to expose the crew to any long-gestation organisms that might still show up.

David and Mariko slept on in their quarters, as unaware of their activity as the rest of the crew. Mariko might have come with them, but Ryan and Sean saw no point in risking more than the minimum number on the ground, either. If she wanted to join them later, that was her business.

The shuttle came to rest in the dock with a squeal and a clang of closing latches. Sean opened the first of the airlock doors, pulled his own bag of tools in after him, and went through the next three doors—one more in the starship and two in the shuttle—into the cargo hold. Ryan followed, shoving his tool bag and the enzyme cylinder ahead of him and closing the doors behind him as he went through.

Sean was already at the controls. "Tie that down and strap in," he said, the helmet muffling his voice. "We launch in thirty seconds."

They had left their suit radios switched off, worried that radio traffic on an open channel—even in the middle of the night—would attract too much attention. Sean had disconnected Mac's shuttle bay sensors, but he couldn't do anything to hide their radio signals.

Ryan tied both bags and the cylinder to the walls in the cargo bay—a bay still missing a rover—and made it to the copilot's seat just as Sean released the airlock latches and fired the attitude jets to move them away from the ship. They drifted a few seconds while Ryan finished strapping in, then Sean aligned them back along their orbital path and fired the main engine to drop them out of orbit. They were in a bad position to reach the island; to get there in any reasonable time would require a long, hard burn.

"That...won't go...unnoticed," Sean said, straining against five gees of thrust.

"Uh-uh," Ryan answered. Without a launch warning, Mac would probably sound a red alert when it detected the hot exhaust plume rushing past the ship. It didn't matter, though, because now it was too late for anyone to do anything about it. In fact, they were kind of hoping for a general alert to let everyone know what they were trying.

Sure enough, just a few minutes later the intercom lit up and Captain Van Cleeve stared icily out at them. "All right, you two," he said. "Just what the hell do you think you're doing?"

Sean lowered the thrust to three gees so they could talk. Switching on his radio, Ryan said, "I think that's obvious, sir."

"I ordered you to stay on the ship."

"With all due respect, sir, you should never order someone to do something they don't already want to do."

"Very funny." The captain consulted something out of the field of view on his right. He was in the control room, Ryan saw, which meant he was probably looking at the remote shuttle controls. He reached for something out of camera range, and a red light began blinking on the panel before Sean.

Sean shook his head at the captain. "I'm on manual. There's nothing you can do about it now except shoot us down or let us go."

"I *ought* to shoot you down," Van Cleeve growled, but a moment later he sighed theatrically and said, "But that would waste a shuttle. We can come get it soon enough when the planet's through with you."

"I appreciate your confidence in our ability."

"As I appreciate your insubordination." The captain paused a second, then said, "You might as well tell me your plan."

The control console beeped for attention, and Sean pushed the throttle back up to four gees. Ryan struggled to keep his voice steady as he said, "It's simple enough. We're going to finish exploring. If we don't find any sign of intelligence, we're going to live there. Build a house, plant a garden, send homey pictures back to the ship. Eventually the rest of the crew will realize they can do it, too."

The captain said, sarcastically, "You're going to try to start a colony on your own."

"Not much of a colony without women," Sean replied. Thrust twisted his smile into a grimace. "Think of us more like the early mountain men. We'll learn the tricks and pass them along to the rest of you pilgrims."

"You sound awfully sure of yourself."

"Captain, half the trick to survival is convincing yourself you're going to make it."

"And the other half is making it." Van Cleeve's frown softened by a millimeter or so. "I don't agree with what you're doing one bit, but all the same, you bastards had better make it."

They landed the shuttle in the clearing closest to the broken-down rover. Removing their intact pressure suits, they donned the protective clothing they had worn on their previous walk through the woods, gathered up the tools and spare parts they needed, and walked back to the rover. Ryan felt his breath coming short as he looked behind every tree for bikers, but the only wildlife he saw was one small, heavily-armored almost-reptile that squealed and rolled into a ball when they surprised it around a curve in the trail. Ryan tossed a few rocks at it, and when it didn't explode he took a close up picture of it and he and Sean went on.

The rover was right where they'd left it, looking no worse than before. Evidently clums didn't attack something they'd already killed. That was comforting. Sean took a quick look around, then pulled off his helmet and slid underneath while Ryan, pistol drawn, kept watch.

"You know," Ryan said, "I remember when Michelle was trying to talk me into becoming an explorer. She made it sound like this; constantly looking over my shoulder for wild animals. That's what I thought it was going to be like when I first signed up it. I get the feeling that's what everybody on the ship expected. So why does it seem so much worse to us now that we're doing it?"

Sean, his legs sticking out from under the rover, said, "Because we had Eden. We got soft. We saw how easy it could be when everything went right, and we forgot that it usually doesn't work that way. Hand me the pry bar." He reached a hand out beside his left leg.

Ryan took the bar out of the tool box and held it down for him, then raised up quickly again to continue his watch. The forest was quiet, but that didn't reassure him much. Just because they hadn't encountered any trouble in their first hour back on the surface didn't mean they wouldn't in the next.

He felt that same unsettled feeling in his stomach that he'd felt when he'd first realized the trip was drawing to a close. Anxiety at the prospect of leaving the security of the ship. Worry over abandoning a comfortable life for an uncertain future. He had never worried before, not really. Now he wondered if he would ever quit.

"Yeah," Sean said, grunting with the effort of straightening whatever was bent, "if we'd landed here first, we'd have probably settled the place without even going to look at Eden." Ryan heard him bang on something, then strain again against the pry bar. "Damn," Sean muttered. "I'm going to need another hand here."

"I can't keep watch from under there," Ryan said.

"And I can't fix it alone." Sean slid out from under the rover and stood up, wiping his hands on his coveralls. "Look," he said. "Nothing's tried to eat us yet. I'm willing to bet nothing does for another few minutes."

A moving speck on Sean's forearm caught Ryan's attention. "What's that?" he asked, pointing.

"What?" Sean turned around, then realized where Ryan's finger was aimed. He held up his arm and squinted at the speck. "Looks like an ant," he said, blowing it off with a puff of breath—toward Ryan. Ryan shied back, examining his clothes to see where it had gone.

"Relax!" Sean said. "It's a bug. The planet has bugs. So does

Earth, and so does Eden. They crawl on things. No big deal."

"Yeah," Ryan said, forcing himself to look away, but feeling thousands of tiny crawling feet through his clothes even so. "Yeah, but some bugs are poisonous."

Sean nodded. "Some bugs are poisonous. Why do you think I blew it off? No sense tempting fate, that's why. But there's no sense in flinching every time you see one, either. You'll wear yourself out." Sean reached out and gently guided Ryan's gun back into its holster. "Save your energy for when you need it."

Ryan sighed. Sean was right; he already felt worn out and the day wasn't even half over. "I'll try," he said.

"Good. Now help me bend the differential mounts back where they ought to be." Sean lay back down and scooted under the rover again.

Ryan took another look around the forest. Still quiet. Cautiously, he took off his helmet and lay down in the dirt beside Sean.

"Okay, that's right. Wiggle under here. Get some leaves in your collar. Smell the dirt. That's what home smells like."

Ryan obediently inhaled the aroma of freshly-scuffed dirt while Sean positioned the pry bar against the differential case. "Okay, grab here," Sean said, patting the end of the bar. Ryan wrapped his fingers around it.

"Now push."

Ryan pushed.

Driving through the forest along the wheelie trail, Sean said, "I just realized something. I bet there's a road already made to wherever we want to go. All over the planet."

"I hadn't thought of that," said Ryan. He was once again running the camera while they continued where they'd left off in exploring the island. They were transmitting to the ship as they drove, just as before, and no one there made any direct comment about their reason for being on the ground, but Ryan sensed a definite degree of tension between ground and ship nonetheless. He tried to ignore it, saying to Sean and anybody else listening, "This could be the only place in the galaxy where cars will fit into the ecosystem."

"Cars, hell!" Sean said with sudden animation. "Use wheelies. If they can be domesticated, we won't *need* cars."

Ryan laughed at the sudden image of Sean, a bandanna around his neck and his pistol at his side, riding off into the sunset on a three-wheeled horse. No, wrong image. Sean would no doubt ride naked except for a breech cloth, bearing slashes of war paint on his face and chest, and waving a bow and arrow.

An arrow with a kamikaze tied to the end of it.

Immediately on the heels of that image came another one: Holly racing across the hard packed sand of the beach on a gold-colored wheelie, her hair flying out behind her in the wind and her laughter echoing across the bay. With Ryan in hot pursuit, of course.

But immediately behind *that* came the image of a biker leaping out from behind a rock and pulling her down. Ryan blinked it away, but the memory haunted him for hours.

They made camp on a rocky stretch of windswept ground at the northern end of the island, about thirty kilometers from the shuttle. Camp consisted of parking the rover beside the stream that emptied into the sea there and folding down the back seat to make room for their sleeping bags, since neither of them felt adventurous enough to sleep in a tent. Sean immediately unpacked his fishing pole and headed for the stream, though, leaving Ryan to keep watch from the rover.

He had hardly been gone a minute before the intercom buzzed for attention and Ryan found Michelle looking out at him with a determined expression.

"Hi," he said.

"Hi. We've got to talk."

He nodded. "Okay."

"Private channel."

"Okay." Ryan tapped the scramble icon on the edge of the screen. Michelle's image lost some of its definition, but she was still clearly unhappy. "What do you want to talk about?" he asked her.

"Your father," she said.

"What about him?"

"I wonder if your intense desire to prove you can live down there has anything to do with his death."

Ryan had expected her to try to talk him out of risking his life, but he hadn't expected that approach. "Why should it?" he asked.

"It occurred to me that you might be subconsciously holding out so he won't have died for nothing."

Sean, on the riverbank, had assembled his pole and was beginning to cast his line upstream. Ryan watched him swing the pole back and forth, line trailing in longer and longer loops, while he considered what Michelle had said. Could that be why he felt so strongly about staying there, despite the dangers? He tried to examine his reasons objectively, but he couldn't find Ken's influence in any of them.

"I haven't even thought of Ken since we got here," he told her. "If he's behind any of this, then it's buried pretty deep."

"It could be," she said. "Compulsions do come from deep down."

"You think this is a compulsion?"

"It acts like one. Ryan, think about it for a minute. When we first got here you didn't even want to be an explorer. Now you've intentionally put yourself in just about the most dangerous situation you could find. That's not exactly normal behavior for you."

"I think my reasons are pretty straightforward," he said. "I don't want to ruin an intelligent species' chance to develop on their own. I think we can live here instead, and I'm trying to prove it to the rest of the crew. That's really all that's going on."

Michelle ran a hand through her hair. "Let me tell you what's going on up here, then. More people than just me are starting to wonder if you're okay. People are starting to ask if we shouldn't just go after you and drag you back. Some people are suggesting we just go bring the shuttle back, and leave you and Sean there. I don't think that's quite what you have in mind, is it?"

"Not exactly," Ryan said.

Sean had hooked his fly in a crack between rocks on the opposite bank. Ryan watched him tug on the line a few times, then walk upstream toward it to try pulling from another angle. One quick shake of the line popped the fly loose, and he cast it again farther upstream.

"Let me ask *you* a question," Ryan said. "If Eden didn't exist, would you come live here?"

Michelle took a moment to answer, and when she did it was only to say, "I don't know. It's not a fair question. Eden *is* there."

"And it belongs to somebody else. For me, that means it doesn't exist as a choice. When you can understand that, then you can understand why I'm here."

"I *can't* understand that, Ryan. That's the problem. Nobody up here can. The customs agents are important, yes, but not as important as my own race."

Ryan shook his head vehemently. "Humanity isn't at risk! *We* are. One hundred and seven people."

"And our descendants."

"And our descendants, most of whom would survive even if this planet were twice as tough as it is. Good grief, look at Earth! People raise children in New York City! They send them to public schools. Compared to that, *this* is Eden."

"Ryan, you're shouting."

"Damn right I'm shouting. I'm tired of arguing about this. I'm tired of being the conscience for the whole damn ship. I've made up my mind; I'm staying here. If people hate me for it, that's too bad, but that's the way it is. If you all decide to go off and leave us here, that's too bad too, but I'm not going to have any part of spoiling

Eden for its rightful owners."

As Ryan spoke, he saw Sean's pole arc down toward the stream, and heard him yell in triumph. A flash of bright green broke the surface in a spray of water.

"Now if you'll excuse me," Ryan said, "I think I'm about to be needed down here." He broke the connection before Michelle could argue further, grabbed the net from Sean's pile of equipment, and jumped from the rover to help land the fish.

It turned out to be not quite a fish after all. Ryan scooped it from the water and held it flat against the ground with the edge of the net while they took stock of its mottled green body and knobby antennae and long, sinuous fins running from nose to tail along its underside. Sean looked dubious at first, but after a moment he smiled and said, "What the hell. They take a fly; that's what counts."

"Yeah," Ryan said, uncomfortably aware that despite his pronouncement to Michelle he still felt as if he were going to be eaten at any moment. "Yeah," he said again. "I guess that's what counts."

CHAPTER TWENTY-FOUR

ACCLIMATIZATION

BUILDING A CABIN PROVED to be tougher work than Ryan had expected. He'd absorbed the theory well enough in his reading on the ship, but when it actually came time to fell trees and split rails, he realized nothing substituted for practice. He kept missing the wedge with the hammer, knocking it sideways and having to reposition it every few swings. The trees didn't cooperate well, either: the spirally-growing ones split in spirals as well, and the straight-growing ones had sharp leaves that had to be carefully trimmed off before he could work with them.

Still, by their fifth long day on the planet, he and Sean had the walls up and a roof on, and they had hauled their gear in from the shuttle to spend their first night inside hand-hewn walls. Their cabin boasted a fusion generator for heat and lights, a stove for cooking, and a refrigerator robbed from the shuttle, but Sean had built an open fireplace out of slabs of rock and he insisted on lighting a fire for atmosphere. Ryan, sitting in a folding chair beside it, found his attention drawn to the flames, just as he had been drawn to their campfires on Eden.

"I wonder how the customs agents are doing," he said quietly.

"Struggling along, I suppose," said Sean. "Learning."

"Yeah." Ryan poked at a pocket of flame with a stick from one of the slicer-dicer bushes. He'd discovered that the high silica content in the wood made them resistant to flame. "You know," he said, "I can't help wondering whether any of this is going to help them any in the long run, though."

"What do you mean?"

"I'm thinking about the next ship from Earth. Even if we win now, what's to keep them or Spacehome from sending another one with specific orders to colonize Eden?"

Sean laughed softly. "About fifty trillion dollars."

"Huh?"

"That's about what this expedition cost them. That's in 2050 dollars, too. It'd be more now. They're not going to send another ship out here unless they've got a damned good reason to."

"Colonizing Eden isn't reason enough?"

Sean laughed. "Not on your life. How do you think a colony on Eden is going to benefit Earth? It's not going to solve their population problem, that's for sure. They might learn something valuable there, but we're already here to do it for them, and they know we're going to study both planets no matter where we wind up living. As long as we stay alive and stay in contact, they're going to spend their money sending ships to stars we haven't explored yet."

"Oh," Ryan said. "I hadn't thought of that."

"That's because you're too busy worrying."

"Maybe."

"No maybe. You're a born worry-wart."

Ryan shoved at a weak spot in a log and watched it collapse in a shower of sparks. "I've got lots to worry about."

"So do I. Including my partner bugging out on me."

"Sorry."

"Don't be sorry; just lighten up." Sean got up and got two bottles of beer from the refrigerator, handed one to Ryan, and sat down again.

"Thanks," Ryan said automatically. He took a sip of the beer and set the bottle down on the floor. It was just a sheet of plastic to keep dirt and bugs out, but it was a floor. Looking back into the flames,

Ryan said, "I appreciate your advice, but I can't help thinking how we're sitting in a log fortress on a planet full of creatures that can kill us, while overhead the rest of the crew is thinking about taking the easy way out and ruining an entire civilization's development. Why should I lighten up with that going on?"

"Because worrying about it isn't going to help anything, that's why. We're doing everything we can do, and we either convince them or we don't."

"And if we don't?"

"Then we stay here by ourselves. Unless you'd rather go live on Eden and teach the customs agents how to build houses."

Ryan looked up at Sean. "You know I don't want to do that."

"Then act like it. We're supposed to be showing everyone how much fun they can have down here. We're not going to do that if you keep jumping at shadows." Sean took a drink and belched theatrically.

"Yeah," Ryan said, looking back to the fire. He poked at the coals again, said, "I just can't help wondering. . ."

"Wondering what?"

"If maybe there is a reason for all this being the way it is. Maybe we really are supposed to go to Eden."

"You're kidding me."

Ryan blushed at the tone of Sean's voice. "Maybe I'm kidding myself. I don't know. It just seems like so many things are stacked up against us. It makes me wonder is all."

Sean leaned back in his chair until it creaked. "You start looking for patterns in random happenings, you'll always find some. A paranoid can find connections between any two events. That doesn't mean there are any."

"It doesn't mean there aren't, either."

"Nope. But it's pretty damned foolish to assume there are unless you know for sure."

"Isn't it just as foolish to assume there aren't?"

Sean gave the question a moment's consideration before he answered. "If it colors your judgment, then I suppose it is, yeah. But David has that much right: you can't base a decision on incomplete information. If there's a purpose to all this, then whoever's behind it will have to make it clear what he wants. Even then he'll *still* have to convince me he's right before I do anything about it."

"How's that again?"

Sean laughed. "Not used to blasphemy, eh? That's the whole problem with religion, the way I see it. Not enough people question God. Or his supposed representatives, anyway. They figure if something is God's will, then they'll do it no matter what, even if it goes against their own moral principles. Well I don't see any reason why God shouldn't have to live by the same morals he requires of others. If there is a God, then I suspect he does. That's why I have a hard time believing anybody who'd try to tell me screwing up an intelligent species is God's will. It sure as hell isn't *mine*, and I've got pretty damned good reasons for thinking so."

"You know what the road to Hell is supposed to be paved with," Ryan pointed out.

"And here we are; is that what you're saying? Well listen, Kemosabe, I'm glad to be here. Better to reign in Hell than die of boredom in Eden, and all that. I'd pick this place even if there weren't customs agents there."

"Would you really?"

"Yeah, I would."

Sean's eyes glinted in the firelight. His defiant expression sent chills up Ryan's spine. "I don't know if I'd have the guts to make that kind of decision," Ryan said. "In a way, I'm glad it's been made for me."

"It hasn't been made for you. You could always go to Eden if you wanted. The question is, how bad do you want to?"

Ryan picked up his beer from the floor and took a long drink before saying, "I'm here, aren't I?"

"Yeah, but what if your sweetie goes there?"

He sighed, but it turned into a belch. A bit sheepishly, he said, "I don't know. She's a complete mystery. Even if I went with her I don't know if she'd have me."

Sean narrowed his eyes. "Kristy? She'd have you in a second. In every sense of the word."

Ryan blushed. While they were building the cabin he'd told Sean about the deal he'd made with her, but now he wished he'd held his tongue. "I thought you meant Holly."

"Holly? Good grief, she's old news."

"I don't think so. She..." He stopped. Did he really want to get into this with Sean?

"She what?"

"She, um, got a little physical with me when we got back to the ship last time."

"Did she now?" Sean laughed. "That must have been a shock."

"It was that."

The fire popped, throwing a hot coal out onto the floor beside Sean. He wet his fingers and tossed it back, saying "Shock to her as well, I'd bet. Hmm. That puts a little different spin on things, but I bet you she's still old news."

"Why?"

"Because you're here."

Ryan felt a shiver run through him. Sean had a good point. Holly was horrified at the thought of setting foot on this planet, horrified that Ryan would even consider it for himself, much less ask anyone else to do it. She didn't understand it any more than he understood her attraction to David, or the religion David believed in.

Sean said, "Maybe the vote will go our way and she'll have to come here too, but even then I wouldn't count on her warming your bed anytime soon. You burned that bridge the moment you came back down."

Ryan looked at the stone fireplace, the rough-hewn log walls, the door and windows barricaded shut against alien predators. He had traded Holly for *this*? "Shit," he said.

Sean took another swig of his beer. "Hey, I may be wrong. I don't know everything about women. But I wouldn't tell Kristy to get lost just yet if I were you."

Ryan sank back in his chair and stared at the flames. Just how badly did he want to live here, anyway?

A roar like that of a shuttle landing woke him out of a sound sleep. Ryan reached for his pistol before his eyes would even focus, cocked the hammer, and looked around the cabin, blinking, for the source of the noise. Had a biker broken down the door? Was a clum trying to smash through a wall?

Sean sat up in his own bed, pistol drawn as well, and Ryan watched a slow grin spread across his face as they both realized what the noise meant. It *was* a shuttle landing.

"Put on the coffee, paleface; we've got company!" Sean said over the roar. He lowered his pistol, slid out of bed, and pulled on his pants and a shirt.

Ryan dressed and started the coffeepot while Sean put on his kamikaze suit and stepped outside into the early dawn. The shuttle's engine noise rose to a peak as it landed only a few dozen meters away from the cabin, then wound down to silence. Ryan hurried into his own kamikaze suit and followed after Sean.

The shuttle's airlock cycled open to reveal Mariko, also dressed for kamikazes and carrying a duffel bag in either hand.

"So, could you guys use an extra hand?" she asked.

In the cabin, over steaming mugs of coffee, Mariko gave them the news. "It's just about vote time up there. We've been arguing about it pretty much non-stop since you left, and I think everybody's getting tired of it. I know *I'm* getting tired of it, anyway. I asked Van

Cleeve to let me come do my job until the rest of the crew decides what the hell they want to do, so here I am, at least for a couple of days. Maybe longer, depending on the vote."

"How close do you think it'll be?" Ryan asked.

"That's hard to say. Coming down here and building this cabin definitely helped your case, but I don't know if it's enough to make a difference in the long run. No matter how livable you make this world look, Eden's still Eden. You're asking people to do something that goes against basic human nature."

Ryan said into the steam above his coffee mug, "I thought maybe humans had evolved a little since we've been in space. I thought maybe now we could afford to make a choice based on intellect rather than emotion."

Sean laughed. "Sorry. I think we're a long ways from that yet."

"So Laura told me. I thought I was doing the logical thing, though, trying to prove to everybody that we could live here."

Mariko shook her head. "For you, maybe, this is logical. For the rest of us, it's a decision made in the pit of the stomach. Which means, of course, that it's subject to change from moment to moment. That's why I don't know how the vote's going to go."

"We're staying no matter what," Sean said. He gazed steadily at Mariko.

Her cheeks reddened, and she said, "Look, I like you guys, but I'm not ready to play Eve to two Adams, okay? I came down here to get a few more specimens and see if I can trace the food chain. Who knows, maybe I can find a better solution to kamikazes than replacing them with Earth organisms. Maybe I can find a more convincing reason for everybody to stay here. The fountain of youth, or a cure for the common cold. I came to help out your cause, but I didn't come here to stay unless we win. All right?"

Nodding, Sean said, "All right. Any help's appreciated."

"That's mutual. You want to show me around?"

Ryan enjoyed playing tour guide. While Sean took care of rearranging the cabin to make room for another bed for Mariko, she and Ryan donned their helmets and he helped carry her camera equipment while he showed her the garden spot he and Sean had begun to spade, the creek where they got their drinking water, the dozens of different types of trees growing alongside it, and the tiny camouflaged nests he had learned to spot in their branches only after finding them in the first trees he felled for the cabin.

"Have you seen what kind of birds live in them?" she asked, peering up into the branches with her binoculars.

"Sean says they're more like flying squirrels than birds. I wouldn't know about that, but I do know they're spooky little guys. They don't come out unless you sit still for ten or fifteen minutes, and even then they go right back inside when they see you."

"Hmm." Mariko looked thoughtfully into the branches. "Maybe later. What else have you discovered?"

"Mice," Ryan said, leading her out into the clearing again. "Sort of, anyway. They're kind of big for mice and they've got an extra set of legs. They showed up the day after I sprayed your biker enzyme on the kamikaze nest. That was, what, four days ago? Yeah." He approached the area cautiously, but nothing flew up from the ground. When they drew closer, four or five tiny blurs of green disappeared into dirt-rimmed holes.

"That dirt wasn't there when the kamikazes were here, was it?" asked Mariko.

Ryan shook his head. "I don't think so. They're evidently remodeling it to suit themselves."

"I wonder where the kamikazes went."

"I think the mice ate most of 'em," Ryan said.

"Oh?"

"There were lots of little bones in the grass after they first showed up. I saved you some."

"Thanks." Mariko bent down and examined the fresh dirt

around the hole, scooped some into a sample bottle taken from a zippered pocket, and stood again. "They must have already been the kamikazes' natural enemies, to have taken over so fast."

Ryan scuffed a toe in the grass. "I don't know. It's hard to imagine anything preying on a kamikaze. One bite and they're both dead."

Mariko cocked her head to the side, considering. "Not in the nest," she said at last. "A kamikaze can't blow up in the nest or it'd take the whole thing with it. So something that attacks them at home only has to be stronger than they are, or faster."

"Maybe so," Ryan admitted. A mouse stuck its head out of a hole for an instant, then disappeared again. Ryan said, "I wonder if they eat the explosive, too."

"Count on it," Mariko said. "An explosive molecule is one of the highest-energy compounds you can get; I bet these guys have a way to burn it just like we burn glucose." She looked up at the forest around her as if seeing it for the first time. "Yeah, I bet they do. And I'll bet everything related to them does, too, including bikers. That's where they get the enzyme to neutralize the stuff."

"I don't follow you."

Mariko laughed. "A belly full of explosive is a pretty dangerous thing to be carrying around, no matter how much energy you get out of it. So the enzyme to bind the molecules a little tighter is probably just the first stage in the digestion process, and it eventually evolved into a defense mechanism for the larger animals. Bikers probably don't eat kamikazes, but I bet they evolved from something small that did."

Mariko cocked her head to the side again, and just as Ryan realized she was listening for something she reached up and pulled off her helmet.

"What are you doing?" he asked.

"I thought I heard something calling in the forest, but who can tell inside this damn thing?"

"But—what about kamikazes?"

"What about 'em? I don't see any around, do you?"

"No, but—"

"You sprayed the whole area with the enzyme, right?"

"Right, but—"

"But nothing. If I see any I'll put the helmet back on, but until then I want to hear." She turned away from the kamikaze nest and started walking toward the trees across the clearing, her helmet under her arm.

Ryan followed her, glancing nervously to all sides. His hand hovered close to his pistol, though he didn't think he could hit a kamikaze in flight. The shuttle's autopilot could, but Mariko had parked her shuttle between the other one and the kamikaze nest, and Ryan was willing to bet she hadn't told hers to keep watch.

"Uh, Mariko, maybe we should—"

"Shhh! And don't walk so heavy. I want to get close enough to see what's singing."

Mariko plunged into the underbrush, heedless of the slicer-dicers scraping against her Kevlar oversuit. Ryan had pulled up all the sharp-leaved plants around the cabin, but he hadn't worked his way out this far yet. He followed her as cautiously as he could, but with his helmet limiting his vision he kept tripping over branches and rocks. After Mariko shushed him another couple of times he took a deep breath, lifted off the helmet, and followed after her more quietly. He felt naked—more so than on Eden—but he had to admit he could see better, and hear better as well.

And smell better. He'd drilled holes in the lower face plate for ventilation, but that still wasn't like breathing the air directly, and after days of wear the helmet reeked of Ryan's own sweat anyway. For the first time since he'd been on Eden, he found himself really noticing the aroma of the forest around him. It was full of spicy, living scents.

Whatever was singing had an incredible set of lungs, if indeed it had lungs at all. Its song went on and on without pause, a complex series of whistling notes that rose and fell seemingly without pattern or repetition. As they drew closer they could see that it came from beyond a fallen log taller than either of them. Mariko found a branch sticking out at a convenient height, stepped up on it, and peered over the edge of the log. Ryan waited for her to let him have a look, but it soon became apparent that she didn't plan to give up her branch, so he sought out one of his own. He tested to see if it would support his weight, then cautiously raised his head up even with the top of the log.

It was all he could do to keep from laughing. In the middle of a circle of scratched-up dirt, a blue and yellow beach ball with a row of spikes protruding from its top quivered as if being squeezed by an invisible giant's hand. The whistling came from the spikes on top—evidently hollow tubes—and Ryan could see how the beach ball expanded on one side while it contracted on the other. It looked as if the creature could breathe in on one side at a time and exhale through its pipes with the other while it did so.

Around the whistler stood three long-necked brown birds, all watching intently and bobbing their heads up and down in time with the music. It took Ryan a minute to realize they sported the same row of spikes on their heads.

Mariko eased back down to the ground. Ryan stepped down too, and leaned close as she whispered, "That's got to be a mating call, and those other three are checking out his rhythm."

"Yeah?"

"Yeah. Here, give me the video camera."

Ryan had to set his helmet down and take off the still camera in order to get to it. He handed it to her, then draped the still camera over his shoulder again and put his helmet back on his head. Mariko, rolling her eyes, dropped hers on the ground and climbed up on her branch again to shoot the birds. Ryan climbed up to watch, feeling silly about the helmet but not silly enough to take it off again.

The whistler continued his courtship song, either unaware or unconcerned that he had two humans in his audience. Even muffled by the helmet, it was a beautiful piece of music. The more he listened the more Ryan thought he detected a subtle theme to it, but it was elusive. It didn't sound at all like something an Earthly bird would sing, nor like human music, either. Some of the notes seemed to split in two, leading off into separate melodies that eventually joined up again, but never in the same way.

Suddenly the bird stopped singing. It was silent a moment, then it blew its air out through all the pipes at once in a loud, cacophonous wail and leaped into the air, wings flapping madly to carry it aloft. Without a full air bag it looked more like the other birds, who followed it onto perches halfway up a tree a few meters away.

Mariko lowered the camera and said, "Hah. Must've just realized we were here." She leaned back to step down, looked over her shoulder, and screamed, "Yaaa!"

Ryan looked down to see a biker coming toward them through the underbrush. It was walking as much as rolling, stepping carefully over obstructions in the trail and moving wide around slicer-dicer bushes. It raised its head at Mariko's shout and stopped with one leg raised. Ryan looked back to Mariko just in time to see her teeter off balance and crash to the ground, but before he or the biker could respond, she leaped back onto her branch and vaulted up to the top of the log in one smooth motion.

His heart pounding, Ryan climbed up beside her, then he pulled his pistol out of its holster and cocked the hammer.

"Don't shoot it," Mariko said. She pointed the camera down at the biker and pressed the record button. It lowered its foot and rolled toward the log, stopping a few meters away to sniff the air and weave its head from side to side. It raised up to its full height and reached toward them with its paws, moving up next to the log as it did so, but they were high enough to be out of its reach and it was obvious that two paws and three wheeled legs weren't the right configuration for climbing.

"I think it's just curious," Mariko said.

"Curious about what we taste like," Ryan said, keeping his pistol aimed at its head. His hand shook enough to make that difficult. He felt sudden sympathy for David, who, like Ryan, must have been wondering if he'd be able to kill the creature or just enrage it and make it attack *him*.

"Maybe," said Mariko, "but I think the bird song was what attracted it."

"Doesn't matter; it's interested in us now."

The biker clawed at the bark less than half a meter from Ryan's feet and growled in frustration. The sound of it brought back the memory of lying on the ground with the other biker on top of him, its jaws biting at his helmet. Ryan nearly fired on the one below him now, but Mariko's calm voice made him pause. "Walk down the log a ways and try to get him to follow you."

"Why?" he asked.

"I want to get a good side view, and get you in the picture for scale. And I'd rather not back up while I'm running the camera if I can help it."

"Look, we're not on a sightseeing trip anymore. This thing could kill us."

"Only if we let it. Go on. It's not going to climb up here."

"You hope."

"I know. I took one of these things apart, Ryan. They aren't built for climbing and they don't have the muscles to jump. We're perfectly safe as long as we don't fall off the log."

"Easily done in my present state," Ryan said, but he began creeping backward, grasping branches for support with his left hand while he kept the pistol aimed at the biker with his right. But the biker didn't follow him; it moved closer to Mariko instead.

"Okay, good," she said when Ryan had moved about five meters away. "Now make some noise or something to get its attention."

Ryan felt almost hypnotized, following Mariko's orders when he'd much rather be jumping down the other side of the log and fleeing for all he was worth, but he supposed she knew what she was talking about. He hoped she did, anyway. He raised his pistol up to point at the sky and squeezed the trigger.

He expected the biker to flinch at the report, but he didn't expect the reaction he got. The biker spun around, howling in terror, and skated madly away, zig-zagging back and forth as if trying to shake pursuit. They could hear its cries fading into the distance long after it disappeared from sight.

Mariko lowered the camera and said, laughing, "That was a little more action than I wanted, but what the heck. I got my side view, and now we know just what kind of motion the thing's capable of, too."

"Yeah," Ryan said. He popped the magazine out of his pistol and jacked the bullet out of the firing chamber before lowering the hammer. He didn't trust his shaking hands to lower it on a live round without slipping. He slid the bullet into the magazine, shoved it back into the grip, and put the pistol back in its holster. Sighing, he said, "I didn't think it would do that. I thought for sure I was going to have to shoot it."

Still laughing, Mariko said, "Evidently it thought you were a kamikaze."

"But bikers don't have to worry about kamikazes," Ryan pointed out.

"Sure they do. Not as much as some other animals, but they're not going to stick around where things are blowing up." Mariko climbed down to the ground and retrieved her helmet, tucked it under her arm again, and said, "We'd better go tell Sean we're okay, or he'll be coming to the rescue."

"We can do that from right here," Ryan said. He switched on his helmet transmitter. "Sean, are you there?"

He listened for a response, but either Sean wasn't wearing his helmet or the distance was too great for the tiny suit radios.

The adrenaline rush was wearing off, to be replaced by a warm glow of easy victory. Ryan imagined Sean listening intently for more shots from the forest, and suddenly grinned. "What the hell," he said, pulling off his helmet. He set it at his feet, took a deep breath, cupped his hands around his mouth, and let go with a two-tone Tarzan yell that echoed off the trees all around.

Mariko raised the camera. "Do it again."

Ryan felt himself blushing. If he did, he knew she would transmit the video to Earth. Billions of people would watch him clowning around on a log on an alien planet.

From off toward the clearing came an answering yell. Sean had heard him.

Screw the audience. Ryan had just scared off a biker. He tilted his head back, closed his eyes, and gave Mariko and Sean and whoever else might eventually watch him the loudest, most sincere chest-pounding howl he could manage.

CHAPTER TWENTY-FIVE

CHOICES

RYAN WAS FISHING IN the stream behind the cabin and trying to remember all the pointers Sean had given him when the shuttle's alarm siren went off. He flinched backward and yelled in surprise, then laughed at himself for doing it. He hadn't seen a kamikaze in days, and if that had been the problem then the first he would have known of it would have been a laser beam from the shuttle anyway.

He turned around and saw Sean dig his shovel into the dirt at the edge of the garden he was planting and jog toward the airlock. Ryan reeled in his line and started jogging back toward it as well, looking around for clums or bikers or some new form of danger, but a moment later Sean emerged again, grinning. "It's for you," he shouted.

It took Ryan a moment to realize somebody had called. It had been days since Mariko had gone back, and almost as long since they'd communicated with anybody else on the ship. "Who is it?" he shouted.

"Your girlfriend."

Ryan was about to ask which one, but stopped himself in time. The shuttle's cameras were still on.

He jogged on in, leaned his fishing pole against the hull by the door, and managed not to look surprised when he entered the shuttle and saw Kristy smiling out from the intercom.

"You owe me five hundred and sixty-three kisses," she said.

He grinned. "That many?"

"It would be more, but I stopped counting after I decided you were right."

Ryan sat down in the pilot's chair. "You did? Great! I mean, not that you stopped counting, but—"

"I know what you mean. Listen, I'm calling to warn you. I'm coming down to collect."

"What? When? Not yet. We don't know for sure if it's safe yet!"

Kristy laughed. "Laura told me you'd say that. She told me to tell you you can't have it both ways. It's time to put up or shut up. "

"But—"

"She's coming down, too."

"Laura?"

"Yes, Laura. And Teigh and your mom and your sister and Mariko and Captain Van Cleeve and about a dozen other people."

"You're kidding."

"Nope. We're bringing one of the big landers full of stuff. We plan to stay."

"That's great!" Ryan howled in triumph. Turning toward the door, he shouted, "Sean! They're coming down!"

Sean had been waiting just outside the open airlock. He came in as far as the inner door and said, "Couldn't bear to watch us having all the fun, eh?"

Kristy smiled, but not wide enough.

"What's the matter?" Ryan asked.

"That was the good news," she said. "Now for the bad news: We're the only ones coming. The rest of the crew voted to go to Eden."

Sean stepped up behind Ryan. "They what? You voted without us?"

"You're not part of the crew anymore. But it wouldn't have mattered anyway. The vote was eighty-seven to eighteen."

That bad? Ryan couldn't believe it. He and Sean had grossly

overestimated their support. And now it looked as if they were going to have to live with their mistake. If they could. "How can we keep a colony going with that few people?" he asked.

"They're being fairly generous," said Kristy. "We get to keep a cargo lander and one shuttle and the backup cell bank. They get the ship and the other lander, three shuttles, and the main cell bank. They'll keep the ship going so we can get back and forth if we have to."

"In case we need rescuing," Ryan said. "Sure. No wonder they're being generous; they expect to get it all back in a year or so."

"We'll see who has to rescue who," Sean said. "Who all is coming?"

Kristy read him the list of names. Ryan listened expectantly, but neither Holly nor Michelle were on it.

"Wait a minute," he said. "I admire your determination and courage and all that, but this doesn't solve a thing. The whole reason for living here was to keep from influencing the customs agents."

Kristy said, "They're going to set up their settlement on the same island we were on before. They've promised not to interfere deliberately, but that's as far as they'll go."

"That's not good enough!"

Sean frowned, but he said, "It's going to have to be good enough. Unless you want to pull the same trick Ken tried and strand us all here."

"You know I wouldn't do that."

"Then we'll have to take what we get."

"Thanks," Kristy said. "You make me feel really welcome."

"That's not what I meant," Sean said. "We're glad to have you. I just wish everybody had decided the same way."

Kristy nodded. "Yeah, well so do I. I've got a lot of friends up here I'm probably not going to see again. None of us are really happy about the way things have turned out, not even the ones going to Eden. But we've made our choices, and we're going to have to live with them." She looked directly at Ryan as she said, "And you're going to have to live with me. Unless of course you'd prefer someone else."

Ryan felt a blush stealing over him. It was apparently a day for making choices. He had been dreading this moment, but now that it was here he found the decision surprisingly easy to make. Neither Holly nor Michelle were coming. But even if one of them were, he didn't think he could turn Kristy down. As she had said, it was time to put up or shut up, and *she* wanted *him*, which was worth more than any amount of infatuation on his part.

"No," he told her. "No, I think you and I will do just fine."

He and Sean went back up to help pack. Ryan expected to find it hard to leave again, but the starship seemed foreign to him, like a place remembered from a dream. His twenty years on board were already becoming just a memory, pushed aside by the more immediate reality of living on a planet. As he stood in his room, the artificial window projecting early morning light over the half-dozen duffel bags containing his belongings, he wondered how he could ever have wanted to stay on board his entire life.

Comfort isn't everything, he thought. It was for a while, maybe, until a person found a purpose, but it wasn't an end in itself. Not if you wanted to make something out of your life.

Evidently quite a few people didn't feel that way, though. Ryan still felt betrayed whenever he thought about it. He'd been the most popular person on the ship, save for Laura, but just how superficial an asset that had been was now all too clear. His popularity had influenced one, maybe two votes, but the rest of the crew had abandoned him the moment he stood up for his principles. Michelle would hardly talk to him, save to tell him he was crazy, and he hadn't even *seen* Holly since he'd been on board.

No use brooding over it. They'd made their choice; they'd all just have to live with it. Ryan stacked his duffel bags on the maglev cart he'd borrowed from the cargo bay, laid his guitar on top, strapped the load down with a bungee cord, and pushed it out into the corridor. He paused at the door, looking back into the empty room, then reached in and switched off the window.

Laura was still packing. Ryan could hear her singing softly as he approached her house, and as he drew closer he heard cats meowing. He leaned in through the doorway and said, "Hi. You're taking the cats?"

"Damn right I'm taking the cats!" Laura said. She was sitting cross-legged amid a pile of books, trying to fit them all in boxes. She pointed to nine more boxes with wire mesh windows in them stacked near the door. Cat faces peered out of all but one of them. "If I can find 'em all, that is. I've got Star and Shadow and Ginger and Rascal and Maynard and Herb and Lewie and Bobby Thumbs, but I can't find Nova anywhere."

"Maybe she's up in the axis," Ryan said.

"I'm going to check there next."

"I'll do it. I'm headed that direction anyway."

"Thanks. I'm up to my ears in last-minute stuff as it is." Laura nodded toward the empty cat carrier, and Ryan strapped it on his maglev.

"I'm going to try to find Holly first," he said.

Laura nodded. "Try Michelle's office."

"Oh?"

"She was here a few minutes ago. I sent her there."

"You did?" In all his years on the ship, Ryan had never heard of Laura sending somebody to Michelle for help.

"I talked with her," Laura said, "but Michelle's going to have to be the nurturer now, at least for their half of the crew. I figured she might as well get started."

"I hadn't thought of that." Ryan considered asking what Holly had come to see her about, but he thought maybe he knew.

Laura confirmed it. "A few kind words from you could really make a difference, you know."

She couldn't have been more succinct with a slap in the face. Ryan felt the heat in his cheeks as the shot hit home. He'd been a grouch the whole time he'd been on board, trying to make people feel guilty enough to change their minds. No wonder Holly hadn't come to see him, knowing what she faced.

"I'll—I'll try to lighten up," he said.

"Good idea." Laura packed another book into the box before her, then looked up and said. "You still here? Go!"

Ryan went.

She wasn't in Michelle's office. Michelle was, though, and she sat up with a guilty start when he parked his belongings in the hallway and stepped in through the door.

"Hi," he said. "I, uh—" He had to clear his throat. "I just wanted to, well, you know. Say goodbye. And say I'm sorry about the way I've been acting lately."

"You don't have to apologize," she said. "We've all been a little hard to get along with."

"Yeah, but I'm supposed to be the ship's nice guy."

She stood up and came out from behind her desk. "You still are."

"Thanks for saying so, anyway. Laura told me I was being a real jerk." Ryan didn't know what to do with his hands all of a sudden. Folding his arms across his chest didn't seem right, and stuffing them in his pockets didn't seem right either. He settled for reaching out and taking Michelle's hands in his own.

"Look, we don't have to act like we're never going to see each other again," he said. "We've still got the ship. And just because we're going to be living on different planets doesn't mean we can't continue to be friends."

"True enough." She took a deep breath, then said, "I guess I knew deep down inside that we wouldn't wind up together, but I never thought we would spend the rest of our lives so far apart, either. It's going to be hard."

"It is." He drew her closer to him, put his arms around her.

"Are you still mad at us for going to Eden?"

He nodded. "Yeah. But I'll probably get over it if you leave the customs agents alone."

"We could do that just as well with you along," she said. "Maybe better."

Still hugging her, he said, "I don't think so. If we all go, people will eventually forget what all the arguments were about. If some of us stay here, we'll be a constant reminder."

"What, now you're staying here to be our conscience?"

He shook his head. "I'm staying here because this is where I want to live. It's more interesting. More exciting. More stimulating. I think humanity's future lies in places like this, rather than places like Eden." He let go of her and stepped back. "I'm not preaching, mind you. I'm just answering your question."

Michelle nodded. She leaned forward and kissed him. "Don't forget to call," she said.

"I won't."

"And be careful."

"You be careful, too. Don't get hit by any coconuts, and watch out for undercurrents."

"Yes, Mom."

Ryan took a step backward toward the door. "I guess I'll see you again...whenever."

"Whenever," she echoed.

He stood there a moment longer, fixing her image in his mind, then turned away and pushed his maglev on down the corridor toward the hospital. Maybe Holly would be there.

She wasn't. Nor was she at Laney's Eatery. So Ryan tried the only other place he could think of: her room.

She answered the door in her bathrobe. It was dark blue terry cloth, cinched tight around her waist with a yellow tie. Her hair was wrapped in a bright green towel. She looked far too festive for her expression, which wasn't happy.

"Hi," Ryan said.

"Hi." She didn't stand aside to let him in.

"I've been looking all over for you" he said. "Laura told me she'd sent you to Michelle's office, but you weren't there, and you weren't in the hospital or the cafeteria either. So I thought I'd try here."

"Well, you found me."

"Uh huh. Can I come in?"

She shrugged and backed away from the door. "Sure, why not?"

He came in slowly, uncertain how to proceed. Her window was simulating a rainy afternoon; gray light and the patter of raindrops filled her living room. "You're, um, I guess you're pretty mad at me, huh?" he asked.

She crossed her arms over her chest. "I'm trying to decide whether or not I hate you."

"That bad?"

"Ryan, you've ripped the crew apart! You gave us an impossible choice and then told us that anybody who doesn't take it is a selfish conqueror. You've abandoned us all to go live in that horrible, dangerous place. With Kristy Crawford! How am I supposed to feel?"

"Oh," said Ryan.

"*Oh?* What do you mean, *Oh?*"

He sat down suddenly on the arm of her couch, not trusting his legs to hold him. "I mean *Oh.* I think I finally get it. Sean was right; I could have had a chance with you if I had stayed here, couldn't I?"

She turned away. "A *chance?* What did you *think?* Do all the women on the ship throw themselves at you the way I did, or are you just dense?"

"Dense, I guess," he said. "I thought you were mostly angry. You told me the next day you wanted to go back to the way we were beforehand. What was I supposed to think?"

She pulled the towel off her hair and clenched it in her hands. Her hair fell over her shoulders, light brown now that it was wet. "I don't know," she said. "I guess at the time I wanted you to sweep me off my feet."

"And instead I ran off to make trouble with Sean." He held his hands to his forehead. "Oh, Holly, I wish you'd told me straight out."

"Would it have made any difference?"

He looked up at her. "What?"

"If I'd told you I loved you, would you have gone back to Eden with me? If I told you *now*, would it make any difference?"

His heart was pounding. The room felt about ten degrees too hot, but it grew even warmer when Holly untied her robe and let it fall to the floor.

"What are you doing?" he asked.

"What do you think I'm doing?" She stepped toward him. Droplets of water sparkled in the hollow between her breasts. "What would you say if I told you I'd marry you? All you'd have to do is give up this ridiculous notion of colonizing Hell and come with me to Eden. Would you do it?"

She stood right in front of him, too close for him to stand up. There was no safe place to look. He swallowed. "I—Holly, you can't be serious."

"Can't I? If you say yes, I'd do it."

He looked up into her eyes. They burned with the same intensity as they had when she had kissed him. She meant it. He could have her for a lover. All he would have to do was betray everything he had stood for over the last few months. His father's death would mean nothing, his own sermonizing about the customs agents would mean nothing, his promise to Kristy would mean nothing.

"You'd hate me inside of a week," he said.

"What makes you think that?"

"Because *I'd* hate me."

She looked at him for another few seconds, then nodded and backed away. "That's what I thought." She retrieved her robe and put it back on.

"Then why did you...?"

"I wanted to make absolutely sure."

He stood up. "And now that you have?"

She laughed softly. "I don't know. That's as far as I'd thought it through." She stepped up next to him again. "Forgive me?"

He had to take a couple of deep breaths before he could trust his voice, and by the time he did he was over the initial shock. "I'm not exactly sure what I'd be forgiving you for. Giving me a second chance?"

"Giving it to you too late to matter. Playing with your head. Not knowing my own mind well enough until it was too late. Take your pick."

"Tell you what," he said. "I'll forgive you if you'll forgive me."

She had to think it over. "I really do hate what you did to the crew. And to me. It still makes me mad every time I think about it. But I can't stay mad at you. If I do, it's going to drive me crazy. So I guess we might as well make our peace while we can still do it in person." She reached out and put her arms around him.

He pulled her close, feeling her body's curves beneath the single layer of soft robe. Her hair smelled of strawberry shampoo, and when she pressed her face into the side of his neck he felt a shiver run up his spine. It wasn't too late, he knew. Not even now. It would never be too late, not if they were both willing to throw everything else away.

She lifted her face from his neck, and he bent down to kiss her. Her lips melted beneath his just the way he'd always dreamed they would. The kiss grew more and more intense, and with each passing moment he knew he should stop, but he couldn't. Neither could she. They kissed one another hungrily, making up for all the time they'd lost during the trip, and all the time they would never have after today. Ryan felt himself grow dizzy. He had to straighten up or fall over, and he knew if they fell on the couch that would be the end of his resolve.

He straightened up.

She tilted her head, then slowly smiled. "Consider yourself forgiven," she said.

"Likewise." He kissed her again, just for a second, then let her go. With a wry shake of his head he said, "Well, that'll give us something to think about on long sleepless nights, won't it?"

"It might cause a few," she replied.

He stepped toward the door. "It might just do that." He turned back at the doorway and said, "Let me know how things go on Eden."

She nodded. "I will. I'll expect regular reports from you, too."

"Deal."

"And be careful down there."

"Always."

They looked at one another for a few more seconds, not speaking, then when it became apparent that neither of them could say goodbye, Ryan blew her a kiss, stepped into the hallway, and pushed his cart full of belongings on toward the ship's central axis.

The door to the astronomy module was open when he got there. There was no gravity now that the ship wasn't under thrust, so Ryan tied his things to the base of the Tree and went through the door, knowing who he would find on the other side.

David sat before a computer monitor, strapped into his chair to keep from drifting away. He looked up when Ryan entered, smiled, and said, "Ah, just the man I wanted to see. I've got something for you."

"You do?"

David took a ream-sized stack of paper from the printer's delivery bin and held it out to Ryan. "Mineral concentration maps," he said. "I ran a spectroscopic survey of the whole planet. Of course it only tells you what's on the surface, but that should help narrow down the search for high-grade ores."

Ryan accepted the printout, stammering, "I—you—I mean, thanks!" He looked at the topmost page, saw what looked like a contour map with splotches of color on it. A legend on the side identified the colors as iron, lead, zinc, copper, and so on. This would be an incredible help when the colony began manufacturing its own goods.

"You're welcome," David said. He turned back to the computer, and a moment later handed Ryan a thin rectangular disk cartridge. "Here's the same thing on file."

"Thanks again." Ryan took that from him as well. He looked out one of the windows, a window that for twenty years had shown only stars, and watched land and cloudscape drift by. After a moment he said, "You're going to be the main explorer for the Eden colony, aren't you?"

David laughed. "A cushy job if ever there was one."

Ryan looked back inside and shook his head. "Don't bet on it. At least, don't bet your life on it. Watch out for surprises, okay?"

"Okay."

David unbuckled his seatbelt and stood, steadying himself with a hand on the computer. "You watch out, too."

"Yeah."

They stood facing one another in the close, instrument-filled room. Both men knew what the other was thinking. Finally Ryan held out his right hand. David took it in his and they shook. "Take care of Holly," Ryan said.

"I'll do that."

"That's all I can ask. That and don't mess with the customs agents."

"You have my promise."

Ryan nodded. Coming from David, a promise meant something.

He wouldn't have thought so a few months ago, back when David was getting religion on Eden, or even a few weeks ago when they had quarreled about it on Ryan's world, but he had come to realize that a man could believe in God without sacrificing his principles. If David said he would leave the customs agents to themselves, he would leave the customs agents to themselves.

That didn't necessarily mean everyone would, but it couldn't hurt. People listened to David. Maybe he *could* keep humanity from meddling in their affairs. Ryan didn't think so, not forever, but it was out of his hands now. He'd done what he could for them.

"Good luck," he said, turning to go. "And thanks for the maps."

"Any time."

Ryan drifted through the doorway into the axis again.

Nova had discovered his maglev. She was using one of the bags as a scratching post, pulling on the heavy fabric and releasing her claws with a sound like popcorn popping. Ryan scooped her up in his arms and ruffled her fur until she began to purr. So the cats were going, too. He felt a wave of guilt at the thought of taking them down to such a hostile environment after their comfortable lives on board the ship, but there was no way to ask them their opinion. All you could do was guess, and Ryan guessed that Nova, at least, would choose to go. She'd always been an explorer. The cats would only be exploring the insides of new houses, at least until Laura was sure it was safe to let them out, so the move would really be no more traumatic for them than a move to Eden would be anyway.

He let Nova climb onto his shoulder, where she hung on with her claws hooked into his shirt while he looked up at the Tree.

Lack of gravity was beginning to show its effect. The Tree's needles were turning brown, not all at once as Ryan had suspected, but starting at the base of each tuft. The oldest growth was going first, evidently, but there was no doubt what the final outcome would be. The trip back to Eden might buy it another few months of life, but no more than that.

The Tree evidently realized that as well, down on some biological level. Ryan didn't know what the stimulus was—a change in sap flow patterns or hormone levels or what—but the tight little tangerine-sized cones at the ends of the branches had begun to open. The Tree was preparing to scatter its seeds before it died.

The cell bank no doubt already held lodge pole seeds, but not from the Tree. Ryan pushed off from its base, pulling his baggage along behind him, and drifted about halfway up the trunk before centrifugal force drew him out against the wall. He kicked off again and caught a branch. Wincing at the sharp prickles on the cones, he twisted two of them free and zipped them into the topmost duffel bag. Here was one old friend, at least, he wouldn't have to say goodbye to. He would plant these seeds outside the house he built for himself and Kristy, and when he was an old man he could lean back against the trunk of the tallest one and play his guitar.

He'd have to learn how first, of course, but this time he didn't think that would be a problem.

About The Author

Jerry Oltion is the author of *Abandon in Place, The Getaway Special,* and the forthcoming *Anywhere But Here,* plus several Star Trek books and over a hundred short stories. He won the Nebula award in 1997 for the novella version of *Abandon in Place.* He lives in Eugene, Oregon, with his wife Kathy, who also writes science fiction.

OTHER TITLES AVAILABLE FROM
WHEATLAND PRESS

ANTHOLOGIES

POLYPHONY 1, Deborah Layne and Jay Lake, Eds. Volume one in the critically acclaimed slipstream/cross-genre series will feature stories from Maureen McHugh, Andy Duncan, Carol Emshwiller, Lucius Shepard and others.

POLYPHONY 2, Deborah Layne and Jay Lake, Eds. Volume two in the critically acclaimed slipstream/cross-genre series will feature stories from Alex Irvine, Theodora Goss, Jack Dann, Michael Bishop and others.

POLYPHONY 3, Deborah Layne and Jay Lake, Eds. Volume three in the critically acclaimed slipstream/cross-genre series will feature stories from Jeff Ford, Bruce Holland Rogers, Ray Vukcevich, Robert Freeman Wexler and others.

TEL: STORIES, Jay Lake Ed. An anthology of experimental fiction with authors to be announced.

EXQUISITE CORPUSCLE, Frank Wu and Jay Lake Eds. Stories, poems, illustrations, even a play; an elaborate game of literary telephone featuring Gary Shockley, Benjamin Rosenbaum, Bruce Holland Rogers, Kristin Livdahl, Maggie Hogarth, and others.

ALL STAR ZEPPELIN ADVENTURE STORIES, David Moles and Jay Lake Eds. Original zeppelin stories by Jim Van Pelt, Leslie What, and others; one reprint, "You Could Go Home Again" by Howard Waldrop.

SINGLE-AUTHOR COLLECTIONS

DREAM FACTORIES AND RADIO PICTURES, Howard Waldrop. Waldrop' stories about early film and television reprinted in one volume.

GREETINGS FROM LAKE WU, Jay Lake and Frank Wu. Collection of stories b Jay Lake with original illustrations by Frank Wu.

TWENTY QUESTIONS, Jerry Oltion. Twenty brilliant works by the Nebul Award-winning author of "Abandon in Place."

THE BEASTS OF LOVE, Steven Utley, Intro. by Lisa Tuttle. Utley's "love stories spanning the past twenty years; a brilliant mixture of science fiction fantasy and horror.

AMERICAN SORROWS, Jay Lake. Four longer works by the Hugo and Campbell nominated author; includes his Hugo nominated novelette, "Int the Gardens of Sweet Night."

NONFICTION

WEAPONS OF MASS SEDUCTION, Lucius Shepard. A collection of Shepard' film reviews. Some have previously appeared in print in the *Magazine o Fantasy and Science Fiction*; most have only appeared online at *Electri Story*.

POETRY

KNUCKLE SANDWICHES, Tom Smario, Intro. by Lucius Shepard. Poem about boxing by a long-time poet and cut-man.

NOVEL

PARADISE PASSED, Jerry Oltion. The crew of a colony ship must choos between a ready-made paradise and one they create for themselves.

FOR ORDERING INFORMATION VISIT:
WWW.WHEATLANDPRESS.COM

Printed in the United States
22377LVS00002B/46-204